He was the man in her dreams

The one who had haunted her all these years, the one she put into every book she wrote. Jared was her pirate—fierce, tender, passionate and proud. The shock of recognition made Kate shiver.

"What's wrong?" Jared stirred lazily, turning onto his back. He looked up at her with eyes that gleamed with the banked embers of a fire that had been only temporarily quenched.

"Nothing's wrong. It's just that I've had this odd feeling I know you."

"You do know me. You said I was perfect. Your very words."

She laughed softly. "I'm not sure you can hold me responsible for that remark. I was under the influence of raging hormones at the time."

"If that's the way you're going to be about it, I'll just have to enrage your hormones until you say it again." He shifted, rolling her beneath him. "And again and again..."

Also available from Jayne Ann Krentz

SERPENT IN PARADISE
STORMY CHALLENGE
RAVEN'S PREY
UNEASY ALLIANCE
THE TIES THAT BIND
THE WEDDING NIGHT
A SHARED DREAM
TRUE COLORS
MAN WITH A PAST
BETWEEN THE LINES
CALL IT DESTINY
GHOST OF A CHANCE
THE FAMILY WAY
A WOMAN'S TOUCH
LADY'S CHOICE
WITCHCRAFT
LEGACY
JOY
FULL BLOOM
TEST OF TIME

JAYNE ANN KRENTZ

The PIRATE, The ADVENTURER & The COWBOY

HQN™

HQN™

ISBN 0-373-77171-1

THE PIRATE, THE ADVENTURER & THE COWBOY

Copyright © 2006 by Harlequin Books S.A.

The publisher acknowledges the copyright holder of the individual works as follows:

THE PIRATE
Copyright © 1990 by Jayne Ann Krentz

THE ADVENTURER
Copyright © 1990 by Jayne Ann Krentz

THE COWBOY
Copyright © 1990 by Jayne Ann Krentz

www.HQNBooks.com

Printed in U.S.A.

CONTENTS

THE PIRATE   11

THE ADVENTURER   219

THE COWBOY   429

Dear Reader,

Those of you who read my books know that these days
I write contemporary romantic thrillers as Jayne Ann Krentz,
historical romantic suspense as Amanda Quick and
futuristics as Jayne Castle. At the start of my career,
however, I wrote classic, battle-of-the-sexes-style
romance using both my Krentz name and the pen name
Stephanie James. This volume contains one or more stories
from that time.

I want to take this opportunity to thank all of you—
new readers as well as those who have been with me from
the start. I appreciate your interest in my books.

Sincerely,

Jayne Ann Krentz

THE PIRATE

For Debbie Macomber,
a generous friend
Who doesn't mind sharing a nifty idea

Prologue

"NO, ABSOLUTELY NOT. YOU CANNOT make me get on that plane. I won't go." Katherine Inskip braced herself in her chair and glared at the two women across the small table. Behind her, the glass panes of the airport lounge window vibrated as a jet roared past on the runway, then climbed into cloudy Seattle skies. "There are laws against this sort of thing. This is illegal impressment or something. You can't do it."

"Save the drama for your next book, Kate. You are going to board that plane in fifteen minutes." Margaret Lark, sleek and cool as always, checked the expensive black-and-gold watch on her wrist. Her voice was calm and authoritative. She had spent several years in the corporate world and could still dominate a meeting when the occasion arose. "Sarah and I have discussed the matter thoroughly and we both agree that you need a vacation. Your doctor has told you that you need a vacation. Even your agent said it might not be a bad idea and you know things are bad when your agent thinks you should take a little time off work."

"It's true, Kate. You know it is." Sarah Fleetwood, on the same side of the table and the argument as Margaret, smiled gently, her fey eyes soft with concern. "You're much too tense and nervous lately. You've said yourself that you're not sleeping well. And your appetite is fading. Why, you haven't felt like making pizza or tacos for weeks, and that's not like you. It's the stress. You've got to do something about it."

Kate scowled at her. "So what if I'm a little stressed? I've just come off a ten-day, ten-city book promotion tour. What do you expect? I'm tired, that's all."

"It's more than just jet lag from the tour," Margaret said. "It's been building up for some time. Kate, you've become a workaholic and if you don't take care of yourself, you're going to pay a price."

"What's wrong with being a workaholic? I like my work. In fact, I love it. You know I do. I'm not happy unless I'm writing. I'll go nuts if you take me away from it."

"There's nothing wrong with enjoying your writing," Sarah assured her in soothing tones. "Margaret and I love writing, too. That's not the point."

"Well, what is the point?" Kate demanded, feeling cornered. "I'm happy just the way I am, I tell you. Happy, do you hear me?" She slapped the small table for emphasis. "I've never been so damned happy."

"The point is that you need to start leading a more balanced life," Margaret announced. "You've been going at a hundred-mile-an-hour pace for far too long. Since your divorce, in fact. You need a break and now that *Buccaneer's Bride* is safely on the stands, you can afford the time to take one. Trust me on this, Kate. When I was working in the business world, I saw plenty of examples of what overwork and stress can do to people. Not a pretty sight." She dug an airline ticket envelope out of her black Italian-leather handbag. "You need to learn how to take time out to relax and enjoy life."

"And Amethyst Island sounds like the perfect place for you to do just that," Sarah announced. Her unsettlingly insightful gaze rested on Kate's set face for a few seconds. Then she reached out and took the ticket envelope from Margaret and pushed it into Kate's fingers. "Margaret and I have looked into this thoroughly. The place has everything: palm trees, warm, tropical seas, a first-class luxury resort, papayas, coconuts…"

"I hate coconuts," Kate pointed out desperately. "You know I do. Remember how I wouldn't eat any of those cookies you made last week because they had those yucky little bits of coconut in them?"

"So you'll eat papaya, instead," Margaret said with a shrug. She glanced at her watch again and stood up, slender and chic in her tailored blazer and fine wool slacks. "Time to head for the departure lounge."

Sarah jumped up beside Margaret, boundless enthusiasm lighting her elfin features. "On your feet, kiddo. You're on your way to paradise and you're going to love it. I just know it."

Kate looked up at her beseechingly and knew she was defeated. It was sometimes possible to argue logically with Margaret, but when Sarah got that expression of intuitive certainty in her deep, knowing hazel eyes, nothing could change her mind. Small, delicate and vibrant, Sarah always made Kate think of a brightly plumed hummingbird. Today, dressed in a lemon-yellow sweater and black-and-white striped jeans, she looked more than ever like some small, exotic bird.

"Sarah, I know you and Margaret mean well, but…"

Sarah took Kate's arm and hauled her to her feet. "Just think of what's waiting for you, friend. You're heading for genuine pirate territory. The real thing. Just like a setting from one of your books. Margaret did the research on this, and she says it's the place for you. You know how accurate Margaret is with her research."

A gnawing sense of fatalism settled over Kate. Sarah was right—Margaret's research was always impeccable. It was one of the things that lent real power to her friend's sophisticated stories of love and intrigue amid the jungles of the modern corporate world.

"And Margaret says Amethyst Island actually has a ruined castle left over from the days when a real live buccaneer lived there," Sarah went on cheerfully.

"A castle?" Kate was intrigued in spite of herself. Sarah had her halfway down the corridor now, plowing along in Margaret's elegant wake. "This island has a castle on it?"

"That's right. And a history of violence and lust. Just think, Kate, you're going to be able to explore a genuine pirate hideaway. No telling what sorts of bloody deeds were done there in the last century. Think of the atmosphere you'll soak up."

"What is this about lust?" Kate asked.

Sarah waved an airy hand. "Oh, there's some legend about how the pirate king who settled the island went back to England once, kidnapped his bride and took her away to the South Seas. I don't know all the details. I write contemporary romantic suspense, not historical romance, remember?"

"He kidnapped his bride?" Clutching the ticket envelope more tightly, Kate allowed herself to be thrust into the crowd of people milling about at the boarding gate. "What pirate? Which legend? I never heard of any stories about Amethyst Island. In fact, I've never even heard of Amethyst Island."

Margaret smiled and impulsively hugged her friend in farewell. "It's part of a small chain in the South Pacific called the Jewel Islands. You'll have plenty of time to find out all about the place. Have a wonderful time, Kate. When you come back, you'll feel like a new woman."

Alarm flared through Kate as the crowd caught her up and carried her toward the jetway. "Wait. What's this about lots of time? When am I coming back? How long am I to be banished to a tropical island, for heaven's sake?"

"You've got reservations for a month at the only resort on the island," Sarah called out just as Kate got hustled through the doorway.

"A *month*? Good grief, that's forever. I'll be bored to tears. I'll be crawling the walls. I'll be a basket case by the time I get back. And it'll cost a fortune. Neither of you can afford to send me away for a month."

"We put the whole thing on your bank charge card," Margaret assured her.

"Oh, Lord, talk about stress," Kate wailed. "I'll never recover."

Sarah chuckled. "Send us a postcard."

Margaret waved farewell. An instant later, Kate lost sight of both women as she was swept up and carried down the ramp to the open door of the waiting jet.

BACK IN THE DEPARTURE LOUNGE, Margaret frowned with faint concern. "I hope we did the right thing."

"We did," Sarah said with cheerful certainty as they both turned to walk back through the bustling terminal. "I have a feeling about this Amethyst Island. As soon as you found out about it from the travel agent, I knew it was the right place to send Kate."

"You and your intuition."

"My intuition hasn't been known to fail yet." Sarah halted abruptly in front of a newsstand and grinned at a display of paperbacks.

One book stood out from all the rest on the rack. Its cover, lush and colorful, featured a powerful, good-looking man dressed in a wide-sleeved shirt that was open to the waist to display an impressive chest. A lethal-looking dagger was thrust into his belt. Locked in his fierce, passionate embrace was a fiery-haired woman clad in a diaphanous gown. The backdrop featured a misty view of a tropical island and a ship with billowing sails. The title, picked out in gold, was *Buccaneer's Bride*. Stamped across the top of the book in bold script was the author's name, Katherine Inskip.

"You know what would really make this a perfect vacation for Kate?" Sarah mused.

"Sure. Finding herself a real live pirate and having herself a nice little adventure." Margaret's brows rose and her mouth curved in wry amusement. "But don't hold your breath, Sarah. She's no more likely to encounter the man of her dreams than you or I are. We three may write about romance and adventure for a living, but we live in the real world."

"I know." Sarah shook her head thoughtfully. "But at least you and I still have our eyes out for the right man. Kate has given up looking for him altogether. I wonder if she'd even recognize him if he came along?"

"Probably not. Even if he did happen along, he'd have a heck of a job on his hands just getting her attention. The only men Kate really sees these days are the ones she puts in her books."

"Maybe. But you know something?" Sarah cast one last glance at the cover of *Buccaneer's Bride*. "I really do have this feeling about sending Kate off to Amethyst Island. Go ahead and laugh if you like, but I think she's in for something more than just a routine South Seas island vacation."

Chapter One

"WHAT ON EARTH DO YOU MEAN, hand over my purse, you little worm?" Kate stood in the narrow, cobbled alley and stared in outraged disbelief at the little man wielding the big knife. It was all too much.

She was hot, tired and thoroughly disgusted. Her canvas-and-leather flight bags hung heavily from her shoulders and her camera felt like an albatross around her neck. The purse the little man was demanding so rudely was slung diagonally across her body and bulged with magazines, guide books, cosmetics and a small statue carved out of lava.

The once rakish-looking safari dress was now damp with perspiration and sadly wrinkled from several hours of sitting in a cramped coach-class airline seat. The traveling had become an endless nightmare. Kate was convinced that owing to some oversight on her part during a previous lifetime she was now doomed to travel through this South Seas purgatory forever, never again to know the comforts of civilization.

The little creep standing in front of her waving the knife was definitely the last straw.

"You heard me, lady."

The small, unkempt man reminded Kate of a rat. He darted a nervous glance over her shoulder and then back over his own. Satisfied that the alley was still deserted except for his victim, he motioned with the wicked-looking weapon. "I said give me your purse. Hurry. It ain't like I got all day, y'know."

"You've obviously spent so much time in this heat that you've fried what few brains you've got. Quite understandable. This place is an oven. But pay attention. If I'd wanted to get mugged, I could have stayed home. I have not endured an endless flight, eaten rotten airline food, had my luggage lost and missed my connections just to wind up turning over my purse to the first two-bit thief who comes along."

"Jesus, lady, will you keep your voice down?"

"Why should I keep my voice down?" Kate's voice, already laced with outrage, rose yet another notch in volume. "I have no intention of handing over my purse or anything else to you. Now get out of this alley and leave me alone."

"Now look here, you crazy bitch." The man waved the knife threateningly, but he took a step back when Kate's eyes narrowed. Once more he glanced anxiously over his shoulder. "I ain't got time to be nice about this."

"Neither do I." Kate grabbed her camera and held it up to one eye. She focused on her target and squeezed the shutter-release button. The man's mouth fell open in shock. "A charming pose. You know, if you knew what I've been through today, I'm sure you'd find yourself another poor helpless tourist to rob. I am not in a good mood."

"I don't care what kinda mood you're in."

Kate ignored his interruption. "Furthermore, I am a person who has been under a great deal of stress lately, according to my friends. People who have been under stress are unpredictable and dangerous. You never know what they're going to do." She squeezed off another shot.

"Hey, what are you doin'?" The little man swore and leaped back another step, instinctively raising a hand to shield his face. "Stop takin' pictures of me. What's the matter with you? Just give me the damned purse."

"Very well. Since you insist." Kate let the camera fall to her waist. Grimly, she let the heavy shoulder bags slide to the pavement. She tugged at the leather strap of her purse.

"That's better. Come on, come on."

"This," Kate said through her teeth, "has been the worst trip of my entire life and I've hardly gotten started. I can't wait to get home and tell my friends what they did to me. Here. You want my purse? Help yourself." Kate turned the bulging bag upside down and dumped the contents at her feet.

The would-be thief swore again in a strangled-sounding voice. "You're crazy, lady. You know that? *Crazy.*"

"Stressed, not crazy. There's a difference. If I were crazy, I might actually be enjoying myself."

"What the hell do you think you're doin'?"

"Getting myself robbed." Kate finished emptying the purse. "Come and get it, you little runt."

"Get outa my way." The man edged cautiously forward. "Get back. Go on, get back."

"Is there a good living in this sort of thing?" Kate watched as the man hunkered and worked his way closer to where her wallet lay on the ground.

"Shut up. Just shut up, will you? Don't you ever close that damned mouth of yours?" The little man lunged toward the wallet.

Kate waited until the last second and then kicked out at the hand holding the knife.

"Aargh!"

Caught off balance, the thief dropped the knife and scuttled to one side like a small, startled crab. Kate took a step forward and kicked him again, this time catching the man in a far more vulnerable spot.

"Damn you, you crazy, stupid woman! You're a real nut, you know that?" The man rolled to one side, hugging himself. He lurched to his feet, backing away from her. Then his nervous little eyes flicked to a point behind her. He cursed, turned and fled.

"That's it!" Kate yelled after him, her hands on her hips. "Run like the coward you are. You remind me of my ex-husband, you little twerp."

But the man was long gone. Grumbling, Kate knelt on the cobblestones to retrieve her belongings. It was not a simple task because her fingers were shaking.

"Did you kick your ex-husband around like that?" inquired a deep, amused male voice from behind her.

With a gasp, Kate shot to her feet and spun around. A man lounged in the alley entrance. He was a very large man, a couple of inches over six feet, lean and hard and broad shouldered. Caught in the harsh glare and deep shadows cast by the intense tropical sun, he looked infinitely more dangerous than the man with the knife. The slashing, wicked grin that revealed his teeth did nothing to soften the impression.

But far more unsettling than the dangerous quality was the fact that the big stranger looked eerily familiar. Yet Kate was certain she had never seen him before in her life. She would not be likely to forget those cool silver eyes.

"Who are you? The little twerp's accomplice?" But even as she asked the question she knew this man did not eke

out a hand-to-mouth existence taking wallets from innocent tourists. If he chose crime as a career path, he'd go
into it in a big way. He'd be a jewel thief or a mob leader.
Two hundred years ago, he would have been a pirate.

"The little twerp doesn't have any friends, let alone
accomplices."

"You know him?"

"Sharp Arnie and I have encountered each other occasionally over the years. We're not exactly pals."

"Oh." Kate frowned. "Did he run off because he saw
you?"

"I believe he ran off because he thought he was going to
get stomped into the ground trying to retrieve your wallet."

"I was certainly going to do my best to stomp him. The
nerve of some people. Shouldn't we be notifying the authorities or something?"

"Sharp Arnie will be taken care of in due time. Don't
worry about him. It's a small island."

"I'll be happy to file a complaint or press charges or
whatever one does in this sort of situation."

"Don't bother. We're not real formal around here. Guess
I'd better give you a hand picking that junk up or we'll be
stuck on Ruby all day."

The man levered himself away from the pink wall and
paced toward her. He moved with an easy, coordinated
stride that bespoke strength.

He was wearing a pair of faded jeans and an equally
faded khaki shirt. The collar of the shirt was open, and
Kate realized she was staring at the crisp, dark hair that
grew there. She caught herself and came back to her senses
instantly as she realized the stranger was reaching for her
valuables.

"Hold on just one second before you touch my things.
Who are you?"

"Jared Hawthorne. You're Katherine Inskip, right?"

She eyed him warily. He didn't look like a fan who might have recognized her from the photo the publisher put on the inside of her book's back cover. "How do you know my name?"

"I've been looking for you. Billy said you'd gotten tired of waiting around for your ride to Amethyst Island and had decided to do some sight-seeing."

"Billy being the Billy of Billy's Ruby Island Dive and Tackle Shop? The same Billy who told me that through absolutely no fault of my own I had missed the one flight a day to Amethyst Island? The Billy who was going to arrange for me to spend the night in that fleabag of a hotel on the waterfront until I informed him that if he did not contact the management at the resort on Amethyst Island at once and tell them to send a boat I would be leaving on the next plane for the States?"

Jared Hawthorne winced. "Sounds like the same Billy, all right. He owns that fleabag of a hotel, by the way. But you're in luck. When his message arrived I decided to come over and pick you up."

"I should think so," Kate said. "I'm booked into Crystal Cove Resort for a solid month. The least the resort can do is provide convenient transportation."

"Take it easy. I'm here, aren't I? You've got your transportation. What do you say we get moving? I've got better things to do than hang around here on Ruby."

"So do I. I certainly hope the Crystal Cove Resort offers a few more amenities than Billy's hotel does."

"Crystal Cove offers everything you'll need for a relaxing vacation on a tropical island," Jared said. "Within minutes after your arrival you will discover that time has slowed to an ancient, unhurried crawl and you are in another world."

"You're quoting directly from the brochure, aren't you?"

"Yeah. I wrote it." He leaned down and effortlessly scooped up a compact, hairbrush and several magazines, which he dumped into the empty purse.

"How long have you worked at Crystal Cove?" Kate asked.

"Since it was built. I own the place." He grabbed the strap of one of her flight bags and slung it over his shoulder. "Ready?"

That explained why he didn't have to bother with snatching tourist wallets, Kate decided. He didn't need them. In his line of work people willingly handed over their credit cards. "The resort must have a very small staff if the owner himself has to make the run to Ruby Island to pick up guests."

"Don't worry. There will be plenty of people to wait on you hand and foot at Crystal Cove, madam."

"I don't need a lot of servants, just air-conditioning. It's hot as hell here." Kate picked up one of the magazines and fanned herself with it. "Right now I would trade just about everything I brought with me for five minutes in front of a real air conditioner."

A glint of what might have been amusement lit Jared's silver eyes. "Sorry. Ceiling fans."

Kate blinked. "I beg your pardon?"

"The resort is built to take advantage of the prevailing breezes. All the rooms have screens and ceiling fans instead of air-conditioning."

"Good grief. You mean I'm going to have to endure this heat for the next month?"

"The afternoon rains cool things off. Nights are balmy. Mornings are pleasantly warm. The heat only gets a little unpleasant during the middle of the day. Smart people stay in the shade or in the water during that time period. They don't run around buying souvenirs." Jared regarded the lava statue with amused disdain.

"I see." Kate snatched the small statue from his hand and dropped it into her purse. "Is it always this hot during the middle of the day?"

"No. Sometimes it's hotter."

"That does it. I'm going to strangle my two best friends the minute I get back to Seattle." Kate hoisted one of the stuffed flight bags and gritted her teeth against the weight.

"Why?" Jared took the bag from her and slung it easily over his own shoulder.

"They're the ones responsible for sending me to this godforsaken place. You know," Kate confided almost wistfully, "I used to have a rather romanticized view of tropical islands. I imagined them as remote, mysterious, exotic locales where anything could still happen."

"What's the matter? Has the image been shattered?"

"You can say that again. I didn't want to take this vacation in the first place, but during the first leg of this trip I tried to be a good sport. After all, my friends meant well. I managed to convince myself I might actually be able to enjoy a few weeks on a tropical island."

"I take it you've changed your mind already?" Jared motioned for her to precede him out of the alley.

"When I discovered in Hawaii that the airline had somehow lost my baggage during a nonstop trip over the Pacific Ocean, I began to change my mind. When I sat in the Honolulu airport for six hours waiting for my bags, I had a few more second thoughts. After I landed here on Ruby Island and discovered I had missed my connection to Amethyst I became seriously concerned. And now, after having nearly been robbed at knife point here in paradise and after discovering that there is no air-conditioning awaiting me at my so-called luxury resort accommodations, for which I am paying a fortune, I realize I am the innocent victim of a malicious joke."

"Don't get paranoid. You're just shaken up from your encounter with Sharp Arnie." A degree of indulgence softened his eyes. "Not surprising, really. That knife of his can be intimidating at first glance. Give yourself a little while to calm down. Just relax."

"Sharp Arnie was merely the last straw. If it wasn't for the fact that I can't bear the thought of getting on one more airplane today, I would turn around and head back for Seattle this minute."

"There isn't another flight out of here until tomorrow."

"And that's another thing I don't like about these remote islands. They're too damned remote."

"Sharp Arnie had a point. Don't you ever close your mouth?"

"Only when I'm working, and I didn't come all this way to work. I'm supposed to be on vacation. Stress, you know."

"Stress makes you mouthy?"

"Among other things." Kate led the way back through quaintly twisted streets to Billy's Ruby Island Dive and Tackle shop where the remainder of her luggage was waiting. She was aware of Jared Hawthorne following behind her like a porter. His dignity did not seem offended, she noticed. He carried the heavy flight bags as if they weighed only a few ounces.

The narrow, sun-drenched streets of the small port village were nearly empty. As Jared had noted, most people were wisely staying indoors to avoid the heat of midday.

Port Ruby was picturesque in its own way, Kate grudgingly decided, but hardly romantic. It was hot, dusty and run-down. An array of ramshackle shops and open-air bars lined the harborfront. Here and there a few dogs of questionable pedigree flopped in the shade of scraggly palms. Everything, including the dogs, looked as though it needed a coat of paint. Kate fervently hoped that Crystal Cove Resort had a bit more to offer in the way of atmosphere.

The door to Billy's shop hung askew on its hinges, the old screen torn and the weathered wood peeling. Kate stepped into the dark interior and breathed a small sigh of relief at the slight reduction in temperature. The now-familiar figure of Billy, who appeared to be somewhere between fifty and seventy and outfitted with skin that resembled tanned leather, stirred from the seat behind the counter. He rose ponderously to his feet, a can of beer in his hand.

"Hey, Hawthorne." Billy's cheerful grin exposed a few missing teeth and some gold ones. "I see you found the little lady."

"Sharp Arnie found her first." Jared dumped the flight bags onto the wooden floor. "He was up to his usual tricks with a knife."

Billy's grin faded. "Sharp Arnie? Is he back on the island?"

"Yeah. Better tell Sam."

Kate glanced at each man in turn. "Everyone seems to be very familiar with Sharp Arnie. If he's such a well-known public menace, why isn't he in jail?"

Billy shrugged. "He winds up in jail from time to time, but mostly he just gets kicked off one island and washes up on another. He makes a sort of circuit around our neck of the Pacific." Billy scowled suddenly as if a thought had just occurred to him. "You all right? He didn't hurt you or nothin', did he?"

"No." Actually, her knees felt quite wobbly, Kate suddenly realized. Delayed shock. Or perhaps it was the heat. Whatever the cause, she wanted very much to sit down.

Just wait until she told Sarah and Margaret about this little incident. "Thank you for your concern, Billy."

"Sure, sure. Sharp Arnie usually don't go around stickin' that knife of his into anyone unless he gets real provoked. Don't worry about your wallet. Sam will get it back from him before he kicks the little punk off the island."

"Fortunately, I am still in possession of my wallet. Thank goodness. Imagine trying to notify all those credit card companies from here!"

Billy looked puzzled. "He didn't take your wallet? Hey, that's real lucky, huh? What happened? Hawthorne get there in time to run him off?"

"No," said Kate.

"Hawthorne," Jared said coolly, "got there in time to watch Ms Inskip kick the, uh, stuffing out of Sharp Arnie. The poor bastard was running for cover last I saw him. Ms Inskip was yelling at him and that seemed to be upsetting him."

Billy swung a startled gaze back to Kate and then gave a crack of laughter. "Nice goin', Ms Inskip. Always did admire a woman who could take care of herself. Here, have a cold beer." He fished a can out of a small refrigerator and slapped Kate on the back as he handed it to her.

"Thank you." Kate staggered a bit under the blow but quickly caught her balance. Out of the corner of her eye, she saw Jared watching her as she pulled the tab on the blessedly chilled can. He had that arrogantly amused glint in his silver eyes again, she thought. It annoyed her. *Dammit,* she thought, *why does he look so familiar? I must have seen him somewhere before this. I know this man.*

"Where did you learn to handle folks like Sharp Arnie?" Jared asked very casually as he accepted a can of beer from Billy.

"I took a two-week course in self-defense techniques for women that was offered at my athletic club last year."

"You've had all of two weeks' worth of training, huh? Impressive."

His condescension was annoying. "It was enough, wasn't it?"

"Enough to terrorize Sharp Arnie, I'll give you that."

"A woman on her own has to learn a variety of skills."

"I'll just bet she does."

Kate gulped the beer and sighed. She was not up to sparring with this familiar stranger just now. Her knees felt a little less wobbly, but exhaustion was hitting her like a wave. "When can we get out of here? Right now even a ceiling fan sounds good."

"It does, don't it?" Billy observed, glancing up to where the shop fan hung motionless in the heavy air. "Hopin' to get mine fixed soon. Parts are supposed to be in any day. Ordered 'em six months ago."

"*Six months.*" Kate was horrified. "You've waited six months just to get a broken fan fixed?"

Billy shrugged philosophically. "Island time."

"Speaking of time, we'd better get going. I've got a resort to run, remember?" Jared set aside his unfinished beer and picked up Kate's bags. He glanced casually at Billy. "You want to cut the cards for the fuel?"

"Not on your life, Hawthorne. I ain't takin' a chance on getting stiffed like last time."

Jared shook his head. "I'm disappointed in you, Billy. Where's your sporting spirit? Suit yourself. Put the fuel on the resort's tab."

Billy grinned widely and scratched his stomach. "I'll just do that. Uh, you want me to help you with the rest of Ms Inskip's luggage?"

"Forget it. I can handle these two flight bags."

Billy cleared his throat. "That's not quite all her stuff."

"It certainly isn't," Kate said. "You couldn't possibly expect me to pack everything I'd need for a month in two small flight bags."

"Where's the rest of it?" Jared asked, looking resigned.

"Got it all back here safe and sound," Billy said, heaving two suitcases up from behind the counter. He bent down for a third.

Jared watched the luggage pile up on the counter. "I take it you don't believe in traveling light, Ms Inskip?"

"Blame the two so-called friends who shanghaied me. They did the packing." Kate smiled blandly. "They weren't sure exactly what I'd need, so they packed for all eventualities."

"No wonder the airline lost your luggage," Jared muttered as he picked up one of the suitcases. "The baggage handlers probably got tired of dealing with it and decided to chuck it. Come on, Billy, let's get this stuff on the boat."

"Sure thing, Jared."

"Wait a minute," Kate said. "Shouldn't somebody be calling this Sam person so he can arrest Sharp Arnie?"

"Plenty of time for that," Billy said, hoisting a suitcase. "Sharp Arnie ain't goin' nowhere."

"What if he leaves the island?" Kate asked worriedly as she followed the two men outside to the dock where a sleek blue-and-white cabin cruiser was tied. The glare off the water hit her full force, and she scrabbled in her bottomless purse for her oversize sunglasses.

"If he's got enough sense to leave the island, good riddance," Billy called over his shoulder. "It'll save Sam some work."

"But if he leaves Ruby he'll only show up on another island. You said yourself he makes a circuit."

Billy chuckled. "If you're frettin' about Sharp Arnie jumping over to Amethyst, don't. Arnie knows better'n to try to work the tourists over there. He tried it once a couple years back and Hawthorne here took him aside and explained he wasn't welcome over there."

"Explained he wasn't welcome?" Kate echoed in disbelief. "I must say the approach to law and order around here is extremely casual."

"Yeah, but it works." Jared tossed her luggage into the back of the boat and bent to untie the lines. "Hop aboard, Ms Inskip. We're ready to leave."

"Not so fast. Just why is Sharp Arnie so willing to spare Amethyst Island?"

It was Billy who answered. "Let's just say Arnie is real respectful toward Jared here. See, Hawthorne owns most of Amethyst. What he says over there goes, don't it, Hawthorne?"

"Most of the time," Jared agreed. "Makes life simple." He leaped lightly on board and reached out to grasp Kate's arm. He hauled her off the dock and into the boat with little ceremony. "Sit down, Ms Inskip." He guided her rather forcefully into a seat and gave her a wicked smile. "Wouldn't want you to fall overboard between here and Amethyst. Something tells me I'd never hear the end of it. So long, Billy. See you later in the week. Thanks for looking after the lady."

Billy grinned. "No problem. Have a nice vacation, Ms Inskip."

Kate opened her mouth to explain once again that so far her vacation was not off to a great start, but she closed it in frustration when Jared Hawthorne rudely gunned the engines.

Abandoning the effort, she sank wearily into a seat and gazed dully out over the water. As she watched, Port Ruby began to shrink in the distance. It occurred to Kate that she could not remember ever having felt so bone weary.

When she got bored with watching Port Ruby, she allowed her gaze to wander back to Jared Hawthorne who was concentrating on guiding the sleek craft through the necklace of small islets that protected Ruby Island from the full force of the sea.

When they got beyond the bits and pieces of land, Kate was suddenly aware of the vast expanse of turquoise sea that lay ahead. She had not spent much time in boats of any size, let alone one as small as the cruiser.

"I assume you're reasonably good at handling a boat?" she called to Jared.

"You'll find out soon enough, won't you?" he retorted cheerfully. Then he seemed to notice the tension in her face. "Hey, take it easy. I make this run three or four times a month. Amethyst is just a short hop."

"I see." The eerie sense of familiarity returned to Kate as she studied Jared's lean profile. Idly she tried to pin down who it was he reminded her of. His hair was dark, nearly black, worn unfashionably long and silvered here and there with hints of gray. He must be nearly forty, she decided. Try as she might, she could not think of anyone she knew who resembled him. Her curiosity overcame her.

"Look," she finally said, pitching her voice above the roar of the engine, "this is going to sound silly, but do I know you from somewhere?"

Jared gave her a curious glance. "No. Definitely not. Believe me, I'd remember if we'd ever met."

"Of course. I told you it was a silly question. It's just that I'm so tired I can't think straight." She ran her fingers through her short hair. The breeze generated by the moving boat was refreshing. "How long until we get to Amethyst?"

"About an hour."

"I think I'll take a nap, if you don't mind."

"Suit yourself."

"Thank you, I usually do," Kate said as she settled back in the shade of the cruiser's canopy.

"What a coincidence," Jared said half under his breath as he watched her eyes close. "So do I, Ms Inskip. And something tells me that could be a problem."

She looked different with her lashes lowered and her mouth closed, he thought, studying her objectively for the first time. More vulnerable, a little softer. Attractive, even.

Damned attractive, if you liked the type.

He decided Kate Inskip was probably only a few years younger than he—thirty-three or maybe even thirty-four. The wide belt of the wilted safari-style dress revealed a slender waist and hinted at full, round hips. The large, button-flap pockets on the front of the dress successfully concealed most of the contours of her breasts, however. That was okay, though, Jared finally decided. A man should have something to look forward to discovering on his own.

A wealth of tawny brown hair styled in a short, sassy fashion made a nice frame for her long-lashed green eyes and tip-tilted nose. It was a strong face, Jared realized, the face of a woman accustomed to making her own decisions and carrying them out, the face of a woman who did not rely on men to smooth her way in the world. But there was an intriguing sensuality about her full mouth, he discovered.

What the hell was he thinking of, Jared wondered in the next instant as he realized with a start where his thoughts were heading. Kate Inskip was definitely not his type. She'd never be his type, not in a million years.

He liked his women soft-voiced, sweet-tempered, gentle and affectionate, preferably with big blue eyes; the old-fashioned type who enjoyed cossetting and cooking for a man; women devoted to hearth and home; women, in short, who reminded him of his lovely Gabriella.

He definitely did not go for the bossy, assertive, independent, prickly little broads who neither needed nor welcomed a man's protection. He was not into modern-day shrews.

Any man who got close to Kate Inskip would have to be prepared for skirmishes and fireworks. She was not a lady who would come tamely to a man's hand. Hell, he'd have to find a way of getting her to stop talking, no mean feat in itself, before he could even kiss her.

Still, that beautiful mouth just might make it worth the effort, he reflected.

The effect of his thoughts on his body made him realize just how long it had been since he'd gotten tangled up with a woman. The fact that he was even taking a second look at this one was proof that it had been much too long. Ms Inskip was right; one of the problems with living this far from civilization was exactly that: it was damned remote and that severely limited the number of his female acquaintances.

Attractive, wealthy, trendy women showed up as guests at the resort from time to time, of course, but Jared had long ago learned that being some rich woman's vacation fling was not his thing. Maybe his reluctance to get temporarily involved with the women who showed up at Crystal Cove stemmed from the fact that he had once been happily married and had learned the comforts of long-term domesticity. No doubt about it, life with Gabriella had spoiled him.

Whatever the reason, he'd never really gotten the hang of casual affairs; never wanted to get the hang of them. He did not like the idea of waking up in the morning with the feeling he'd become one more souvenir.

He studied Kate's gracefully sprawled form more closely. She didn't really look like the type of woman who collected sexual souvenirs, he told himself. Nor did she look like the overindulged, trendy, jet-setter type. She appeared to be exactly what she'd implied she was, a stressed-out businesswoman who badly needed a vacation. The thought was vaguely reassuring.

Then he flashed again on the memory of Sharp Arnie's expression of shock when the little man had finally realized he'd chosen the wrong tourist. Jared grinned. The tale of Ms Inskip's fearless stand in the alley would make a good story, and a good story was always a welcome diversion on Amethyst Island.

When you lived this far from civilization, he reflected, you learned to get a lot of mileage out of old-fashioned forms of amusement.

Chapter Two

KATE AWOKE IN FLOWER-SCENTED DARKNESS.

For a long, confused moment she tried to figure out what was wrong. The bed felt unfamiliar and the soft, balmy air wafting through the room was definitely not coming from her apartment furnace.

In the next moment reality returned, and she rolled over with a heartfelt groan. She was trapped in paradise for four interminable weeks. She wondered if she would survive.

She sat up slowly and cautiously, prepared to sink back into the pillows if the effects of jet lag had not yet fully worn off. But she got to her feet with minimal difficulty and realized she felt infinitely better than she had several hours earlier when she'd collapsed shortly after her arrival on Amethyst.

She had only a bleary memory of what the island and the resort had looked like as she'd trudged up the path from the dock. Glistening white ultramodern buildings elegantly sprawled above a crystal clear cove had been the dominant impression. She'd been blindly following the two bronzed, dark-haired, dark-eyed young men who were carrying her luggage, and as soon as she'd gotten rid of them she'd fallen into bed.

Why wasn't the sun shining, she wondered in growing annoyance as she fumbled her way across the room. Everything felt out of kilter. A glance at the clock showed it was only 10:00 p.m. She had been asleep for several hours but not all night. What she really ought to do was go straight back to bed. Unfortunately she felt wide awake and hungry.

She turned her head and was transfixed by the view of moonlight on water that filled the screened opening on the far side of the room. Fascinated, she crossed the cool bare floors and stood staring out at the silvered sea. Palm fronds rustled softly on the other side of the screen. The fragrance of the night filled her head, and images danced in her brain.

With very little effort she could envision a tall-masted sailing ship in the cove and hear the shouts of its rough crew as it went to work unloading the captured cargo.

She could almost see the figure of the captain. He would be tall and broad shouldered with a lean, strong body and a harshly etched face. High cheekbones, gray eyes and thick, dark hair. Perhaps a bit of silver in the hair for character, Kate decided. Ever since she herself had passed thirty, she'd noticed her heroes had started showing hints of gray in their hair.

A rumble in the region of her stomach reminded her that she hadn't eaten in over twelve hours. Reluctantly Kate turned away from the screened wall and found a light switch.

The room was surprisingly pleasant, she had to admit as she surveyed the spacious suite. The rattan and wicker furniture with its flower-spattered cushions looked comfortable and appropriate in a way it never did when she looked at the stuff in the import shops in Seattle. The dreaded ceiling fan was spinning lazily overhead, coaxing the balmy breezes into the room. There was even a private veranda on the other side of the screen.

It wasn't really so bad.

All in all, Kate decided, she might be able to get through the next four weeks, providing she didn't expire from boredom. Maybe she could entertain herself by working on characters for her next novel. After all, the setting alone should provide inspiration.

Cheered by that thought, she rummaged through her suitcases until she found a jungle print blouse and a pair of khaki slacks. She could only hope that the Crystal Cove restaurant would still be open at this hour. She was starving.

She opened the door of her room and found herself on a narrow, torch-lit path that wound through a garden past other guest-room doors. She followed the gravel walk through lush, heavy-leafed foliage until she came to a small lagoon. Here the path turned and traced the edge of the water until it reached the wide, open-air lobby of the resort.

Lights, laughter, music and a number of hotel guests dressed in flowered shirts and colorful muumuus assured Kate she had come to the right place.

She was about to cross the narrow bridge over the lagoon when a small, dark-haired figure dressed in jeans and a T-shirt darted out of a clump of ferns and collided with her.

"Oops, sorry." The boy, who looked to be about nine years old, stepped back instantly and peered up at her. "Didn't mean to run into you like that. I was chasin' my friend, Carl. You okay, ma'am?"

"I'm fine," Kate assured him, aware there was something familiar about the youngster. This time she didn't have to rack her brain for the answer. She smiled. "I'll bet I know who you are."

"Yeah?" The boy looked immediately intrigued. "How much?"

"I beg your pardon?" Kate said in confusion.

"How much do you want to bet?" the boy clarified patiently.

"Good grief, it was just a figure of speech."

"You don't want to bet?" The boy appeared disappointed.

"Well, I suppose I could go as far as a quarter, since I'm so sure I know who you are."

"A quarter? That's nothing."

"Fifty cents?" This was getting ridiculous, Kate decided.

"Okay. You've got a bet." The boy grinned. "Who am I?"

"Are you by any chance related to Jared Hawthorne?"

The slashing grin was a mirror image of Jared's. "He's my dad." There was a wealth of pride in the statement. He immediately dug two quarters out of his rear pocket and handed them to her. "My name is David. How did you guess who I was?"

"It wasn't hard." The combination of dark hair and silver-gray eyes would have been difficult to mistake, Kate thought wryly. She carefully dropped the coins into her shoulder bag. "I'm Kate Inskip."

"Oh, wow." David Hawthorne's eyes lit up with genuine excitement. "You're the lady who kicked the knife out of Sharp Arnie's hand today, aren't you? My dad told me all about it. He said you looked like some kind of lady commando in action. Man, I wish I'd been there to see you do it."

Kate wrinkled her nose. "Lady commando? Your father certainly has a way with words."

"My dad kicked Sharp Arnie off our island a couple of years ago. Ol' Arnie's never come back," David said.

"I'm not surprised. Probably found out he couldn't get a room with air-conditioning."

"Huh?"

"Never mind." Kate smiled again. "Know where I can get a bite to eat?"

"Well, the main restaurant closed fifteen minutes ago, but the bar serves snacks and stuff most of the night. You can get just about anything you want there."

"Thanks, I'll do that. Are you always up and around at this hour of the night?"

"Sure. Except on school nights. But there's no school tomorrow."

"I see."

"Dad says as long as I'm living in a resort, I might as well keep resort hours as much as possible. People stay up late at places like this, you know."

"I see."

David chewed on his lip for a second, looking torn. Then he appeared to come to a decision. "Would you do me a big favor, Ms Inskip? Would you teach me how to do that special kick you used on Sharp Arnie? Dad said you knocked the knife out of Arnie's hand, then stomped him right into the pavement with your high heels."

Kate looked down at the boy. "Is that exactly what your father said? I stomped Sharp Arnie into the pavement?"

"Yeah," David assured her with relish. "Right after you kicked Arnie in the...uh–" He broke off abruptly and coughed. "That is, well, you know. Anyhow, I'd really like to learn how to do that."

The kid was irresistible, Kate decided. Pity the father was such a loudmouth. "All right. One of these days I'll show you how I did it."

David brightened. "That'd be great. Maybe I could show you something in return."

"Like what?"

"How about the reefs? Know how to use a snorkel?"

"I've never tried."

David grinned. "Then we've got a deal. You show me how to stomp a sucker like Sharp Arnie into the pavement, and I'll show you how to use a mask and snorkel around the reefs."

"Deal."

David nodded, satisfied. He led the way over the small bridge into the wide lobby. "Bar's that way."

"Thanks. Nice meeting you, David."

"See you around real soon." David took off in the direction of the front desk where he greeted one of the clerks and promptly disappeared into a back room. He was obviously very much at home.

An odd way to raise a child, Kate reflected as she made her way through the lobby, but then, she was hardly an expert. She thought wistfully of the plans for children she had once made, plans that had gone up in smoke on the day her husband had filed for divorce. She wouldn't have minded a little boy like David Hawthorne; a child full of life and mischief and the future. But you couldn't have everything, she reminded herself firmly. Fate had dealt her a different hand than the one she had originally intended to play, and she had learned to live with it.

With the ease of long practice, she pushed the emotional images aside.

Her mind instantly zeroed in on another matter entirely. If there was a junior Hawthorne around, there must be a Mrs. Hawthorne. It gave Kate an unexpected jolt to realize Jared might be married. Then she told herself it was hardly an important issue to her.

She glanced at the paneled lobby walls and noticed that they were covered with several ethereal watercolors. It didn't take a trained eye to tell they were excellent. Which only went to prove that art was where you found it, she thought. She paused to examine two or three of the soft, translucent seascapes and wondered if the artist lived on Amethyst.

After a few moments of scrutiny, Kate made her way into a darkened, thatched-roof bar that hung out over the water's edge. Huge fan-backed wicker chairs clustered around small tables, providing islands of privacy for couples. The tiny candles burning on each table revealed that the lounge was comfortably busy.

Kate quickly located an empty fan chair, sat down and grabbed the small bar menu. A sarong-draped waitress appeared a minute later, smiling in welcome.

"I'd like one of these pineapple-and-rum drinks," Kate said, deciding to be adventurous. "And a bowl of the conch chowder." Was that going to be enough? She was really hungry. "Some of the fried plantains, I think. And how about a salad?"

"Missed dinner?" the waitress asked with a smile as she jotted down the order.

"Afraid so."

"No problem. I'll be right back. Say, are you by any chance the lady Jared picked up this afternoon over on Ruby? The one who knows karate or something?"

"No. You must be thinking of someone else."

"Oh. All right. But I could have sworn… Never mind. Be back in a few minutes."

Kate settled back and automatically tuned in on the conversations going on around her. It was hard not to listen to others in a restaurant or bar when you were sitting alone. The storyteller in her could never resist listening to someone else's stories.

She did not have to wait long to hear a familiar voice drifting in her direction from the vicinity of the bar. There was no mistaking Jared Hawthorne's deep, dark, amused tones. He was telling a tale and obviously enjoying himself in the process.

"So she turns her damned purse upside down and dumps everything out on the ground. You shoulda seen Arnie's face. But wait, it gets better. She tells Arnie to come and get the wallet, and the stupid little jerk makes a try for it. Then—get this—she kicks the knife out of his hand."

"You're joking." The second male voice had the cultured grace of an English accent. "She kicked him?"

"I swear. Twice. The second time right in the family jewels. Sharp Arnie didn't know what hit him. I wish I'd had a camera. She did, though. She took a couple of pictures of Arnie."

"My word. If that's her idea of a souvenir photograph, she must have a very interesting album at home."

"That thought did cross my mind."

Kate got to her feet as her drink arrived. "Thank you," she said crisply, taking the tall glass out of the waitress's hand. "I'll be right back."

Drink in hand, Kate marched the short distance to where Jared was lounging on a stool. His back was to her as he sat, elbows folded in front of him, one foot casually propped on the brass rail that ran around the bottom of the bar. He was intent on telling his story to the bartender, a square-jawed, balding man who carried himself with a distinctly military bearing. The crisply ironed khaki shirt with its array of epaulets, buttons and pockets added to the overall effect. He was polishing a glass as he enjoyed Jared's tale.

"I'd have given a great deal to have seen the entire affair," the bartender mused, shaking his head in wonder. "What's the lady like? She sounds most remarkable."

"Interesting, but definitely not my type. A real spitfire. Has a tongue that can tear a man to shreds from twenty paces. You should have heard her chewing out Arnie. Took a real strip off him. Even told him he reminded her of her ex-husband, heaven help him."

"Who? Arnie?"

"No, the ex-husband. At any rate, after she'd sent Sharp Arnie running, she started talking about filing a complaint."

"Sam will take care of him."

"That's what I told her. I don't think she was impressed with our brand of local law enforcement, though. She's one prickly little broad, I can tell you that. Not the kind who'd cook your dinner and then fetch your pipe and slippers for you."

"You employ three professional chefs, you don't smoke a pipe and I've never seen you wear a pair of slippers in all the time I've known you. I fail to see the problem."

"Wait until you meet her. You'll see what I mean. A man could get scratched if he wasn't real careful. Ask Sharp Arnie." Jared took a sip from the drink in front of him. "Not bad-looking, though," he added thoughtfully. "I was thinking this afternoon there might be possibilities if you could just figure out a way to get her to close her mouth for thirty seconds or so."

The bartender suddenly sensed Kate's presence. He glanced over Jared's shoulder and his bushy brows climbed. "Short, light brown hair? About five foot five. Nice eyes?"

Jared set down his glass in surprise. "How'd you know?" Realization dawned. "Oh, hell." He groaned and swung slowly around on the stool to face Kate. His smile was deliberately charming. "Good evening, Ms Inskip. Feeling rested?"

"I was feeling much better," Kate murmured, idly stirring her drink with the little parasol that decorated it. "Until I realized I have apparently become a major topic of conversation around here. You folks living on tropical islands must be awfully short of entertainment if you have to resort to gossiping about your paying guests."

In the glow of the candlelight, Jared's starkly carved features looked taut and strained in spite of the smile. Kate was willing to bet he was probably turning a dull red. She wished the lighting was better so she could be certain.

"I was just, uh, telling the colonel here how you took on Sharp Arnie this afternoon," Jared said carefully.

"I was very impressed, Ms Inskip," the bartender said, sounding genuinely admiring. "Very impressed, indeed."

"In spite of the fact that I'm one prickly little broad?" Kate smiled sweetly and sipped her drink. "In spite of the fact that I can tear a man to shreds with my tongue at twenty paces? In spite of the fact that I can't be relied on to fetch a man his pipe and slippers?"

"Unlike our friend Jared here, I've always admired a female who speaks up for herself," the colonel declared gallantly. "Never did care for lady wimps."

"Then we have something in common. I myself am not fond of wimps, male or female." Kate allowed her glance to flicker assessingly over Jared. "And there is certainly nothing more useless than a man who arrives too late to be of assistance to a lady in distress, is there?"

"Christ," Jared muttered. "You want to dig your claws in a little deeper? Maybe draw some blood this time?"

"Pay no attention to him, Ms Inskip. He's just the boss around here. I hope you will allow the management to buy you another drink. After what you've been through today, you deserve a second." The colonel reached for a glass.

"How kind of you." Kate inclined her head in a gracious gesture. "Have it sent over to the table, please. And do thank the *management* for me, will you? I wouldn't want anyone to think I wasn't properly appreciative."

"I'll pass the word along," the colonel promised on a soft chuckle.

Still smiling, Kate removed the little parasol from her glass and stuck it into Jared's shirt pocket. He didn't move. "Very nice," she said, stepping back to admire the effect. "No home-cooked meal, pipe or slippers, I'm afraid, but don't ever say I lack the feminine touch. Now if you'll excuse me, I'll get back to my dinner." She turned away, pointedly ignoring Jared, who sat grim mouthed on his stool.

"Seems very nice to me, Jared," the colonel remarked loudly enough for Kate to overhear. "But then I've always had a certain appreciation for the feisty type myself. Never boring, you know."

Kate did not hear whatever it was Jared mumbled in response. She was quite satisfied with having made her feelings known. Jared Hawthorne might think twice next time before he entertained others with outrageous stories about innocent tourists.

Kate's full attention was captured by the bowl of steaming conch chowder that awaited her at her table. She resumed her seat, took a last swallow of the pineapple-and-rum concoction in her glass and prepared to dig in. She'd taken no more than two spoonfuls of the chowder when she realized she was no longer alone. It didn't take a great deal of intuition to guess who was impinging on her privacy.

"Here's your free drink," Jared said, looming up out of the shadows to stand beside her table. He put it down in front of her. "I'll have the chowder put on the house tab, too."

Without asking permission, he sprawled gracefully in the other fan chair. Kate noticed he was still wearing the tiny parasol in his shirt pocket. His hooded eyes met hers across the candle flame.

"I suppose you'd like an apology?" Jared said.

He looked right at home framed by the exotic wicker backdrop, Kate observed. The glow of the candle gleamed off his long, dark hair and highlighted his harsh, bold features. The unwavering intensity of his gaze was startling. For a moment she stared at him and saw an island lord who lived just beyond the reach of civilization; a man who could indulge himself by playing by his own rules; a pirate. Frowning, she dismissed the mental image.

"An apology?" Kate considered that. "No, I don't think you have to bother giving me one. Apologies only work when they're genuine, you see. In your case we both know you'd just be offering one out of fear of having insulted a paying guest who might pack up and leave in a huff. You're only thinking of the resort's cash flow. Don't worry, the free drink and chowder will suffice. I'm not going to stage a grand exit just because you think I'm a prickly little broad. I have two brothers and an ex-husband. Believe me, I've been called worse."

"I'm greatly relieved to hear that."

"And don't lose any sleep over that crack about me not being your type, because I assure you the feeling is mutual."

Jared swore softly, his expression one of chagrin. "I'm sorry. I never meant to offend you."

"I know. You were just telling a good story. Don't worry, I understand. Sometimes it's hard to resist the impulse. I should know. I make my living telling stories."

"What kind of stories?"

"I write historical romance."

"Published?"

"Yup."

Jared looked momentarily at a loss. "I don't think I've ever read anything by you," he finally admitted.

Kate smiled brilliantly. "What a pity. One more thing we don't have in common."

"Are you trying to get rid of me?"

"I'm trying to eat my dinner. I happen to be extremely hungry. Stomping knife-wielding assailants into the pavement always has that effect on us lady commandoes."

"Trying to apologize to a prickly little broad has the same effect on me." Jared helped himself to one of Kate's fried plantain slices. "So tell me, Ms Inskip, do all the ladies back in the States take two-week classes in self-defense these days?"

"More and more of us are. How long has it been since you've been back?"

Jared shrugged. "I go once a year to take my son to see his grandparents. That's about it. I'm not too fond of the mainland. I moved out here to Amethyst a long time ago and I've never wanted to leave."

"You like it out here where you get to play king of the island, right?"

Jared smiled slowly, white teeth glinting. "Right."

"What did you do before you built Crystal Cove?"

Jared shrugged. "I was born into the hotel business and I grew up in it. My father was a vice president with one of the big international chains. We lived all over the world. Later I decided to follow in his footsteps. But I soon realized that, although I loved the business, I wasn't cut out to work for a corporation. One day I chucked it all and went out on my own."

He definitely did not look like a corporate animal, Kate thought. "Is your wife equally satisfied with island life?" Kate could have kicked herself for asking, but she suddenly had to know for certain if he was married.

Jared's smile vanished. "My wife died five years ago. And yes, she loved living here. But then she would have been happy anywhere as long as she was with me and David. Gabriella was that kind of woman."

"I see." Kate didn't know what else to say. Jared had obviously been married to a paragon, and now he was alone. "I'm sorry."

"Thanks, but don't worry about it. Five years is a long time. David doesn't remember her and, as for me, I've adjusted."

Kate was very sorry she had given in to her curiosity. She felt as though she had intruded on something very private within this man. Instinctively she backed off, looking for a way out of the overly personal conversation. "I ran into your son a while ago. A nice boy."

Jared's eyes reflected paternal satisfaction. "Yeah, he's a good kid." He paused. "Got any of your own?"

Kate struggled to find another exit. "No. My husband and I talked about it a few times, but he wasn't exactly enthusiastic about the idea. Kept saying we should wait, and then one day he was gone altogether and that sort of changed my plans." She scowled at him. "Are you going to eat all my fried plantains?"

Jared glanced down, apparently surprised to discover the inroads he had made into the stack of chips. "Sorry. Again. I seem to be saying that a lot tonight. Want some more? On the house?"

"No, thanks. I'm finally getting full." At least the overly intimate mood was broken, Kate thought in relief. "Now if you'll excuse me, I'll be on my way." She stood up and reached for her purse.

Jared got slowly to his feet. "Look, if you're rushing off on account of me…"

"I'm not," she said flatly. "I'm rushing off so I can take a walk around the resort gardens. I'm supposed to be doing relaxing things. As I explained to Sharp Arnie, I've been under a lot of stress lately. I'm here to unwind. I assume it's safe to walk around at night?"

"Sure, it's safe." Jared was clearly offended. "You can even go down to the beach. The path is well lit. Just don't try to follow any of the paths that lead into the jungle or up to the castle ruins. They're not lit, and unless you know where you're going you could get lost at night."

Kate's attention was riveted instantly. "There really is a castle here?"

Jared's expression was edged with humor. "Yeah, there's really a castle. But no one is allowed up there except on guided tours. The place is crumbling to pieces and it's extremely dangerous."

"I wouldn't be able to see much at night, anyhow. But I'll certainly want to see it while I'm here."

"We schedule regular tours once a week."

Kate nodded absently, thinking it would probably be far more interesting to explore the place on her own. She had never been enamored of tour groups. "Fine."

"And you'll probably want to see about a costume for the masquerade ball the night after next," Jared added quickly as Kate turned to leave.

She halted and tilted her head inquiringly to one side. "What masquerade ball?"

"In honor of the pirate who discovered this island and built the castle," Jared explained. "The day after tomorrow is supposedly his birthday and the resort makes a big deal of it. We also use his wedding date and the date he arrived on the island and Christmas as excuses to hold the damned ball three more times during the year. The masquerades have become an institution. The guests get a kick out of them. Everyone dresses up in early nineteenth-century costumes."

"I don't have a costume."

"A lot of the regulars bring their own, but for those who don't, the gift shop rents them."

"How nice for the resort's bottom line," Kate observed.

"We try to be a little more subtle than Sharp Arnie, but the goal is similar."

"To part the tourist from his dollar? I understand. I'll check with the gift shop tomorrow. I've never been to a masquerade ball. Wouldn't want to miss anything on my vacation. I have friends at home who will expect a complete report. Good night, Mr. Hawthorne."

"Good night, Ms Inskip." He echoed her mocking formality with a courtly inclination of his head that seemed to suit him.

The Old World grace of the small gesture triggered another fleeting sense of recognition. For an instant longer Kate studied Jared, trying to place him. Then she turned on her heel and left.

Jared stood where he was for a long moment, watching the unconsciously elegant swing of her hips as she walked out of the bar. Then with a small rueful sigh, he headed back to his stool.

"Did you dig yourself back out of that pit you were in the last time I saw you?" the colonel asked as Jared sat down.

"She didn't dump her chowder or the drink over my head, did she? Payoff time, Colonel." Jared held out his hand.

The colonel sighed and reached into the till for a five-dollar bill, which he reluctantly dropped onto Jared's palm. "I'm not sure you really won that bet fair and square."

"Hey, you can't back out of this, pal. You bet five bucks I'd get the chowder or the drink dumped all over me, and you lost."

"But you did not precisely charm her, did you?"

Jared shrugged. "I wouldn't go that far, but I think I made some progress."

The colonel poured a glass of whiskey and set it in front of his boss. Then he picked up a cloth and began to polish bar ware with fine precision. "I thought you said she wasn't your type."

"True." Jared took a sip of his whiskey.

"You don't usually get involved with paying guests."

"For a lot of good reasons."

"Granted. So why do I get the feeling you're about to break a few of your own rules?"

"There's something different about this one, Colonel. Something that interests me. I can't quite figure out what it is."

"A man who allows himself to get overly curious about a woman is a man headed for deep water."

"I can swim." Jared raised his glass in an ironic salute. "But as usual, you speak words of great wisdom, my friend."

"And as usual, I'll probably be ignored," the colonel said. "But you might want to watch your step around that lady. You yourself saw what happened to Sharp Arnie."

"Sharp Arnie got what he deserved. But I'll bear your warning in mind."

"Do that."

"Besides, what's the worst that can happen to me?" Jared asked with a nonchalance he didn't really feel. "She's only going to be here for a month."

"What if she doesn't go home when she's supposed to?"

"The tourists always go home, Colonel. You know that. Sooner or later they all get back on a plane and leave."

"What if that turns out to be the worst that can happen?" the colonel asked quietly.

Jared slanted him a derisive glance. "You worried about me getting my heart broken?"

"Should I?"

"Nope. Like I said, she's definitely not my type. She just happens to interest me, that's all."

"But not seriously."

"Not a chance."

The colonel planted both hands flat on the bar and leaned forward. "Want to bet?"

"You just lost five bucks. Haven't you learned your lesson?"

"Jared, my friend, we both know you've been looking for a wife for the past couple of years. In all this time I haven't seen you get this *interested* in any of the other ladies who've caught your eye. Maybe you shouldn't be so quick to write her off as an unsuitable candidate."

"She said herself we've got nothing in common, and she's right. Take my word for it, Colonel. She'd be all wrong for the job."

"Because she's not like Gabriella?"

"You know, little Ms Spitfire Inskip isn't the only one around here with a big mouth," Jared growled. He was about to change the subject when a movement at the edge of his vision gave him the excuse he needed to end the uncomfortable conversation with his bartender.

He turned his head slightly to watch as a bulky man impeccably dressed in a white straw hat, white slacks, white sandals and a white shirt settled heavily into one of the fanback chairs. The candlelight glinted on the many rings on the pudgy fingers.

"Butterfield's here," the colonel noted, his aristocratic voice turning cooler than usual.

"I see him." Jared reluctantly pushed himself away from the bar. "Guess I'd better go say hello."

"You want to take him his drink?" The colonel was already pouring out a hefty portion of straight rum.

"Sure. Why not? Save him the trip. You know how Max feels about exercise. Make it a double."

Picking up the rum, Jared left his own whiskey on the bar and made his way through the gloom to the table where the portly man sat. Max Butterfield had removed his hat, displaying a pink scalp surrounded by a fringe of gray.

The overweight man looked up expectantly as Jared joined him. He took the glass of rum and downed a swallow before saying a word. Then he beamed, displaying dimples. "Ah, manna from heaven. Just what I needed, my boy."

"I figured it might be." Jared took the other seat. "Is it still on for tonight?"

"Most definitely, most definitely. I've been counting on this little inspection tour you've arranged." Max lifted his glass in a toast. "To our successful completion of this project."

"The sooner it's over, the better, as far as I'm concerned."

"Such impatience, my boy. You must learn to control it. Everything in due course. Matters will be resolved soon enough."

"How soon?"

"Oh, I'd say sometime during the next month. The fish have taken the bait. It's just a matter of time."

FORTY-FIVE MINUTES AFTER SHE'D LEFT the hotel, Kate rose from the moonlit rock where she had been sitting and started slowly back toward the lights of the resort. She thought she would be able to get back to sleep now, though her body still seemed confused.

It wasn't just her body that was mixed up, she reflected. Her mind was definitely off track, too.

She'd been sitting on the dark beach dwelling on the subject of Jared Hawthorne, of all things, and for the life of her, Kate could not figure out quite why. It was disturbing because the man was clearly not her type.

She was wise enough to know she did not *have* a real-life type when it came to men. The man she longed for existed only in her dreams and between the covers of her books.

On some intuitive level, Kate had always accepted that she would never actually meet her fantasy hero. She frequently joked to Sarah and Margaret that she probably wouldn't like him if she did happen to meet him. He would be too arrogant, too proud and infuriating and much too macho for a twentieth-century woman to tolerate.

When she had eventually decided to fall in love and marry at the age of twenty-nine, Kate had deliberately chosen the sort of man modern women were supposed to covet. Harry had appeared to be a sensitive, supportive, intellectually stimulating male. There had been poetry and candlelight, art films and a shared interest in writing. What more could any woman realistically want, Kate had asked herself.

But things had gone steadily wrong, and after the divorce, Kate had been consumed for a time with a sense of failure and guilt. She knew in her heart she should never have married Harry in the first place. It had been wrong for both of them.

To exorcise the demons, she had turned to the one true love she could always count on—her writing. She knew now that Sarah and Margaret had been right when they said she had allowed her work to consume her these past two and a half years. One needed balance in life if one was to survive and stay sane.

Amazing how clear that was tonight, Kate thought with a smile. Perhaps her friends had been right. A vacation was exactly what she had needed.

Holding her sandals in one hand, she trudged through the sand toward the path that led up from the cove. It was an easy, well-lit walk, and she would have been back in her room within fifteen minutes if she'd stayed on it.

But she didn't stay on it because she came across a fork in the path. One branch was barred with a heavy chain and a sign that warned trespassers not to proceed any farther unless accompanied by an approved guide from the hotel staff.

Kate knew instantly that she had just found the path that led to the mysterious private castle.

There was no way in the world she could resist taking a peek. She was no fool, however. She certainly wouldn't risk her neck exploring the ruins alone at night. But she couldn't see the harm in catching a glimpse of the castle. An old pirate fortress drenched in moonlight was more than any romance writer worth her salt could possibly ignore.

She slipped under the heavy chain that barred the way and managed to get several feet along the steep, dark path before she heard the soft, masculine voices behind her. She froze, recognizing one of the voices instantly.

Discretion, at times, was the better part of valor, Kate decided as she ducked into a clump of thick ferns.

She could not really explain, even to herself, why she decided to hide rather than confront Jared Hawthorne. Kate just knew that in that moment she really did not feel up to defending her reasons for flagrantly violating his edict.

Besides, it would be embarrassing to be chewed out in front of a stranger, and she could hear the second man quite clearly. She was fairly certain that Jared would have no compunction at all about reading her the riot act in front of others for daring to climb the castle path.

The rich, humid jungle scent of the ferns enveloped her as she crouched motionlessly. She smiled as Jared and an overweight man dressed all in white went past within a yard of where she hid. Jared was moving easily, but the portly man was breathing heavily. Kate hugged herself and grinned. She suddenly felt as if she were involved in a small, delightful adventure.

It wasn't until the two men had vanished along the trail and Kate had quickly escaped back toward the resort that she found herself wondering why Jared was breaking his own house rules.

She could think of no reasonable explanation for the owner of the Crystal Cove resort to be escorting anyone up the dark, forbidden castle path at this hour.

Chapter Three

KATE PICKED UP THE SKIRTS OF HER diaphanous, high-waisted gown, adjusted the silver mask that concealed the top portion of her face and crossed the small bridge over the lagoon. She walked into the lantern-lit resort lobby and was instantly transported back to a time and place she had frequently visited in her imagination.

It gave her a disorienting sense of déjà vu. Things looked remarkably familiar, even though she knew she had never walked into such a scene before in her life.

She had stepped into a charming recreation of a Regency-era ballroom. Men dressed in austere black and white circled the room to the strains of a waltz. The ladies in their arms were all wearing low-necked off-the-shoulder gowns that floated around their ankles. Here and there a variety of other costumes added flavor to the colorful mix. Wealthy nineteenth-century planters, pirates, grass-skirted ladies and one or two ship-wrecked sailors bobbed amid the elegant crowd. Everyone wore a mask.

No doubt about it, the costume rental business was a thriving one here on Amethyst Island.

Kate instantly dismissed the exorbitant price she had paid to rent her own lovely yellow gown. It was worth every penny, she decided as she moved into the airy room.

She was asked to dance before she got halfway across the lobby. Smiling, she stepped into the arms of a masked stranger and found herself waltzing for the first time in her life. It was surprisingly easy, she discovered. It was as if she had always known how to waltz.

"This is really something, isn't it? I mean, I came here to go diving, and I end up at a masquerade ball. I almost didn't spring for the costume, but at the last minute I decided to give the thing a whirl." The redheaded stranger grinned beneath his mask as he swung Kate around in a wide circle. "I'm glad I did. Been here on the island long?"

"No." Kate really didn't feel like talking. It broke the spell. She just wanted to drift around the room to the glorious strains of the waltz and pretend she was in another world.

"Diving's terrific around here. You dive?"

"No. I've never had the opportunity. I wouldn't mind learning, though."

"The resort provides instruction, if you're interested. Even if you don't want to go the whole route, you could rent a snorkel and mask. The reefs are unbelievable. It's like being inside a saltwater aquarium filled with the most spectacular fish in the world."

Kate smiled at the man's enthusiasm. "I'll give the snorkeling, at least, a try," she said as they drew to a temporary halt and waited for the music to resume.

"Do that. I'll be glad to show you the ropes. Unless you're, uh, here with someone special?"

"No. There's no one special, but I do have a snorkeling instructor lined up."

"Just my luck. Maybe I could buy you a drink in the bar instead?" the redheaded man persisted.

"Later, perhaps."

"The name's Jeff Taylor."

"Mine is Kate Inskip." She was searching for something else polite to say and wishing the music would start again, when a miniature pirate tugged on her arm. She looked down to see Jared's son, David, in an elaborate costume complete with eye patch and plastic cutlass.

"Hi, David."

"Hi, Ms Inskip. You recognized me, huh? I recognized you right away, too. You look great tonight."

"Thank you. You look pretty sharp yourself."

David glanced at Jeff Taylor and Kate could have sworn she detected a hint of disapproval in the boy's eye. "Seen Dad, Ms Inskip?"

"No, I haven't."

"He's supposed to be around here someplace."

"I'll keep an eye out for him," Kate promised. The more she got to know David, the better she liked him. They had become instant friends. Twice during the past two days he had turned up to chat with her while she sat on the beach in the shade of an umbrella. He'd settled in next to her for some time this afternoon and rattled on about everything from the small island school he attended to his shell collection. He had even taken her beach-combing, and she'd returned to her room with some lovely specimens.

Now David seemed disinclined to leave, though he was supposedly looking for his father. The boy eyed Jeff Taylor again. "So," he said, clearing his throat and trying for a nonchalant pose. "You having a good time, Ms Inskip?"

"I certainly am. Mr. Taylor and I were just talking about the great snorkeling around here."

"Right," David said quickly. "Remember I'm going to teach you how to snorkel."

"I wouldn't mind giving her a few lessons," Jeff volunteered.

"No offense, Mr. Taylor, but you're just a visitor here. I've lived here all my life, and I know the waters around here like the back of my hand."

"I'm sure you do," Jeff Taylor said diplomatically. "But I'd kind of like to show Ms Inskip some of the places I've discovered on my own."

"Perhaps after I've had my lessons from David, I could see some of the reef with you, Jeff," Kate said, making her own attempt at diplomacy.

"My dad could show you the reef," David said quickly. "If you want to snorkel with a grown-up, that is."

So much for diplomacy. "I'm sure he's a very busy man," Kate murmured.

She prayed that much was true. More than once during the past two days she had felt a strange tingling sensation at the back of her neck. When she'd turned around, she'd found Jared Hawthorne watching her with a narrowed, intent gaze. It had happened at poolside and two or three times in the restaurant where Jared apparently ate lunch and dinner with his young son. It had also happened again last night in the lounge. She had gone back to her room, aware of an unsettling sensation of being pursued.

A writer had to work hard to keep her imagination under control, Kate thought.

"I'll bet he could find the time." The boy glanced at Jeff Taylor again and then back at Kate. "Maybe we should go ahead and set a time for the lessons. How about tomorrow morning?"

"Well," Kate began hesitantly. Then she saw the anxious look on David's face. "Tomorrow would be fine."

"Great. It's all settled. Guess I'd better say hello to my friends Travis and Carl. They're here tonight with their parents, along with some other folks I know. They always come to these masquerade parties."

"That's nice. Do you have a lot of friends here on the island?" Kate asked.

"Lots," David assured her brightly. "Dad and I know everyone here on Amethyst."

"I see. I'm sure they're all very nice."

"Yeah, they are. Well. See you later."

Kate nodded. "Goodbye, David."

The boy still looked reluctant to leave her alone with Jeff Taylor, but he finally turned and darted off through the crowd. Jeff chuckled. "I think the kid's got a crush on you."

"Unfortunately, he's a little young for me."

"I, on the other hand, would appear to be just about the right age. Shall we try another waltz?"

For the next hour Kate danced to her heart's content, first with Jeff and then with a very nice middle-aged man who had obviously been wedged into his evening clothes with a shoehorn. After him she found herself in the arms of a nineteenth-century sailor who wore a gold earring in one ear.

Kate lost track after the sailor. The truth was she didn't care who partnered her. She was lost in the fantasy. She floated around the floor in the arms of strangers and imagined herself to be a fine Regency lady who had been kidnapped and carried off to the island kingdom of a wealthy, dangerous pirate, who was secretly the son of an earl.

The man had his reasons for turning pirate, Kate decided, automatically plotting a novel in her head while she danced. Vengeance, perhaps. Whatever the reason, someday he would return to England to claim his title and his estates. But in the meantime he lived a life of violence and elegance here on a tropical island. And he was tired of living it alone. Hence the kidnapping of the lovely lady. How else was such a man to obtain a bride?

At the end of the first hour of steady waltzing, Kate finally allowed herself to take a short break. Edging through the crowded lobby, she made her way outside into the scented, balmy night.

She just wanted a few minutes alone in the moonlight to catch her breath, she decided, as she moved along the garden path. She was feeling oddly enthralled, almost lightheaded. She wanted to savor the fantasy. Tomorrow she would dig out a notepad and jot down all the plot ideas that were occurring to her tonight.

For a moment she thought she was dreaming when she rounded a bend in the garden path and saw the rakish, dark-haired buccaneer waiting for her. He lounged in the shadows of a palm, his wide-sleeved white shirt giving him a ghostlike appearance in the moonlight. He wore a leather belt and gleaming leather boots. The handle of a surprisingly lethal-looking dagger gleamed at his hip. His black half mask shielded the upper portion of his face. The polite inclination of his head was both elegant and arrogant. Kate halted a few feet away.

"I trust you are enjoying yourself, madam?" Jared asked, smiling faintly. He didn't stir from the shadows.

Did he know who she was, Kate wondered. Possibly. She had recognized him instantly, even before she heard his distinctive, rough-textured voice. She realized with a small shock that she would have known him anywhere.

"I am enjoying the evening very much." Kate was suddenly afraid to move lest she shatter the shimmering magic.

"Did you know the ball is in honor of my birthday?"

Kate regarded him with deep interest. "I was told the ball was in honor of a certain pirate's birthday."

"I never liked the word *pirate* myself. Too difficult to define. One man's pirate is another man's loyal privateer, still another's hard-working sea captain."

"Now I myself have never had any trouble spotting a true pirate the minute I see one," Kate said.

"Have you ever actually seen one?"

She thought of the man who had haunted her dreams most of her adult life, the pirate who existed only in her imagination. "Oh, yes. I've seen one."

"Ah, so you consider yourself an expert on the subject?"

"I like to think so."

"But even experts make mistakes." Jared held out his arm. "Will you walk with me in the gardens, Madam Expert?"

Kate hesitated for an instant, a delicious sensation of adventure making her cautious. The entire evening was beginning to feel like something out of a dream, and though she was in the business of creating dreams she had never before found herself in the middle of one.

But dreams, she was discovering, had a power all their own. On impulse she stepped forward and curled her fingers around Jared's arm.

"Tell me about yourself, my lord pirate," she said as they began to stroll through the scented tropical greenery.

"What would you like to know?"

"Well, to begin with, why did you come here to Amethyst Island?"

"I think you know the answer to that."

She nodded. "You wanted to carve out your own kingdom."

"There are not many places left in the world where a man can do that. Some men were not born to live in cities or to work for corporations or to answer to others. Some men prefer to live on their own terms and keep civilization at arm's length."

"I can understand that."

"Can you?" Jared sounded intrigued.

"Of course. I write about such men all the time."

"Ah, yes. The heroes of your books. Maybe you do understand. Tell me, Kate, why do you set your stories in the past?"

She smiled. "That's a good question. I'm not certain of the answer, but it's probably because so many modern men seem unsure of themselves, so easily intimidated by strong women." Kate thought briefly of her ex-husband.

"Do you prefer strong men?"

"Most of the women I know prefer strong, centered men. I'm no exception."

"Tell me something, Kate. Do you think you could ever stop doing battle with a strong man long enough to let him make love to you?" Jared asked softly. "Could you take the risk of letting such a man touch you?"

Kate caught her breath. She looked up at him quickly and was dazzled by the sensual warmth in his gaze. "I'm not sure I should answer that."

Jared gave a muffled exclamation that could have been part laughter and part oath. He drew her closer to his side, so close that Kate's hip brushed his muscular thigh and her bare shoulder grazed his arm. He was a hard, powerful man, and underneath the physical strength was an equally fierce sexuality. She could feel that raw energy radiating from him. It enveloped her, enthralled her, excited her. She sensed the primitive response deep within herself, and the knowledge that she was capable of such a reaction shook her to the core.

"Maybe you're not quite as daring as you think you are," Jared said.

Kate shrugged lightly in the low-necked gown and saw his pirate's gaze drift to the curves of her breasts. She felt suddenly very exposed. The gown was no worse than a swimsuit, she told herself firmly, but that didn't lessen the vulnerable sensation. "Maybe I just haven't had a lot of experience with strong men. There never seem to be very many around."

Jared drew her to a halt in the shadows of a wide-leafed tree that towered over the path. "Women like you are rare, too. Maybe we both have a few things to learn."

She looked up at him and experienced another jolt of awareness. She was startled to feel herself trembling with anticipation. "Are you going to kiss me?"

"Yes," Jared said slowly, as if he had reached an important decision, "I am. I have to do it. I've been thinking about this for two solid days and it's been driving me crazy."

He bent his head and brought his mouth slowly down on hers. There was no hurry about it. It was as if he was content to take his time and discover all he wished to know about her.

Kate closed her eyes as the compelling fantasy in which she was moving suddenly became as solid as reality. A deep, sensual tug in the pit of her stomach caused her to almost lose her balance. Instinctively she wrapped her fingers around Jared's upper arms, seeking support.

He groaned in response and eased her back against the trunk of the tree. His mouth was warm, strong and searching, and when he moved close, Kate could feel the heat in his body. The fire in him was lighting a blaze within her.

She sensed his hands moving up from her waist, gliding along her rib cage until his thumbs rested just beneath the curves of her breasts. The touch was exquisitely intimate, inviting a response.

Kate parted her lips and surprised herself by nearly panicking for a brief, nerve-shattering moment. The hungry, captivating manner in which Jared took deep possession of her mouth was a revelation to her. She had never had any man's kiss jangle her senses this way. It set off distant alarm bells.

The panic subsided almost at once, to be replaced by a longing unlike anything Kate had ever known. Her arms tightened around Jared's neck, and she whispered his name in a small, choked voice when he freed her lips. She clung to him more tightly and kissed his throat.

"You're full of surprises," he muttered, as if making an important discovery. He nibbled passionately on her earlobe. "A man never knows what he's going to encounter next."

"You're not quite what I expected, either." She pulled slightly away from him, searching his gaze in the darkness.

She could see nothing beyond the glint of moonlight in Jared's eyes. It occurred to her that she was just as well hidden from him. There was something reassuring about the sense of anonymity provided by the masks. It was as if they were both unaccountably free to play this reckless game tonight.

"Well, Madam Expert, what's the verdict? Am I truly a pirate?"

"Yes, my lord, you are. There is no doubt about it."

"Then that makes me an expert," Jared said with a slow smile.

"On what?"

"Ladies like you, of course."

It was Kate's turn to smile. Never had she felt so full of such sweet, seductive, feminine power. It gave her a heady thrill. "Your logic is very profound."

"The way I see it, contrary to your earlier opinion, we do indeed have something in common."

"Do you think so?" she asked with mocking doubt.

"I'm very sure of it."

Without releasing her, Jared swung around so his back was against the tree trunk. He deliberately widened his stance and drew Kate between his legs. The skirts of her yellow gown drifted over his thighs. She put her hands on his waist and felt the hilt of the dagger. She was aware of cold metal under her palm. Definitely not plastic, she thought with a start.

"Is this real?"

"The dagger or me?" He nuzzled her throat.

Kate laughed softly. "Both."

"Yes."

"Where did you get it?" She touched the dagger again as she leaned her head against Jared's shoulder.

"He left it behind when he sailed away from the island for the last time. I found it along with some other stuff in an old chest a few years ago."

"Who left it behind? The pirate who built the castle?"

"Umm-hmm." Jared slid his fingers tantalizingly over her bare arm and dropped a small kiss on her shoulder.

"Is this really his birthday?"

"Yes."

"You said this was your birthday."

"It is."

"You're teasing me. Whose birthday is it really?"

"His. And mine." Jared's tongue touched the pulse of her throat.

"That's too much of a coincidence. What was his name?"

"Whose?"

Kate tugged at the crisp hair that filled the neck opening of his shirt. "The pirate's."

"Ouch. That hurts."

"Tell me his name."

"Such a demanding little creature." Jared lifted his head and looked down at her. Then he caught her face between his strong fingers. "His name was Hawthorne. Roger Hawthorne."

Kate was mesmerized. Her mouth fell open. "Really?"

Jared grinned. "It's the truth."

"You're related to him?"

"The connection is a little distant after all these years, but yes, I'm a descendant. I found out about this island through some old records that had come down through the family. One day about fifteen years ago I chucked everything and came out here to find Amethyst Island."

"That's wonderful," Kate breathed.

"You, my sweet, are obviously a sucker for pirates. But who am I to complain? Come closer and let me show you my dagger." He captured her hand and began to guide it slowly down below his belt.

She pulled her fingers free quickly. "Don't get carried away. I'm not a complete pushover for the species."

"How do you know? You've never met a real one. The only pirates you know are the ones you invent in your imagination."

"But I told you I'm an expert." Kate was suddenly tense as the atmosphere became more highly charged. "As much as I may be attracted to pirates, I should warn you that I am not equally attracted to the idea of a vacation fling with one."

The teasing humor went out of him in an instant. "I'm not into flings, either. And as a rule, I don't get involved with paying guests. But I think I'm going to make an exception in your case."

"Is that right?" Kate felt something come alive within her, something that might have been hope.

"Please don't play games with me," Jared said quietly. "We're both old enough and single enough to be able to admit we're attracted to each other. And this..." He stroked her arm in a slow caress and shook his head in silent wonder. "This is something special. I'm old enough to know that, too."

"What happens next?"

"Let's find out." Jared started to kiss her again but halted when a loud, youthful voice called from the garden path.

"Hey, Dad, where are you? Lani says to tell you it's time for the cake. Everyone's waiting."

"Tell her I'll be there in a minute, Dave," Jared called back.

"Okay. Hey, where are you, anyhow? How come you're... Oh. Hi, Ms Inskip."

There was a rustle of leaves and Kate turned in Jared's arms to see David peering in through the foliage. "Hi, Dave."

"What are you guys doing out here in the bushes?" David asked with the perfect innocence only a nine-year-old can muster.

"I was showing Ms Inskip the Hawthorne dagger," Jared said calmly as he released Kate and stepped out from under the heavy leaves.

"Oh, yeah? It's neat, huh, Ms Inskip? Dad uses it to cut the first piece of cake at these parties."

"That's wonderful," Kate murmured. "It's always nice to see an antique get some use. I was afraid the Hawthorne dagger might be nothing more than a useless museum piece after all these years."

Jared bit back a laugh, his eyes glinting with sensual warning. "I'm a great believer in the old adage, use it or lose it. Come on, you two. Let's go cut my birthday cake." He waited until David had run ahead down the path before pulling Kate briefly close once more. "And as for you, my sweet shrew..."

Kate heard the sexy threat in his voice and shivered with anticipation. "What about me?"

"Just be sure you stick around. When I've finished with tonight's festivities, I intend to show you what happens to smart-mouthed, feisty heroines who can't remember their manners. That crack about the antique Hawthorne dagger is not going to go unpunished."

"You expect me to stick around after a threat like that?"

"How can you resist? You're a feisty heroine, aren't you?"

Ten minutes later, the wicked-looking dagger flashed as Jared took the first slice out of a giant cake. The crowd cheered and champagne flowed. Spelled out in red icing across the top of the cake was the name Hawthorne. Beneath it was a carefully picked-out reproduction of the dagger. Kate stood to one side and sipped from a fluted glass as Jared led a salute to his ancestor.

"The guests love these affairs," drawled a voice behind Kate. "I always said this was a smart bit of theater on Hawthorne's part."

Kate turned to look at the man who had spoken. He was not wearing a mask, but even if he had been, she would have recognized him by his girth and his pristine white attire. This was the man who had accompanied Jared on the midnight walk up the castle path the other night. An uneasy chill chased off some of her pleasure.

"You seem to know a lot about these masquerade balls. Are you a regular guest here at Crystal Cove?" Kate asked. She pushed her silver mask up on top of her head to get a better look at the heavyset man.

"I'm not precisely a guest," he responded judiciously. "More like an old friend of the family. I've been living out here in the islands for longer than I can remember. Even longer than Jared. I'm a writer. Allow me to introduce myself. The name is Butterfield. Max Butterfield."

"Katherine Inskip." Kate racked her brain but could not think of anything she had ever read by a Max Butterfield. She smiled to herself. Now she knew how other people felt when they were introduced to her and could not claim to have read her books. "I write, too."

"So I hear. Romance novels."

"What about you?"

"I'm working on a novel, but in the meantime I keep body and soul together by doing the odd travel piece here and there. You know how it is."

Yes, she knew. She felt a wave of sympathy for Max Butterfield. She also wondered how long he had been working on his novel. "Have you known Jared a long time?"

"Years." Max took another long drink. "It's a small world out here in the islands."

"You can say that again, Max. Too small at times." The colonel, nattily attired in an early nineteenth-century British officer's dress uniform smiled benignly as he approached. He had an attractive, vivacious woman in her early forties on his arm. She was wearing a gown similar to Kate's in style, but done in mint green. "Ms Inskip, allow me to present my fiancée, Letty Platt. Letty, this is the heroic Katherine Inskip who leveled Sharp Arnie with but a single blow."

"This is getting embarrassing," Kate complained as she shook the other woman's hand. "What did Jared do? Give the story to the local newspaper?"

Letty Platt grinned, her blue eyes sparkling. "Better than that. He just told it to a couple of people, and within an hour it was all over the island. Out here we thrive on interesting tidbits like that."

Kate realized immediately that she was going to like this woman. "I'll keep that in mind. Do you live here on the island, Letty?"

"Oh, my, yes. My husband brought me out here a long time ago when he took a notion to live on a tropical island. He was Jared's mechanic and general handyman for years before he died."

"I see. And you've been living alone out here for some time now?"

"Not for much longer. The colonel and I will be tying the knot soon." Letty beamed up at the colonel, who patted her hand with proud affection.

"Do you work here at the resort, Letty?" Kate asked.

"Officially, I'm the bookkeeper, but in reality I help out where I'm needed. Enough about me, though. I'm delighted to meet you, Kate," Letty confided. "When the colonel told me you were on the island, I was so excited. I've read all your books except for *Buccaneer's Bride*, which I just bought today in the resort gift shop. Can't wait to start it."

"Thank you." Kate felt herself going an awkward shade of pink, as she always did when she met an enthusiastic fan. This was a part of the business she never quite got accustomed to handling. One of the things she liked about writing for a living was that for the most part she could be quite anonymous.

"The colonel says that in addition to stomping Sharp Arnie, you've managed to shake up Jared a bit, and that's great news as far as I'm concerned," Letty confided cheerfully. "It's wonderful to see Jared take an interest in someone like you. He's been very lonely for a long time, though he'd never admit it."

"If you're playing matchmaker, Letty, I think I should warn you you're wasting your time. I got the distinct impression I don't fit Jared's image of the ideal woman," Kate said. Although that certainly hadn't stopped him from making a very heavy pass a few minutes ago, she reflected. Just as knowing what he thought of her had not kept her from responding.

She must have been out of her mind out there in the garden.

"Nonsense. Come with me, my dear." Letty winked at the colonel as she took Kate's arm and led her a short distance away from the two men. She halted and said in a low voice, "I hope you won't take anything Jared Hawthorne says about women too seriously. Like most men, he doesn't really know what he wants."

"I'm not sure we should be discussing this," Kate said uneasily.

"Probably not, but I've already talked to David and I feel obligated to plead his case. He's decided he wants you and his father to get to know each other better, you see. He's quite taken with you. Told me all about how you're going to teach him your special karate trick."

"This is getting more embarrassing by the minute."

"Don't be embarrassed," Letty said. "The colonel is very observant, a real student of human nature, you know, and he says Jared's fascinated by you. The details of that little scene between the two of you in the bar the other night are making the rounds and, frankly, the whole thing sounds delightful. Just like something out of one of your books. I'm sorry I missed it."

"I doubt if Jared found it delightful."

"Nonsense. It's no secret that Jared bases his notions of what he wants in a woman on his memories of his first wife. And it's quite true that Gabriella was an angelic creature. Just ask anyone. But Gabriella died five years ago and Jared is a normal, healthy man in his prime. He needs a woman, and to be quite honest, I don't think he needs another angel."

Kate studied her champagne glass. "Why do you say that?"

Letty smiled knowingly. "It can be hard to live with an angel when a man has as much of the devil in him as Jared has. Enough said, hmm?"

Kate cleared her throat. "Please, Letty, before you get any more ideas, I think I should remind you that I'm only going to be on Amethyst for a month."

"That's precisely why I took the liberty of speaking to you tonight, my dear. There isn't a moment to waste, is there?"

Chapter Four

"COME ON, DAD, YOU CAN TELL ME. I won't tell Travis, or even Carl, honest. You were kissing Ms Inskip under that tree last night, weren't you?"

Jared glanced speculatively at his son, who was sitting at the kitchen table, kicking his sandaled feet and grinning hugely. Behind David the entire wall was open to the morning breezes and a sweeping view of the cove.

"Why do you want to know?" Jared sliced two ripe papayas in half and picked up a lime.

"'Cause. I just want to, that's all."

"Son, you're getting old enough to be told a few of the rules men have to live by when it comes to dealing with women."

"Yeah? What rules?" David was obviously fascinated.

"The first one is that a gentleman never discusses in public what he does with a lady in private."

David's face fell. "That's dumb. Who made that rule?"

"The ladies all got together and made it a long time ago."

"Can they do that?"

"They did it."

Jared squeezed the lime over the papaya and brought the plates to the table, just as he had every morning since Gabriella had been gone. Somehow, without his or David's being aware of it, breakfast had become an important ritual over the years, something they both unquestioningly shared and took for granted.

The other meals were inevitably eaten in the hotel restaurant. Slicing papayas and making toast was about the limit of Jared's capability or interest in the kitchen, though he could make a decent cup of coffee. There was not much point in having three gourmet chefs on the staff if one didn't make practical use of them, he reasoned.

Jared looked at his son's new jeans and realized they were already getting too short. He made a note to buy a new pair soon. Time went by so blindingly fast, even out here in the islands. David was almost ten years old, Jared reflected. There would be more and more of life's hard rules to learn. The trick would be to teach him how to tell the good rules from the bad.

For a moment Jared watched his son stewing silently over the rule regarding women. Then he gave David a wry grin.

"I'll tell you something, kid. If you value your hide, you'll remember this particular rule. Ladies such as Ms Inskip have a way of getting even with a man who gossips about them."

David giggled. "What would she do to you if you told me about kissing her?"

"I'm afraid to even hazard a guess," Jared said darkly as he sat down and poured himself a cup of coffee. "Probably deck me with one of her karate kicks."

David's humor turned to outright shock. "She couldn't deck you, Dad." He paused, digesting the unthinkable. "Could she?"

A loud, enthusiastic squawk came from the yellow-fronted Amazon parrot sitting on top of its large cage. Jared scowled at the bird. "Keep your opinions to yourself, Jolly." He looked at his son. "Feed your bird. He's turning nasty again."

"Here you go, Jolly." David handed the bird a bite of papaya. Jolly glowered at Jared for a moment and then took David's offering with great dignity. David turned back to pin down his father. "Ms Inskip couldn't really deck you, could she?"

"With any luck I will never have occasion to find out." Jared smeared guava jelly on his toast, wielding the knife with some force.

"Hah. I bet three dollars she couldn't do it," David finally decided. "You're bigger than she is."

"Size is not always a factor, but nevertheless I appreciate your faith in me."

"Are there rules the ladies have to follow?"

"A few. The trouble is, they get to make up a lot of them as they go along." *Such as whether or not they'll still be around when a man comes back to collect what had been promised with a kiss.*

"That's not fair."

"That's another rule, kid. Sometimes life isn't fair."

"Did the ladies make that one up, too?"

"No. That one got made up without anyone's approval, and we're all stuck with it." Jared bit down hard on the toast.

David kicked his feet while he contemplated that. "I think Ms Inskip plays fair. She's going to show me how to do that special kick today and maybe some other neat self-defense stuff she knows. I'm going to show her how to use snorkeling gear."

"Is that right?" It occurred to Jared that his son was making faster progress than he was. Maybe he should have offered a few free snorkeling lessons. He had certainly gotten nowhere fast last night.

When the cake-cutting ceremonies had finally ended, Jared had looked around and discovered that Kate had disappeared. Like a fool, he had been unable to resist walking through the gardens past her room. Her light had winked out even as he'd stood in the shadows and watched. Jared had spent a restless night, and he was still feeling generally annoyed this morning.

"Yup. We made a deal last night. Some guy she was dancing with offered to show her the reefs, but I reminded her we'd already agreed I'd do it."

Jared looked up. "Who was the guy?"

"A guest. I think his name was Taylor or Tyler or something." David munched papaya, watching Jared out of the corner of his eye. "You know something? I kinda like Ms Inskip, Dad. She looked real pretty last night, didn't she?"

Like a lady out of a dream. "Yeah," Jared said. "She looked pretty last night." And the dream lady had turned into a sensuous creature of heat and shadow when he'd taken her into his arms. But instead of waiting for him after the last dance, she had vanished, the way a dream vanishes in the night. "When are you going to give her the snorkeling lesson?"

"This morning. Right after she shows me some of her self-defense tricks." David finished his papaya and jumped to his feet. He rubbed Jolly's head as he headed toward the veranda. The bird endured the caress with regal condescension. "Gotta go. I'm supposed to meet Ms Inskip in a few minutes."

"Wait a second. You didn't finish your toast."

"I'll take it with me." David snatched up the slice of toast and loped out of the kitchen, out across the veranda and down onto the path that led to the cove.

Jared was left alone with Jolly. The bird eyed him assessingly for a moment and then climbed slowly down from the cage, jumped to the back of David's chair and hopped onto the table to investigate the remains of the papaya.

"What the hell do you think you're doing, you old pirate? You know you're not supposed to be on the table. Get away from that plate or I'll sell a few of your tail feathers as souvenirs to the tourists."

"Wanna bet?" Jolly picked up the papaya in one claw and began to nibble delicately.

"It's always nice to know who's the boss around here." Jared got to his feet and started clearing the table. "Why do you think she ducked out after the masquerade ended last night? I was sure she'd be waiting for me. After the way she responded under that tree, what the hell else was I supposed to think? She wanted me every bit as much as I wanted her, and I know it. I think. Who can figure women? Especially a lady commando with two whole weeks of self-defense training under her belt. Maybe she just got off on proving she could turn me on. I'll tell you one thing, pal. If that's the case, I'm going to put a stop to her game real quick."

"Wanna bet?"

Half an hour later, Jared stood in the open expanse that was one wall of his office and gazed down at the glistening white sands of the cove. From here he could see a smattering of early risers, some with scuba and snorkel gear and some dressed for strolling. At the far end of the beach he saw the two people he was looking for. David was standing on one foot, lashing out toward an invisible target with the other. Kate, dressed in a green maillot, was standing nearby, coaching the boy.

Jared didn't bother to take his gaze off the pair when someone knocked on the office door. "Come in."

The door swung open. "Morning, Jared," the colonel said as he walked into the room. "A fine day, isn't it?"

"Yeah." Jared frowned as he watched Kate demonstrate another quick, striking kick. "But then it always is, isn't it? Come here and watch this, Colonel."

The colonel walked over to stand beside Jared. He peered down into the cove. "Ah. The redoubtable Ms Inskip, I presume?"

"Who else? She's teaching Dave some mishmash of judo and karate."

"The sort of thing she used on Sharp Arnie?"

"Right."

"Nice technique," the colonel observed.

"Too stiff. She needs to loosen up, be more flexible."

"Are we talking about her self-defense skills or something else?"

"Forget it." Jared watched in silence for a few more seconds. "I wonder how she is at baking cookies? Five will get you ten she can't even boil water."

"David doesn't seem concerned with Ms Inskip's possible lack of culinary talents. He appears to be enjoying himself immensely."

Jared narrowed his eyes. "He couldn't wait to get out there on the beach this morning to take the lesson."

"He's becoming quite fond of Ms Inskip."

"I know."

"You don't sound pleased by the prospect," the colonel said.

"She'll be gone in a month."

"That would depend, I suppose, on whether or not she had a reason to stay." The colonel moved over to the desk. "I brought last night's receipts and a couple of bar and restaurant requisitions that need your signature."

Jared didn't turn away from the scene in the cove. "Leave them on the desk. I'll take care of them later."

"Have plans for the morning, do you?" the colonel inquired with a polite tilt of his bushy brows.

"My son is going to give Ms Inskip a snorkeling lesson. Thought maybe I'd supervise."

"Excellent idea." The colonel beamed.

KATE STOOD, FEET PLANTED WIDE APART in the sand, hands on her hips, and studied David's form with pursed lips. The boy made two more kicks before she nodded in satisfaction.

"Good. You've got the hang of it now. Watch your balance. Balance is everything. It's what gives you the advantage. My instructor said almost everyone is off balance most of the time. The trick is to make use of that fact."

David grinned and kicked out one more time. He accompanied the kick with a loud shout. Then he looked up at Kate. "Think I could take Sharp Arnie now?"

"People like Sharp Arnie are best avoided rather than confronted," Kate said. She ruffled his hair affectionately.

"You didn't avoid him. You clobbered him."

"I was under a certain amount of stress at the time. The smart thing to do would have been to hand over my wallet and run."

"You wouldn't run from anything, I bet. You're like my dad. I asked him this morning if you could take him in a fight."

Kate blinked. "What did he say?"

"He said he didn't want to ever find out."

"How very wise of him."

"Huh?"

"Never mind. Ready to give me my snorkeling lesson?"

"Sure. I've got all the equipment. You can leave your towel and stuff here on the sand." David bent over to scoop up two masks. Then he glanced down the beach.

He straightened almost immediately and waved. "Hey, look, there's Dad. Hi, Dad."

Kate deliberately quashed the little shiver of awareness that went through her as she turned her head to watch Jared stride toward them over the sand. He was barefoot, wearing a pair of faded, low-slung denims and a white cotton shirt. His hair was brushed straight back from his forehead and gleamed in the morning light.

He might be wearing jeans this morning, but he looked as much like a buccaneer as he had last night in full costume, Kate realized. She wondered what would have happened if she'd found the reckless courage to wait for him after the ball. But at the last moment she had known she was not ready for that kind of risk. Facing the Sharp Arnies of this world was one thing; getting involved with a man like Jared Hawthorne was a whole different kettle of fish.

"Good morning, Kate." Jared's slashing grin was a cool challenge. "How did the self-defense lesson go?"

"It went great," David said before Kate could respond. "I can deck Sharp Arnie now, just like Ms Inskip did."

"A chilling thought," Jared murmured, his silver eyes meeting Kate's over the top of his son's head. "Enjoy yourself last night, Kate?"

"Very much." Aware of Jared's intent gaze, she picked up the towel and draped it over her shoulders; the ends covered her breasts.

"I was just curious. You disappeared so quickly someone might have gotten the impression you had gotten bored."

"Not at all."

"No? Then perhaps you just lost your nerve?" Jared smiled thinly.

"It was after midnight and I was tired. Just call me Cinderella." Kate felt something within her rise to his blatant challenge.

"I can think of better names."

"You're right. Calling me Cinderella might imply you're Prince Charming, and we wouldn't want a case of mistaken identity here, would we?"

"Prickly." Jared shook his head ruefully. "Even at this hour of the morning."

"Say, Dad, you want Ms Inskip to show you some of her self-defense tricks?" David asked, impatient with the conversation going on over his head. "She knows all kinds of stuff."

"Are you kidding? You think I want to end up like Sharp Arnie?" Jared demanded.

"Ah, come on, Dad, let her show you. You won't hurt him, will you, Ms Inskip?"

"Oh, I'd be very gentle," Kate promised, her sense of humor getting the better of her. "But I'm sure your father has more interesting things to do this morning than take a self-defense lesson from me, Dave."

Jared's eyes glinted in the sunlight. "Well, I guess I can spare the time to take one short lesson. I have a feeling you know all sorts of tricks, don't you, Kate?"

"Lots and lots," she assured him blithely.

Jared nodded. "I thought so. Including a very good vanishing act. All right, show me something really clever."

Kate saw the taunting laughter in him and was suddenly determined to replace the masculine amusement with respect. She stood facing him, her arms relaxed at her sides. "We'll keep this nice and simple. With all this soft sand, nobody will get hurt. Go ahead, Jared, pretend you're, uh, assaulting me."

"Whatever it takes." Jared didn't hesitate. He walked straight toward her, his hand outstretched to grab her wrist, his silvery eyes alight with mischief.

At the last second Kate wondered if she was being set up, but it was too late to retreat. She glided forward, reached for his arm, pivoted smoothly around and tugged hard just as she had been taught.

It was a textbook throw; much too easy, in fact. Jared came off his feet with no resistance at all and wound up flat on his back in the sand. He groaned once, closed his eyes and did not move.

"Dad." David rushed forward and fell to his knees beside his father. "Dad, are you okay? Ms Inskip, is he all right? What's wrong with him?"

Kate's satisfaction transformed into instant concern. She hurried forward and knelt down beside Jared. "I don't know. I didn't hurt him. He just took a light fall. I wonder if he hit his head on a rock or something under the sand."

She reached over to check the back of Jared's head and knew she had made a bad mistake when she felt iron fingers circle her wrist. Too late she realized she'd been had. Jared's dark lashes lifted lazily to reveal his wicked anticipation.

"Gotcha."

"You rat." She sighed, fully aware that Jared was going to enjoy whatever happened next.

"Hey, Dad, you were just joking, right?" David's expression skipped from worried to delighted in the blink of an eye. He stood up. "Are you going to show Ms Inskip some of your self-defense stuff now?" He turned to Kate and said proudly, "Dad knows some tricks, too."

"No kidding?" Kate twisted her hand in Jared's grasp and discovered there was no way on earth she was going to pull free.

"I'll be delighted to show you a trick or two, Ms Inskip." Jared rolled over and surged to his feet, dragging Kate up beside him.

"Now, wait just a minute," Kate gasped, aware that pleading was useless but desperate enough to try it, anyway. She was curiously torn between laughter and outrage, and for some odd reason the laughter was winning.

"Hey, Dad, what are you going to do with Ms Inskip?"

"She wanted a lesson, right?" Jared caught Kate around the waist and tossed her lightly over his shoulder. He started toward the water.

"Right," David agreed, trotting along beside his father.

"Put me down this instant," Kate ordered, very much afraid she was wasting her breath.

"So what do you say we give her the lesson she's been asking for since last night?" Jared concluded, ignoring Kate's struggles.

"Don't you dare," Kate yelped as she saw water foaming around Jared's feet.

Jared waded out until he was knee-deep. He didn't seem to care that his jeans were getting soaked. "The first thing you do when you go snorkeling," he said in an instructional tone as he slid Kate down off his shoulder and into his arms, "is get wet."

"You're doing this because of last night, aren't you? This is very petty behavior, Jared."

"I just like to keep the scales balanced. Any man who lets you get the upper hand too often is asking for trouble." He waited three more seconds until the next wave peaked and then he opened his arms and let Kate fall.

The pirate's grin on Jared's face was the last thing Kate saw before the roiling water closed over her head. It was also the first thing she saw when she surfaced again a few seconds later. She managed to get to her feet only to be sent spinning by a wave she hadn't seen approaching behind her. She gasped, kicked forward into shallower water and stood up again.

"Dad, wait, she didn't get a chance to put on her mask," David said, splashing toward Kate with the snorkeling equipment.

"Heck," Jared said, "I knew I forgot something. You want to try it again, Kate?"

Kate slicked back her hair and held up one palm in surrender. "Not your way, thanks. I think David will make a much better instructor."

"This is your lucky day, Kate. You get both of us." Jared unfastened his jeans to reveal a pair of swimming briefs. He waded toward shore and tugged off the wet denim and his soaked shirt while David helped Kate put on the mask.

Jared took over the instruction when he returned, giving orders in a crisp, efficient manner.

A few minutes later, all three of them were swimming toward the reefs. Jared and David kept Kate between them as they guided her through the underwater wonderland.

Kate forgot all about Jared's teasing revenge as she came face-to-face with one spectacular fish after another. The colors were glorious. Jeff Taylor had been right when he said swimming around the reefs was like swimming inside an aquarium. Each amazingly tame fish was more outrageously beautiful than the last.

The morning sun danced in the crystal clear water, creating a fabulous underwater garden of coral and sand. Kate lost track of time as first David and then Jared drew her attention to yet another beautiful scene. When Jared finally tugged her ankle and motioned her to surface, she did so with reluctance.

He raised his mask and grinned down at her delighted expression as they stood waist-deep in the water. "You like that, huh?"

"It's fantastic. I've never seen anything like it. Absolutely beautiful. You're so lucky to live in a place where you get to do this every day."

Jared eyed her for a moment and then nodded. "Dave and I like it, don't we?" He looked at his son, who was standing in shallower water.

"Yeah, it's great. But I like Disneyland, too. Dad took me there last year."

"I'll take this, even over Disneyland. Well, I thank you both for the lessons, though I will do the polite thing and refrain from commenting on the first step." Kate wrinkled her nose. "Do we have to stop now?"

Jared shook his head. "You two don't have to quit, but I've got work to do. Some of us are not on vacation. I'll see you both later. Dave, don't forget to take care of the equipment when you're done here."

"I won't, Dad. Come on, Ms Inskip. Let's go look at another section of coral."

"Sounds like a wonderful idea."

Kate lowered her mask and turned to follow the boy back under the water. She was aware of Jared standing in the shallows watching them for a few minutes, but when she surfaced a while later, he was gone.

The small, aching sensation of regret she felt startled her.

THE INVITATION TO DINNER IN JARED and David's private quarters arrived late the next afternoon. Kate had been lazing in the shade on her veranda, telling herself she ought to be doing something useful, such as plotting a new novel, when the knock sounded on her door. She got to her feet and went to answer the summons. A young man in the resort's livery of white slacks and a flowered shirt stood on the threshold. He was obviously having a hard time containing a grin.

"Message for you, Miss Inskip. From the management. I had special instructions to wait for a reply."

"Thanks." Kate glanced curiously at the childish print on the outside of the envelope. She unfolded the single sheet of lined binder paper and read the short, painstakingly lettered message.

"Please come to dinner tonight. We will have it at seven." It was signed David Hawthorne.

"Just a minute," Kate told the messenger. "I'll give you a reply."

She found a piece of stationery with the resort's crest on it and carefully wrote a short note of acceptance. Then she folded it, slipped it into an envelope and sent the courier off with it.

As soon as she closed the door behind the young man she went straight to her closet and examined her wardrobe. Sarah and Margaret had done an excellent job of packing. Kate smiled to herself as she made her selection.

At precisely seven o'clock that evening, dressed in a demure ankle-length sheath of polished green cotton and gold sandals, Kate walked down the path to the gracious, airy home where Jared and David lived.

The house was set a short distance from the resort. It was nestled in the lush island foliage on the top of a bluff and commanded a sweeping view of the cove and the small outlying shoals and islets that protected Amethyst Island.

Kate hesitated briefly before raising her hand to knock at the front door. She'd never accepted an invitation quite like this one before, and her curiosity was aroused. She wondered if Jared knew what his son had planned for the evening. Cautiously she tapped on the door. A moment later she heard pounding footsteps and then the door was flung open.

"Hi," David said. "I knew you'd come. Everything's ready. Dad's in the living room."

Kate stepped inside the cool foyer and glanced curiously at her surroundings. There was a subtle harmony to the bleached wood floors, the sisal matting and the graceful greenery. The front of the house seemed to be one vast open window that caught the breeze and the spectacular view.

David led the way toward a large room furnished in rattan. Kate followed her host down two steps and looked across the room to see Jared standing at a brass and glass beverage cart. He turned to glance at her as she walked slowly toward him. His gaze was appreciative and his smile was slow.

"I'm innocent," he said. "This was all David's idea."

"I believe you." Kate smiled at the boy, who was looking enormously pleased with himself.

David looked at his father. "Come on, Dad, you're supposed to pour her a drink. Then I'll introduce her to Jolly."

"Thank you for reminding me, Dave. What will you have, Kate?"

"A little sherry will be fine."

Jared nodded and picked up a bottle. "When is the restaurant kitchen sending dinner over, son?"

"I told them to send it at seven-thirty. Is that okay?" David looked momentarily anxious.

"That sounds fine." Jared handed the glass of sherry to Kate, his gaze a mixture of amusement and sensual intensity. "Dave tells me he has arranged everything this evening."

David nodded in satisfaction. "Come on, Kate. I want you to meet Jolly."

"Who's Jolly?" Kate obediently followed the boy out of the living room and into a spacious kitchen. A large green-and-yellow bird crouched malevolently on top of a black wrought-iron cage. "Oh, I see. He doesn't look especially Jolly."

"Jolly is short for Jolly Roger," Jared explained.

Kate laughed. "Now that fits. Will he take off my finger if I try to scratch his head?"

"Of course not," David said.

"Wanna bet?" asked Jolly. But he stretched his neck out demandingly.

Kate scratched cautiously. "He's beautiful. Does he talk a lot?"

"You've just heard his entire vocabulary," Jared said.

"Wanna bet?" Jolly turned an annoyed eye on Jared.

"Fortunately," Jared said, "the two words he knows are very useful here on Amethyst."

Kate glanced around the kitchen and saw a number of pencil drawings tacked up on the refrigerator. She went for a closer look and discovered they were astonishingly charming sketches of the cove and the resort. "These are wonderful. Did you do them, Dave?"

"Yeah. You really like 'em?"

"Very much. You have a lot of talent."

David blushed happily. "Thanks. Well." He looked from one adult to the other and started to back out of the room. "Guess everything's under control, so I'd better be going."

Kate looked at him in surprise. "Aren't you staying for dinner?"

David shook his head quickly. "Carl Shimazu invited me to spend the night at his house. His mom said it was okay. Carl and I are going to study together." He looked at his father. "You don't have to worry about anything, Dad. I told the kitchen staff to take care of everything."

"Thanks, son." Jared's mouth quirked. "I appreciate that."

"Sure. Well, good night. See you guys later." With one last look around, David turned and bounded into the hall. A moment later the front door closed behind him.

Jared swirled the whiskey in his glass and led the way back into the living room. "What can I say? He means well. He likes you."

"I like him, too."

Kate wandered over to the expanse of open wall and took a deep breath of the fragrant night air. An odd nervousness was settling on her now that she was alone with Jared. When she had accepted the invitation she had been certain David would be around to act as a buffer. Instead, she was on her own.

The nervousness alarmed her. This was not like her at all. The only other time she could remember feeling nervous around a man in recent years was the time she had been stopped by a grim-looking motorcycle cop. She had been sure she was going to get a ticket. In the end she had given him an autographed book for his wife, instead. He'd been thrilled.

Jared came up behind her, not touching her. "The other night in the garden I got the impression you liked me, also. Did I get the signals mixed?"

"You're very direct, aren't you?"

"I don't have time to string this out, but even if I did, I probably wouldn't. You're right. I am a direct man, Kate. I don't like games."

"Your friend Letty says we strike sparks off each other."

"I guess we do. Is that so bad?"

Kate shook her head. "No, but I'm not sure it's good, either. Sparks can be dangerous."

"They can set fires," Jared agreed. "But I'll be honest with you, Kate. I've never had any woman set quite this kind of fire in me. I'm not sure exactly how to handle things, but I know I can't walk away and pretend this never happened. Can you?"

There was silence for a long moment. Then Kate said softly, "I told you I wasn't interested in a vacation fling."

"Is that why you disappeared so fast after the masquerade ball? You just aren't interested? I don't believe that."

She tilted her head thoughtfully to one side. "You want the truth? I got cold feet."

"I thought that might be it. At least you're honest about it."

"I also decided you were taking a lot for granted on the basis of a few kisses."

"And you wanted to put me in my place?"

Her fingers tightened on the glass. "No, not exactly. I just decided things were happening too quickly."

"If things don't happen quickly between us, they won't happen at all. Within a month you'll be gone."

"Yes." She moved uneasily, stepping away from him and turning to smile coolly. "Which is the best reason of all for not getting involved, isn't it? What's for dinner?"

"I don't know." Jared's mouth curved faintly. "David ordered everything. One of the side benefits of raising a kid around a resort is that he gets very sophisticated about such things as ordering up room service."

"I see. David does this for you a lot, then?"

"For your information, this is the first time he's ever tried his hand at matchmaking."

Kate winced. "Sorry, didn't mean to annoy you."

"Didn't you? I think you enjoy annoying me, Kate."

"Careful, you're getting paranoid."

"I'm not so sure about that. Sometimes I almost have the feeling I'm being tested in some way."

Kate's eyes widened in astonishment. "Good grief, what a weird thing to say. You really are paranoid." But she sensed some blundering masculine insight in his accusation and wondered silently what was happening to her.

Jared smiled again and held up his palm. "You're probably right. Let's call a truce, okay? The food will be here any minute and I'm hungry."

"So am I. I did some more snorkeling this morning and it gave me an appetite."

He eyed her warily. "About the snorkeling lesson yesterday. Can I assume you're not holding a grudge?"

"Just because you faked that fall and then dropped me into the sea? Heavens, no. Why would I hold a grudge over a little thing like that?"

"Beats me. It wasn't as if I didn't have grounds for revenge or anything. But some women aren't as fair-minded as you are. David took pains to point out to me what a good sport you were about the whole thing."

Kate laughed softly, beginning to relax. "All right, I'll admit you might have had grounds for revenge. I shouldn't have ducked out the night of the masquerade without saying anything. I should have told you I'd changed my mind."

Jared grinned. "That's probably as close to an apology as I'll get, so I'll take it and be satisfied." He started to say something else and then paused as a knock sounded on the front door. "Ah, there's dinner. Let's see how creative the kid is."

David, with the help of the resort's restaurant staff, had outdone himself. The Brie-and-sun-dried-tomatoes appetizer was followed by impeccably fresh fish cooked in parchment and a beautifully arranged plate of exotic tiny sautéed vegetables. It was all lavishly served by a waiter who couldn't seem to hide his delight as he went about his duties. It was obvious the staff was enjoying the entire event.

When the excellent Chardonnay had been served, the linen napkins unfolded and the candles lit, the waiter bowed himself out the front door. Jared waited until he was gone, then he lounged back in his chair and looked across the table at Kate.

"You realize, of course, that this will be all over the resort by midnight, if it isn't already?"

"Uh-huh."

"Certain assumptions concerning our relationship will be made."

"Probably."

"Just thought I'd warn you." Jared nodded once and raised his wineglass. "Here's to us and the month we have. Let's not waste it, Kate."

Kate felt her insides tighten, but at the same time a thrill of anticipation was soaring through her. She looked into Jared's silvery eyes as she obediently raised her own glass and the poignant sense of familiarity nearly overwhelmed her. "To us," she whispered.

"Why don't you tell me how you go about writing a book?" Jared suggested when the toast was finished.

"All right. If you'll tell me how you go about running a resort."

"It's a deal."

To Kate's surprise, it was suddenly easy to talk to him. The conversation flowed so effortlessly now. She felt lighter than air, caught up once more in that dangerously seductive certainty that she knew Jared far more intimately than could possibly have been the case.

When they had polished off the white-chocolate-and-macadamia-nut dessert, Jared got to his feet. He reached down to grasp Kate's wrist and drew her up beside him. "Come on, I want to show you something."

"Not your etchings, I hope."

"I think you're going to find this a lot more interesting than etchings. And I want you to remember I thought of this angle all on my own. David didn't have anything to do with it."

"Where are we going?" Kate asked as he led her down the hall.

"To my study."

Not his bedroom. Kate wondered at the sense of wistful disappointment she felt.

When Jared opened the door into a book-lined room, she stepped inside and gazed around with deep interest. "Very nice."

He released her wrist and went over to a glass-fronted cabinet that housed several very old leather-bound volumes. On one of the shelves was the black dagger Jared had been wearing the previous evening.

"What are those?" Kate's attention was instantly captured by the sight of the old books.

"Some journals, business papers and a ship's log belonging to Roger Hawthorne plus a diary that his wife, Amelia, kept."

Kate's eyes widened in astounded delight. "Are you serious?" She flew across the room to stand in front of the cabinet. She stared longingly down at the aging volumes.

"Take a look." Jared opened the glass doors, smiling with satisfaction as Kate reached carefully inside for one of the journals.

She stroked the cracked leather cover lovingly. "Do you realize what you have here? A pirate's personal journals. What an incredible thought. And the diary of the bride he kidnapped. I would sell my soul for these volumes."

"I wasn't planning to ask such a high price, but if you insist, I won't turn you down."

Her head came up swiftly as she sensed the sensual meaning in his softly spoken words. The expression in his eyes made her catch her breath, and she forgot about the treasure she held in her hands.

"Jared?"

"You can examine the journals any time you like while you're here on Amethyst."

"Thank you." She was breathless. The heat in his gaze was warming her from the inside out, "Thank you very much." Kate put the old volume carefully back into the glass cabinet and stood very still.

After a long, shuddering moment of silence, Jared reached out to touch her cheek. "Whatever else it will be, Kate, it won't be just a fling. You know that, don't you?"

She felt his fingers tremble slightly on her skin. When he dropped his hand, she was trapped by the molten silver of his eyes. Surely she had known this man all her life. "Yes," she said. "I know."

He picked up a blanket that lay folded on the end of the sofa, took Kate's hand again and led her out of the study onto the shadowy veranda that overlooked the sea.

Chapter Five

THE NIGHT WAS HEAVY AND WARM. Kate fell silent as Jared led her out into the darkness. She was back under the same spell that had captured her the night of the masquerade ball, she realized. But tonight there would be no escape. Jared's hand wrapped hers in a strong, sure grip, and she had no desire to be freed.

Without an explanation he tugged her down the steps of the veranda to a path that led toward the water. They walked through a grove of shadowy palms and out into a small, secluded moonlit cove. This was not Crystal Cove, the main hotel beach, but a private, hidden place that Kate sensed was not open to the public. Wavelets foamed softly on the shore, glistening in the pale light.

"Where are you taking me?" she asked, not particularly concerned with the answer.

"To a special place I know. And, no, before you ask, I don't take a lot of female guests there."

"I wasn't going to ask."

"Starting to trust me?"

"I just don't feel like asking too many questions tonight," she said.

His hand tightened around hers. "Good. It's probably better that way."

At the edge of the sand they stopped and took off their shoes. Then they walked to the end of the beach. There Jared drew Kate into the shadows of a palm. He spread the blanket on the ground and stood looking at her, his face taut with controlled hunger. When he made no further move, Kate knew he was waiting for her to make the final decision.

She hesitated a moment and then walked into his arms. They closed around her, safe, strong and wonderfully familiar, wonderfully right.

"Promise me you won't regret this in the morning," Jared said into her ear, his fingers tangling in her hair. "I want this to be right for both of us. No recriminations, no reprisals, no apologies."

"I wouldn't have come this far with you if I had any more doubts."

"The other night I thought you knew what you wanted, but you still left without a word."

"I told you, the other night there were other complications. Things were happening too fast. Nothing felt real. Then I realized your friend Letty was matchmaking and I really got nervous. I needed time to think."

"No more thinking. I've tried to think this through for the past couple of days. It got me nowhere." Jared groaned and pulled her close. Kate's body reacted instinctively to the hard, demanding male strength in him. His kiss was a heavy, drugging caress that intoxicated her with emotion and sensual excitement. His mouth moved on hers as his hands moved on her body—slowly, intimately, hungrily.

Kate felt the zipper of her sheath slide down the length of her spine to her waist, and the dress crumpled to her hips. Her small, lacy bra fell away under his touch. Jared leaned his forehead against hers and looked down at her breasts.

"I knew you would be this lovely. I want you so much. I haven't been able to think of anything else since I saw you in that alley on Ruby." He touched her nipples, sliding his thumbs across them slowly until they flowered into firm peaks. "You make me ache in a way I haven't ached in a very long time."

She trembled under the warm honey of his words. "I have never ached this way." The honesty in her own words amazed her. She hadn't meant to say them, but now that they were said it was all right. It was the truth.

"Letty was right about us striking sparks off each other. But some of the sparks are very, very exciting."

"Yes." Kate slowly unbuttoned his shirt until it hung open and then she pushed it off entirely. The garment fell to the sand, and she stroked Jared's sleek shoulders, loving the feel of the strong, muscled flesh.

Jared finished undressing her carefully, his hands gliding down over her hips, taking the dress and her panties with them. Then he was stroking her bare, rounded buttocks, cupping her and lifting her up against him. She felt rough denim and the cold metal fastening of his jeans against her stomach. The heaviness of his manhood thrust against the fabric. The fullness of his arousal was almost shocking.

"You feel so good," Jared whispered as he eased her down onto her back on the blanket. He knelt beside her and stroked the length of her bare leg. "Warm and soft and sexy."

"Not prickly?"

"Not prickly at all." He bent his head and kissed the hollow of her stomach. "I should have guessed all the prickliness was designed to protect something very special."

Unable to help herself, Kate arched sensuously under his touch, closing her eyes and moaning softly. Her fingers tightened on his shoulders and she urged him closer. He was hard all over, the contours of his back defining his physical strength.

Jared came down on top of her, his bare chest crushing her gently. So much crisp, dark hair on that chest, Kate thought.

He was still wearing his jeans, and Kate found the texture of the cloth against her naked leg strangely exciting. It became almost unbearably so when Jared slid down the length of her. His mouth was all over, tasting her, exploring her body, covering her with hot, damp kisses. She gasped and her head tipped back over his arm when she felt his teeth lightly graze her breast. Then she felt his tongue curl around her nipple and she laughed in soft delight, lightheaded with the thrill of it all.

When he moved lower still, she thought she would fly apart into a million glittering pieces.

"Jared."

"I'm not going anywhere. You taste like the sea."

"I can't stand…Jared, wait. Come here. Please." She coiled one leg around his thigh and tightened her grip on him, pulling him upward again. Her hands slid down his back. "Your jeans."

"I know. I'll get rid of them." He rolled to one side, unfastened his denims and slid out of the last of his clothing. He paused long enough to draw a small packet from one pocket, fumbled with it for a few seconds and then he came back to her in a hot, enveloping rush.

"This is so perfect," Kate said, looking up at him through

half-closed lashes. His body was lean, hard and beautifully male. "Maybe too perfect." The strength in him was controlled and all the more powerful because of that control. "You're so perfect."

His smile was slow and deeply sensual as he bent over her. "Remember that in the morning. Promise?"

"I promise."

He caught his breath as he put his heavy thigh over one of her twisting, restless legs, pinning her gently. "Now put your arms around me and open yourself for me. I want you more than I can ever remember wanting anything in my life."

"I want you, too." She was stunned at the depths of her own need. Such incredible passion would have a high price. Nothing came free in this world. She looked up at Jared, studying his shadowed face.

"I'm glad you want me. I need you to want me. Lord, how I need it," he said fiercely. His expression was stark in the moonlight; the desire in him unmistakable. His eyes glittered with it. The hand that covered her stomach shook with it.

Jared slid his warm palm down to the soft hair above her thighs. Kate parted her legs for him, lifting herself helplessly against his hand. She felt his fingers slip down into her softness and search out the growing dampness between her legs. Slowly he explored her secrets with roughened fingers, coaxing more of the liquid heat from her until she could not think of anything except the mind-spinning passion. He kissed her, filling her mouth and then withdrawing in a tantalizing rhythm that set up the more intimate pattern that would soon follow.

When Jared moved at last, settling himself deliberately between her legs, Kate cried out and sank her nails into his shoulders.

"Yes, sweetheart. Show me how much you want me." He pushed himself slowly, relentlessly into her heat. "So good," he muttered hoarsely. "So tight and hot and sweet. I'm going to lose my mind."

She clung to him, wrapping herself around him as he filled her completely and then he began to move, pulling almost free of her, hesitating and then driving as deeply into her softness as he could.

Over and over, Jared repeated the excruciatingly exciting rhythm until Kate was lost in her need. She could no longer think clearly or question or talk. She could only feel, and what she felt was unlike anything she had ever known in her life. She was on fire with passion, a white-hot banner of searing flame that threatened to consume her. It would have been terrifying if it hadn't been so totally irresistible; so totally right.

Together they twisted and writhed on the blanket, clutching each other as if locked in mortal combat. They rolled over and over, fighting for the release that was racing toward them out of the darkness.

As the sensual battle moved toward its inevitable conclusion, Kate experienced a wild, surging sense of freedom and exhilaration that was beyond anything she had ever known in her life. She cried out with it.

"Jared."

"Now," he muttered against her throat as he pushed her onto her back. He grabbed her wrists and anchored them above her head, muttering hot, encouraging words into her ear as he held her. "Let it go. Give it to me. All of it. *All of it.*" His muscles bunched and his back arched. "I've waited so long for you, sweetheart. Too long."

Pinned beneath him, Kate opened her eyes just enough to see that Jared's face was set in a rigid mask of emotion. She didn't think he even knew what he was saying. His words were thick and hoarse, almost anguished. He surged deeply into her one last, shattering time and she was spun outward into the shimmering sea.

And suddenly she knew without a shadow of a doubt where she had seen him before. He was the man in her dreams, the one she had first begun to know when she had changed from girl into woman; the one who had haunted her all these years; the one she put into every book she wrote. This was her pirate—fierce, tender, passionate and proud.

The shock of recognition merged with the sensual storm that was sweeping through her and blotted out everything from Kate's mind. She cried out and then she was lost.

REALITY TRICKLED BACK SLOWLY, MIXING with moonlight and the soft sounds of the sea. Kate was aware of Jared's arm across her breasts and of the dampness of his warm skin. He was sprawled beside her, one leg still flung over her thighs, his chin just touching her head. He was heavy, but his weight made her feel protected and safe.

She remembered the fleeting instant of recognition a few minutes earlier and shuddered.

"Cold?" Jared stirred lazily, turning onto his back, one hand behind his head. He looked up at her with eyes that gleamed with the banked embers of a fire that had been only temporarily quenched.

"No." She touched his moonlit-etched face with curious fingers.

"What's wrong?" He kissed her fingertips as they traced his mouth.

"Nothing's wrong. It's just that I've had this odd feeling I know you."

"You do know me. In fact, I'd say that you know me very well now."

She crossed her elbows on his chest and studied him. "Better than you think."

He laughed, his voice husky and replete with satisfaction. "Is that a warning?"

She shrugged. "Maybe."

"I'll keep it in mind." He stroked her bare shoulder. "You know something? You're not prickly at all when you're in this mood."

"I'm glad you approve."

"I approve, all right. I can see the trick will be to keep you in the right frame of mind as much of the time as possible."

"That could take a lot of work on your part."

"I'll devote every spare minute to the job." Jared snagged his fingers in her hair, pulled her mouth down to his and kissed her hard. "Damn, but you're a delight. You make me feel like a million bucks. Two million."

"I feel pretty good myself."

"What piece of good luck brought you to my island, sweet Kate?"

"The combined effects of overwork and two well-intentioned, interfering friends. Left to my own devices, I would never have made it as far as Amethyst Island. I'd still be sitting at home, staring at a computer screen."

Jared framed her face with his hands, his expression turning serious. "What's your home like? A snazzy little apartment in Seattle?"

"I like it."

"How long have you lived there?"

"Since my husband went off to devote himself to his talent."

"What was he like, this ex-husband of yours?"

"He's a man who has the soul of a poet. A writer of great undiscovered literary potential, or so he told me."

"Why did you marry him?"

"Good question. When we were first introduced we were both aspiring writers. I thought he was sensitive, intelligent and supportive," Kate said slowly. "And he was. At first. He liked the fact that I had a full-time job and could support him while he devoted himself to his writing. But then I got published and he didn't, and he blamed me for his failure and things went downhill from there. I now realize, of course, that he was really weak, neurotic, self-centered and a whiner. Goes to show how one can change one's opinion of a person, doesn't it?"

"Where is he now?"

"I'm not sure. Last I heard he was hanging out at an elite writers' colony, reading his poems to other writers who all agree with him that the only reason they're unpublished is because the world does not appreciate true genius."

"Miss him?"

"No." Kate smiled. "And I know he doesn't miss me. Toward the end of our relationship, I had gotten tired of coddling his overinflated ego and even more tired of dealing with his nasty little remarks about my writing. I'm afraid I turned a tad shrewish."

"I'm shocked. You? A shrew?"

"That was how Harry saw me."

"Probably because he didn't know how to deal with you," Jared said easily. "So your ex turned tail and ran, hmm?"

"Packed his bags and walked out after making a suitably dramatic farewell speech. I cried for about fifteen minutes, and then my friends Sarah and Margaret came over and took me out for champagne and pizza. They told me I was lucky to see the last of good old Harry, and within forty-eight hours I knew they were right. But it took a while to put it all behind me."

Jared nodded soberly. "Harry was not the man for you."

"Truer words were never spoken." The man for her existed only between the covers of her books and here on Amethyst Island, Kate reflected silently.

Jared grinned. "On the other hand, be sure you remember what you yourself said earlier."

"What's that?"

"Unlike your ex-husband, I am perfect. Your very words."

She laughed softly. "I'm not sure you can hold me responsible for that remark. I was under the influence of a lot of raging hormones at the time."

"If that's the way you're going to be about it, I'll just have to enrage your hormones until you say it again." Jared shifted, rolling her beneath him. "And again and again."

"We could be here all night."

"That thought had occurred to me." He lowered his head and took her mouth.

A long time later Kate sighed and snuggled close. "Perfect," she murmured.

THE NEXT FEW DAYS PASSED IN a haze of passion and laughter. Kate went snorkeling in the cove with David, toured the island with Jared and his son in a Jeep, ate papaya and impossibly fresh fish and spent every possible stolen hour in the arms of her dream lover.

Those hours had to be grabbed when they were available because Jared, Kate soon learned, in addition to being a father, was a very busy man. His schedule was unpredictable and usually very full. One moment he was going over special banquet arrangements with his food and beverage manager and the next he was dealing with a crisis involving the pool filter machinery. Kate sought him out one afternoon and discovered him helping his staff fold a huge stack of towels in the resort's hot laundry room.

"The assistant housekeeper's daughter is having her baby. She went over to Ruby to be with her and two of the laundry room staff went along. They're all family. None of them made it back this morning, so we're short-handed," he'd explained tersely, folding a towel with precision.

"Want me to give you a hand?" Kate asked, picking up a fluffy white towel that bore the Crystal Cove crest.

Jared blinked in surprise and then grinned broadly. "I'll take any help I can get."

"Just be sure you also take a few bucks off my room bill for today, okay?"

"You bet. Want to flip a coin for the day's tab? Double or nothing?"

"Not on your life, Hawthorne. Unlike everyone else around here, I only bet on a sure thing."

The housekeeping staff had found the exchange hilarious, and the story was soon all over the resort. Afterward Kate found extra towels every day in her room.

Jared made no secret of their liaison and Kate soon realized that everyone, from the resort staff to David, Letty and the colonel, was delighted with the way events were unfolding.

It should have been a perfect island affair, and Kate told herself it would have been if it weren't for two things. The first was that the end was preordained. She was, after all, holding a return ticket to the States. Whenever she allowed herself to dwell on that fact, she got restless and depressed and had to consciously push aside the emotions.

The second factor that stood in the way of her total enjoyment of the affair with Jared Hawthorne was a little harder to pin down, but it filled her with increasing unease. It had to do with the fact that she had seen him make another midnight trek to the Hawthorne castle with Max Butterfield and she had begun to realize she did not particularly care for Max. His incessant references to the great novel he had not yet written reminded her too much of her ex-husband.

On the night Jared and Max made the second trip to the castle, Jared had taken Kate back to her room right after dinner in the hotel dining room. He had made hot, urgent love to her and then told her he had to go home early because the baby-sitter couldn't stay with David past midnight.

Something had not rung true. She had known Max was back on the island, however, after being away for a few days. Kate had lain awake for a long time after Jared had left, questions and doubts and pure curiosity tumbling about in her brain. Then, drawn by a premonition, she had dressed in jeans and a dark shirt and walked down the path through the jungle to the point where it branched off to the castle.

She had stood concealed in the shadows for a long time before she had heard Max's complaining voice and the sound of his labored breathing. A moment later the fat man and Jared had passed her on their way to the castle.

Kate had waited a long time for them to return, but finally had given up and gone back to her own room. She did not get much sleep that night.

No matter how she looked at it, Jared had lied to her. He had not hurried home to his son.

The next morning, Kate sat in a lounger on a terrace overlooking the cove and wondered what to do next. Over and over again she toyed with the idea of confronting Jared and asking him what was going on, but she always backed off from that approach when she remembered that he had deliberately misled her. It was obvious he did not want her to know what he was doing with Max Butterfield. If she confronted him, he would probably lie to her, and she didn't want to hear his lies.

She had to face the knowledge that, though Jared might appear to have stepped straight out of her fantasies, the truth was, she knew very little about him.

"Good morning," sang out a familiar, cheerful voice. "How's the antistress campaign going?"

Kate shook off her somber mood and smiled at Letty Platt. "Terrific. I feel like a new woman. And I've got some fascinating reading." She indicated the diary of Amelia Cavendish that lay in her lap.

Letty glanced at the leather-bound volume. "So Jared has let you actually touch his precious old Hawthorne journals, I see. Congratulations. He's very protective of those books. Keeps them in a locked glass case."

"I know and I don't blame him. They're fascinating, once you decipher the handwriting. They're in amazingly good condition, too. But that's because the paper used in the old days was of such fine quality, not like the cheap, disposable stuff we use now."

Letty nodded, sitting down on a nearby lounger. "Discover anything interesting about our founding father?"

"This is Amelia's diary, not Roger's, and yes, I'm finding out a lot of interesting tidbits. For example, did you know that she had been in love with Roger Hawthorne since she was a young girl?"

"Really? I thought he just happened to spot her when he went back to England looking for a bride."

"Nope. She was the daughter of the lord who owned the estates that bordered his father's lands and she'd had a crush on him for years. He was well aware of it, the cad. Used to tease her unmercifully. But he also danced with her when she made her come out in London. He kissed her that night. Listen to this, Letty."

I was transported the moment his lips touched mine. I did not dream such unbearable joy existed. I know I should not have allowed him such liberties, but I vow I was helpless to resist him. It seems I have loved Roger forever, and at long last he is discovering he loves me. Surely he loves me. He is too much the gentleman to have kissed me otherwise. I am in heaven as of this moment. I cannot wait until he makes an offer for me.

"Uh-oh," Letty said. "Let me guess what happened next. The rogue left England and poor Amelia never got her offer."

"Afraid not. Hawthorne didn't actually seduce her, but he certainly got passionate on a number of occasions and led her to believe he was going to ask for her hand in marriage. Then, without any warning, he ups and leaves the country without a word of explanation and doesn't return for three years. Amelia was devastated. Cried inconsolably for days."

"Poor girl."

"She turned out to be the feisty type, though. When she finally recovered from her heartbreak she was determined never to give her heart to another man. She scorned all offers of marriage, though her family pleaded and threatened when she turned down one eligible male after another."

"She'd really had it with men, hmm? Can't say that I blame her. Why did Roger Hawthorne leave England so suddenly?"

"I don't know yet. Amelia just says he split without bothering to say goodbye. He was a second son and so couldn't inherit. I expect he decided to go off and make his fortune as a pirate, and the thought that poor Amelia would get her heart broken didn't occur to him."

"Or didn't bother him too much if it did occur to him. Typical male in many respects."

"I'm at the part now where he's just returned. Amelia has found out he's in London and that he's asked her father for her hand in marriage. Apparently he's quite wealthy now and society is willing to overlook the little matter of how he got so rich. Amelia writes that her parents are delighted with the offer. But she refuses to even see him. Says she is not about to trust him with her heart a second time. Can't wait to see what happens next."

"Well, we can guess, given the fact that the legend says he eventually kidnapped her and brought her back here."

Kate closed the book. "Something tells me she put up a good fight. She's really furious with him at this point."

"Maybe her relationship with Roger went the same way your relationship with Jared is going. I must tell you, Kate, we are all having a great time watching you two."

"I can tell. I feel as if I'm conducting a relationship inside a goldfish bowl."

"You don't know how good it is to see Jared getting involved emotionally at long last. He's been alone with only David for too many years. He needs a wife."

Kate stirred uneasily. "Come on, Letty. You know as well as I do that the kind of thing Jared and I have is probably going to end the day I catch my plane home."

Letty smiled complacently. "If Jared takes after Roger Hawthorne as much as I think he does, he won't let you get on that plane."

"He can't stop me," Kate said automatically.

Letty chuckled without opening her eyes. "Don't be ridiculous. Jared all but owns this island. He can do anything he wants around here. Just ask anyone."

Kate thought about Jared's midnight treks to the Hawthorne castle and went cold. What if Letty was right, she wondered. What if Jared really did run this island as if it were his own personal kingdom? What if the power he wielded around here had gone to his head and he had gotten involved in something dangerous or outside the law?

Her imagination was running wild, she told herself. "Letty, what do you know about Max Butterfield?"

"Max?" Letty opened one eye. "Not a lot. But then there isn't a lot to know. He's been out here forever. He's the kind of guy who imagines himself to be another Hemingway and does a good enough job with the booze, but not an equally good job with the writing. Why? Did old Max make a pass?"

"No. I was just curious." She was about to ask another question when Jared's voice interrupted.

"There you are, Kate." He walked up behind Kate and leaned down to drop a hard, possessive kiss on her forehead. "I've been looking for you. Hi, Letty, how's it going?"

"Just fine, Jared. Kate has been filling me in on all the details from Amelia Cavendish's diary. It's about time someone read it cover to cover."

"I tried once, but I didn't get far. Pretty dull going. Roger's journals and log are a lot more interesting." Jared dropped lightly down onto the foot of Kate's lounger. "Who wants to read a woman's diary?" he added plaintively.

Kate punched him lightly in the ribs. "I'm having a great time reading it, I'll have you know. It's a heck of a lot more interesting than a ship's log."

"Ouch." Jared gave her a reproachful look as he massaged his injured ribs. "That's a fine way to treat a man who's just come out to invite you to a nice home-cooked dinner."

"Has David lined up the restaurant staff for us again?"

"Uh, no, not exactly."

Kate's brows rose as she saw the speculative gleam in Jared's eyes. "Really? Who's going to do the cooking? You and David?"

"As a matter of fact, we planned to let you do it." Jared gave her his best buccaneer's smile. "Dave hasn't had a home-cooked meal in ages. Neither have I."

Letty gave a muffled laugh from her lounger. "Be careful, Kate. Sounds like they're planning to take advantage of you."

"I'm supposed to be on vacation," Kate pointed out loftily.

"Yeah, well, if you can't cook, just say so. Dave and I will understand. It's not too late to order dinner from the restaurant."

"I can cook," Kate retorted, feeling challenged.

"Are you sure?" Jared looked doubtful.

"Of course I'm sure," she snapped, thoroughly irritated now by his skeptical expression.

"It's okay to admit it if you can't. I mean, this being the late twentieth century and all, there are probably a lot of women who never really learned to cook. They've got their careers and stuff to think of first, I guess and…"

"I told you, I can cook."

"Well, if you really think you can handle it…"

"I can handle it."

"You're sure it's not too much trouble?"

"It's not too much trouble, dammit. Haven't you got some work you should be doing?"

"Yeah." Jared got to his feet and leaned down for another quick, satisfied kiss. "There's a major plumbing disaster going on in the south wing. I'd better check on the repairs. See you around six. You can pick up any supplies you need at Chan's grocery in town. Letty will show you the place. Tell Chan I sent you and he'll give you the resort discount."

Jared sauntered off, whistling.

Kate stared after him. "Correct me if I'm wrong, Letty, but did I just let myself get bamboozled into cooking a free meal for Jared and Dave?"

"That's what it sounded like to me." Letty looked over at her curiously. "Can you cook?"

"You're looking at the best pizza maker this side of Seattle."

"Pizza!" Letty looked first astounded and then delighted. "If David isn't already half in love with you, he will be after tonight. Since Gabriella died, that boy's been eating restaurant food for just about every meal of the day except breakfast. When you stop and think about it, you realize he's been practically raised on such things as pâté-stuffed mushrooms and seafood curries. Not normal kid food at all."

The question was whether David's father would be as easily impressed, Kate decided. And if Jared did fall in love, would he admit it, either to her or himself?

The fact that she was even pondering such a question shocked Kate. It meant she had to face something she had been deliberately shying away from for the past few days. She was tumbling head over heels into love with the pirate of Amethyst Island.

Chapter Six

THE SHORT TRIP INTO THE TINY ISLAND TOWN of Amethyst was a disturbing confirmation of everything Letty Platt had said about Jared's power on the island. Even more unnerving for Kate was the realization that even though this was the first time she had left the resort grounds, she was already a well-known figure, and not because of her reputation as an author, she soon discovered to her chagrin.

"Ms Inskip, it is indeed a pleasure to serve you." The beaming owner of the small grocery brushed aside his young assistant who appeared to be his son and handled the transaction personally. "Allow me to give you the usual resort discount," he insisted as he bagged Kate's purchases.

"I think I can handle the regular prices." Kate reached for her purse.

"No, no, no. Impossible. I will not hear of it. Jared Hawthorne does a great deal of business with my small shop and the discount I give him is my way of thanking him. You understand?"

"Yes, of course, but these are my groceries, not Mr. Hawthorne's. I'm buying them for personal use, not for the resort."

"But you are a close personal friend of Jared's and I must insist you accept the discount."

"But I really don't want it or need it."

Letty stepped close and murmured, "I wouldn't argue with him if I were you, Kate. Mr. Chan will be hurt, Jared will be annoyed and you'll lose the battle, anyway. This is Jared's discount and you're entitled to it. Let it go at that."

Kate sighed. She knew it wasn't worth an argument. She summoned up a properly grateful smile. "Thank you, Mr. Chan. You're very kind."

"Not at all, not at all." He rang up the sale on a cash register that looked as though it had been around since before one of the less recent wars. "Please give my best to Jared."

Kate took the paper sack full of pizza fixings and turned to follow a grinning Letty out of the store. Several people glanced at her with open curiosity and big smiles.

"What, exactly, do you think Mr. Chan meant when he called me a close personal friend of Jared's?"

Letty shot her a slanting glance. "What do you think he meant?"

"I was afraid of that. Does everyone on the island know that I'm…that Jared and I have been that—" she cleared her throat "—that close?"

"Probably. Does it bother you?"

"It annoys me," Kate snapped as she dumped the sack of groceries into the back of the small Jeep Letty was driving. "It's an invasion of personal privacy."

"If you wanted a lot of personal privacy," Letty said as she put the Jeep in gear, "you shouldn't have gotten involved in an affair with the biggest honcho on the island."

Kate closed her eyes in brief frustration. "You've got a point. Getting involved with Jared is probably not the brightest thing I've ever done. Maybe the tropical heat has warped my brain. Where are we going now?"

"Thought we'd make a quick stop at a dress shop run by a friend of mine. She carries some nice things, and her prices are a lot better than the ones in the resort's gift shop."

Kate perked up. "Sounds like a great idea."

But twenty minutes later when Kate selected a colorful full-length island dress and asked to have it hemmed, she was confronted with another example of Jared's inescapable presence. He might as well have been looking over her shoulder, she thought wryly.

"I'll have my seamstress hem it immediately," the shop owner promised. "It will be delivered to the resort this afternoon. Will that be soon enough?"

"There's no great rush," Kate said quickly. "I can pick it up tomorrow."

"I wouldn't hear of it." The woman waved the idea aside with a graceful movement of her hand. "You're a personal friend of Jared's, and I insist. It's the least I can do. After all, Jared was the one who loaned me the capital I needed to open this shop. I'm delighted to be able to do a favor for a friend of his. Heavens, just about everyone on the island is happy to extend a few favors to Jared. Isn't that right, Letty?"

"I'm afraid so." Letty's eyes brimmed with amusement. "Come on, Kate. Let's take a peek inside the gallery next door. You might see something you like."

"And get it at a Hawthorne discount?" Kate asked dryly.

"Probably. Mary Farrell, who runs it, gets most of her business from the resort visitors. She undoubtedly feels she owes Jared a favor, too. Her artists would all be starving if it weren't for the customers Crystal Cove sends her way."

Kate threw up her hands. "I give up. Why don't you all just admit you're living in a feudal kingdom and buy Jared a crown?"

"Not exactly a feudal kingdom," Letty said, laughing. "Just a very small town on a very small island that's tucked away in a very far-off corner of the world. If it weren't for Jared Hawthorne and his resort, Amethyst would either be completely deserted or look a lot more like Port Ruby, a run-down, sleazy dump. People around here know that."

"And they're suitably grateful."

"You could say that."

"You know something, Letty? I'll bet things around here worked very much the same way back when Roger Hawthorne was in charge."

"I wouldn't be surprised."

KATE CAME TO A HALT ON THE PATH, glanced quickly back over her shoulder and then ducked under the heavy chain that guarded the route to the Hawthorne castle.

She felt extremely daring as she slipped past the barrier. She was now on forbidden territory.

There was no real reason to worry about being seen, though she continued to glance back over her shoulder. There was no reason to be nervous, either, she reminded herself. She had been at Crystal Cove long enough to learn the routine. It was barely dawn and no self-respecting guest at the resort arose at this hour. Neither did members of the staff, as far as Kate could discern. Life was definitely more relaxed on a South Seas island.

She would have the castle to herself, and that was exactly what she wanted. Her curiosity had become overwhelming.

Earlier in the week she had dutifully signed on for the official tour of the castle and had been bitterly disappointed. An enthusiastic guide had led the small group of

interested guests along the winding path to the picturesque ruins, but no one had been allowed to do any in-
depth exploring.

The young man had told everyone the story of Roger
Hawthorne, a rather sanitized version compared to the edi-
tion Kate was reading in Amelia's diary.

The Hawthornes had lived on Amethyst Island for
many years and had produced several children, despite
Amelia's initial opposition to the marriage. That information had amused the small crowd. The family had
eventually moved back to England when Roger's older
brother had died without an heir, leaving the estates and
a title to Roger.

The castle had remained empty ever since.

"And in such a dangerous state of disrepair that the resort management allows visitors only as far as the front hall
at the present time," the guide had concluded. "Renovations are planned and someday soon large sections of the
castle will be open for viewing."

But Kate had seen no sign of the renovations, nor any
evidence of workmen around the place. She had, however, seen two sets of fresh footprints in the dust on a circular staircase at the back of the shadowy hall. Something
told her the prints had been left by Jared and his large
friend Max.

Kate had awakened this morning with the sure and certain knowledge that she could no longer contain her anxious curiosity. She had to know what was going on. Her
intimate relationship with Jared made it impossible to ignore his mysterious comings and goings any longer.

The castle was supposed to be a crumbling ruin, forbidden to everyone, yet Jared had taken Max Butterfield
up to it at midnight on at least two occasions, and the two
men had apparently gone well beyond the front hall.

Kate was rapidly becoming convinced that whatever was going on at the castle at night was either illegal or dangerous or both. She had to know the truth.

It was a long hike along the narrow path to the Hawthorne castle. The route wound through the dense tropical growth above Crystal Cove and continued on for some distance through more heavy foliage until, with no warning, it ended abruptly in front of the old stone ruin.

Kate came to a halt and caught her breath while she studied the dark pile of stone in the dawn light.

The Hawthorne castle was more of a well-fortified stone house than a true castle, she decided. It was not a huge place, just a three-story structure pierced with narrow windows. There were no outer walls protecting a courtyard, gatehouses, moats or ramparts. There was, however, a tower that rose above the main building from which Roger Hawthorne had no doubt kept an eagle eye on the sea. From his aerie he could have watched for both opportunities and competitors.

The section of the castle that faced the sea was a solid wall of stone that merged with the dark lava that rose out of the waves. On the sea side, the castle was impregnable. The only approach was from the jungle side of the island.

During the tour, the guide had explained that Hawthorne and his crew had used the beach above Crystal Cove as a wharf. Cargoes had been unloaded, goods had been traded and business had been conducted on the spot where the resort now stood. The wealthy planters and others from nearby islands had been eager to buy whatever Hawthorne managed to get hold of and no one worried too much about the original owners of the goods.

Kate took a deep breath and walked cautiously through the massive stone entryway, following the path the tour guide had used the previous day. A moment later she found herself in the shadowy, high-ceilinged hall.

An eerie sensation rippled through her as she switched on her small flashlight. When she had stood in this room with a crowd full of curious resort guests, everything had seemed quite interesting. But this morning she felt as if she were standing in a room full of ghosts.

"Not exactly an English country house, Amelia," Kate whispered. "How did you stand it? I'll bet you were really annoyed when you realized you were supposed to set up housekeeping in this joint."

Kate walked across the floor to the circular stone staircase at the far end of the hall. The footprints were still there. She had not imagined them. The staircase went down, not up to the next level.

She leaned forward and splashed the light over the steps. They twisted and vanished into a forbidding darkness.

She had known the answers weren't going to come easily. She took a deep breath and considered her next move. There was no real option. If she wanted to know where the footsteps led, she would have to follow them.

When she started slowly down the narrow steps, she learned firsthand the meaning of having the hair on the back of her neck stand on end. Her fingers trembled as she grasped the flashlight. Her every instinct was alive with warning.

But she forced herself down the steps, following the muddled prints in the dust. It crossed her mind that the guide had emphasized several times that the castle was not structurally safe, but she decided that as long as she followed the footprints she would be reasonably safe. Jared and Max had come this way more than once, she reminded herself. And at midnight, too.

The gloom thickened around her as she descended below the level of the entry hall. Down here there were no slits in the walls to provide air and light. A dank, damp odor swirled around her. When she paused to flash the light around, Kate saw only more stone.

Then, without any warning, the stone steps came to an end in a tiny cell of a room. Perhaps this was a storage cellar, she thought. But when she examined the floor, she found that the footprints continued on, straight into a wall. There must be some sort of concealed doorway in the stone, she decided, but she had no idea of where to begin hunting for the hidden lock.

There were more prints leading off in the opposite direction back under the staircase. Kate followed these to a dark opening that proved to be a doorway. The door itself was long gone. When she flashed her light down the dank hall that was revealed, she saw a barred room that must have been used as a dungeon or secured storage room at one time.

Her uneasiness grew. The more she studied the barred room, the more it looked like a dungeon cell. Kate suddenly wanted very badly to get back upstairs into the light. She started quickly up the steps, stumbling in her haste.

When she was within sight of the last step, Kate switched off the flashlight and quickened her pace. She couldn't wait to get out into the warm light of the new day. Later, when she was safely back in her room, she would try to figure out what to do next. Perhaps she should confront Jared, after all. But what would she do if he simply denied everything? She could not bear the thought that he might be a real-life pirate.

The questions hammered at her, driving her forward until she practically leaped up the last step.

She was so intent on getting out of the hall that she didn't even see the man who stood concealed in the shadows at the top of the dark staircase. When his arm closed suddenly around her, snagging her and pulling her back against a solid male body, Kate opened her mouth on a terrified scream.

There was no scream: a large hand clamped over her mouth. Kate reacted in fear and rage, driving her elbow back into what felt like a very solid midsection. The blow brought a muffled curse, and for an instant the man's grip slackened.

That was all the time Kate needed. She moved, grasping his arm and stepping to one side in an effort to yank her assailant off balance. He went readily in the direction she wanted, too readily—the way Jared had that morning on the beach. Instead of losing his balance, he added so much force to the momentum she had established that Kate was thrown off her feet. In that instant Kate finally realized who she was dealing with.

"Jared."

He came down on top of her, pinning her to the floor. "Oh, Christ, it's you. I should have known. Quiet, you little fool. Sound carries. Are all romance writers so damnably curious?"

A new kind of anger surged through Kate. How dared he treat her like this? How dared he sneak around in the dark and grab unsuspecting people who were merely trying to get to the bottom of a few crucial questions?

"Let me go, you bastard. Let me go, dammit. You're a liar. A *liar.*"

"Stop it," he ordered roughly. "Will you just stop struggling, for crying out loud? Listen to me, you little shrew. Settle down or you'll hurt yourself."

But Kate was too incensed to stop. She had never been so angry. She felt betrayed.

The battle was short and frantic, and Kate knew she had lost it before it had even begun. Nevertheless, she fought desperately, aware that she was overmatched. All two weeks' worth of self-defense lessons were discarded in a moment as she realized none of them would work. Instead she fought like a small, terrified creature that has become the prey of a much bigger, more dangerous predator.

She tried to kick out and found her leg anchored to the floor by Jared's thigh. She tried to punch and got her wrists captured for her troubles. Jared did not hurt her, but he eventually succeeded in immobilizing her.

"That's enough," he said through his teeth. "You can't win, so stop wasting your energy."

A few minutes later, exhausted by her struggles, Kate followed his advice. She lay still, fighting to catch her breath. Her wrists were pinned on either side of her head in a parody of the way he had held her when he had made love to her. He was sprawled on top of her, using his weight to hold her still.

"That's better," he said after a minute's tense silence. He sat up slowly, releasing her carefully. His eyes never left her face. "Are you all right?"

"No." She sat up, aware that she was trembling with outrage. She brushed the dust from her shirt, concentrating on the small, useless task so that she would not have to meet his eyes. "I am not all right. How dare you manhandle me like this?"

He muttered something short and explicit under his breath as he got lithely to his feet. He reached down to haul her up beside him. His face was taut with anger.

"What the hell are you doing here?" Jared spoke through clenched teeth.

"What do you think I'm doing here? I came to take a closer look at the castle. The guided tour was a joke. We barely got to glance inside this hall. I wanted to see the rest of the place."

"You've been told the rest of the castle is off-limits."

"Yes, well, as you said, romance writers are a curious bunch."

Jared regarded her in silence for a few seconds. "Cut it out, Kate. I want the truth. Why are you here?"

"How did you know I was here?" she countered.

"I went by your room to see if you wanted to go for a dawn walk on the beach. It seemed so *romantic*. Thought it would appeal to you. You weren't there, so I figured you might have gone down to the cove on your own. You weren't there either, but the chain across the castle path was still swinging and I knew someone had come this way. When I walked into the hall I heard someone coming up the stairs."

"How very alert of you. I'm lucky you didn't break my neck."

"How was I to know it was you, dammit? I'm not in the mood for any of your sass, lady. I want some answers and I'm going to get them, but not here and not now."

"Why not here and now? I'd like a few answers, too."

"You've pushed your luck far enough today. The first thing we're going to do is get you back to the resort. I don't want you hanging around here any longer than necessary." He took hold of her arm and propelled her out of the hall and into the morning sunshine.

"Now, just one damned minute." Kate stumbled and tried to pull free of his grip. Jared ignored her efforts. He dragged her swiftly along the path until they reached the chain that barred the way. There he paused long enough to push her underneath the metal links. He followed, ducking quickly beneath the barrier.

"All right," he said a moment later as they hit the main path back to the resort. "We're safe now. If anyone sees us here we can say we were down at the beach."

"Why do we have to make any explanations at all?" Kate cast him a furious glance.

"Because I said so."

"And whatever you say is law around here, is that it?"

"Now you're catching on."

He had hold of her hand now. To anyone else it would look like an affectionate grip, but Kate was thoroughly aware of the force behind it. She was relieved to be away from the castle ruins, but the wariness she felt around Jared was not making her feel much better. She began to think longingly of her cozy little apartment in Seattle.

"Where are we going?" she demanded as Jared walked her swiftly past her room and on toward the main resort building.

"My office. We can talk there without worrying about someone interrupting us."

She said nothing more as he led her through the empty lobby and down an open hallway to a room that over-looked the cove.

"In here." He closed the door behind them and pushed her toward a chair. "Sit down and talk." He went over to a side table and switched on a coffee machine.

"I think you're the one who should be doing the talking." Kate absently rubbed her wrist where he had gripped it. "What's going on at that castle, Jared? What are you and Max involved in?"

"Damn. You know about Max, too? You have been busy, haven't you?" He seemed totally wrapped up in watching the fresh coffee drip into the glass pot.

"I know you and Max have been paying some midnight visits to the castle." Kate decided she had nothing to lose at this point by admitting what she had seen.

"You're in this deeper than I realized. Who are you, Kate?"

The implied accusation infuriated her. "I'm exactly who I told you I am, a stressed-out writer on vacation. Nothing more and nothing less. Unlike you, I'm not living any lies."

"The weird part is that I believe you. I think I'd know if you were lying to me."

"I've got news for you—you're not the only one who can tell when someone is lying."

Jared sighed. "What made you start spying on Max and me? Research?"

"Hardly. I was coming back from the beach late my first night on the island and I decided to take a quick look at the castle. I had to hide in the bushes because you and Max were on the same path. When I spotted both of you going that way again a second time, I got curious."

"I'll just bet you did. Lord save all men from curious females."

Jared poured two cups of coffee and carried one over to her. When she took it without a word, he went around behind a massive carved desk and sat down.

"What's going on, Jared? What's the big secret?"

He sipped his coffee, looking very thoughtful. "To put it bluntly, my sweet, it's none of your damned business."

"Are you up to something illegal?"

"No."

"Then what's going on?" Kate was slightly relieved to hear the denial, but she was still thoroughly exasperated.

"It's nothing that concerns you, Kate. Furthermore, I'm ordering you to stay out of it."

"I don't take orders from you. If it's nothing illegal, then you won't care if I call the police."

"What police? Sam over on Ruby Island? Give me a break. He'd laugh himself silly. Even if you got him to listen to you, what would you tell him? That I made a couple of midnight trips to Hawthorne Castle? I own the place, remember? I've got a perfect right to go there any time I want. You're the one who was illegally trespassing."

He was right, of course. She had absolutely nothing to report to any official. "Jared, something is going on, I know it."

"I don't care what you think you know so long as you keep your mouth shut and don't give me any trouble. That means staying away from Hawthorne Castle. Understood?"

She jumped to her feet. "No, it is not understood. I want to know what's going on. I insist you tell me."

"Just because your curiosity is running wild doesn't mean I have to satisfy it, Kate."

"But if it's something illegal…"

"I've told you, it's not illegal."

"Why should I believe you?"

"I've never lied to you, have I?"

"Yes, you have. Last night is an instance that comes immediately to mind. You told me you had to go home early so David wouldn't be alone. But you didn't go home. You went to the castle."

"Oh, yeah. I forgot."

"You *forgot?* Forgot you lied to me? Very convenient."

Jared sipped his coffee. "I didn't actually lie to you, you know. I did have to get home early last night. But I allowed myself enough time to make the trip to the castle."

"I'm supposed to accept that as an explanation?" Kate yelped.

"You're really worked up about this, aren't you?"

"Yes, dammit, I am. I've got reason to be worked up. I've been lied to, misled and physically assaulted by the man with whom I'm having an affair."

"Let's not get carried away here. I didn't actually set out to assault you. It was dark in that hall and I wasn't sure who was coming up the steps. I just grabbed the first warm body that appeared. The next thing I knew, I was forced to defend myself against all two weeks' worth of your self-defense lessons. Which reminds me, you need a little work in some areas, Kate. I might be able to give you a couple of tips. I studied karate for a few years."

Kate folded her arms across her chest and stood stiffly in front of the entrance to the veranda. "I don't believe this. You're not going to explain any of it, are you?"

"No."

She whirled around and slammed her fist against the nearest wall. "You can't do this to me. I'm having an affair with you, dammit. That gives me some rights. I demand an explanation, Jared."

"Well, you're not going to get it, so you might as well calm down. The only thing you are going to get is my personal guarantee that what I'm doing is legal. You are also going to get a few strict instructions. From now on, you stay way from the castle."

"I could try cornering Max Butterfield and asking him what's going on." It was a weak threat, but it was all Kate had.

"Max left the island yesterday afternoon."

That stopped her for a second, but only a second. "I could tell Letty or the colonel what I've seen."

"Go ahead. They'll come straight to me and I'll tell them everything's under control. That will satisfy them. You'll just wind up making yourself look foolish."

"Because as long as you're in charge, everything's just hunky-dory here on Amethyst Island, is that it? I don't believe this."

"Believe it." Jared set down his cup and leaned back in the leather chair. "It's the way things work around here."

"So I've been told." Kate massaged her temples and tried to clear her head. "This is crazy."

"Can't you trust me, Kate?" Jared asked gently.

"That's unfair," she snapped. "You know if the situation was reversed, you'd jump on me with both feet, demanding explanations."

"Only because I'd be worried about you getting yourself into trouble."

"Okay, so I'm worried about you."

He smiled grimly and put his feet up on the desk. "There's no need. I've been taking care of myself for a long time."

"Jared, I don't like this. You've been living out here beyond the reach of civilization for so long that you're starting to think you're a law unto yourself, the way Roger Hawthorne thought he was."

"Not quite. I haven't started locking people up in dungeons yet."

"That's not very funny. Roger did that?"

"Sure. He was the only law on the island and the bunch that worked for him was rough, to put it mildly. He occasionally needed a dungeon, so he had one built at the bottom of those stairs you were exploring this morning."

"That little cell? That's some sort of dungeon?" Kate's eyes widened. "I knew it. But there's more down there than just that barred room. I know there is. I saw the way the footprints just disappear near the wall."

"Did you?" He eyed her speculatively.

"There's something else down there, Jared."

"Yeah. There is. But it's got nothing to do with you. One of these days, I'll show you the whole place, honey, but not today. Not for a couple more weeks, at least. Until I give you the word, you are not going to set foot on the castle path."

"You can't stop me from going wherever I want to go."

"Yes, I can. Here on Amethyst, I can do just about anything I want."

She stared at him for a long, measuring moment and knew he was right. "You really mean that, don't you? You really think you can give me orders and make me obey them."

"Kate," he said wearily, "even if you went back to the castle, you wouldn't see anything more than you did this morning. There's nothing more to see except a few other empty rooms."

"Then why can't I go there and explore to my heart's content?"

"Because it's unsafe, that's why. I've told you that."

"It's more than just structurally unsafe, isn't it? Whatever you're involved in there is dangerous. I know it is."

Jared swung his feet down from the desk, his eyes narrowing. "Look, I've had enough of this. Whether you like it or not, I'm the boss around here. Hawthorne castle belongs to me. That makes it private property. I don't want you anywhere near it and that's final."

"And you really don't feel you owe me any explanations at all?" she asked in stunned, helpless disbelief.

"Just because I'm sleeping with you? No."

Kate looked at his implacable face and realized further argument was useless. Furious, she went to the door and yanked it open. "You arrogant, overbearing, dictatorial, son of a… You know something, Jared Hawthorne? You're no better than your ancestor. You're just a twentieth-century pirate who thinks he's lord of all he surveys."

She slammed the door on her way out. When she was safely back in her room, she cried for the first time since Harry had walked out the door.

On that occasion she had been feeling hurt and humiliated and very much a failure. This time it was much worse. This time she was afraid her heart might break.

Chapter Seven

JARED WALKED INTO THE NEARLY EMPTY BAR that afternoon and realized immediately that the news of his quarrel with Kate had spread even faster than the news of his affair with her. He also knew that if it was all over the resort, it would be all over the island by now, too.

"Well, well, well, decided to come out of hiding, eh?" The colonel rested both hands on the bar and grinned in masculine commiseration. "Don't worry, it's safe enough in here for the moment. The lady's nowhere in sight. Haven't seen her all day."

"Is that right? And how do you know I've been in hiding?" Jared dropped onto a stool and hooked his foot over the brass rung.

"Lani was behind the front desk this morning when Kate came out of your office. I gather Ms Inskip looked more than mildly annoyed after her early morning interview. She didn't say anything, according to Lani, but it was obvious she'd just gone toe-to-toe with someone and the only other person in your office, Lani says, was you. You yourself have apparently been snapping off heads right and left all day. Everyone agrees that makes it official: you and Kate must have quarreled."

Jared swore, knowing there was no stopping the local rumor mill. "Is everyone else enjoying this as much as you are, Colonel?"

"Far as I can tell."

"Where's Kate?"

"I have no idea. Haven't seen her."

"She's probably sulking in her room. I'll give her a little while longer and then I'll go see if I can smooth a few feathers."

"You think it's going to be that easy?"

"She'll calm down. She's just a little pissed at the moment."

"I'd say she's more than a little pissed."

"Only because she lost the argument. She'll get over it."

"I wouldn't count on that happening anytime soon. I get the impression Ms Inskip is not accustomed to losing an argument. And since you're not exactly an expert at losing, either, I'd say we're in for a long siege."

"What's she going to do? Spend the rest of her vacation in her room? She's not that silly or irrational."

The colonel polished a glass and contemplated that. "She might decide there are more pleasant places to spend a vacation than Amethyst Island."

That jolted Jared. His jaw tightened. "You think she'd leave just because I put my foot down with her over something that was none of her business in the first place?"

"Is that what you did?"

"Yeah, that's what I did. Apparently she hasn't had too many people do that to her."

"I can see why," the colonel said. "As far as her getting ready to leave the island, I can't say for certain one way

or the other. Haven't heard a thing on that score. Guess
we'll find out soon enough, though, won't we? Hank will
be making his usual afternoon run back to Ruby in about
an hour. If she's on the plane we'll have our answer. A lot
of people have a lot of money riding on it, you know."

"Who's handling the bets?" Jared asked, resigned to the
inevitable.

"Jim at the front desk."

"Figures." The news irritated Jared but did not particularly surprise him. He was suddenly far more concerned
about another matter. Until that moment it hadn't occurred to him that Kate might actually leave the island because of the quarrel. He thought about that possibility a
moment longer and then stood up quickly. "See you later,
Colonel."

"Where are you going?"

"To catch Hank. I want to make sure he knows he hasn't
got a spare seat on that Cessna of his."

"Hank almost always has a spare seat on the afternoon hop."

"Not today he hasn't."

TWENTY MINUTES LATER JARED DROVE swiftly back from
the small paved strip that served as Amethyst Island's airport. He killed the Jeep's engine in the resort driveway with
a quick, savage motion of his hand.

He wasn't in a good mood, but he was momentarily satisfied. Hank Whitcomb had been willing to see reason the
moment Jared had pointed out that there were other island
pilots who wouldn't mind getting a guaranteed daily schedule between Amethyst and Ruby.

"Sure thing, Jared," Hank had said with a grin when
Jared handed him enough cash to cover the cost of one
empty seat to Ruby. "No seats available on this here flight.

None whatsoever. Good luck with that little lady, pal. Sounds like she's got you running around in circles."

He was not running around in circles, Jared assured himself as he stalked into the lobby. He was simply drawing a few lines for a woman who needed them drawn.

He found the front desk vacant and promptly hit the bell to summon a clerk.

"What can I do for you?" asked the thin young man who emerged from the office. He had started talking before he realized who it was that stood at the front desk. When he saw Jared, he blinked a little nervously. "Oh, it's you, boss. Sorry, I was just checking something on the computer. We had some last-minute bookings."

Jared leaned his elbows on the polished desk and waved a twenty in front of the desk clerk's nose. "Forget the last-minute bookings, Jim. I want to place a last-minute bet."

"Uh, sure thing, boss. Whatever you say." Jim smiled weakly. "What exactly did you want to bet on?"

"The same thing everyone else around here is betting on: whether or not Ms Inskip leaves with Hank this afternoon."

The clerk had the grace to turn red. He cleared his throat with a couple of coughs. "How did you want to place your bet, boss?"

"I've got twenty that says she won't be on the plane."

"Yes, sir. Twenty it is." The clerk leaned forward conspiratorially. "You know something the rest of us don't?"

"Of course not." Jared smiled grimly. "I just feel lucky."

"HEY, DAD, WHERE HAVE YOU BEEN? I've been looking all over for you." David dashed down the hall and skidded to a halt as Jared walked into the house. The boy looked worried.

"I ran out to the strip for a few minutes. Had to talk to Hank." Jared ruffled his son's hair.

"You didn't take Kate out to the strip, did you?" David demanded, thoroughly alarmed now.

Jared scowled. "No, I did not take Kate out to the strip. Why?"

"'Cause everyone knows she's mad at you and we're all afraid she's gonna leave on account of you yelled at her. It'll be all your fault if she goes, Dad."

"I did not yell at her. And where did you hear about her being mad at me?"

"Everyone says so. Hey, it's not because of that bet you and I made about her cooking, is it? Is she mad because we did that?"

"No, it's not because of the bet. Kate doesn't even know there was a bet. And if the subject comes up I want it clear that it was all your idea."

"You're the one who said she probably couldn't cook," David reminded him. "You bet me a dollar she couldn't, remember?"

"Yeah, but you're the one who suggested we con her into fixing dinner so we could find out for sure. You are also the guy who won a buck off me because she could make pizza. I'd appreciate it if you would not forget your part in all this."

David chewed his lower lip. "She'd probably really get mad if she ever found out, huh?"

"Yes," Jared said, "I think she would be very mad."

David sighed. "She sure made a great pizza, didn't she? You said she'd probably burn it, but she didn't."

"Pizza is probably the only thing she knows how to cook. I don't think Ms Inskip is the homey type."

"Anyone who can make good pizza can probably make lots of good stuff."

"Maybe," Jared agreed cautiously.

"Think she'll leave the island because you yelled at her?"

Jared lost what was left of his patience. "I told you, I did not yell at her, and no, Kate's not going to be leaving the island. Not today, at any rate."

David's expression relaxed instantly. "That's great. In that case, I'm going to win another buck."

"I should have guessed." Jared swore under his breath but without much heat. "You'd think everyone around here could find something more interesting to bet on than the status of my love life."

David's gaze widened with interest. "Is that what you have, Dad? A love life?"

"Had. Past tense."

Jared went into the kitchen and dug a cold beer out of the refrigerator. Then he walked out onto the veranda, dropped onto a lounger and started wondering how he was going to get his love life back. It was amazing how fast a man could get used to having a certain prickly little broad around.

KATE PACKED AND UNPACKED HER suitcase three times before sinking dejectedly onto the bed. She knew she ought to leave on the afternoon flight. If she had an ounce of self-respect, not to mention common sense, she would get off the island. She could not possibly stay here after what had happened this morning.

It amazed her to think she had spent years fantasizing about pirates. Having met one in the flesh, she now realized they were an infuriating breed. Give her a nice, sensitive, understanding, *civilized* male any day.

The knock on the door brought her head up with a start and her heart leaped. As she went to answer the summons, she steeled herself to be firm. If this was Jared come to apologize and explain his actions, she would not make it easy for him. The man deserved to do some groveling. Head high, she opened the door.

"Oh, hi, Letty."

"I take it you were expecting someone else?" Letty's expression was one of sympathetic female-to-female understanding.

"Not exactly expecting, more like entertaining a fleeting hope. Come on in."

Letty walked in and glanced at the open suitcases. "So you're going to leave," she said softly. "I wondered if you might be thinking of it."

"To be honest, I haven't made up my mind."

"Better hurry." Letty glanced at her watch. "Hank takes off in half an hour."

"The thing is, I hate to let that arrogant, dictatorial clod run me off the island this easily." Kate started to rehang some of her clothing. "It goes against the grain."

"Said arrogant, dictatorial clod being Jared?"

"Yes."

"Good." Letty settled into one of the chairs near the screened window. "Glad to hear it. The staff is taking bets, and I've got five dollars riding on your decision."

Kate wrinkled her nose. "There's certainly not much privacy on this island, is there?"

"Afraid not."

"Everyone knows I'm furious with Jared?"

"Uh-huh. Believe me, no matter which way they're betting, they're all praying you'll stay."

"Why?"

"Because no one wants to deal with Jared's temper after you leave. He's in one heck of a bad mood and they all figure it's going to get worse if you run off."

"I'm supposed to do everyone a favor and soothe the savage beast?" Kate was outraged anew. "Forget it. The quarrel was one hundred percent his fault."

"Was it?"

"It most certainly was." Kate rehung another dress. "Furthermore, I have absolutely no intention of apologizing to the man. But you can go collect your winnings, if you like, because I've just decided for certain that I'm not going to let him chase me off this island. I came here for a vacation, by heaven. I'm going to get one. Lord knows I've paid enough for it."

Letty grinned. "Somehow I rather thought you'd take that attitude."

"Don't look so delighted, Letty. I'm not hanging around so that I can placate Jared. I've got better things to do on my vacation. The big affair is at an end."

"Did you inform Jared yet?"

"He'll find out soon enough."

"Can't wait." Letty got up and headed for the door.

"Where are you going?"

"Now that I've got a little inside information, I thought I'd go double my bet."

Kate stared as the door closed behind her friend. All in all, she did not think she was getting cured of her stress problems.

THAT NIGHT KATE DRESSED FOR THE evening ahead as if she were preparing to go into battle. She went through everything she had brought with her and finally selected a flame-colored gown with an artfully draped bodice and a full, flouncy, flirty skirt. A pair of red heels and a silver collar at her throat completed the effect. She surveyed herself in the mirror and decided she had the look she wanted—cool, regal and totally self-contained.

When she walked into the crowded bar for an aperitif, she could feel the speculation, approval and open relief emanating from the staff. The colonel arched one thick brow and inclined his head in a silent salute. Kate smiled demurely and took one of the fan-backed chairs near the rail-ing. A few minutes later a rum-and-fruit concoction mate-rialized at her elbow. She looked up to smile at the waitress.

"Glad you didn't leave," the woman said in a low voice.

"Don't tell me, let me guess. You had a bet riding on my plans for the future, too?" Kate was long past the outraged stage. She had moved on to a sort of fatalistic acceptance of the inevitable.

"I bet ten dollars you wouldn't be going back to Ruby with Hank Whitcomb," the waitress admitted, "but that's not the real reason I'm glad you stayed."

"You think I'm going to somehow wave my magic wand and put Jared back into a good mood?"

The waitress laughed. "You'd have the eternal gratitude of the entire staff of Crystal Cove."

"Has it occurred to anyone that the only reason I might have hung around here is so that Jared can exert himself to put *me* back into a pleasant frame of mind?"

The waitress considered that angle. She appeared to have trouble grasping the concept. "Is that why you stayed? To bring Jared to his knees?"

"You look doubtful."

The waitress's smile broadened. "Let's just say it should be interesting. Good luck, Ms Inskip. Oh, and I just fin-ished your last book. It was great. Loved that part where the hero goes into the bedroom thinking the heroine is going to be meekly waiting for him in bed and she dumps the chamber pot over his head instead."

"I'm glad you enjoyed it."

Kate allowed the waitress's parting remark to warm her as she sat gazing out at the darkening sea. But the good feeling didn't last long. It was obvious everyone at Crys-tal Cove was finding the situation between herself and Jared vastly entertaining, but Kate knew better. There was nothing funny about her quarrel with Jared; this was no amusing battle of the sexes. The stakes were too high.

She went cold whenever she allowed herself to speculate on what Jared might be involved in up at Hawthorne Castle.

Jared had the natural authority and innate arrogance of a man who was accustomed to running his own domain, but she knew him well enough by now to know he was neither vicious nor totally unreasonable. Vicious, unreasonable men did not build thriving resorts capable of supporting the economy of an entire island. Vicious, unreasonable men did not incur the kind of loyalty and friendship Jared had locally.

Or did they?

Something serious was going on up at Hawthorne Castle, and Jared was deeply involved. He did not want her anywhere near the place and as far as Kate could tell, there could be only one reason for forbidding her to take the castle path: Kate was very much afraid Jared was following in the footsteps of Roger Hawthorne, and because she was also very much afraid she was in love with him, she knew she had to stop him.

She was lost in thought when a shadow fell across the table. She looked up, half expecting to see Jared standing there, but it was Jeff Taylor who was smiling hopefully down at her.

"I see you're alone tonight. Mind if I join you?" He was dressed in a pair of slacks and a flower-printed aloha shirt. His red hair was still damp from a shower.

Kate smiled. "Not at all."

Jeff's smile widened with satisfaction. "Thanks." He took the chair across from her and lifted a hand to catch the waitress's attention. "Haven't been able to catch you alone since the night of the masquerade ball. You been hanging out with the local boss man, I hear. How come he's left you on your own tonight?"

"I'm on vacation," Kate said. "I hang out with whoever I want to hang out with."

"Hope that means me tonight."

Out of the corner of her eye, Kate saw Jared saunter through the door and head for the bar. She tensed, preparing for a scene. "Why not?" she said, smiling brilliantly.

Several hours later Kate finally decided Jared was not going to make a scene, after all. She told herself she was glad, but some small, very primitive part of her was hurt, she had to admit.

It was not that she didn't enjoy herself with Jeff Taylor. They had dinner together and danced afterward. Jeff was charming, funny and more than willing to follow her lead. When she eventually pleaded weariness and said she wanted to go to her room, he quickly volunteered to walk her back through the gardens. She wondered briefly if she would have trouble with him at the door, but when she dismissed him gently, he went with good grace.

"Maybe we can do this again," he murmured, brushing a quick, light kiss across her cheek.

"Maybe." She smiled a good-night sort of smile that made no promises. Behind her the room was shrouded in darkness.

"Say, you want to go snorkeling in the cove tomorrow morning?"

She hesitated and then asked herself why not. She was supposed to be on vacation, after all. "Sounds great."

Jeff grinned. "I'll meet you right after breakfast."

"That will be fine."

Kate smiled again and then closed the door gently but firmly in his face. She turned around and walked into the room without bothering to switch on the light. She went to the screened wall and stood looking out at the silvered sea. She was learning to love the island night. The fragrant, velvet air drifted through the open windows, caressing her and bringing back poignant memories of the nights she had spent in Jared's arms.

The familiar feeling of awareness went through her and she hugged herself. It was ridiculous, but she could almost feel him nearby. There was that curious tingling at the back of her neck…Kate gasped and whirled around.

"Lucky for all of us you didn't invite Taylor into the room," Jared said from the shadows of the bed. "Could have been a little awkward trying to explain the crowd in here."

"*Jared.*" Kate took hold of herself immediately. "What are you doing here?"

"What do you think I'm doing here?" His hand moved negligently, and the pale moonlight glinted off the brandy snifter he was holding. He was propped up against a couple of pillows, wearing a pair of low-slung jeans and nothing else.

"How did you get in here?"

"I own the place, remember? I have a key."

Kate drew a deep breath, unable to move. This was not fear, she told herself firmly. She was just feeling naturally wary of the big, dangerous man on her bed. "Did you stop by to apologize and explain yourself?"

Jared sipped meditatively from the snifter. "No. What about you? Finished playing games with Taylor?"

"I'll play games with whoever I feel like playing games with."

"Then we have a problem, don't we?"

"I don't see why. You and I are no longer involved, remember? We had a major quarrel this morning. That was the end of our famous affair as far as I'm concerned."

"You're lying. If you thought things were over between us, you would have bought a ticket on the afternoon plane to Ruby. You didn't even try."

"I said things were over between us, I didn't say my vacation was over."

"Go ahead and tell yourself whatever you like. We both know you're still here because of what's happening between us."

"You are so damned arrogant."

"And you're not?"

"Not like you," Kate shot back.

He laughed softly and sat up on the side of the bed. He put the snifter down on the end table and got to his feet, facing her. "You're more like me than you want to admit and that's why we've got a few problems. But I'm beginning to think we can fix all that."

She instinctively stepped back as he came around the end of the bed and started toward her. Then she refused to retreat any farther. Her chin lifted even as she felt herself turning hot and vibrant with the fierce emotions coursing through her.

"Now just one blasted minute, Jared Hawthorne."

"Let's get something clear right from the start. This is just between you and me," Jared said. "You want to go to war, we'll go to war. You want to make love, we'll make love. But we don't involve any third parties. No more Jeff Taylors."

"You really are a pirate, aren't you?"

"If I'm a pirate, you were born to be a pirate's woman." His hands closed over her shoulders and his mouth found hers in a searing kiss.

He was right, Kate acknowledged silently as she felt the passion rising swiftly; some part of her had been born to respond to him. He was the man she had been waiting for all her life. Her arms went around his neck and she shoved her fingers through his thick, dark hair.

Jared exhaled heavily, his body going hard at her touch. "I knew when you didn't try to get on that plane today that you realized this was special." He pulled her down onto the bed and sprawled across her. "Neither one of us can walk away from it now."

His arrogance appalled her. "All right," Kate said, looking up at him through her lashes, "I'll admit the sex is good. And I've heard it's a great cure for stress. I might as well enjoy it."

Jared's eyes glittered with sudden anger and his hands tightened on her. "It isn't just the sex and you know it."

"What else is there? It's not as if there's a lot of trust or love between us."

"Damn you, stop trying to manipulate me. I'm not the kind of man you can push and prod until I collapse in a heap of jelly and tell you whatever you want to hear. One of these days you're going to learn that."

"Just as you're going to have to learn that I'm not the kind of sweet, soft, meek little woman who will let you pat her on the head and tell her to mind her own business."

He stared down at her, his mouth inches from her own, his hands locked on her shoulders. "One of us is going to have to back down and I can tell you right now, it won't be me, Kate. I know what I'm doing and I know what's best for you. You're going to have to trust me and that's final."

"Nothing is final," she told him, pulling his head down to hers. "But there's no point talking about it tonight."

"On that we agree."

His mouth took hers once more in a kiss that demanded everything from her. It was as if he had decided that in place of the capitulation he could not quite wring from her, he would take her very soul instead.

Kate trembled with the force of her passion, clinging to Jared as he thrust her legs apart with his own. Her red skirt foamed high up on her thighs. He freed her mouth with a husky groan and buried his lips in the curve of her shoulder.

She felt his hands on the zipper of the red dress and a moment later the silky material was being pushed down over her hips. She was alive with her own desire and infinitely aware of his. The combination was electric. Kate wondered why there were no visible sparks flaring in the darkened room. The invisible ones were everywhere, igniting a wildfire.

Jared's hands moved hungrily on her, tugging off the red dress, the red shoes and the panty hose. When she was wearing nothing except the silver collar and moonlight he sat up and unfastened his jeans. He stepped out of them in a series of quick, jerky movements that spoke volumes about his restless impatience. When he was free of the denims he stood beside the bed for a long moment, staring down at her. His body was heavy with arousal.

"You want me, don't you?" he asked.

"Yes."

"Don't ever again say it's just good sex," he ordered as he came down beside her. His palm closed over her breast.

"That really bothered you, didn't it? Why?"

"Because it's a lie and I won't let you lie to me."

"But it's all right for you to lie to me?" she asked.

"I've never lied to you, but there are some things you don't need to know." He stroked his hands through her hair. "You'll just have to learn to trust me."

"Jared—"

"Hush. Not now." He cut off her words with a hot kiss, his tongue plunging between her lips. His fingers roamed over her, awakening her nipples and moving lower to find the dampening warmth between her legs.

Kate's head was spinning with the euphoric excitement. She touched him wonderingly, loving the feel of his beautifully contoured back and the sleek muscles of his thighs. She let her nails slip into the rough hair below his waist and when she found the hard, thrusting shape of him she circled him gently.

"Yes," Jared said, his voice hoarse with barely controlled need. "Touch me. Harder. That's it. So good. So damned good."

She raised herself on one elbow and pushed him gently onto his back. He went over easily, watching her through hooded eyes as she leaned down to kiss his throat.

His fingers kneaded her shoulders as she trailed small, damp kisses over his bare skin. She felt his hips lifting urgently against her.

In this, at least, there was total honesty between them, Kate told herself. Jared made no effort to conceal his desire. The wanting in his eyes was blatant and implacable.

The excitement roared through both of them. Kate could feel her own passion feeding off Jared's. The energy of their lovemaking dampened their skins with as much perspiration as if they had been engaged in a battle.

Jared, apparently growing impatient with the sweet warfare, finally shifted onto his back and pulled Kate across his thighs. He guided her down, pushing himself slowly up into her softness until he was deep inside.

Kate sank her nails into his skin, closed her eyes and gave herself up to the white-hot passion. Jared's hands were all over her, moving on the insides of her thighs and up into the hidden places. He seemed to know exactly how to touch her. His fingers thrummed gently and she cried out.

"Come on, honey. Let me see you come apart for me. You know you will. You know you want it. That's it. *That's it.* Tight. Tighter. So beautiful. *Yes.*"

Kate gasped and collapsed against his chest as the sweet, shattering finale took her. Jared's damp hands clenched into her rounded buttocks and he lifted himself against her one more time. He bared his teeth, caught his breath and shuddered heavily.

Afterward they lay together for a long while without speaking. Kate had her head on Jared's shoulder and his arm was around her, pinning her close to the length of him.

"I can't stay," Jared said at last, his reluctance to leave clear in his voice. "I have to get back to the house. Beth won't be able to watch David all night."

"I know."

"He won a dollar today betting you wouldn't leave the island."

"I think everyone had a bet on whether or not I'd get on that plane."

"They all wanted you to stay."

Kate sighed and moved her head restlessly against the pillow. "They don't understand. They think we had a simple lovers' quarrel and that's all there was to it."

"It *was* just a simple quarrel. Given your stubbornness, I expect there will be plenty of others."

"Not a cheerful thought."

"We don't have to argue, you know." Jared sat up slowly and reached for his jeans. "I'd much rather make love with you."

She lay watching him as he dressed. "Would you?"

He fastened his jeans and leaned over the bed to cage her between his hands. "Yes," he said. "I would. But if you want to fight occasionally, I'll fight with you. I'm an accommodating man, Kate."

"Gee, thanks."

"There's just one thing you ought to know before you launch too many more battles."

"What's that?"

"You can't end any of them by getting on a plane and flying home."

"Who's going to stop me?" As usual, she could not resist rising to the bait.

Jared smiled slowly in the shadows. "Take a wild guess." He kissed her again, straightened and walked out the door.

Chapter Eight

KATE SURFACED, PUSHED BACK HER MASK and snorkel and laughed up at Jeff Taylor, who stood in the water beside her. "This is great," she said. "I could get used to doing this every morning before going to work."

"If you think this is good, you should try the diving." He indicated his gear on the beach. "Fantastic. I'm going out in a while. Going to do a little underwater photography."

Kate nodded as she started toward shore. "It sounds fascinating." She wondered if she could write off the expense of diving lessons if she used the information in a book.

That thought unfortunately only served to remind her that soon she would be returning to Seattle. She tried to push the unwelcome realization aside as she walked up onto the beach. She halted beside Jeff's diving gear, eyeing the yellow-and-black wet suit.

"Do you need a suit for diving in these warm waters?"

Jeff nodded, picking up a towel. "You do when you're going to be in the water for a long time. Any water, no matter how warm, saps your body heat after a while."

"Who will you be diving with today?"

"No one. I go by myself."

"Aren't you supposed to always dive with a buddy?" Kate dried her hair with the towel.

"Technically. But I know what I'm doing in the water and I prefer to go down by myself. I don't take stupid chances. Do me a favor, though, and don't tell the resort management I dive alone, okay? Someone is almost bound to feel obligated to give me a lecture on the subject of diving safety, and I hate lectures."

Kate smiled. "I won't mention it. Be careful, though."

"I'm always careful."

"Have a good dive and thanks for joining me this morning." She draped her towel around her neck, turned and waved as she started up the beach.

"Maybe I'll catch up with you later in the bar," Jeff called.

"Maybe."

A few minutes later Kate halted at the top of the path and looked back. Jeff was busy adjusting his wet suit. She waited awhile longer and watched as he strapped on the rest of his gear and finally slipped into the water. He disappeared at once. The whole business looked like a lot of fun, Kate decided. If she lived here on Amethyst, she would definitely learn how to dive.

But she did not live here on the island, and somehow she couldn't work up a lot of interest in diving back home in the cold, dark waters of Puget Sound. She had gotten accustomed to warm, clear, turquoise seas.

You can't have everything, Kate reminded herself. The affair with Jared would eventually end and she would be left with real-life memories to match her dreams. There were a lot of women who never even got that much.

She was contemplating the dismal prospect of returning home alone when she rounded a corner into the hotel gardens and nearly collided with Max Butterfield.

"I beg your pardon," Kate apologized quickly and hurriedly stepped back. She looked with chagrin at the damp spots she had left on Max's pristine white shirt.

"Please don't concern yourself." Max fastidiously brushed his shirt and then the white pants. He was obviously not pleased with the wet patches she had left behind, but he managed a gracious smile. "Should have been watching where I was going. Been swimming, I see?"

"Yes. Great morning for it. But then, I guess all the mornings around here are pretty terrific, aren't they?"

"Endless paradise," Max said, glancing over her shoulder and out to sea. "Hard to believe one could ever actually tire of it, isn't it? Would you care to join me for a cup of coffee on the pool terrace, Ms Inskip? We can talk shop. It's been a long time since I conversed with a fellow writer. One tends to lose touch."

Kate hesitated and then nodded, unable to think of a suitable excuse. "All right. That sounds nice. Thank you."

They made their way through the open lobby to the tiled terrace that surrounded the pool. A waiter in sunglasses took their order and returned with a silver pot of coffee, two croissants and a Bloody Mary for Max.

"When did you first come out here to the islands, Max?" Kate buttered a croissant and popped a flaky bite into her mouth.

"So long ago that I can no longer remember the exact date, but I do remember the marvelous sense of adventure I felt at the time. Quite extraordinary. Everything seemed so exotic, you know. I was certain I was destined to be famous and in the little biographical notes at the end of my books it would be mentioned quite casually that I lived and worked on a tropical island."

"That sort of thing always makes a nice touch in an author's biography," Kate conceded. "Gives the writer a larger-than-life image, doesn't it?"

"It does, indeed, and when I first arrived here I fully intended to live a larger-than-life sort of life. But somehow time has gone by so much more quickly than I had planned. My novel is still waiting to be written, but in the meantime I have had to support myself with small jobs on the side and here and there a travel piece." Max shrugged massively and polished off the rest of his croissant. "Life seldom turns out as one had thought it would, does it? But one learns to adapt. Tell me about yourself, Ms Inskip."

"Not much to tell. I live and work in Seattle. I've managed to make a living doing something I love, so I consider myself lucky." *You can't have everything.*

"You are. I consider people like you and Jared Hawthorne extremely fortunate, and I must confess I envy you. I cannot tell you how much I envy you. You are both making a living doing what you love."

And we both worked hard to earn our luck, Kate thought, glancing around at the beautiful resort and thinking of what it must have cost Jared in terms of time, work and money. Then she reflected on the frustrations she had endured in her writing career and recalled the number of rejections she had received over the years.

It was odd to think that she and Jared actually had something in common in terms of their success. Neither of them had been handed anything on a silver platter. They had both paid their dues.

"I still have a few faint hopes," Max went on, sipping his Bloody Mary. "One never gives up entirely, I suppose.

Once in a while we are fortunate enough to be given a golden opportunity to reshape our private destinies. I'm keeping an eye out for such a chance."

"I wish you the best of luck, Max." Kate smiled at him, willing herself to be a little more understanding. She knew how she would have felt by now if she had never gotten published.

"Thank you, my dear. You are very kind."

"I SAW YOU ON THE TERRACE HAVING coffee with Kate this morning," Jared said as he sat down across from Max in the bar. "Why?"

"So blunt. Are you jealous of me, by any chance? I am truly flattered. When one reaches my age, jealousy from a younger man is always welcomed, even if there is no cause."

"You know damned well this isn't a question of jealousy." Jared leaned back in the fan chair and studied Max through narrowed eyes. "What did you talk about?"

"Nothing that need concern you, my boy. We merely chatted about our shared interests."

"What shared interests?"

"Writing."

"Don't give me that. You haven't written a thing except one or two obscure travel articles in all the years I've known you, Max."

Max's eyes went cold. "That does not mean I have no intention of writing again. I was a good writer once, Jared. Editors said I had potential. A great deal of it."

"Well, you're in another business now, aren't you?" Jared was feeling annoyed and when he got annoyed, he got a little ruthless. "And you've dragged me into it, too. The sooner this whole thing is over, the better. I don't like it."

"You've made your feelings on the subject quite clear right from the start." Max smiled benignly. "My supervisors are aware of your attitude. They understand that you are doing us a very big favor and they have asked me to convey their appreciation."

"Screw their appreciation. I want this thing brought to a quick end and then I don't want to hear from you or your supervisors again. When you write up your final report, Max, I want you to make it clear that there will be no more favors from me. We're even."

Max lifted his glass of rum in a short, mocking toast. "Understood. No more favors."

"When is it going to be over, Max? I'm tired of being kept on the line. This is my island and I don't like you and your friends playing games on it. I want a day and a time."

"Calm yourself, my friend. Everything is scheduled for the regular cruise ship day at the end of the month. Our little fish will swallow the hook at that time, as planned."

Jared stood up. "The sooner the better."

"I could not agree with you more," Max said. His gaze was on the sea as he sipped his drink.

Jared started to walk away, paused and turned back. He leaned down, one hand planted on the table and spoke softly. "No more cozy little chats with Kate, Max. I don't want her to be touched by any of this, not even indirectly."

Max was both amused and offended. "You think I am so unprofessional as to let something slip to a pretty lady?"

"I think," Jared said, spacing his words for emphasis, "that the pretty lady is also pretty smart and it wouldn't take much to make her curious. Stay away from her."

This time Jared did not pause as he walked away from the table. He nodded briefly at the colonel on the way out of the bar and then headed for the lobby.

He spotted Kate and David as soon as he crossed the small lagoon bridge. They were standing together looking up at one of the watercolors on the wall. They didn't notice him right away and he stopped to watch them for a moment.

David was talking very seriously about the painting, and Kate had her head tilted in the familiar way that meant she was paying close attention. Jared studied the graceful line of her throat and shoulder and something deep within him tightened as memories of the previous night trickled back. She had only to be in the same room with him to arouse him, he realized. The intensity of his feelings amazed him. She stirred a part of his nature that he had never fully explored and the knowledge that he could feel such an aching need at this stage of his life was unsettling.

She was so different from Gabriella in every way. His wife had been like the watercolor on the wall, a soft, gentle creation of pastels and light. Kate was vibrant and strong, full of color that was so hot and bright that it could, on occasion, singe a man's fingers.

But what was life without a few burned fingers, Jared asked himself with an inner smile as he went toward Kate and his son.

"What are you two up to this morning?" he asked as he came to a halt beside them.

"Hi, Dad. I was just telling Kate that it was my mother who painted this picture."

Kate smiled gently at Jared, her eyes searching his face. "Your wife was a very talented woman."

Jared glanced at the soft seascape and nodded briefly. "Yes, she was. She did all the lobby paintings."

"That's what Dave was just telling me."

"Yeah, I was explaining it to her, Dad. But I got to go now. Carl's expecting me. See you guys later." David dashed out of the lobby and across the small bridge.

Jared watched his son until the boy was out of sight and then he turned back to find Kate studying him. "I told you once, Dave doesn't really remember his mother, but he takes a lot of pride in knowing she did these paintings. It gives him a way of feeling his connection to her."

Kate nodded. "I understand. She must have been a very lovely woman to have created such lovely art."

"She was." Jared glanced at his watch. "What do you say we go get some lunch in the restaurant? It's almost noon."

"All right."

A few minutes later Kate put down her menu and looked across the table at Jared. "I'm very different from her, aren't I?"

Jared, who had just been wondering why Kate had been so abnormally silent for so long, suddenly understood. "Night and day," he said casually. He plucked the menu out of Kate's fingers and turned to the waitress who had bustled up to take their orders. "Bring us the fresh tuna, Nancy. I know Marty got a delivery this morning."

"You bet, boss. Be right back."

"I didn't come all this way to have tuna fish," Kate complained.

Jared grinned. "The difference between fresh tuna and canned tuna fish is also night and day. Relax, you're going to love it, especially the way Marty does it."

"Is that why you're sleeping with me, Jared? Because I don't remind you of Gabriella?"

Jared drummed his fingers on the table and wondered why it was women asked such ridiculous questions. "Are you sleeping with me because I don't resemble your ex-husband?"

She turned faintly pink, which surprised him.

"Never mind," Kate said, moving a few inches back from the table in a small action that said more than words she was pulling back from the entire conversation. "I shouldn't have asked you such a personal question." She

smiled brightly. "I understand there's a cruise boat coming in next week."

"We get a ship through every few weeks. And the answer
is no, I'm not sleeping with you because you are so different from Gabriella. I'm sleeping with you because you're
you and you have a way of making me get as hard as an
eighteen-year-old kid every time you're in the vicinity."

"Last night you said there was more to our relationship
than just sex."

Jared realized he had not phrased his reassurance in the
best possible way. "Kate, don't twist my words. I meant
what I said last night and I mean what I'm saying now. I
like going to bed with you and I like being with you when
we're not in bed, even when you snap at me. Look, I'm
not good at this kind of conversation. Could we change
the subject?"

She propped her elbows on the table, laced her fingers
and rested her chin on the back of her hands. Her eyes
were very clear and green as she looked at him. "Of course,
Mr. Hawthorne. Whatever you say, Mr. Hawthorne. Far
be it from me to try to dictate our conversation. What
would you like to discuss, Mr. Hawthorne?"

Jared swore softly. "You're mad at me again, aren't you?
I was right the first time I met you. You are one prickly
broad."

"Yes," Kate said. "I am a bit prickly. But that doesn't seem
to keep you from wanting to climb into bed with me. An
insightful observer could conclude that my prickliness might
be one of the things that attracts you to me and you just
don't want to admit it to yourself because you decided long
ago you liked sweet, biddable, mild-mannered women."

"I don't think I followed the logic there, but don't bother
running it by me again. I'm sure I'd get just as lost a second time. What are you going to do this afternoon?"

"Read some more of Amelia Cavendish's diary."

"Working your way through it, hmm?"

"It's fascinating."

"Only to a woman. I told you I couldn't get through it, even if she was the wife of a distant ancestor of mine. All that nonsense about her social life in England in the beginning and later that endless litany of complaints about the way Roger Hawthorne treated her. I never bothered to finish."

"Then you missed a lot of the good parts. She had legitimate grounds for all those complaints about your ancestor. He treated her abominably. First he woos her and then abandons her without so much as a goodbye note and then he returns three years later and expects her to marry him. When she doesn't instantly leap into his arms, he kidnaps her, brings her out here and forces her to marry him. Yes, I'd say she had a reason to gripe."

Jared laughed. "I'll let you in on a little secret. Roger's journal contains a couple of references to what he called his sharp-tongued little shrew. I gather she made life hell for him on board ship after he kidnapped her. He said at one point in the journal that he was probably the only man alive who could claim to have been nagged halfway around the world. Amelia complained about everything from the food on board ship to the way Hawthorne made a living."

"Amelia did not approve of his chosen profession," Kate said austerely.

"I gather she made that real clear. You know, you're beginning to remind me of her in more ways than one. I'm starting to appreciate just what poor Roger had to go through." Jared broke off as the tuna arrived. When the waitress disappeared again he looked up from his plate to find Kate studying him with her intelligent eyes. "What's the matter?"

"Nothing."

"Then eat your fish."

"Yes, sir."

"Do us both a favor and don't start baiting me today, okay?"

She shrugged. "Okay. Why did Roger Hawthorne leave England so suddenly the first time?"

"A little trouble resulting from a duel. He killed his opponent and had to get out of the country in a hurry. Dueling was illegal. There would have been a hell of a scandal for his family if he'd been caught."

"Why didn't he take the time to explain that to Amelia?"

"He left her a note explaining everything and asking her to wait for him, according to the journal. But apparently she never got the message or if she did, she didn't pay any attention."

"Really?" Kate's eyes were riveted on his face. "He left her a note? She knew nothing about any note."

"And didn't believe him three years later when he tried to explain. So he gave up explaining and kidnapped her instead."

"Very interesting," Kate mused. "There's no mention of a missed message in Amelia's journal."

"Like I said, she didn't believe Roger's story." Jared looked up, seeing a golden opportunity to make a point. "She didn't *trust* him."

"How could she? The man was a pirate."

"Depends on your point of view. He didn't attack English ships. Just those of England's enemies. Enjoy your swim this morning?"

"Yes."

"You went snorkeling with Taylor, didn't you?"

"Yes." She forked up her tuna and sampled it tentatively, then nodded in approval.

Jared sighed and put down his fork. "Did you do it just to show me that you could get away with seeing Taylor after I told you I didn't want you hanging around with him?"

"No. I went swimming with him because I had already made the arrangement last night. You probably heard me make it, since you were lying on my bed eavesdropping at the time."

"You're not really interested in him, are you?" Jared was sure of that, which was the main reason he hadn't gone down to the cove this morning and interrupted the snorkeling activity.

"No, I'm not seriously interested in him. He's a nice guy who asked me to swim with him, and I'm supposed to be enjoying myself on vacation, so I went."

"Meaning you don't enjoy yourself with me?"

"I wouldn't say that. I like being with you when you're not grilling me or giving me orders or telling me to mind my own business. Unfortunately, that leaves a very small amount of time in which I can actually enjoy myself."

"Now I know how Roger Hawthorne felt when he realized he'd kidnapped a professional shrew."

"But the good time we do have together makes it all worth it," Kate concluded, her eyes flashing with feminine mischief.

Jared felt himself slipping under the spell of her provocative smile. He took a firm grip on himself and picked up his fork. This was neither the time nor the place to take her into his arms. He had work to do this afternoon. "All right, I'm ready to change the subject again."

"What would you like to discuss now? Ready to tell me what's going on up at the castle?"

"No, dammit." His temper erupted in a flash. The woman did not know when to quit. "And furthermore, I don't want to hear one more word about it. Clear?"

"Clear." She went back to eating and made no effort to introduce another subject.

Jared gave her five minutes of silence. Then he could no longer resist asking the question that had been at the back of his mind for several days. "I'm not like him at all, am I?"

She did not pretend to misunderstand. "My ex-husband? No, you're not like him at all. As you said, night and day."

He heard himself ask the next question before he had the good sense to think about what he was saying. "If you were ever to get married again, would you want someone like him? I mean someone like the man you thought he was when you married him? A sensitive, literary type? A guy with the soul of a poet or whatever it was you thought he had going for him?"

"Nope." Kate worked steadily on her tuna, apparently relishing every bite.

"I see." Jared found himself stewing in unaccustomed frustration. He hadn't wanted to ask the question in the first place, but having asked it, he had certainly expected a more complete answer than the one he had gotten. Kate was normally chatty as hell. "Do you, uh, know what you'd want the second time around?"

"No, but I expect I'll know it when I see it. Think you'll ever find someone who will fill Gabriella's shoes?"

That startled him. "I don't know." He frowned down at his tuna, trying to sort through his jumbled thoughts. "I'm not sure if that's really what I want, anyway. I used to think it was. But maybe it's not such a good idea. Lately, I've started wondering. I loved her. If she were still alive, I would still love her. But she's gone and I've done some changing and nothing stays the same, does it?"

"No." Kate smiled with a curious understanding. "That's the one sure thing in life. Nothing stays the same."

Jared nodded and then found himself saying aloud something he had never admitted to a living soul. "I had to be so careful with Gabby. She was very fragile. So gentle. You could crush her with just a look. I treated her like rare crystal most of the time, but once in a while I didn't and then I'd feel guilty for days."

"I know what that kind of guilt is like. I wasn't always gentle enough with my husband," Kate said. "I would get impatient with him. His ego was so fragile and he used to get so depressed so easily. I don't think I was as understanding and compassionate as I should have been. It must have been hard on him watching me get successfully published while he kept accumulating rejections. Especially when he was convinced that what he was writing was infinitely more important than what I wrote."

Jared let the silence that followed her comment hang for a while. He realized he felt at peace with Kate for the first time that day. He replayed his own words in his head and saw the truth in them. Somewhere along the line he had stopped looking for a replacement for Gabriella. He wanted a wife, but he wanted someone who was a unique individual, a person in her own right, not a clone of Gabby.

"You really don't know what you want in a second husband?" Jared asked again.

"Like I said, I'm sure I'll know it when I see it."

That comment shattered his feeling of being at peace with her. He scowled across the table, annoyed. "What are you expecting to happen? You think some guy will walk into your life and you'll take one look and know he's the right man?"

"Sure. Why not?"

"You know what your problem is? You've written one too many romance novels," Jared muttered.

"WELL?" LETTY DEMANDED A FEW days later when she happened across Kate curled in a shaded lounger. "Fill me in on the latest. How's Amelia doing with her pirate?"

Kate glanced up from the diary in her lap. "Whipping him into shape, I'm happy to say. She locked him out of her bedroom on her wedding night because he showed up drunk after too much carousing with his crew. She made it stick, too. Mostly because Roger was too drunk to find the key, which she had wisely hidden."

"I love it. What happened next?" Letty sat down nearby and poured herself a glass of iced tea from a pitcher Kate had ordered earlier.

"Roger was too embarrassed the next day to admit he hadn't made it into his wife's bedroom. So he tried acting as if everything was normal between himself and Amelia. Pretended there wasn't a thing in the world wrong. Unfortunately Amelia fell for the act. She went for a walk with him down to a secluded little cove." Kate wondered privately if it was the same cove where Jared had first made love to her.

"I'll bet Amelia soon found herself flat on her back in the sand."

"Eventually. It wasn't as bad as it sounds, though. Here's how she puts it:

"Roger apologized very prettily for his uncouth behavior of the previous night and began a very learned discussion concerning the marital obligations of husbands and wives. I informed him that I was very well aware of those obligations, and having found myself wedded, however unwillingly, I intended to do my duty. He then explained in a rather awkward fashion that he would prefer it if I did not act entirely out of a sense of womanly duty. I knew then that he loved me and I was content."

"That's sweet," Letty said.

"Maybe. Maybe not. I can't help wondering if Roger had finally figured out that charm would work better than a lot of loud, blustering machismo."

"I prefer to think he had learned his lesson and wanted to please Amelia."

"More likely he just didn't want to spend another night locked out of his bedroom." Kate closed the book, wondering if she would have believed Jared loved her if he had tried the same line on her.

Probably. He was, after all, the man of her dreams. He just didn't know it. She remembered their discussion over lunch a few days earlier and knew she had not been exactly truthful with him. But she was not about to confess to Jared that he was exactly what she wanted in a second husband. Not yet, at any rate.

Before this relationship could go any further she had to find a way to save him from his own piratical tendencies. She had to discover what was going on at Hawthorne Castle.

The next day she got her first real clue. It was late in the afternoon, shortly before she was due to meet Jared for dinner in the hotel restaurant, when Kate came across the most interesting portion of the diary that she had yet encountered.

Amelia Cavendish, inquisitive lady that she was, had discovered the mechanism that unlocked the hidden door at the bottom of the stone staircase.

Amelia, Kate decided as she carefully memorized the instructions, was definitely turning out to be a kindred spirit. She had been unable to resist finding out what was behind the locked wall and Kate was filled with the same gnawing curiosity.

According to the diary, Roger Hawthorne had built the hidden room as an emergency escape route to the sea. There was, according to Amelia, a wharf inside a natural cave adjoining the castle. Hawthorne had widened the entrance so that a small boat could get through to the sea and then concealed the enlarged opening with a movable section of stone that blended with the lava.

It is a very large opening, quite large enough to permit a boat to enter and dock at the small wharf inside the hidden chamber. I fear the room is not merely to be used as an emergency escape route. I believe Roger uses this secret place to unload his most valuable cargoes. I also fear these cargoes are not such as result from the honest shipping business in which he is supposedly engaged. I shall have to put a halt to such practices immediately. Roger Hawthorne is the son of an earl and I am a daughter of a respectable family. We do not indulge in this sort of thing. I will make that quite clear to him.

"Attagirl, Amelia," Kate whispered. She closed the diary and wondered more than ever if Jared was following in his ancestor's footsteps. If so, she must be as firm as Amelia had been.

Chapter Nine

"WHAT THE HELL DO YOU MEAN, YOU can't repair that railing today? Tomorrow is Thursday, remember? By tomorrow this place will be crawling with cruise-ship people. We'll need all the extra bar seating we can get. I don't want to have to block off this area just because you couldn't get the damned railing fixed in time." Fists on his hips, Jared confronted the two workmen in front of him. They both shrugged.

"Take it easy, boss," said the taller of the two. "Not much we can do without the teak. You know that. Hank said he checked over on Ruby this morning 'fore he left and it hadn't come in from Hawaii yet."

"That teak was due two weeks ago."

"Island time, boss," the second man said philosophically. "Hey, you know how it is out here. Two days, two weeks, two months. Don't make much difference. It'll get done one of these days. No hurry."

"I don't want that railing repaired one of these days, I

want it fixed by this time tomorrow. I didn't get this place built by running it on island time, and I'm not going to lose the seating capacity on that terrace tomorrow just because the damned teak didn't leave Hawaii yet." Jared studied the broken section of terrace railing. He was used to improvising. Out here in the islands, a man either learned how to get creative or he didn't survive in business.

The two workmen stood on either side of Jared, examining the broken railing with grave concern.

"Okay, Mark, I think I've got an idea," Jared finally announced. "Remember the lumber we had left over after we finished the new changing rooms?"

"Sure. We stored it in the back of the maintenance shed." Mark's face lit up. "Think there's a piece that'll fit?"

"Go check. It's not teak, but who's going to notice?"

"Right, boss."

The two men ambled off the terrace just as Letty and David came around the corner. Letty smiled.

"Still waiting on the teak for the railing, Jared?" Letty surveyed the broken section.

"Hi, Letty. Yeah, still waiting. Far as I can tell it hasn't left Hawaii. The usual story. It'll get here one of these days." He looked down at his son. "How was school?"

"Same old thing. You seen Kate?" David's face was screwed up with concern. "I've been lookin' all over for her. We were gonna practice my kicks again today and then go snorkeling."

"Haven't seen her since lunch," Jared said, deliberately quashing the memory of Kate's oddly distracted air earlier. It had irritated him because he was almost certain she was already starting to make plans for her trip back to Seattle. This was the final week of her stay and that fact was eating at him. Thus far, neither of them had brought up the subject of her imminent departure.

"Maybe she went swimming," Letty suggested.

"She wouldn't have gone down to the beach without me," David said, obviously certain of that much. "She promised she'd wait for me. She always keeps her promises."

His son was right about that, Jared thought. If Kate made a promise, she would keep it. He wondered what it would take to get Kate to promise she'd wait for him.

Then he wondered for the hundredth time how a supposedly intelligent, mature woman could entertain the silly romantic notion that she would recognize her perfect mate the moment he walked into her life. It was a particularly ridiculous and infuriating example of feminine logic and he intended to point that out to her again tonight. He himself was rapidly learning that the right person didn't always show up packaged as expected.

"She'll turn up soon. Don't worry about it," Jared told his son.

Letty smiled at David. "Your father's right. If Kate said she'd be around to work on those kicks this afternoon, then she'll be here. Why don't you go try her room again?"

David brightened. "I will. See you later, Dad."

Jared nodded. "Right. Don't forget we're going to have dinner at home with Kate tonight."

"I won't. Is she cooking again?"

"Uh-huh. Said she'd make tacos."

"Oh, boy!" David whirled and dashed off the terrace.

Letty's mouth curved in amusement. "First pizza, then hamburgers, then macaroni and cheese and now tacos. Kate certainly knows the way to a little boy's heart."

"You can say that again. If she hangs around long enough we may get hot dogs and peanut butter sandwiches." Jared made a production out of studying the broken railing. "Ten to one that's the only kind of stuff she knows how to make."

"I doubt it. But Kate's too smart to fix coq au vin or rabbit *provençale* for a kid."

"She's smart enough, all right. About some things."

"Speaking of little boys' hearts, how is yours doing?"

"I'm not a little boy, Letty."

"Oops. Sorry. Didn't mean to stomp on any toes."

"Don't worry about it." Jared heard the roughness in his own voice and stifled an oath. "My toes are tough."

"I won't worry a bit about it. You've always been very good at taking care of yourself. Time's running out, though. Are you really going to let her just up and leave in three days, Jared?" Letty wandered over to the unbroken portion of the terrace railing and leaned her elbows on the teak.

"If she wants to go home like all the rest of the tourists, there's not much I can do about it."

"I guess not. Pity, though."

"I don't need your sympathy, Letty."

"I know." She gazed out to sea. "I'm not sure it's you I was feeling sorry for. I think Kate is going to miss Amethyst. She fits in well around here, doesn't she? She's adapted very nicely to island life."

"She's stopped complaining about the lack of air-conditioning, if that's what you mean."

"Not quite. I think it goes deeper than that. The island suits her. But I suppose that's only to be expected from a woman who writes so many books featuring pirates and tropical islands."

Jared gripped the railing. "I've heard about her pirates." He paused and slanted Letty a close look. "You ever read any of her books?"

"Oh, yes. All of them. I just finished her last one, in fact—*Buccaneer's Bride*. It was wonderful. I've still got it in my purse."

Jared found himself staring at Letty's colorful, oversize canvas bag. "You do?"

Letty smiled slowly. "Umm-hmm. You know, they say you can tell a lot about an author by reading her books. A perceptive person could probably get a feel for how Kate thinks and what she fantasizes about by reading her work."

Jared swore and stretched out his hand. "Okay, let's see it."

Letty slowly unzipped the canvas bag and reached inside. "You sure you want to read a historical romance novel, Jared?"

"No, but I'm getting desperate," he admitted. He gazed down at the couple on the cover. "The heroine has red hair. Kate doesn't have red hair. She said she had something in common with all her heroines."

"Obviously it isn't her hair color," Letty said dryly. "At any rate, that's not important. Take a look at the hero and then read the first couple of paragraphs."

Jared studied the hero without much enthusiasm. "The guy needs a haircut." He opened to the first page and started to read.

His eyes were the color of the evening mist, and his hair was as dark as midnight shot with silver. There was a cruel twist to his mouth and an elegant knot in his cravat. He moved easily among the glittering guests, secure in the knowledge that Society accepted him for what he claimed to be: the wealthy, powerful Earl of Hawkridge.

But Elizabeth knew the truth about the cold and arrogant Hawkridge. Beneath his fine evening clothes the man was a pirate. Three days ago he had vowed to make her his prisoner.

KATE HELD HER BREATH as she stood at the foot of the stone staircase. This was the first time she had dared to sneak back to the castle after her initial foray ten days earlier. Jared had been keeping such a close eye on her lately that Kate had begun to feel like a goldfish in his private bowl. But today he had finally been distracted by a problem with the terrace railing. She had seized the opportunity.

She let the flashlight beam dance briefly around the small room, checking for any obvious sign that someone else might be nearby. A heavy stillness greeted her. Then, very cautiously, she followed the instructions in Amelia Cavendish's diary and pushed the metal baluster on the third step from the bottom. It gave easily—so easily that Kate knew it was kept well-oiled. But that made sense, she reminded herself. Jared apparently used the secret room frequently.

There was a soft, mechanical grinding sound from deep within the stone walls and very slowly a small section opened up to reveal inky darkness.

Along with the darkness came a rush of cool air, the tang of the sea and the sound of water lapping at stone. Kate edged forward and aimed the flashlight into the hidden room.

The light bounced on the rippling surface of dark seawater then skidded a few feet to the right to reveal a short stone quay. Several large cartons were stacked beside the water. Kate stepped through the entrance and peered around with the aid of the flashlight.

She was looking at the inside of a natural cavern that had been formed aeons ago out of cooling lava. The room, as Amelia claimed in her diary, had been converted into a docking facility. She knew the chamber had an opening to the sea, but when she aimed the light at the far end of the cavern she saw only solid stone. Amelia's diary had not mentioned where to find the mechanism that opened the stone wall at the far end of the room.

It was clear there was plenty of room to tie up a small cruiser or similar boat here inside the hidden chamber. Back in Amelia and Roger's day, a row boat, an outrigger canoe or a sailboat could have been kept inside, ready for an emergency escape. Especially sensitive cargoes could be stored here, far from prying eyes.

There was a chill in the dark room that was not entirely from the sea. She did not want to hang around here for very long, she decided. There was something eerie about the place.

It didn't take long to convince herself that there wasn't much more to see. She darted the flashlight beam over the twisted lava walls and along the far side of the man-made quay and was about to turn back into the stairwell when she caught a glimpse of yellow at the edge of her light.

For an instant Kate went very cold. She had a sudden vision of someone lurking in the shadows of the hidden room, waiting to pounce on her. The memories of Jared discovering her the last time were all too clear.

But a few seconds later, as she still stood motionless in the opening, she realized the bit of yellow was not moving. She aimed the beam directly at it and saw a bright yellow stripe that was very familiar. It was part of a black-and-yellow wet suit.

Jeff Taylor's tanks and the remainder of his gear lay nearby.

Kate waited no longer. She backed out of the room, ran to the stone staircase and shoved hard at the baluster. The opening in the wall creaked shut.

She switched off the flashlight and bounded up the stairs.

It wasn't until she was safely outside and on the path that led back to the resort that Kate's jumbled thoughts finally slowed and settled down into meaningful patterns.

Trusting Jared was one thing. A part of her was surprisingly willing to do exactly that, though that same part did not approve of the mystery. But surely she was not obliged to blindly trust all these other people who appeared to be involved in whatever was going on around here.

JARED INHALED DEEPLY AS HE WALKED into the cool tiled hall. The aroma of simmering taco filling emanating from the kitchen was delightful. He hadn't had tacos in ages. It made him realize how much he had missed the pleasure of walking into the house after a day's work and finding dinner cooking on the stove. Kate would probably be quick to tell him that was a sign of outdated male chauvinism. Jared decided he'd better enjoy it while he could.

There was no telling where his next all-American home-cooked meal was coming from, he realized. Unless he did something about it, he and David would be back to eating the creations of the restaurant's three gourmet chefs. That meant back to marinated goat cheese, sun-dried tomatoes and seafood pâtés. David would never forgive him.

Jared ambled into the kitchen and found it empty except for the gently steaming pot on the stove. He walked past Jolly's cage and the big bird mumbled an aggrieved squawk. Jared stopped long enough to scratch the parrot's head.

"I still say she can't bake cookies," Jared confided to the bird.

"Wanna bet?"

"No. The way my luck is running lately, I'd lose and I am not about to start losing to a birdbrain like you."

Jared headed down the hall and heard his son's voice emanating from the study. Then he heard Kate's soft, husky tones. He smiled and went to the open door.

For a moment he stood there unnoticed. David and Kate were at the desk, intently examining a drawing the boy had apparently just finished. Jared watched as his son carefully rolled up the large sheet of paper and secured it with a rubber band.

"Are you really going to frame it when you get home?" David asked, handing the rolled drawing to Kate. His eyes were large and questioning as he looked up at her.

"Oh, yes," Kate said gently. "I know a place where they frame art. It's just down the street from my apartment. I'll take it there and have them put it in a red frame and cover it with a sheet of glass. Then I'll hang it in my living room."

"Just like a real picture, huh?"

"It is a real picture. Signed by the artist, too. And no matter how much anyone offers to pay for it, I'll never sell it."

"Really?"

"Really."

Jared heard the small catch in Kate's voice and it tugged at his insides. He opened his mouth to announce his presence, but she turned her head in that moment and saw him in the doorway. The soft, damp shimmer in her eyes told him she was near tears. Even as he stared at her in stunned amazement, she blinked away the evidence.

"I'm home." Jared couldn't think of anything else to say.

"Hello." Kate didn't move. Her smile was tremulous. She clutched the rolled-up drawing as if it was very precious.

David glanced up eagerly at the sound of his father's voice. "There you are, Dad. I just gave Kate one of my drawings. She's going to frame it."

"So I hear." He smiled deliberately at Kate. "Whenever you look at it, you'll think of us, won't you?"

"Yes." She moved toward the door. "Excuse me, I've got to check on dinner."

Jared stepped aside and she slipped past him. He turned back to David, who was staring after Kate. "What's wrong, son?"

"She says she's going back to Seattle in a few days."

"That's her home, Dave."

"But she likes it here, she said so. She hasn't even complained about the heat in ages."

"A lot of people like it here, but not many of them stay. You know that."

"I bet she'd stay if you asked her to," David said, a stubborn set to his chin.

"You think so?"

David brightened. He nodded his head vigorously. "Why don't you?"

"I'll think about it." Jared smiled. "Go wash your hands. I think dinner's about ready."

SEVERAL HOURS LATER, JARED GUIDED Kate off the dance floor and steered her out through the hotel lobby into the gardens. He was aware of a strange restlessness and a feeling of urgency. As far as he was concerned, it was all Kate's fault.

She had been moody since dinner, he reflected, and he strongly disliked moodiness in women. A man always felt he was supposed to do something about the condition and he never knew what it was he was supposed to do.

Dinner had gone well, as far as Jared could tell. Kate had been cheerful while everyone was involved in building tacos, but afterward, when they had said good-night to

David and headed for the lounge, her cheerfulness had vanished like snow in the tropics.

The balmy air in the gardens soothed Jared's uncertain temper. He made himself calm down and think clearly. Letty and David were right, there wasn't much time left. In three days, Kate was going to be gone. He needed to start laying the groundwork for whatever future they had. As luck would have it, they both opened their mouths to speak simultaneously.

"Jared, I…"

"I've been thinking…"

"Sorry," he said. "What were you saying?"

"Nothing. Go ahead. What have you been thinking about?"

"Us."

She flashed him a quick, questioning glance out of the corner of her eye. "What about us?"

They were almost at the door of her room. Jared cleared his throat. "You'll be going home soon."

"Yes."

"Yeah, well, you remember I told you I get back to the States at least once a year so David's grandparents can see him?"

"I remember." She stopped and fished her room key out of her small purse.

He took the key from her. "Normally we go in August. That's a slow month around here." Jared opened the door and stood back while she entered. "But I think this year maybe we'll go a little earlier. Maybe in a month or two." He closed the door behind him.

"Is that right?" Kate did not bother to turn on a light. She dropped her purse on the bed and kept walking out onto the veranda.

Jared moved after her, struggling for the right words. He did not know how to deal with a woman who fully expected to recognize the man of her dreams on sight, but who clearly had not done so. "Anyhow, I was thinking we could stop over in Seattle." There was no response from Kate. Jared plowed on, attempting to clarify the obvious. "We could see you." Maybe if he gave her a little time, she would come to her senses.

Kate leaned on the railing, her eyes on the darkened sea. "That would be nice," she said carelessly. "Let me know when you settle on the exact dates. I'll try to clear my calendar. Maybe we can do lunch."

Jared came to an abrupt halt. He stared at the back of her head in disbelief. *"Do lunch?"*

"Sure. Why not? For old times' sake. Assuming I'm not busy, of course."

"Do lunch." Rage boiled up inside him, hot and fierce and fueled by frustration. He crossed the short distance between himself and Kate in one long stride, grabbed her arms and swung her around to face him. "I don't believe you said that. What the hell do you mean, we'll *do lunch*?"

Her eyes locked with his, cool and distant in the shadows. "What did you have in mind? Did you plan to send David off to the Space Needle while you and I have a quick toss in the sack?"

"Dammit, you know I didn't mean it like that."

"No? Then what did you mean?"

"I thought we could see each other again, that's all."

"And I said, fine. Just let me know when you'll be in town."

"Stop making it all sound so damned casual." He released her abruptly and clamped his hands around the railing.

"But that's exactly what it is, Jared. Casual."

He looked at her through hooded eyes, trying to get a handle on whatever game it was she had chosen to play with him tonight. "It's not casual. It couldn't possibly be casual. Not for you."

"Why not?"

"Because I'm the man of your dreams." He felt the sudden stillness in her and moved in ruthlessly for the coup de grace. "You couldn't possibly feel casual about me. Not now, not ever. You might hate me or you might love me, but you would never, ever feel casual about me."

"What makes you so damned sure of that?"

He smiled thinly. "I'm reading your book. Letty gave it to me. It was a real revelation, Kate. Because I'm the hero of that book, aren't I?"

"Not very likely. I didn't even know you when I wrote it."

He shook his head, feeling more sure of his ground now. He had her on the defensive; he could feel it. Relentlessly, he stalked her. "I'm not a fool, Kate. And I'll admit I don't generally read romance novels, but it doesn't take a genius to figure out that I'm what you want and need in a man. You just haven't admitted it to yourself yet."

"Your ego is astonishing."

"Look at me, lady. Look at me and tell me I'm wrong. You want someone who is as strong as you are. You want someone who wants you so much, he can't think of anyone else. You want someone who doesn't run when you stand up to him. Hell, I even look like one of your heroes, right down to the dark hair and gray eyes. I live on a tropical island and you half believe I'm a real-life pirate. I'll bet you fifty bucks, a hundred bucks, a thousand, that you can't walk away from me without a backward glance. You're going to dream about me for the rest of your life."

Kate stared at him, her eyes wide. "The fact that you're the man of my dreams doesn't do me much good if I'm not the woman of yours."

Jared reeled. "You admit it?"

"Admit what? That you're a fantasy come true for me? Yes, I admit it. I've known it since the first time you made love to me."

Jared let go of the deep breath he had been holding. "Kate, honey, listen to me…."

"No, you listen to me, Jared." She smiled gently. "You've done enough damage tonight. I think it's time you left."

"You can't kick me out. Not now."

"I think I'd better. If I don't I'm only going to get hurt worse than I already am. I realized that this afternoon when David gave me his beautiful drawing. I've got to start pulling back."

"Kate, I don't want to hurt you. That's the last thing I'd want to do."

"Then leave."

He couldn't believe she was kicking him out. "What do you want from me?"

"Nothing."

"That's not true. You're lying. I can see it in your eyes."

"You're suddenly very perceptive for a pirate." She shrugged and leaned on the railing again. "All right, I'll admit I want something from you, but it's something I don't think you can give me, so it's better if I don't ask for it."

"Stop talking in circles. Be honest with me, Kate. That's all I'm asking."

"I'm not sure you deserve a lot of honesty. You haven't been overly honest with me, have you?"

"Kate, stop baiting me."

"All right, I'll tell you exactly what I think. I think I am in love with you, but I'm afraid of that fact precisely because you are too close to being the living image of the man of my dreams."

Heady relief washed through him. "Honey, don't be afraid to let yourself love me."

"Furthermore," she went on as if she hadn't heard him, "I think that you could learn to love me, but you're afraid to try because I'm *not* the image of the woman of your dreams."

He absorbed that in silence for a long moment. "I hadn't thought about it that way. You think I'm so hung up on Gabriella's memory that I could never love you?"

"Not exactly, but I think that because you were happy with her, you've decided you'd only be happy again with a woman who was a lot like her. Maybe you're right. We both know I'm not at all like her, Jared. In fact, I'm her opposite in many ways. You said it, yourself: night and day."

"I don't want another Gabriella. *I don't want another angel.*" The words shocked him as much as her with their intensity. "I want a flesh-and-blood woman who understands that a man can't always be a saint. A woman who can put up with me when I lose my temper, one who won't crumple like a flower when I argue with her, one who can love me for what I am."

She stared at him, her eyes luminous in the shadows. "I want a man who can love me for what I am, a man who's not constantly searching for some image of the past."

"Maybe it's time we both stopped thinking in terms of preconceived dream images," Jared said. He touched her cheek. "I'm not still pining for Gabby. I swear it. I'll admit she left an impression in my mind of the sort of woman I could love. But that's all it was, just an impression, an idea. And you've trampled all over it. In fact, I don't think there's much left of it. When I think about the kind of woman I could love now, all I can think about is you."

Kate looked up at him, her eyes clear and deep. Jared thought he could see her heart. Her fingers closed around his wrist as he stroked the line of her cheek.

"Do you mean that, Jared?"

He framed her face with his hands and was instantly captivated by the undisguised longing he saw in her gaze. "I mean it."

He brought his mouth down onto hers, aware of an odd and unexpected rush of tenderness. She responded to it immediately, her lips softening under his, her body pressing close. For a long moment he savored the taste of her, letting himself drown in the knowledge that she wanted him. It felt so good, he thought; so right. Whatever had made him think she wasn't his type?

The tenderness caught fire and blazed into the stark need Jared always seemed to feel when he took Kate into his arms. It was exhilarating to know that he did not have to temper the force of his desire with her. He could let himself go and she would respond fully and completely. She was a woman whose passions matched his own.

"I want you, sweetheart. I've wanted you since the first time I saw you. You make me crazy, you know that?" He caught her around the waist and lifted her up off her feet. She clung to his shoulders, her green eyes brilliant with silent laughter.

"I'm glad," she said. "You do the same to me and you know it. In fact, I'm beginning to think you know entirely too much about me."

"Not a chance. I could spend the rest of my life getting to know you as well as I'd like." *The rest of my life.* Jared lowered her until her feet touched the veranda deck. He took one step over to the lounger, sat down and tugged her tenderly down beside him.

He deliberately settled her full-length on the cushions, pushing her skirt up high on her thigh. Then he reached down, circled her delicate ankle with his hand and slowly stroked his palm upward. He loved the smooth curves of her legs and the deep, mysterious shadows that waited under the silk of her skirt. In a few minutes he would undress her and touch all those fabulous, hidden places and she would grow hot and moist with her need of him.

The anticipation made him hard. Part of him urged him to make the moment last, but another part wanted to race recklessly toward the soul-stirring conclusion. It was the devil's own choice.

"What's the matter?" Kate reached up to curl her arm around his neck, urging him close. "You look as if you can't make up your mind about something."

His answering laugh was more like a heavy groan that was torn from his chest. He started unbuttoning the bodice of her dress. "I always feel like a kid with an ice cream sundae when I'm with you. I want it all and I want it right now, but I also want to make it last."

"There's nothing that says we can only do it once," she murmured.

"Such a demanding female." Jared smiled with deep pleasure as he slipped his hand inside the open bodice. He touched the sweet curve of her breast and sucked in his breath.

Kate lifted herself against his touch, moving under his palm like a sleek cat. The honest, uninhibited desire sent the blood pounding in his veins. When she fumbled with the zipper of his jeans he shifted, gathering her beneath him so that he could lie on top of her.

He tried to undress her slowly, taking his time and enjoying every inch of skin he exposed along the way. But she kept whispering his name and sighing with such fevered longing that he knew he would not be able to last much longer. When she pushed his jeans down over his hips, leaving him wearing only his unbuttoned shirt, he decided he'd had enough of the pleasures of anticipation.

The next few minutes were hurried and a little frantic as Jared got rid of the last of Kate's clothing. He loved the way her breath quickened and her skin got slick with her excitement.

At long last Jared was where he wanted to be, sliding between Kate's legs, bracing himself on his elbow as he reached down to guide himself into her. His fingers tangled briefly in the soft hair that shielded her delicate secrets and then he was opening her gently. She cried out as he positioned himself and surged fully and deeply into her. When she closed around him he thought he would lose his sanity.

"*Jared*. Yes, please, oh, my love, please. I want you so much."

"Hold me, sweetheart. Close. Tight." The words were thick in his mouth. He was almost incoherent now as his passion roared through him. She clung to him, giving herself to him with the wholehearted generosity that never ceased to amaze him.

Jared took everything he could, knowing that even as he claimed her, he was being claimed. In those last split seconds before release he was aware of nothing except the overwhelming need to make himself a part of the woman in his arms. He had to bind her to him, make her realize that she would never be free of him.

And then Kate was convulsing gently around him, shivering exquisitely, calling to him in that soft, husky voice. Jared went rigid, hovered for an endless, mindless moment in the eye of the storm and then collapsed slowly against her.

It was a long, languid time before he reluctantly rolled to one side. He inhaled deeply, feeling his energy flowing back along his nerve endings. He could not let her leave. That was all there was to it. *He could not allow her to leave.*

"Jared?"

"Hmm?" He felt affectionate and indulgent now, the urgency and passion magically converted into a pleasant, drowsy satisfaction.

"If we're agreed that tonight marks some sort of turning point in our relationship…"

"It does. Definitely. A turning point. No casual lunches in Seattle."

"Yes, well, then I think it's time we talked honestly about a few things."

Jared immediately felt his indulgent mood begin to disintegrate. "You're going to bring up the subject of what's going on up at the castle again, aren't you? I can hear it coming. How many times do I have to tell you that it's none of your sweet business? You're just going to have to contain your curiosity and learn to trust me."

"I think I could trust you, Jared, even though I don't like being kept in the dark."

"Thanks." He felt a measure of relief at having gained that much from her, at least.

"But I see no reason why I should trust Max Butterfield or Jeff Taylor. I really feel you owe me an explanation on this."

"*Jeff Taylor.* At the castle?" Alarm shot through him, shattering what was left of his relaxed, indulgent mood. Jared jackknifed to a sitting position and grabbed Kate by the shoulders. He hauled her up to face him. "What in hell are you talking about?"

Chapter Ten

KATE WAS STUNNED BY JARED'S REACTION. She stared up at him in shock. "What's the matter? I know you don't like me prying into this, but I really think I deserve an explanation, don't you?"

"Kate, listen to me. I'll give you all the explanations you want, but first you've got to tell me what makes you think Jeff Taylor is involved in this."

"You're not going to like it."

"That goes without saying. Just talk. And fast."

Kate drew a deep breath. "I found the secret to opening the wall in the castle."

"Where?" Jared's expression was grim.

"In Amelia Cavendish's diary."

"Damn. I should have known. All right, go on. I take it you couldn't resist going back to the castle to see if the secret worked? Never mind. Stupid question. Of course you couldn't resist. Of course you wouldn't think of doing the sensible thing and come to me to ask me about it."

"Why should I ask you?" Kate shot back, stung. "Every time I've tried to ask you about what's going on at the castle, you tell me to mind my own business."

"Okay, okay, we'll argue about this later, I can promise you that. Right now I have to know what you saw."

"I got the wall open and I took a quick look inside. I saw some crates and cartons and the wet suit and equipment Jeff uses."

"How do you know it was Taylor's?"

"The wet suit was yellow and black. The same colors as the suit he wore diving the other day." Kate frowned. "I suppose it could belong to someone else. Does the resort rent yellow-and-black suits?"

"No." Jared released her and drove a hand through his dark hair. "What the hell is going on?"

"That's what I'd like to know. Jared, if you're involved in something illegal, now is the time to tell me. We've danced around this matter long enough."

"I've already told you, it's not illegal. But it is getting to be a damned nuisance." He stalked to the edge of the veranda and stood gazing out into the darkness for a long moment.

"Please. What is this all about?" Kate asked.

"It's about a favor I was doing for Max Butterfield."

"Max? What kind of favor?"

"It's a long story. The short version is that Max sometimes does odd jobs out here in the Pacific for the government."

"I don't get it. He's a spy or something?"

"Nothing that exciting," Jared said evenly. "Or that formal. He's not exactly on the government payroll. He's what you might call a stringer. He started out selling bits and pieces of information when he realized several years ago that he wasn't ever going to get around to writing the

Great American Novel. Over the years he's had his uses, I guess."

"But what was he doing here? Why were you helping him?"

Jared reached for his jeans. "He did me a favor a couple of years back when I needed a little muscle to get rid of some rounders who decided they were going to settle here on Amethyst. He got his buddies in the department to send some professional leaners."

"Leaners?"

"Yeah. Leaners. You know. They lean on people." Jared zipped his jeans and started buttoning his shirt. "They asked a lot of pointed questions about tax-filing status and things like that. Made our unwelcome guests generally uncomfortable. They leaned until the troublemakers decided to go to some other island. The long and short of it is, I owed Max and his friends."

"And he came around to collect?"

"A couple of months ago."

"Well?" Kate followed him as he finished dressing and stepped back into the darkened room. She grabbed her dress and held it in front of her. "What did he want?"

"The guys he sells information to wanted him to set up a trap here on the island." Jared glanced over his shoulder, his mouth twisted wryly. "You should appreciate this part. Seems they were having trouble with some real modern-day pirates. Someone's got a racket going using the cruise ships."

"How?"

"They've been hijacking sophisticated electronics equipment from military and construction sites here in the Pacific. They use a small, fast boat or a plane to bring the stuff to remote islands where it's stored until the guys who are running things arrive to repackage and ship the stuff to a new destination."

"How are the cruise ships involved?"

"Max's friends figured out who was running the first stage of the operations, but they couldn't get a handle on the ringleader. The head man, disguised as an innocent tourist from one of the cruise ships, apparently arrives at the islands where stuff is stored. He takes care of business while everyone is souvenir shopping and then he leaves on the boat. In some cases the equipment is smuggled right on board."

"When a cruise ship arrives, an island like Amethyst is temporarily swamped with strangers," Kate said slowly. "It would be easy for someone to conduct some illegal activity and then leave with no one the wiser."

"Max and his pals arranged to sucker these pirates into using the hidden dock inside the castle as a temporary storage facility for the illegal shipments. They fell for it. Tomorrow when the ship arrives the boss man is supposed to hit the island and head for the castle where Max and some of his buddies are going to be waiting for him." Jared was at the door.

"Wait, where are you going?"

"To find Max. As far as I know the government people are coming in on a private plane tomorrow. There shouldn't be anyone hanging around that castle now. But apparently someone is. Jeff Taylor, if you're right about what you saw."

"You're going to tell Max something's happening there?"

"Right. This is his operation. He should know why Taylor is involved in this. I want an explanation. I don't like being kept in the dark."

"I know exactly how you feel."

Jared gritted his teeth. "I'm never going to hear the end of this, am I?" He was halfway out the door but he halted abruptly and looked back at her, his eyes intent. "Kate, listen to me. I may be busy for a while. I don't know what's going on or what's going to happen next. But if I'm not back in an hour, I want you to call Sam Finley on Ruby, you understand? The number's in the card file on my desk."

Kate was feeling more uneasy by the second. "It would take him a long time to get here."

"With any luck we won't need him at all. Max probably knows what's going on and has everything under control."

"You don't believe that or you wouldn't be acting like this. Jared, I'm worried."

Jared came swiftly back into the room and caught hold of her arms. He pulled her close and kissed her hard. When he raised his head, his silvery eyes were gleaming. "Just stay put and try not to get into any more trouble, okay? I should be back soon."

"I don't like this. Not one bit."

He flashed her a brief grin. "Look at it this way, if you hadn't gotten so curious, we'd still be out there fooling around on the veranda at this very moment. Any way you slice it, it's all your fault."

"Don't you dare blame this on me."

"Why not? Things were so calm and peaceful around here until you showed up. Nothing's been the same since you hit the island." Jared headed back to the door. "I'll be back as soon as I can."

"Jared, wait, I'm not sure this is the right—"

But it was too late. He was gone, closing the door firmly behind him.

Kate dressed slowly, her mind churning. She didn't like any of this, and most especially she had not cared for the gleam in Jared's eyes as he had walked out the door. There was enough pirate in him to enjoy this whole thing, she decided, even if he was one of the good guys.

And of course he was one of the good guys, she reflected, aware of a definite sense of relief. Her pirates might walk close to the line at times, but they always managed to redeem themselves. They adhered to their own codes of honor. When the chips were down, you could count on them.

When she had pulled on a pair of jeans and a shirt she went to stand out on the veranda. Her insides were knotted with tension. She wondered if Max was in the bar as usual and if Jared was talking to him at that very moment. Would they head for the castle? Would Max try to contact his superiors? Or would he and Jared try to take matters into their own hands?

That last possibility sent a jolt of alarm through Kate. She could just see Jared doing something like that. And if Max was in the business of dealing with modern-day pirates, he'd probably go right along with the whole stupid idea.

At the very least, they'd go up to the castle to check out the diving equipment and see what else they could find.

Kate's uneasiness grew. There was always the possibility that Jeff Taylor was at the castle himself by now. If Max and Jared walked in on him, there could be real trouble. Unless, of course, Jeff, too, was one of the good guys. But who would know until it was too late?

Kate came to a decision and headed for the door. The sensible, logical thing to do was call Sam Finley at once. Just in case.

She made her way quickly through the gardens to Jared's house where she found the lights on and the door unlocked. No one ever bothered to lock doors on Amethyst, she had learned. She let herself into the hall.

"David? Beth? Anybody home?"

"Wanna bet?"

Kate went into the kitchen. "You the only one here, Jolly?"

The bird cracked a sunflower seed and studied her as if she were a specimen under glass. Kate gave his head a quick scratch and headed for Jared's study. The phone numbers were filed on a neat little series of cards, right where he had said they would be. Without hesitation she looked up Sam Finley's number and dialed it.

There was no answer.

Kate slowly replaced the receiver and wondered what to do next. She was getting an unshakable feeling that Jared and Max were walking into trouble. It was ridiculous to allow herself to get too nervous. Max, at least, was supposedly a professional at this sort of thing. And Jared was surely not totally devoid of common sense. But she could still picture the gleam of suppressed excitement in his eyes. Kate found herself staring at the Hawthorne dagger in the glass case.

It occurred to her that Jared had gone merrily off unarmed tonight. The dagger wasn't much of a weapon by contemporary standards, but it would have been better than nothing.

Without giving herself time to think about it, Kate opened the case, picked up the dagger and stuck it into her jeans, under her shirt. The old metal lay cold and hard against her skin. She felt a bit melodramatic, but she didn't hesitate. Her mind was made up now. She had to do something. She went to the desk and rummaged around until she found a small flashlight and then she headed for the door.

Her first stop was the lounge, but as she suspected, neither Max nor Jared was there. That only confirmed her feeling that they had both gone to the castle to see what was happening. She reminded herself that Max was apparently a pro, but that didn't kill the uneasiness she was feeling. The fact that Jeff Taylor was nowhere around did not make her feel the least bit better.

"Evening, Kate. How are you tonight?" The colonel nodded from the bar where he was busy pouring drinks for the throng.

"Fine, Colonel. Seen Jared?"

"He was in here a while ago, looking for Max. Haven't seen him since. Thought he'd be with you."

"He was earlier." Kate debated saying anything else and then decided Jared would not thank her for blabbing to the entire bar about what was supposed to be some sort of top-secret operation. "Tell him I'm looking for him if you see him," she said lamely and hurried back outside.

There was nothing else to do except go on up to the castle herself and see what was happening. If she didn't, she'd go crazy with worry.

The walk along the torch-lit path toward the beach was not too bad. But when she turned off the main trail to follow the dark path to the castle, chills shot all the way down her spine.

It seemed to take forever to reach her destination. When the tower finally loomed into view, a dark mass of stone silhouetted against a dark sky, she breathed a sigh of relief.

There was no sign of light showing through the narrow windows, but that did not tell her much. She walked quickly through the shadowed courtyard and slipped into the main hall.

It was darker than midnight inside. For a moment she stood in the doorway, listening intently. When she detected no sound at all she finally switched on the small flashlight and went over to the circular staircase.

She started down the steps with great caution. The black stairwell seemed bottomless and because of the way it twisted as it wound downward she could not see more than a few paces ahead, even with the light.

She was on the bottom step when she heard the smallest of sounds and then it was too late. A rough male arm coiled around her throat, dragging her off the step and back into the dungeon hallway. The flashlight clattered to the floor.

Frantically Kate lashed back with her foot. She was rewarded by a muffled oath.

"Hell, not again," Jared muttered in her ear. He sounded thoroughly disgusted. "I should have guessed." He relaxed his grip only slightly. "Hush. Not a sound. Not one sound."

Kate nodded quickly, the rush of adrenaline making her stomach queasy. Jared must have felt the motion of her head. Either that or he assumed she had the sense to keep quiet. He grabbed the flashlight and switched it off. Then she felt his hand close tightly around her wrist and she was being dragged deeper into the darkness behind the steps.

Kate stumbled along until Jared stopped without any warning. She immediately collided with him.

"Did you see anything at all when you came in?" Jared's mouth was next to her ear.

"No. Nothing. Can we talk in here?"

"Yes, but keep your voice down."

"I suppose it would be asking too much to turn on the flashlight again?"

"Definitely." He shifted slightly beside her but remained invisible in the pitch darkness. "What the hell are you doing here or is that a dumb question?"

"Why do you think I'm here? I tried to call Sam Finley and there was no answer. I went to the lounge and there was no sign of you, Max or Jeff Taylor. All in all, I figured things might be getting just a teensy bit out of control, so I thought I'd come see what was happening." Kate paused to catch her breath. "Jared, what *is* happening? This is getting scary."

"You were right. Things have gotten just a bit out of control. I couldn't find Max in the bar, so I decided to check out the castle myself. He was waiting for me."

"What do you mean? Max is here? Then why are we sneaking around alone in the dark like this?"

"Max was waiting for me with a gun," Jared explained patiently. "What's more, the fat little bastard took away mine and put me into the dungeon cell. Damned embarrassing."

"He took away your gun?" Kate's voice rose on a squeak. "You had a gun with you? Where did you get it?"

"I picked it up from the house before I came up here, of course. Where do you think I got it? Amethyst is a long way from the nearest 911 operator. Out here we have to look after ourselves."

"And a fine job you seem to be doing."

"Don't start nagging now. Save it for later, okay?"

"Okay, okay. I'm trying to put this together. I take it Max has turned renegade or something?"

"Or something. Looks like he's decided to quit nickel and diming the government and go for the big time. He's involved with the pirates."

Kate was shaken. "You're lucky he didn't kill you."

"He plans to. But he wants to do it at sea so he doesn't have to worry about anyone finding the body and linking him to this mess. I was put into one of the cells to wait until they're ready to move the cargo. I was going to get shipped out along with the electronics."

"Oh, Lord," Kate whispered. "He was going to kill you. How did you get out of the dungeon?"

"Roger Hawthorne was a cautious man. He'd lived through enough mutinies to know enough to plan ahead. He considered the possibility that he might someday be forced to occupy his own dungeon so he designed a way out that only he knew. He put the information into his journal. I discovered the secret years ago after I started reading the books he'd left behind."

Kate was dazed. "I can't believe this. Max a traitor and potential murderer."

"You know, I never really felt a lot of warmth for old Butterfield, but I figured since his supervisors trusted him, there was no reason I shouldn't. Just goes to show—in case anybody ever doubted it—that the government is as good at making mistakes as everyone else."

"Better, probably. Poor old Butterfield. I suppose there's no predicting what the trauma of never getting his novel into print will do to a writer's mind," Kate said soberly.

"Don't be an idiot. Max never even got the damned book written." Jared was silent for a moment, obviously deep in thought.

"What about Jeff Taylor's wet suit? Why was it in the hidden chamber earlier today?"

"Max was kind enough to fill me in on that. He said Taylor has been making regular visits to the chamber. There's an underwater entrance through a lava tunnel. He could come here any time and not risk being seen."

"That explains why he liked to dive alone."

"Right. Seems he was doing some last-minute work on those crates this afternoon and wanted to consult with Max about some details. He was in a hurry and didn't want to take the time to get back into his gear and swim out around the point and into the cove. He just left his stuff here and went down the path. It was safe enough on a one-shot basis. No one noticed him, but it's damned lucky you didn't happen to be coming up the path at the same time he was going back to the resort."

"Yes. Isn't it, though." Kate's fingers trembled.

"Your being here changes things. I was going to wait for Max and Taylor to return, but now I think our best bet is to get back to the resort and try to track down some assistance from Ruby. Sam is over there somewhere. I'll start calling around until I find him."

"Good idea. Let's get out of here." Kate put out a hand to find the wall.

"This way." Jared took hold of her arm and guided her through the darkness back to the tiny room at the foot of the stone stairs.

Kate was fumbling with the first step when she felt him go very still behind her. He tugged on her arm and she obediently stopped.

Then she heard the footsteps ringing on the stone above. Adrenaline flooded her veins all over again.

Jared was already tugging her back down the stairs. She felt him moving about in the darkness and then she heard the faint groan from deep inside the stones. She whirled around, but could see nothing. The cool rush of air and the soft sound of water told her the wall was now open.

Jared pushed Kate in front of him, urging her into the hidden cavern. She moved cautiously, relying on his knowledge of the place.

A moment later she felt the rough lava wall beneath her extended palm. Jared pushed her down until she was crouching behind an outcropping of rock.

"Don't move," he breathed into her ear. "With any luck no one will see you in the shadows."

She knew then that he was going to try to surprise whoever was coming down the staircase. "Jared, wait." She caught his hand while she yanked the dagger out of her jeans. "Here."

His hand closed swiftly around the hilt of the dagger. "You, my love, truly were meant to be a pirate's lady."

He moved away from her and Kate huddled into herself. After a moment it seemed to her she heard a faint, whispering sound near the edge of the quay, as if a body were sliding into the water, but she could not be certain.

An instant later she heard the footsteps on the staircase and then a beam from a flashlight darted into the room. It slid rapidly over the stone wharf, but did not come close to her hiding place.

Kate held her breath as a familiar figure walked swiftly into the cavern, calling out commandingly.

"Butterfield? You in here?" Jeff Taylor's voice reverberated off the cavern walls. "What's going on? Why did you open the wall before I got here? So help me, if you think you're going to get away with pulling a fast one on me the way you did on your government people, you're crazy. Nobody cheats me, Max baby. Nobody at all."

The beam of the flashlight bobbed eerily about in the darkness, but it did not find Jared or Kate. It did, however, reveal the small cabin cruiser tied up at the quay near the pile of crates and cartons.

Taylor scanned the interior of the boat and then, apparently satisfied that it was empty, he propped the flashlight on one box and began loading crates into the cruiser.

That was when Jared staged his reappearance. Kate had to admit it was done in a suitably dramatic fashion, just like a scene out of one of her novels.

He came up out of the water only inches away from Jeff Taylor's foot. Jared had the dagger between his teeth so that his hands remained free and in the glow of the flashlight he looked incredibly dangerous. His dark hair streamed back from his forehead and his teeth flashed around the handle of the knife. In that moment he was every savage buccaneer Kate had ever created.

At the last instant Jeff Taylor sensed what was happening. He tried to jump back out of reach, simultaneously grabbing for the gun in his shoulder holster.

But he was too late. Jared had already wrapped one hand around Taylor's ankle. He jerked the man off his feet and into the water. The gun sank beneath the dark surface.

The struggle in the water was short and merciless. Even as Kate darted forward from her hiding place, Jared was subduing Taylor. By the time she reached the edge of the quay and turned the flashlight beam on the two thrashing men, she saw that Jared had the dagger's point firmly lodged near Taylor's throat. Taylor stopped struggling.

"Stand back," Jared ordered as he pulled an unresisting Taylor out of the water. "Bring me that yellow nylon line sitting in the stern of the cruiser."

Kate did as she was instructed and watched in fascination as Jared neatly bound his captive with a lot of very businesslike nautical knots.

"You're a fool, Hawthorne." Taylor looked up at Jared with furious, sullen eyes. "You should have stayed out of this."

"Tell me about it." Jared stepped back, satisfied with his knots.

"Now what?" Kate asked.

"Now you go back to the resort and try calling Sam again."

She didn't like the expression in his eyes. "What about you?"

"I'll go find Max Butterfield," Jared said. The glow of the flashlight rendered his face in stark, chilling lines.

"No need to come looking for me, Jared." Max Butterfield spoke from the shadows of the open wall. Another flashlight beam penetrated the darkness. "I'm right here. Together with my insurance policy, of course. No, don't bother reaching for that old dagger. Leave it right where it is or someone will get hurt." He motioned with the gun in his hand.

"Dad." David stood at Max's side, held fast by Butterfield's grip on his arm. The boy's eyes were huge in the shadows. "What's going on? Max said you wanted to see me right away. He said you were in trouble. Are you and Kate okay?"

"As you can see, my boy, they're just fine," Max said. "For now, at any rate. Although I am saddened to see that my rather inept friend has not fared so well. You always were a trifle too precipitous, Taylor. You're an excellent planner, but you lack creativity."

Kate felt something very cold squeeze her stomach and she could only imagine how Jared must be feeling as he realized his son was now a hostage. The carefully controlled tension in him lapped at her in waves.

"Let David go, Max." Jared gazed unwaveringly at Butterfield. His voice was very quiet. "You don't need him. Get in the cruiser and go. No one will stop you."

"Now we both know it's not quite that simple, Hawthorne." Max sounded mildly regretful. He glanced at Kate and shook his head. "A pity about your curiosity, my dear. This entire matter could have been handled far more neatly if you had not gotten involved. Now I fear it will be rather messy. But a writer's life is filled with ups and downs, is it not?"

"Your life has definitely gotten a lot more messy than most," Kate said. "What made you decide to turn traitor?"

"Such a dramatic turn of phrase, my dear. I don't quite see it that way. Remember our little philosophical discussion at poolside concerning fate? I believe I mentioned then that once in a while one is given a golden opportunity to reshape one's destiny. I have been handed such an opportunity and have decided to take it."

"You really believe your own bull, Max?" Jared asked conversationally.

"Dad?" David tried to pull free of Max's grip and looked up angrily when he was not released. "Hey, Max. Let me go. Come on, let go of me."

"Not yet, David, my boy. I'm afraid I need you to ensure your father's good behavior." Max looked at Kate, paying little attention to his small hostage. "And also that of Ms Inskip. Come along, boy." He started to drag David toward the cruiser, motioning with the gun to urge Jared and Kate out of the way.

"I'm not going anywhere with you." David started to struggle.

"Behave yourself, boy, or I'll put a bullet through your father right now. Do you understand?" Max jerked David forward.

David looked at Jared, his small face taut with fear. "Dad?"

"Don't fight him, son," Jared said, his voice calm. "Just go along quietly, okay?"

"But, Dad, I don't want to go with Max." David was near tears as he was dragged toward the boat.

"Everything's going to be all right. When this is all over, you and Kate can practice some of those things she taught you. Remember what you learned from her?"

David blinked a couple of times and the tears were halted. He glanced at Kate and she could see awareness dawning in his eyes. She nodded reassuringly.

"You might even want to start practicing right away, Dave," Jared said.

"Yeah," said David, gathering himself.

"This is all very touching," Max Butterfield said as he started to step into the boat, "but I'm afraid we really don't have time for these sentimental farewells. Jared, go open the sea wall. Come along, David."

"I'm not going anywhere with you," David announced in the distinctly stubborn accents only a nine-year-old can manage.

"Of course you are."

"Wanna bet?" David lashed out without warning, slamming the sole of his right foot squarely against Max's kneecap.

For the next few seconds, everything happened very quickly. Max yelled in pain and surprise and lost his balance. He clutched his knee and then flailed wildly for his balance. He missed the boat and toppled with slow grandeur into the black water.

David ran straight to his father. Jared caught him close in a short, fierce hug. "You are a hell of a kid, you know that?"

"It was Kate's trick," David reminded him.

"Kate is a hell of a woman. And I am one hell of a lucky man." Jared gently pushed the boy toward Kate, who held him tightly to her. Then he walked over to the edge of the quay and stood looking down at Max, who was bobbing about and sputtering seawater.

"Jared, we've been friends for a long time." Max splashed toward the stone wall. "I ask that you consider our long acquaintanceship before you do anything rash. Consider also the cash involved here."

"I have considered it, Max. I considered it while I was locked in that dungeon cell. And I considered it very closely when you threatened Kate and my son. And after due consideration I have decided I never did like you all that much, anyway."

Chapter Eleven

"FURTHERMORE, I WANT YOU TO KNOW I feel some serious errors in judgment were made around here. Serious errors that were compounded by a ridiculous macho approach to the entire event." Kate reached the end of the terrace, swung around and paced back. The morning was magnificent, as usual. Out in the bay lay the sleek, white cruise ship, its passengers still at breakfast on board. "I think it was absolutely unpardonable of you not to tell me what was going on right from the start."

"It had nothing to do with you and it was potentially dangerous. The whole thing was supposed to be a secret operation. Fat lot of good it does trying to explain the concept of *secret* to women." Jared concentrated on the repair work being done on the terrace railing. He had been concentrating on it ever since Kate had finally tracked him down that morning. "Mark, watch out for the tile. It cost me a fortune to have this stuff shipped in and I don't want it chipped."

"Right, boss." Mark and his assistant exchanged quick grins as they dutifully spread a protective cloth over the expensive Italian tile. They had been listening unabashedly to the exchange between Kate and Jared for several minutes. When they finished here on the terrace, the entire resort would know every detail of the argument.

"The very fact that it was dangerous is precisely why you should have told me what was going on."

"The idea was to keep you out of it." Jared examined the lumber that was to be used for the makeshift railing. "This isn't going to look great, but it should do the job."

Kate glowered at Jared's back. "What's going to happen to Max and Taylor?"

"Sam Finley collected them bright and early this morning. He'll turn them over to the authorities." Jared frowned at his men. "Let's get moving on this, you two. This should have been completed yesterday. Those people from the cruise ship will be pouring in here in another couple of hours. Where's the colonel? He was supposed to be digging some extra tables and chairs out of storage."

"Saw him a while ago, boss. He's working on it."

"Jared," Kate began determinedly, "I would appreciate your undivided attention. I am trying to talk to you." But it was a losing battle and she knew it. They had all gotten to bed very late last night and there had been little chance to rehash the affair. Kate had awakened bright and early this morning with every intention of doing so, but thus far she had been thwarted at every turn.

"Hi, Dad, how's the railing going?" David bounded up the terrace steps and skidded to a halt near his father.

"We're getting there," Jared said.

David grinned at Kate. "You still yelling at Dad?"

"I am not yelling at your father. I am trying to have an intelligent, coherent discussion and I am being stonewalled."

"She's yelling," Jared said.

"What does stonewalled mean?" David asked.

"Never mind." Kate turned back to Jared. "Jared, I would like to talk to you in private, if you can manage to spare a few precious minutes of your valuable time."

"Not right now, Kate. Maybe I'll have some time later to let you nag me but I've got more important things to do at the moment. Okay, Mark, let's get that new section in place and see how it fits."

"This is impossible," Kate said.

"No, I think it will be just about right." Jared studied the length of wood that had been sanded down to form the new railing. "Maybe a quarter inch more off that end, Mark."

"Right, boss." Mark picked up the power saw.

"I'm wasting my breath," Kate said. "I should have known there was no point trying to have a serious conversation about this with you. You wouldn't talk to me last night and you won't talk to me this morning. I'm beginning to get the idea you just don't want to talk to me at all."

Jared must have caught the new note of resignation in her voice. He shot a quick glance over his shoulder. "There's nothing to talk about that can't wait until after that cruise ship sails. Look, why don't you go have a nice swim in the cove? Dave, take her swimming."

"Sure thing, Dad."

Kate smiled slightly at David. "No, thanks, Dave. Maybe some other time. I think I'll go back to my room for a while."

"Good idea. Have a nice nap or something," Jared said. He grabbed hold of the railing and helped his men lock it into place. "You must be exhausted after all the excitement last night."

Kate watched him for a moment. Then she looked down at David, who was studying her anxiously. "See you later, Dave. Thanks again for the drawing." She turned and walked off the terrace.

The colonel was setting out sparkling glasses on the bar as she went through the lounge. Letty was helping him.

"Morning, Kate," Letty called. "Finished chewing Jared out for not telling you about what was going on up at the castle?"

"Yes. I'm finished."

"Well, I want you to know I'm on your side in this. Men. They think they should make all the decisions and keep the ladies in the dark. For their own good, of course."

"Now, just one minute," the colonel interrupted. "Jared was doing a favor for a government man and he had been told to keep his mouth shut. He couldn't tell Kate what was going on. He couldn't tell anyone, not even me. Give the man a little credit. He was doing what he had to do. How could he have known Butterfield had turned bad? No one knew. I heard what the government man who came over with Sam Finley this morning told Jared. He said Butterfield had always been useful and they'd never had cause to suspect him."

"Naturally you'd take Jared's side in all this," Letty said. "You're a man. Seems to me that if Kate hadn't gone up to the castle with the Hawthorne dagger, Jared might have been worse off than he already was. You can't tell me that dagger wasn't very useful."

"Excuse me," Kate murmured. "I have to be on my way. I've got a lot to do this afternoon before Hank leaves for Ruby." She gave both the colonel and Letty a fleeting smile and headed for the door.

"Oh, my goodness," Letty breathed. "Did you hear that, Colonel?"

Satisfied, Kate did not linger to hear the colonel's response. She slipped out the door and into the gardens, heading for her room.

Ten minutes later Kate had all her suitcases open on the bed. She started taking clothes out of the closet.

There were some risks a woman had to take, she told herself as she worked. And if she failed, then she failed. It was better to know the truth than to live on in false hope.

By noon, Kate had to face the fact that Jared was not going to come pounding on her door demanding that she stay on the island. Perhaps he hadn't yet heard she was leaving. Or perhaps he simply didn't care.

When she went into the restaurant for lunch she discovered it was already filled with cruise-ship people who were thoroughly enjoying the stopover on Amethyst. She wandered past the gift shop and saw that it, too, was crowded. The colonel was swamped in the bar and the extra seating on the terrace was jammed. Snorkelers and swimmers swarmed down on the beach and the resort Jeeps were busying ferrying people into town for souvenir hunting.

Obviously the owner of Crystal Cove Resort had more important things on his mind today than whether one particular guest was getting ready to fly home.

Kate ate her lunch in a leisurely fashion, chatting with the waitress and the rest of the staff. Jared was nowhere to be seen. When she wandered out into the lobby she was greeted by Lani and Jim at the front desk. They looked stunned when she asked for her bill so that she could settle it.

"You're leaving? Today?"

"On the afternoon plane to Ruby," Kate explained as she signed her name on the credit card slip.

"Jared never said anything," Jim said uneasily.

"He may not have heard yet." Kate smiled as she handed back the slip. "He's got a lot on his mind today."

"That's for sure." Jim glanced at Lani, who gave a small, helpless shrug. "We're going to miss you around here."

"A lot," Lani said, her dark eyes wistful. "Things have been much more interesting around here since you showed up. It just won't seem the same after you leave."

"I've had a wonderful time, but all good things must come to an end."

"Would you do me a favor and autograph your book for me?" Lani whipped out a copy of *Buccaneer's Bride* from behind the desk. "I just loved it."

"Of course." Kate scrawled her name and best wishes inside and handed the book back. "Thanks for asking." She turned away from the desk and walked out onto the little lagoon bridge. It occurred to her that it was hot today but she didn't mind. The heat no longer seemed to affect her much. Apparently she'd acclimated.

Two hours later she and her luggage were standing on the tarmac near Hank's twin-engine Cessna. A small group of people who were preparing to leave the island milled around, waiting for Hank to load the bags.

There was still no sign of Jared.

She had known this was going to be a risk, Kate reminded herself as she nudged one of her bags toward the pile Hank was assembling. She had gambled and she had known there was a chance she would lose. Betting was a way of life here on Amethyst, but she hadn't had a lot of practice at figuring odds. She wished the stakes weren't quite so high this time.

"You ready, Ms Inskip?" Hank asked as he started boarding his passengers.

"Yes."

Hank looked down the road that led back to the resort. "You know, I kinda thought Jared might show up this time the same way he did last time."

"He showed up the last time I was preparing to leave?"

"Yes, ma'am. Showed up and paid me the price of a seat just to make sure I'd say I didn't have room for you on board. In case you showed up here at the strip, that is. Which you didn't."

Kate smiled briefly. "I guess he didn't want me to go that time."

"So what about this time?"

Kate shrugged and walked toward the plane. "Looks like he doesn't care this time."

"That can't be right. Not from what I hear." Hank scowled. "You sure he knows you're leaving?"

"If he's paying any attention at all to what's going on around him today, he knows." Kate put one foot on the bottom step.

The roar of a Jeep engine shattered the serenity of the flight field. Hank grinned in sudden relief and turned his head to look down the road again.

"Well, well, look who's here," Hank said softly.

Kate stood on the bottom step and watched the Jeep tear through the gate and race toward the plane and the small group of people clustered around it. Jared was at the wheel. Beside him sat David, looking very fierce.

Everyone stopped talking abruptly and turned to watch as the Jeep slammed to a halt in a cloud of dust. Jared switched off the engine and vaulted out of the vehicle. He stalked swiftly toward Kate, his expression taut with anger.

"Where the hell do you think you're going?"

"Home." Kate braced herself and lifted her chin defiantly. "It's time, Jared."

"You're not due to leave until tomorrow."

"Twenty-four hours either way isn't going to make much difference, is it?"

"Are you out of your mind? It makes a hell of a difference."

"Why? What was going to happen between today and tomorrow that's so important?"

"I was going to ask you to marry me!" Jared roared. "That's what was going to happen."

Kate's heart leaped, but she forced herself to stay calm. "Were you really? How odd. You couldn't even find time to talk to me this morning. And you're going to be swamped with cruise-ship people until late tonight. How were you ever going to find a spare minute in which to ask me to marry you?"

"That's my business." Jared reached up and took hold of her wrist. "Get out of the way. Hank's trying to load his passengers."

"I'm one of them."

"Not anymore you're not." Jared looked over at David, who was sitting on the hood of the Jeep. "Come give me a hand with the luggage, Dave. Kate does not travel light."

"You bet, Dad." David leaped down and dashed forward. He was wearing a huge grin now. "I knew you'd make her stay."

Kate dug in her heels at the foot of the steps. "Jared, it isn't going to be this easy. There are one or two matters we have to deal with before any commitments are made."

"Later, Kate."

She ignored him. "First, I do not appreciate the cavalier treatment I've been subjected to today. Second, I think it's high time you stopped fooling around and told me flat out that you love me. I'm sick and tired of pussyfooting around the subject."

"I love you. Dave, get those two flight bags, will you? I'll take these suitcases. Hank, could you give us a hand? We're in kind of a hurry here."

"No problem." Hank smiled genially and bent to pick up two large suitcases.

The three males started toward the Jeep with the luggage. Kate stared after them in annoyance and then hurried forward. "Not so fast, dammit."

"Honey, I've got a resortful of people trying to spend money." Jared tossed her luggage carelessly into the back of the Jeep. "I'm too busy to stand around here restating the obvious."

"What's so damned obvious? You've never bothered to tell me you love me. How was I supposed to know?"

"You wouldn't have headed for the airport this afternoon after making sure everyone except me knew where you were going unless you were damned sure I'd come after you. Okay, you've made your point. Now get into the Jeep. I've got things to do back at Crystal Cove. If you're going to be the wife of a resort owner, you're going to have to learn that sometimes the paying guests come first."

"Your wife?" She smiled brilliantly up at him.

"Yeah, my wife. Get into the Jeep, lady. Now."

"Not until I've been properly asked. You can't just order me about as if I were one of the staff, Jared Hawthorne."

He towered over her. "Ask you? Are you kidding? I'm not asking, I'm telling you you're going to marry me. You think I'd be dumb enough to ask politely and give you a chance to say no?" He took one step forward, scooped her up into his arms and tossed her into the passenger seat. "With women like you, a man has to be assertive or he'll find himself running in circles. If you don't believe me, look at me right now. Circles within circles. I'm getting dizzy."

"Ready, Dad?" David hopped into the back seat.

"Ready."

Jared turned the key in the ignition and swung the wheel. The Jeep leaped toward the road to the combined cheers of the small crowd around the plane. Kate turned in the seat to wave goodbye to Hank, who waved back before he returned to the business of loading his passengers.

"Everything's okay now, huh, Kate?" David asked, leaning over the front seat.

She grinned and reached back to ruffle his hair. The breeze was warm with the scent of exotic flowers and the sun was so bright on the sea that it almost hurt her eyes. She felt gloriously alive and sure of herself. The pirate of her dreams had just swept her off her feet and was carrying her away to his island hideaway where he would make hot, passionate love to her just as soon as he got a spare minute. The boy in the back seat of the Jeep was going to be the son she had never had. She just knew her career would flourish because living here on Amethyst Island was going to inspire her as nothing else could ever have done.

"Yes," said Kate with complete certainty. "Everything is okay."

"Wanna bet?" Jared cast a sidelong glance at Kate.

"You got a problem, Hawthorne?" Kate smiled serenely.

"Yeah, I've got a problem. It seems to me I'm the only one who's making a public commitment around here. I've declared my love in front of a whole planeload of passengers, but I haven't heard much in the way of response from you."

"Oh," Kate said, as if it had just slipped her mind for a moment, "don't worry about it. I love you, too."

Jared laughed, his satisfaction ringing loud and clear in the crystalline island air. "Yeah, I kind of figured you did."

THE TELEGRAMS ARRIVED AT TEN O'CLOCK in the morning. Margaret Lark was just switching on the kettle to make her customary morning cup of tea when her doorbell rang. She accepted the message, skimmed it hurriedly and grabbed the phone to dial Sarah Fleetwood's number.

"Did you get one, too?"

"Sure did. Can you believe it?" Sarah laughed with delight.

"No. This is incredible. What a cure for stress."

"I knew Amethyst Island was the right place to send her. I just had a feeling." Sarah carefully unfolded her copy of the telegram and reread it once more.

Have found my pirate. He's got everything: dark hair, gray eyes and a real dagger. Married yesterday. Will see you soon when we return to the States for a visit. Regards, Kate.

THE ADVENTURER

Prologue

"DOES IT OCCUR TO YOU THAT YOU might have become a little obsessed with this matter of the Flowers, Sarah?"

"Kate has a point, Sarah. During the past few months, you've talked about nothing else except the Fleetwood Flowers and that man Gideon Trace. Trace may be real enough, but I'm sure the Flowers are just an old legend. There are probably thousands of tales just like it and none of them has much basis in truth. Why get excited about this one?"

Standing at the window of her bright, cheerfully cluttered apartment, Sarah Fleetwood gazed at the street ten stories below and smiled to herself. "Because this legend is mine," she said enigmatically.

"You mean, because the woman who once owned the Flowers is a distant ancestress of yours?" Margaret Lark shook her sleek head. "That's no reason to think there's any more truth in this tale than there is in any other lost treasure story."

"If you ask me," Katherine Inskip Hawthorne said with a knowing wink, "it's not the tale of the Fleetwood Flowers that has you enthralled, Sarah, it's this man, Gideon Trace, the one you've been corresponding with lately, who really interests you."

Sarah felt the familiar little glow of excitement that always accompanied the sound of Gideon's name. *Gideon Trace*. She had never met the man but already she knew a great deal about him. After four months of exchanging letters with him she was quite certain he was the real-life version of one of her own heroes, a man straight out of one of her novels of romantic suspense. Dark, enigmatic, mysterious and rather dangerous—the Beast waiting in a haunted garden for Beauty to rescue him from some curse.

Sarah knew she was no great beauty but she figured she could handle whatever curse had been put on Gideon Trace. In fact, she looked forward to the task with her usual boundless self-confidence and optimism. She glanced over her shoulder to where her two best friends sat on her shiny new, black leather Italian sofa.

"I can't explain it, Kate, but I know that the legend of the Flowers and Gideon Trace are linked. I'm going after both of them," Sarah said.

"You have no experience in treasure hunting."

"Gideon Trace will help me. I have a feeling about this particular treasure. It's mine. I'm going to find it with Trace's assistance."

Margaret raised her eyes to the ceiling. "Out of all those treasure hunters and salvage operators you contacted five months ago when you were researching *Glitter Quest*, why on earth did you fixate on Trace?"

"Something in his letters told me he was different from the others."

"Well, who am I to discourage you?" Kate said. "I wish you luck, my friend. I've had enough good fortune of my own recently. It's time you had a little, too."

Kate was dressed for travel in a flower-splashed turquoise cotton dress. She looked remarkably fit and healthy, Sarah noticed with great satisfaction. Her friend's eyes sparkled vivaciously and her tawny-brown hair gleamed. The tense, stressed-out look that had been hounding Kate had gone. There was nothing like a couple of months on a tropical island and marriage to a pirate to give a woman a shot of energy and the sheen of happiness.

"I suppose Kate has a point," Margaret said slowly. "We probably shouldn't try to talk you out of this. If a treasure hunt is what you want, go for it. Your intuition has always been extraordinary. Maybe it will lead you to the Flowers."

"Or at least to Gideon Trace," Sarah said, thinking, not for the first time, that her friend Margaret had that wonderfully elusive, subtle quality known as panache. Margaret managed to appear casually elegant just sitting there with one leg tucked under the other. She was dressed with her usual restrained flair, the collar of her pale yellow silk blouse turned up to frame her attractive face. Her black slacks had been beautifully tailored by an expensive designer and her fashionable black pumps had been made in Italy.

"And meeting Trace is the more important goal?" Margaret asked, her gaze shadowed with faint disapproval.

"Oh, yes, definitely. There's something in his letters, something I must..." Sarah paused to glance out the window again, her eye caught by a flash of yellow on the street. As she watched, a cab pulled over to the curb and a lean, dark-haired man dressed in jeans and a casual cotton shirt got out. He was followed by a miniature version of himself. "Jared and his son are here, Kate."

"So much for their whirlwind tour of the Space Needle and the waterfront. Guess it must be time to head for the airport." Kate got up to walk over to the window. Her eyes were warm and soft as she watched Jared Hawthorne lean down to say something through the window to the driver. Then he vanished with his son into the lobby ten floors below.

"How does it feel to have found your pirate?" Sarah asked softly.

"What can I say? I'm a new woman."

Margaret laughed from the couch. "That's certainly true. I take it Sarah and I are forgiven for having shanghaied you into that trip to Amethyst Island three months ago?"

"Given the way it all turned out, I'm more than willing to let bygones be bygones. What's a little matter of kidnapping and impressment among friends?" Kate's wedding ring gleamed in the reflected glow of a late afternoon sun. "I just wish you two could be as fortunate." She looked at Sarah. "Do you really think this Trace person is going to be someone special?"

"Yes." Sarah knew her sense of serene assurance was evident in her voice. "Very special."

"Don't be mislead by a few cryptic letters," Margaret advised. "The man publishes a low-budget, treasure-hunting magazine, for goodness sake. It caters to a bunch of gung-ho males of questionable intelligence who actually believe they're going to find a lost gold mine or Amelia Earhart's plane. Frankly, that puts Gideon Trace just one notch above a con artist."

"That's not true," Sarah said quietly. "He sells dreams. Just like I do."

"Never discount the value of a good dream," Kate added with a note of satisfaction as the doorbell rang. "I'll get that."

Sarah watched her friend walk across the room to open the door for her husband. No doubt about it, Jared Hawthorne was just right for Kate. Those gray eyes and that wicked grin made Hawthorne a real-life, walking, talking pirate who could have stepped straight from the pages of one of Kate's historical romance novels. What was more, he had the forceful personality a man needed to run a tropical resort or deal with a woman like Kate. Jared did both very well.

"Hi, honey," Jared bent his head to give his wife a brief, enthusiastic kiss. "All set? I told the cab to wait. We've got a plane to catch."

"I'm ready." Kate smiled at her stepson. "How was the Space Needle?"

"It was great. You could see the whole city and the mountains and everything," David Hawthorne enthused. "I told Dad we should build one on Amethyst but he said all we had to do was climb to the top of Hawthorne castle and look out."

"He's got a point."

"Yeah, but I like it here. I hope we come back to Seattle, soon."

"So do I," Sarah said from the other side of the room.

"You and Margaret will have to come on out to Amethyst one of these days," Jared said easily. "Don't worry, we've got plenty of room."

"A whole resort," David clarified. "I'll show you how to snorkel, just like I showed Kate."

"Sounds terrific," Sarah said.

"Promise me you'll both make plans to visit us soon," Kate said. "I miss you both."

Jared's brows climbed as he glanced at his wife. "I don't see why. You spend enough time on the phone talking to them."

"Got to keep in touch with the business," Kate informed him loftily.

Jared grinned at Sarah and Margaret. "As I said, come on out for a visit. The airfare's bound to be less than the phone bills the three of you are running up."

Kate wrinkled her nose. "That's not true."

"Wanna bet?" Jared moved toward the pile of luggage in the corner. "Come on, Dave, give me a hand with this stuff. You know Kate never travels light."

"Okay, Dad." David threw a quick grin at Kate as he hurried toward the luggage.

Sarah hugged Kate at the door. "Don't worry, we'll get to Amethyst, one way or the other," she promised as she blinked back a few tears.

"Thanks," Kate whispered. "And thanks again for sending me on that first trip to the island. I owe all my happiness to you and Margaret."

"Oh, Kate, I'm so happy for you." Sarah smiled mistily and stepped back as Jared and David started through the door with the luggage.

"It's been great to see you these past two weeks, Kate," Margaret added, getting to her feet to give her friend a farewell embrace. "It's good to know we'll be able to visit with you at least once a year when Jared brings his son to the States to see his grandparents."

"Don't worry, you'll see her more often than that," Jared said from the doorway. "But right now I'm taking her home to Amethyst. I've got a resort to run. Place has probably started crumbling into the sea during the two weeks I've been gone."

"It wouldn't dare." Kate slung her purse over her shoulder and followed Jared and David through the doorway. "Goodbye, you two. It's been a wonderful visit. Can't wait to see you on Amethyst. Sarah, good luck with your treasure hunting. Margaret, take care. And thanks again."

Sarah went out into the hall to wave the small family into the elevator and then she returned to her apartment. She shut the door behind her with great care and walked over to where Margaret stood at the window.

"Well, you were right when you said Amethyst Island was the place to send Kate," Margaret remarked. "She looks radiant."

"She's happy and relaxed." Sarah watched Kate, Jared and David pile into the waiting cab.

"Good for her. Now, about your plans for the immediate future…"

"What about them?"

Margaret frowned, turning away from the window. "You're really going to look him up?"

"Gideon Trace? Absolutely. I'm driving over to the coast at the end of the week to try to find him."

"You've got an address?"

"Just the post office box number on the envelopes he's sent me. The towns on the coast are all small. The one he's in is barely a dot on the map, the kind of place where everyone knows everyone else. Someone will be able to tell me where the publisher of *Cache* magazine lives."

"You haven't told Trace you're coming, have you?"

"No, I plan to surprise him."

Margaret looked at her ruefully. "You're always so bliss-fully sure of that intuition of yours, aren't you?"

"It's only failed me once. And that was my own fault. I wasn't paying attention to the warnings it was giving me." Sarah walked toward the kitchen. "How about a glass of wine before dinner?"

"Sounds good. Well, at least Trace hasn't tried to talk you into investing a few thousand dollars in some crazy expe-dition to find a lost World War II plane that supposedly crashed on a Pacific island with a load of gold on board."

Sarah giggled. "You mean the way that guy Slaughter did?" Jim Slaughter, owner of a business called Slaughter Enterprises, had been one of the professional treasure hunters she had contacted five months earlier. She had found his ad along with several others in the back of a sleazy adventure magazine for men.

He had written her several letters on impressive letter-head and tried phoning a few times in an attempt to in-terest her in his scheme to find the plane full of gold. Sarah had politely declined several times.

"He was a slick one, wasn't he?"

"I'll say. But that's my whole point, Sarah. People in-volved in the business of treasure hunting are probably all borderline hustlers or outright crazies. They just want you to pour thousands into their projects to find lost gold mines or something. Then they take your money and disappear."

"Not Gideon Trace. He's different." Sarah managed to find two clean wineglasses in the cupboard. She made a mental note to run the dishwasher soon. She was almost out of clean dishes. "Trace certainly hasn't tried to con-vince me to invest a dime in any crazy treasure-hunting scheme. In fact, he's tried to discourage me from wasting my time going after the Flowers."

"I don't know, Sarah. I just don't like the whole idea. But it's your decision." Margaret sauntered after her, pausing to glance at the evening paper that was lying on the counter amid a motley collection of yellow pads, romance novels and pens.

Sarah felt a twinge of uneasiness. Hand on the refrigerator door, she turned her head just as Margaret flipped through the newspaper to find the business section. "Margaret, wait, I don't think you ought to read that section."

But it was too late. Margaret was already staring down at the photo of a hard-faced man in a western-style business suit. "Don't worry about it, Sarah," she said quietly. "He makes headlines in the business world. He always has. You can't expect me to stop reading the paper just because I'm occasionally going to run across an article about him." She refolded the paper and raised her head, smiling grimly. "Besides, that's all in the past."

"Yes." Sarah busied herself with a bottle of Chardonnay and sought a way to change the subject. "Want to go out for a bite to eat in the Market?" she asked as she tossed the cork in the vague direction of the trash basket. It missed. Sarah promised herself she would pick it up later.

"All right. Then I think I'd better go back to my own apartment and get some writing done. I haven't accomplished much in the two weeks Kate's been visiting us and I've got a deadline coming up next month."

"You'll make it. You always do." Sarah poured two glasses of the clean, polished Washington Chardonnay and handed one to Margaret. "Here's to Kate and her new family."

"And here's to your treasure-hunting expedition," Margaret added as the glasses clinked. She took a sip and her gaze turned serious. "Promise me you'll be careful, Sarah."

"Hey, my middle name is Careful."

"No, it's not. Your middle name is Impulsive and I'm afraid that one of these days that intuition of yours, which you trust entirely too much, is going to land you in a heap of trouble."

"I'm thirty-two years old, Margaret. Trouble is starting to look promising. Now, no more lectures. Let's get down to serious business. What do we want for dinner and where do we want to go to eat it? I vote for pasta."

"You always vote for pasta."

TWO HOURS LATER, PLEASANTLY STUFFED with hazelnut tortellini, Sarah turned the key in the lock of her front door. She wandered through the cheerful, vividly decorated one-bedroom apartment, turning on lights as she went.

When she reached the desk where her computer sat like some ancient monolith rising from a sea of notes, magazines, empty tea mugs and research materials, she stopped.

It only took her a minute to find the stack of Gideon Trace's letters. Margaret was right, Sarah thought with a small smile as she reread one of them. Gideon's notes did tend to be a bit cryptic. An uncharitable observer might even call them somewhat dry. There was certainly very little hint of the fascinating man she just knew he had to be.

Dear Ms. Fleetwood:
In regard to your most recent inquiry concerning the legend of the Fleetwood Flowers, I'm afraid I have very little to tell you that you don't already know. The tale dates from the late eighteen hundreds and is not unlike many other stories of lost treasure.

Such stories tend to become greatly exaggerated over the years.

The Flowers were supposedly five pairs of earrings fashioned from gemstones. According to the legend, Emelina Fleetwood, a spinster schoolteacher, spent a summer searching for gold in the Washington mountains near her cabin. It was not unknown for women to try their luck at gold mining on the frontier and some gold was found in Washington, as you probably know.

At any rate, she is said to have discovered a small vein, worked it all summer and then went back to teaching the following year. She never told anyone where her strike was or if she'd gotten anything out of it. But the legend claims she had the earrings, which she always referred to as her Flowers, made up by a San Francisco jeweller and that she paid him with gold nuggets.

Before she died, Emelina Fleetwood is said to have buried her earrings somewhere on her property and drawn a map showing the location. If there ever was a map, it has long since disappeared.

I'm surprised you are familiar with the legend. It is an extremely obscure one. My professional opinion is that there is not much merit to the tale. Any search for the Flowers would probably be a waste of time.

If I can be of any further help, please feel free to contact me. Thank you for your check. I have renewed your subscription to *Cache* for another year.

Yours,

G. Trace

P.S. Thank you for the recipe for pesto sauce.

"Well, Mr. G. Trace," Sarah said as she put the letter back down on the desk, "I appreciate your professional opinion but I'm not going to abide by it. I'm going to find the Flowers and what's more, you're going to help me."

Chapter One

IT WAS THE BIGGEST, UGLIEST CAT SARAH had ever seen. A true monster of a cat, twenty or twenty-five pounds at least and none of it fat.

Its fur was a mottled, blotchy color somewhere between orange and brown with here-and-there patches of black and tan for added color interest. It had one torn ear and a few old scars, but otherwise looked to be in excellent physical condition. Sarah decided this particular cat probably won most of the fights it chose to start. She doubted it had ever purred in its life.

"Excuse me," Sarah said to the cat, which was sprawled across the top step, effectively blocking the entrance to the porch. "Would you mind if I knocked?"

The cat did not bother to lift its head but its tail thumped once in warning. It opened its eyes to mere slits and regarded her without enthusiasm. Sarah found herself pinned by a stone-cold, green-gold gaze.

"I can see you're not the eager, welcoming type. Somebody should have traded you for a Beagle years ago. What are you? Some kind of guard cat?"

The cat said nothing but continued to watch her with its remote, gemlike gaze. Sarah glanced around, hoping for signs of human habitation, but there weren't many.

The big, weather-beaten Victorian-style house she had finally managed to locate after much diligent searching was perched on a bluff overlooking the sea. The view of the Pacific was hidden this morning behind a veil of fog that hung over the water like a sorcerer's dark spell.

The house with all its aging architectural embellishments was as faded, forbidding and aloof as old royalty.

The nearest neighbor was some distance away, concealed by a heavy stand of trees. The distant roar of the sea and the whisper of restless pines were the only sounds. For all intents and purposes, Gideon Trace's home was isolated in a universe of its own, with only the cat to indicate that anyone actually lived here.

Sarah took another look at the large cat. "I'm very sorry," she said firmly, "but I am going to knock on the door, whether you like it or not."

The cat stared at her.

Sarah cautiously moved to the farthest edge of the steps so that she would not have to actually step over the creature. She went briskly up to the wide porch, ignoring the irritated thumps of the cat's tail. But the animal made no move to stop her as she went over to the door.

She had her hand poised to knock when a faint tingle of awareness went through her. The door was suddenly opened from the other side. Sarah looked up and found herself pinned for a second time that morning by a pair of icy, green-gold eyes. This time, at least, the eyes were human. Sort of.

"Who the hell are you and what do you want?"

For an instant Sarah felt as if time had been temporarily suspended. She stood there on the porch, staring up at the man in front of her, mesmerized by his jungle eyes and the gritty, rough-textured sound of his voice. For the first time since she had set out on her quest it occurred to her that she might have bitten off a little more than she could chew.

Gideon Trace looked large, cold-eyed and dangerous.

"Yes, of course," she said finally. "It makes sense that you would look a little like the cat."

The man's gaze narrowed in a way that reminded Sarah of the beast on the porch step. He did not move—just stood there in the doorway, big and unwelcoming. He was clad in jeans and a faded blue work shirt. "Are you selling something, lady?"

Sarah rallied quickly and summoned up her most engaging smile. She held out her hand. "In a way. I'm Sarah Fleetwood. I've been looking forward to meeting you. You are Gideon Trace, aren't you?"

His gaze dropped to her outstretched hand as if he didn't know whether to shake it or bite it. When he glanced up again Sarah thought she saw a barely concealed flare of surprise in his eyes. "Yeah, I'm Trace." His big hand closed briefly around hers, nearly crushing her fingers. He let go of her instantly, frowning. "You're the Fleetwood woman who's been writing to me for the past few months? The one who wrote me about the legend of the Flowers?"

"That's me." Sarah clutched the strap of her oversized black, white and yellow shoulder bag. "I wanted to talk to you in more detail about the legend because I've decided to look for the Flowers. To be perfectly honest, I'm hoping to convince you to go with me as a sort of consultant.

That's what I meant when I said I was here to sell you something. In a way, I am. I'm hoping to sell you on this great idea I've got. You see, I..."

"Hold it." Trace held up a hand to silence her.

Sarah ignored the upraised palm, much too excited to stop now that she had located her quarry. "I haven't had any experience with treasure hunting and I thought you could advise me. I'll pay you, naturally. What do treasure-hunting consultants go for these days? Is there a price break if I buy you for a week at a time, or is it the same as the day-to-day rate? I'm sure we'll be able to work something out. I've given this a lot of thought and I..."

"I said, hold it." Gideon Trace's expression was as austere and forbidding as that of his cat. "Are you always this, uh, enthusiastic?"

Sarah blushed. "Sorry, I was kind of rushing into things, wasn't I? My friends say I'm sometimes a little too impulsive. But what do they know? At any rate, I'm so glad to have found you, Mr. Trace, because I just know our association is going to be an extremely advantageous one for both parties." She gave him another of her most winning smiles.

The smile appeared to make Gideon Trace more wary than ever. His strong face was set in distinctly unenthusiastic lines. His green-gold eyes glittered as he looked down at her. "How did you find me?"

"I asked at the gas station."

"Maybe I should go ask someone at the gas station what I'm supposed to do with you now that you're here."

"I think what you should do next is invite me in for a cup of tea."

"Is that right?"

Sarah swallowed. "I think it would be an excellent idea."

"I don't drink tea. I haven't got a tea bag in the house."

"No problem. I always travel with my own." Sarah plunged a hand into her oversized shoulder bag and whipped out a tea bag with the words English Breakfast on the tag. "All I need is some hot water. You do have that, don't you?"

Gideon was clearly searching for an appropriate response to the question when a soft, inquiring meow sounded from the vicinity of his feet. Sarah knew that gentle tone could not have emanated from the great beast on the front steps. She glanced down to see a small, delicately built silver-gray cat watching her with warm, golden eyes.

"Oh, isn't she lovely?" Sarah crouched and offered her fingers in greeting.

The silver-gray cat stropped her tail once or twice against one of Gideon's well-worn boots and then glided forward. Politely she investigated Sarah's fingers and then rubbed her sleek head against the proferred hand.

Sarah looked up a very long way to where Gideon was scowling down at the scene taking place around his legs. "What's her name?"

"Ellora."

Sarah was delighted. "After the mysterious cave temples in India?"

"Yeah." There was another flicker of surprise in his eyes.

Sarah scratched Ellora's ears and the cat began to purr. "I hardly dare ask the name of that monster on the front steps."

"Machu Picchu."

"Oh, yes, the lost city of the Incas." Sarah turned to look at the big cat who hadn't moved from his position in the middle of the step. "The name sort of fits, doesn't it? Massive and immovable."

Gideon ignored that. "I take it you drove over from Seattle this morning?" He made it sound as if she had done something exceedingly stupid.

"Yes, it was a lovely drive. Hardly any traffic."

"Well, as long as you've made the trip, you might as well come in for the tea."

"Thanks." Sarah gave Ellora one last pat and rose to her feet. "Your two cats certainly have different personalities, don't they? How do they get along?"

"Ellora keeps Machu Picchu wrapped around her little paw." Gideon sounded resigned to the situation.

"Hard to believe," Sarah muttered.

"What do you expect? He's just a simple-minded male. Ellora has no trouble with him at all. This way." Gideon Trace turned to lead her into the house.

Sarah followed quickly, glancing around with deep interest. The inside of the old Victorian seemed dark and forbidding. It was also chilly.

"Must cost a fortune to heat one of these old houses."

"Yeah, but I don't need a lot of heat."

Sarah eyed the faded drapes, unpolished wooden floors and aging furniture. It was obvious publishing *Cache* did not provide a high profit margin. Either that or Gideon Trace simply didn't believe in investing in his personal surroundings. The place did not appear neglected, she finally decided, just dark and gloomy.

It was also incredibly tidy.

Magazines were filed in a terrifyingly orderly fashion in a rack. There was a huge assortment of books but they were all arranged with great precision in the floor-to-ceiling bookcases. The surface of the coffee table was completely clear, unmarred by so much as one empty coffee mug.

Even the chess game that had been set up on a table in one corner looked neat and orderly. Sarah glanced at the carved wooden pieces and wondered who Gideon played chess with. From all appearances he was a very solitary man.

She hurried after her reluctant host as he went through the living room into the kitchen. Here the windows all faced the sea, providing a ringside view of the dark fog that hovered over the water. The room itself was spacious in the manner of old kitchens and somewhat lighter and more inviting than the living room. But the impression of grim orderliness still prevailed.

Sarah realized she had not anticipated that her hero would be quite so organized. But she refused to be daunted by petty details.

"Have a seat."

Sarah needed no second urging. She dropped her huge bag onto a ladder-back chair with a thud and took a seat at the old claw-footed table. "This is certainly an interesting place you have here."

"I like it." Gideon filled an old steel kettle at the sink.

"Have you lived here long?"

"Almost five years."

"Is that how long you've been publishing your treasure-hunting magazine?"

"About."

The man obviously was not good at small talk. That didn't surprise Sarah. Gideon Trace was not a small talk kind of person. "I certainly have appreciated your help during the past few months, Mr. Trace. The inside information you provided on the subject of treasure hunting was invaluable to my story. You'll be happy to know I sent the manuscript of *Glitter Quest* off to New York on Tuesday."

"Delighted," he agreed caustically. "You said in one of your letters that it was some sort of romance novel?"

"That's right. I write romantic suspense."

"Sounds like a contradiction in terms."

"Not at all. I think romance and suspense go together beautifully. Danger and adventure heighten the sensual tension in the story and vice versa."

Gideon looked distinctly skeptical as he set out two cups and spooned instant coffee into one.

"I take it you don't read in the genre?" Sarah ventured, a little disappointed after all these months of corresponding with her he had apparently not bothered to buy one of her books and read it.

"No, can't say that I do." Gideon put the kettle on the stove.

Sarah studied him as he turned to face her. He leaned back against the edge of the counter and folded his arms across his broad chest. Either a forbidding scowl was habitual for him or else she had interrupted something important. Perhaps he had been in the middle of one of his articles for *Cache*. She knew how it felt to be interrupted in the middle of writing.

"Look, if I've caught you at an awkward moment, I could come back later," she offered.

"Good idea. How much later?"

"In a couple of hours, say?"

The edge of his mouth lifted faintly. The hint of amusement vanished almost instantly. "Forget it. Might as well get this over and done. I get the feeling you're the persistent type. Tell me why you've suddenly decided to go treasure hunting, Ms. Fleetwood."

"It's time," Sarah said simply.

"What do you mean, it's time?"

"I just have a feeling about it."

"How long have you known about the legend of the Flowers?"

"Almost a year. The story has been handed down through the women of my family for years but no one ever paid much attention to it. When my aunt died a year ago, however, she left the map to me."

Gideon didn't move but there was a new intensity in his eyes. "What map?"

"The map Emelina Fleetwood made. You mentioned it in your letter, remember? You said you doubted its existence, but it's quite real. My aunt had it most of her life until she willed it to me." Sarah reached for her purse and started scrabbling about inside. "I made a dozen copies and put the original in a safe-deposit box. I brought one of the copies with me." She hauled out a clear plastic envelope that protected a sheet of paper with a crude sketch and some words written on it.

Gideon reached for the envelope with the first show of genuine curiosity he had yet exhibited. He frowned over the cryptic drawing. "Treasure maps are a dime a dozen. Someone's always claiming to have one or trying to sell one. Ninety-nine point nine percent of them are fake. What makes you think this one is genuine?"

"My aunt once had the map analyzed by a lab to make sure the paper at least dated from the right period. It did."

"That doesn't mean the map is genuine or even that it was ever meant to lead anyone to the Flowers. It could have been drawn for any number of reasons."

"It's the real thing."

Gideon's head came up, his eyes brilliant. "You sound very sure of that."

"I am. I have a feeling about it." *And I've also got a feeling about you, Gideon Trace, but we'll get to that eventually.*

"Even if it's genuine, what makes you think you'll be the Fleetwood to find it?"

"I've got a—"

"A feeling. Right. Do you get these feelings often, Ms. Fleetwood?"

"Often enough to know I should pay attention when one hits." There was a soft meow from the floor. Sarah looked down as Ellora jumped lightly into her lap and proceeded to curl up.

"I think I should point out that I don't do the kind of consulting work you're looking for," Gideon stated, his gaze on Sarah's hand as she stroked his cat.

"I know you're in the business of publishing *Cache*, but I thought you might be interested in this project. Right up your alley. It's such a fascinating legend. Think what a great article it would make for your magazine."

"I've heard plenty of other tales just as fascinating, if not more so. Few of them ever lead to a real find. The most anyone ever actually uncovers is an old bit of rusted metal or a button or a stray rifle ball. Treasure hunting is just a hobby for most people. No one gets rich. Believe me, there's more money in publishing *Cache* than there is in actually hunting for the goodies."

"Well, I'm going to give this a whirl and I really think you should consider coming along with me, Gideon."

He blinked. "Me? Why?" Then he quickly held up a palm to forestall her answer. "Wait, don't tell me. You've got a feeling, right?"

"Right," she said, delighted he understood. "Now, how soon can we leave? I've got enough stuff packed in my car to last for a couple of weeks. I figure if you're not particularly busy on an issue of the magazine, we could take off tomorrow morning."

He stared at her. "Just like that? Are you out of your mind? You don't even know me. I could be a mass murderer, as far as you're concerned."

"Don't be ridiculous. I feel like I've known you for months. Ever since I got your first letter, in fact."

Gideon looked slightly stunned. "You're either incredibly naive or amazingly foolish. You shouldn't be allowed out except on a leash."

"I promise you, I'm neither particularly naive nor foolish. I know what I'm doing. I usually do."

"You're serious about this, aren't you? You materialize out of thin air on my doorstep, wave an old map in my face and expect me to immediately sign on for the duration of your idiotic expedition?"

"I like to think of it as a quest. All quests need a knight-errant. You're elected."

"Who are you? The beautiful princess or something?" He slapped the envelope with the map down on the table.

Sarah grinned. "What you see is what you get. I left my tiara at home. How about it, Mr. Trace? Are you available for hire?"

"No, I'm not available," he muttered as the kettle began to whistle. "I write about lost treasure. I don't waste my time looking for it."

"But you won't be wasting your time. I'll pay you."

"Look, lady, treasure hunting costs money. A lot of money. People have poured millions into projects aimed at locating sunken ships and lost gold mines." He picked up her tea bag and dropped it into a cup. Then he poured boiling water over it. When he was finished he poured water over the instant coffee in his own cup. Every movement was economical and controlled. It was the kind of motion that indicated underlying strength and power.

"I'm not suggesting we attempt a major expedition to find a sunken treasure ship. I'm only after Emelina Fleetwood's Flowers. And I've got a map. What could be simpler?"

Gideon shook his head in disgust as he carried the cups over to the table and sat down across from her. "Listen carefully, Ms. Fleetwood, while I spell out a few facts of life. Treasure hunting is almost never successful. At least not today. A hundred, two hundred years ago it was still possible for an amateur to stumble across something like the temple caves of Ellora or a forgotten pharaoh's tomb. Today, the only people who get that kind of thrill are professional archaeologists and even for them, the thrills are few and far between."

"I'm only trying to find a few pairs of earrings, not a lost civilization."

"Then that puts you in the ranks of the hobbyists. You'd be better off buying yourself a metal detector and heading for the beach to hunt for lost change."

"You're really determined to be difficult about this, aren't you?"

"I'm attempting to give you a realistic picture of what you're contemplating."

"Where's your spirit of adventure? You must have a genuine interest in treasure hunting or you would never have started a publication like *Cache*. Don't you feel the lure of the lost treasure? The excitement of the search? The lust for a dazzling fortune in lost gems?"

Gideon's eyes glittered briefly behind harrowed lids. "I try to focus my lust on more accessible objects."

Sarah blinked and then smiled. "Are you trying to frighten me, by any chance?"

He sighed. "I get the feeling that would be difficult."

"Impossible," she said crisply.

He watched apprehensively as she yanked the tea bag out of her cup, squeezed it quickly between thumb and forefinger and glanced around for a place to toss it. When she showed signs of hurling it across the room into the sink, Gideon moved.

"Here, I'll take that." Gideon plucked the tea bag from her fingers and got to his feet. He went over to the sink, opened a cupboard door underneath and carefully dropped the dripping tea bag into a trash bin. Then he came back to the table and sat down again.

"Everybody's afraid of something, Ms. Fleetwood."

"True. And I'm no exception to the rule. But I'm not afraid of you."

"Because you've got a feeling about me?"

"Right."

"You know something, Ms. Fleetwood?"

"Call me Sarah. What?"

"You're one very bizarre female."

"Yes, I know," Sarah admitted humbly. "My friends have often told me that."

"Wise friends. Have they attempted to diagnose your condition?"

"They say my problem is that I tend to think sideways. As I said, what do they know? Now, about our project."

"Already it's *our* project?"

"I've been thinking of it as our project right from the moment the idea occurred to me."

"When was that fateful moment?"

"I believe I was in the shower at the time. I get many of my best ideas in the shower, you know."

"No, I didn't know." Gideon looked unwillingly fascinated.

"At any rate, I suddenly knew that it was time to look for the Fleetwood earrings and that I was the one to search for them. I got out of the shower, put on a robe and walked out into the living room. Your latest letter with the research data on salvage operations that I needed for *Glitter Quest* was on my desk. I glanced at it and immediately knew I wanted you to help me in my search."

"This is amazing."

"Isn't it, though? I expect it will be a lot of fun, too. And very educational?"

"Educational?"

"Sure. The material you sent me on treasure hunting for *Glitter Quest* was extremely interesting, but rather academic, if you know what I mean. This way I'll have a chance to learn about the process of a real-life treasure hunt from the ground up, so to speak."

Gideon sipped his instant coffee. "What if I tell you I'm not free at the moment to take off for two weeks?"

"Well, I could come back at a later date, I suppose."

"How much later?"

"Tomorrow?"

"Or the next day, maybe? Never mind. It's obvious you're not going to go away for good."

"I really could postpone this for a while if it was absolutely necessary. After all, those earrings have been lost for a long time. But I sort of thought this was the right moment to start the search. And something tells me you have to be involved in the hunt. I really can't explain it, but I sense it's inevitable. I trust my intuition."

"You do realize that financing this little expedition is going to be a major project in itself? Two weeks in the mountains including meals, lodging and gas are not going to come cheap. Can you afford it?"

"I've budgeted for it. I'm a reasonably successful writer, Gideon, and I assure you I can handle the tab for this venture. I'll consider it my annual vacation."

"You want to spend your annual vacation digging around in the dirt for something that probably doesn't even exist?"

"You have to learn to think positive, Gideon," she said earnestly. "The earrings exist and we'll find them."

"Tell me, Sarah, do you usually have to strong-arm some man into accompanying you on your annual vacations?"

"Now, don't be sarcastic. To tell you the truth, I've never met one who was worth the effort before. And it does appear to be an effort, doesn't it? I didn't realize it would be quite this difficult."

Gideon fixed her with a strangely baffled look. "I'm worth the effort because I can show you how to read that map or something?"

"Sarah pursed her lips and scratched behind Ellora's ears. "Not exactly. Maybe. You've certainly had more experience with treasure maps than I've had. But I'm not sure if that's why I need you along. It's hard to explain. I just know I want you with me. Somehow the Flowers and the map and you are all linked together."

He frowned suspiciously. "You're not under the impression you're psychic or something, are you?"

"Of course not."

"Are you sure?"

"You're teasing me, aren't you? Don't worry, I'm not weird or anything. Just sort of intuitive. The minute we started corresponding, for example, I knew I was going to like you very much. I certainly hope you feel the same way about me."

"I'll be blunt, Sarah Fleetwood. I can't even begin to figure out how I feel about you."

"Well, you don't need to make up your mind this instant."

"I don't? What a relief."

She smiled sunnily and dove into her oversized bag for a piece of paper and a pen. "Here's the name of the place where I'm staying tonight. It's a tiny little motel a couple miles down the road." She jotted down the name. "Know it?"

He scowled at the slip of paper. "Sure, I know it. We don't have that many motels around here. What about it?"

"I suggest you pick me up for dinner around six o'clock.

The motel clerk said there was a nice little restaurant nearby. You'll probably be more relaxed if we settle the details of our association over dinner."

"Dinner."

"You do eat dinner, don't you?" Sarah gently lifted Ellora from her lap and set her on the floor. The cat purred more loudly than ever.

"Yeah, I eat dinner. That's not the point. The point is…"

"Don't worry, I'm buying." Sarah picked up her bag. "Please, Gideon? This is very important to me and I feel certain that once you've had a chance to think about it all, you're going to want to accompany me on my search for the Flowers. Have you got anything else you have to do tonight?"

"What if I said I had a date?"

Sarah was thunderstruck. "Good grief, I never even considered that. Have you got a date?"

Gideon groaned. "No."

"Wonderful. Then it's all settled. See you at six." Sarah whipped around and headed toward the front door, digging the car keys out of her pocket. "Just give me a chance, Gideon," she called back over her shoulder. "I know I can talk you into this. And you won't lose by it, I promise. I'm prepared to pay you a very decent wage. You can apply it toward the heating bill for this house."

She waved from the doorway at Gideon, who was still sitting at the kitchen table, and then she turned to lope down the porch steps. Machu Picchu had not moved from his throne. He slitted his eyes as Sarah stepped carefully around him.

"It's okay, beast. I know what I'm doing. I'll take good care of him." Sarah grinned at the cat and went down the walk to get into her car.

Inside the house Gideon sat unmoving until the cheerful hum of the compact's small engine had faded into the distance. Then he looked down at Ellora.

"You know something? She reminds me of you. She moved right in on us the same way you moved in on me and old Machu a year ago. What the hell am I supposed to do now?"

He got up slowly and carried the cups over to the sink. He had long ago discovered that if he didn't pick up the dishes, they never got picked up. He was willing to bet that Sarah Fleetwood's apartment would be littered with old tea mugs that needed washing.

"The Flowers. Why in hell did it have to be the Flowers? And why her?" Gideon stalked into the living room and paused for a moment beside the unfinished chess game. He had carved the pieces himself. They weren't great art, but they were functional. He picked up the queen and turned it over and over in his hand, examining it from all angles.

He was interrupted in his contemplation of the queen by a grumbling roar from the front door. Gideon went to open it. Machu Picchu ambled inside, pausing briefly to slap his tail heavily against Gideon's boot before he heaved himself up onto his favorite indoor position on the back of the sofa.

"Dinner. I'm supposed to drop everything and pick her up for dinner. Where does she get off giving orders like that? Who the hell does she think she is?"

The cats blinked lazily and watched as Gideon strode along the hall to his study. There, carefully weighted down by a big chunk of rose quartz, he found the stack of letters he had received from one Sarah Fleetwood. For some reason he couldn't explain why he'd kept them all.

The earliest dated from four months ago when she had first contacted him for information on modern treasure hunting. The latest dated from last week. He picked it up and scanned it again. It was in the same style as all the rest, breezy, enthusiastic, cheerful and inexplicably captivating.

Dear Mr. Trace:

It's midnight but I had to let you know I am nearly finished with *Glitter Quest*. I want to tell you how much I appreciate your research assistance. It really made a difference. The plot is much more intricate and involved because of some of the details you provided. It's been fascinating working with you. This has been such a fun book to write.

I must tell you I have truly enjoyed our correspondence these past few months. In fact, I have been inspired, but I'll explain just how at another time.

By the way, if you're still suffering from that cold you mentioned in your last note, I suggest you try hot tea with a shot of lemon and honey. Works wonders.

　　　　　　　　　　　　　　　　　　Yours,

　　　　　　　　　　　　　　　　　　Sarah

P.S. Am enclosing a cartoon I cut out of the paper this afternoon. I thought you would enjoy it.

The cartoon featured a pair of cats. It was only a coincidence that the cats, one beefy and one quite small, vaguely resembled Machu Picchu and Ellora, Gideon told himself. After all, he'd never mentioned either feline in his letters to Sarah.

He glanced at the old clock in the corner. It was still early in the day. Plenty of time to find an excuse for not taking Sarah Fleetwood to dinner.

But the woman knew too damned much about the Fleet-wood Flowers, Gideon reminded himself. And now she had managed to locate him. That made her a distinct threat to the quiet, well-ordered existence he had carved out for himself.

Gideon had learned long ago that it was good policy to neutralize potential threats before they got to be real problems.

He'd better take the lady to dinner.

Chapter Two

IT WASN'T AS IF HE HAD ANYTHING better to do, Gideon told himself as he climbed out of his car in the motel parking lot. It was either this or another evening alone with Ellora, Machu Picchu and a good book. Not that the evenings alone were all that bad. For the most part he found them comfortable.

But a part of him still hankered after an occasional shot of excitement and, for better or worse, Sarah Fleetwood had managed to whet his appetite. He had to admit it was the first time in a long while that a woman had been this interesting. What few relationships he'd gotten involved in since his divorce had tended to be quiet and extremely low-key.

There was nothing quiet or low-key about Sarah Fleetwood.

The door of one of the motel rooms was flung wide as he started toward the office to inquire about Sarah's room number.

"Hi, Gideon," Sarah called out across the parking lot. "I'm ready."

He turned at the sound of Sarah's voice and saw her furiously locking the door behind herself. She must have been watching for him from the window. Gideon couldn't remember the last time a woman had waited impatiently for him at a window. Leanna had always been much too poised or preoccupied with her work for that sort of thing, at least when it came to waiting for him.

Of course, he should bear in mind that Sarah Fleetwood was not just waiting for a dinner date. She was after five pairs of jeweled earrings known as the Fleetwood Flowers. That was bound to make any woman eager.

"You're late," Sarah informed him as she hurried across the parking lot. Her high heels clicked on the pavement in a way Gideon found surprisingly sexy. The sound made him think of soft feminine sighs and sudden passion in the middle of the night.

Annoyed with himself, he took his mind off sex and glanced at his watch. "Five minutes. You going to fire me for a lousy five minutes?"

She gave a gurgle of delighted laughter as she hopped into the car without waiting for him to get the door. "Does that mean you've decided to let me hire you in the first place?"

He slid behind the wheel and turned the key in the ignition. "I'm thinking about it."

"Then it's all set." Sarah sat back, clearly bubbling over with satisfaction.

"Not quite." He spun the wheel and drove out of the small lot. "I said I'm thinking about it. I'll let you know my answer when I'm ready."

"Okay, okay. Be that way. In the meantime, I'm hungry. Does this place called the Wild Water Inn have pasta?"

"I've never noticed. Whenever I go there, I order fish. That's the house specialty."

"Maybe they have some pasta and fish dishes. Linguine with clams or something."

He slanted her an appraising glance. "I wouldn't be surprised. Even if it's not on the menu, I'll bet the chef will bend over backward to make a special."

Sarah's eyes widened in surprise. "Do you really think so? He must be a very accommodating chef. What's his name?"

"Mort."

"Mort. I'll remember that. What a nice man."

"You've never even met him and you don't know for sure yet if he'll go to the trouble of preparing something special for you." But Mort probably would do it, Gideon conceded. There was something about Sarah Fleetwood that made a man want to please her just to see the delight reflected in her face.

Any man or just him? he wondered with a sudden sense of foreboding.

Gideon studied her out of the corner of his eye as she watched the rugged coastline sweep past. He knew he was checking to see if his first impression had been wrong. But his earlier reactions this afternoon did not undergo any drastic revision now.

He guessed her age at around thirty, give or take a couple of years, although she might have been younger. Those clear, deep hazel eyes were just as unsettling now as they had been when he'd first opened his door to her, her small, elfin features just as piquant.

The red silk sheath she wore played lightly over a slender, surprisingly sensuous body. There were veins of gold running through her light brown hair. She had brushed the heavy mass straight back from her forehead and tied it in a cascading ponytail that somehow managed to look chic instead of youthful. There was a sleek delicacy about her that would make anything she wore look stylish.

All in all, she still reminded him of Ellora. Gideon briefly regretted that he hadn't put on a tie. He suddenly felt vaguely underdressed in his jeans and white shirt.

"This scenery is magnificent, isn't it?" Sarah said, turning away from the window reluctantly. "I'm going to have to set a book here. It's the perfect backdrop for a romance with intrigue and suspense. Lots of drama and impending danger. Where did you live before you moved to Washington, Gideon?"

"Here and there."

"Ah-ha. A world-weary wanderer who's finally decided to settle down. I knew it. What did you do before you started publishing *Cache*?"

"This and that."

"Real-life treasure hunting, I'll bet."

He gave her an irritated glance. "What makes you say that?"

"Well, we already know you're not a mass murderer and I don't see you as a sales rep. So what else would give you a background in this and that?"

"The inability to hold a good job for any length of time?"

"Nah. You could do just about anything you wanted to do. If you wanted to hold down an ordinary job, you'd have done it. But I don't see you as an ordinary sort of man, Gideon. You're like one of the heroes out of my books and I never write about ordinary men."

"Look, Ms. Fleetwood, we'll probably get along a whole lot better if you don't try to romanticize me."

"How can I help it? You're a very romantic figure."

"You call being forty years old and living alone in an old house with two cats romantic?" He glanced at her in sheer disbelief.

"Very."

"You've got the wrong man. You want someone like Jake Savage."

She was immediately fascinated. "Who?"

"Jake Savage." Gideon wasn't surprised by her reaction. Women always reacted that way to Savage. Just the sound of his name was enough to do it for this particular female, apparently.

"What a terrific name. Do you think he'd mind if I used it some day in a book?"

"I doubt it, he's dead."

"Too bad. What was he like?"

"He was the kind of guy you're trying to make me into. Savage was a real-life adventurer. Liked to live life on the edge. Ran a business called Savage and Company."

"What did Savage and Company do?"

"Just about anything in and around South America and the Caribbean that paid enough. Flew supplies into the jungles for various governments, including our own. Transported equipment up rivers for tourists, photographers and scientists. Handled shipments of medicine and clothing for charitable organizations. Acted as guides and outfitters for archaeologists and the occasional team of journalists. And once in a while Savage and Company did some actual treasure hunting. Oh, you'd have loved Jake Savage, all right."

"What happened to him?" Sarah demanded.

"The story is he went off on a particularly dangerous job one day and never came back out of the jungle."

"And thus passed into legend. Great story."

"Thought you'd like it."

"Did Jake Savage go alone on his last expedition?"

Gideon hesitated. "Savage had a partner who usually accompanied him."

"Did the partner die in the jungle, too?"

"Apparently. He didn't return, at any rate, but hardly anyone noticed. Savage was the big name."

"So his obit got all the attention."

"Right. Without him the company folded."

"All very interesting, but we don't need Jake Savage along on our expedition. We've got you."

"You must drive people nuts with all this boundless optimism and enthusiasm."

She bit her lip. "Am I driving you nuts?"

"Yeah. But don't worry about it. I haven't got anything better to do tonight."

She grinned. "I didn't think so."

Ten minutes later when he walked into the restaurant with Sarah Fleetwood beside him, it seemed to Gideon that every head in the place turned in his direction.

That wasn't strictly true, of course. The customers from out of town had no interest whatsoever in the very ordinary sight of a man walking into a restaurant with a woman. But all the locals, from the hostess to the busboy, were instantly intrigued. Gideon swore silently. He was not accustomed to being the center of attention and he didn't like it. It was all Sarah's fault.

"Nice to see you again, Gideon. It's been a while. Follow me, please." Maryann Appley, the young hostess, smiled very brightly as she led the way to a seat by the window. "I hope you enjoy your dinner, ma'am," she added to Sarah as she pulled out the chair.

"Thanks, I will," Sarah said cheerfully, reaching for the menu. "Look, they do have linguine and clams. What luck." As soon as the hostess disappeared she leaned forward. "Why is everyone staring?" she asked in a stage whisper.

"It's been a while since I brought a lady here." Gideon picked up his menu.

"Oh." She looked thoughtful. "Does that mean you don't date much?"

"It's a small community. Not many single women around. They all head for Portland or Los Angeles because there aren't many single men around here, either."

"There's you."

Gideon looked up. "What are you trying to do? Figure out why I'm not married?"

Sarah blushed a charming shade of peach and looked down at her silverware. "I suppose so. Frankly, I couldn't believe my good luck when I realized from your first letter that you weren't married."

"I don't recall mentioning the fact."

"No, but I could tell. In my age group the men always seem to be married. Or if they're single it's because they've just recently been divorced and are all messed up in the head. Or they're gay." She looked briefly anxious.

"I'm not gay and I'm not recently divorced."

She relaxed back into her infectious smile. "Perfect."

"You think so?"

"Definitely. Have you ever been married, Gideon?"

"You get real personal, real quick, don't you?"

"Not normally but I feel like we've known each other for four whole months."

"Funny. I feel like I just met you today."

"I'm going too fast for you, aren't I?"

"That's one way of looking at it. What is all this personal stuff leading up to? You planning to propose marriage to me?"

Sarah cleared her throat delicately and studied her menu. "Don't be ridiculous. It's much too soon for that."

Gideon stared at her, his head reeling. "Maybe we'd better take this one step at a time."

"My thoughts exactly. We don't want to terrorize you."

"I'm beyond terror. I'm in the Twilight Zone. I feel the way Machu Picchu did the day Ellora arrived on the doorstep."

Sarah laughed and closed her menu with a snap. Her eyes sparkled as she studied him across the table. "What did Ellora do first?"

"Moved right in on Machu's feed bowl. Normally, Machu would have bitten off the head of any intruder who got within twenty yards of his food."

"But not Ellora."

"No. That's when I knew we were done for. I think she baffled him at first. By the time he figured out what was going on, it was too late. She was a permanent resident. You ever been married?"

That caught her off guard. Gideon experienced a definite twinge of satisfaction at having finally achieved the near impossible. He had a feeling Sarah was almost never caught flat-footed. She was too quick, too animated, always one step ahead. A sideways thinker. He watched as she played with a fork for a minute.

"I was almost married once," she said finally. "About four years ago."

"What happened?"

"Got stood up at the altar."

He was astounded. "Literally?"

"Literally. Very embarrassing, to be honest. Church full of people. Spectacular dress. Reception waiting. And no groom. It was all very dramatic, I assure you. Enough to put a woman off marriage for life. But nothing is ever wasted for a writer. One of these days, I'm going to do a romance that starts out with the heroine being left at the altar. Snappy beginning, don't you think?"

"How's it going to end?"

"At the altar, of course. With the right man this time."

"But you're not ready to write that story yet?" he asked on a hunch.

"No. The whole experience left me feeling a little raw, if you want to know the truth. Even if it was all my own fault."

Gideon scowled. "What do you mean, your own fault?"

"You're suddenly full of questions. Does this mean you're not bored?"

"You might be a pain in the neck at times, Sarah, but I seriously doubt you could ever manage to be boring."

"I'll take that as a compliment."

"You didn't answer my question."

She sighed and appeared to be marshaling her thoughts. Gideon got the feeling she was just about to open her mouth when Bernice Sawyer, the waitress, arrived to take their order. He swore silently.

"I'll have the linguine and clams," Sarah announced. "And please tell Mort I was thrilled to see it on the menu. I love linguine and clams."

Bernice blinked. "Uh, sure, I'll tell him. How about you, Gideon?"

"The salmon," he told her dourly, wishing she would go away so he could get the answer to his question.

"Right. Salmon. As usual." Bernice smiled, undaunted by his obvious irritation. "Glass of wine?"

"Yes, please," said Sarah instantly.

"Why not?" Gideon thrust the menu at Bernice, hoping she'd take the hint and leave quickly.

"Be right back," she promised and sauntered off in the direction of the kitchen.

"Really, Gideon, there's no need to be rude," Sarah murmured in a low, chiding tone.

"Was I?"

"Yes, you were."

Bernice materialized again with the wine. Gideon possessed himself in patience until Sarah had taken a sip. When her gaze went toward the view of rocks and crashing surf, he tried again. "So why was it all your fault?"

"I beg your pardon?" She looked politely blank, as if she hadn't followed his train of thought.

Gideon knew instantly she was faking it. "Getting left at the altar. Why was it your fault?"

"Umm. Well, I should have seen it coming." She took another sip of wine.

"You've already told me you're not exactly psychic. How could you have seen it coming?"

"For a man who thought I was coming on a little too strong a while ago, you're awfully interested in my private life all of a sudden."

"Think of this as an interview. I'm still trying to make up my mind about whether or not to accept your offer of a job."

Sarah smiled. "How is my answering your question going to tell you what sort of employer I'll be?"

"I won't know until I hear the answer."

She drummed her fingers on the table, contemplating that. "It's hard to explain. I just knew later that I should have understood Richard didn't really want to marry me. He was on the rebound and he only thought he wanted to marry me."

"How did you feel toward him?"

"Well, you have to understand that I was at a point in my life when I was trying to be terribly realistic about relationships. I had convinced myself that the man of my dreams was pure fiction and I would only get hurt looking for him. Richard was sexy and charming and very nice, really. We had a lot in common and he gave me a whirlwind courtship. Very romantic."

"What happened?"

"The night before our wedding his ex-wife decided she had made a mistake and called him up. He went to meet her. I thought he was going off to his bachelor party. Some bachelor party. At any rate, he didn't show up the next day in church. All for the best, of course. Imagine getting married and then having him change his mind."

"Richard sounds like a real son of a—"

"That is, naturally, one point of view. I'm inclined toward it, myself." Sarah's eyes gleamed with mischief. "The reason the whole thing shook me up so much was that I'd never really made that kind of mistake before. I had plenty of warning and enough hints that he was still emotionally tangled up with his ex-wife, but I didn't pay any attention to them. I felt like an idiot later."

Gideon eyed her thoughtfully. "It threw a scare into you, that's what really happened. You'd always relied heavily on your intuition and it failed you."

"No. I keep telling you, my intuition was fine. I just wasn't paying attention."

"You got a scare. It should have taught you a good lesson about trusting your so-called intuition, but I'll bet you didn't learn a damn thing from the experience."

For the first time since she had landed like a whirlwind in his life, she looked genuinely annoyed with him. "Look, Gideon…"

"Forget it," Gideon said. "This brings us to the little matter of your hiring me as a treasure-hunting consultant."

"It does?"

He was finally beginning to feel like he was catching up with her. At this rate, he might even gain the upper hand for a few breathless minutes. "It does," he confirmed. "It's obvious that you can't really be any more sure of me than you were of this jerk, Richard."

"Not the same thing at all."

"How do you know?"

"I know."

"Got a feeling, right?" he mocked.

"Yes, I do, damn it. Don't make fun of me, Gideon."

"I wouldn't think of it."

She glowered at him. "And don't, whatever you do, turn out to be one of those people who *lectures*."

"God forbid." He sat back and swirled the wine in his glass. So much for trying to make her think twice about the whole project. He wasn't sure why he had bothered. Maybe just to see how deep her certainty ran.

"That was the only thing that worried me a tad, you know," she said finally.

"I've lost you again. What was the only thing that worried you?"

"That you might have a tendency to lecture. I picked that up here and there in some of your letters. But it's a relatively minor flaw and one I'm sure we can work around."

"You think so?" Gideon met her mischievous gaze and the vague tension that had been gnawing at him for several hours suddenly coalesced into a powerful urge to take her into his arms and wipe some of that feminine assurance out of her eyes. He knew just how he would kiss her. Hard and deep and very thoroughly.

"I think so. Say, I've been meaning to ask, did you ever try that recipe for buckwheat noodles I sent you last month?"

"No. The local stores don't run to fancy stuff like buckwheat noodles."

"You should have told me. I'd have sent you some."

"I was thinking about it," he admitted. "But you showed up on my doorstep before I got around to writing the letter." No point telling her that all the recipes she'd sent him during the past four months were neatly filed in a kitchen drawer. He took them out and read through them regularly but he had never actually tried one.

"I see."

Gideon watched her closely. "You're determined to go after the Flowers, aren't you?"

"Absolutely."

"What will you do if I don't agree to come along?"

"Gideon, I'm counting on you to help me."

"Forget the big-eyed approach. I don't respond to it." Like hell. His whole body was responding. "Any idea how much the earrings are worth?" he asked casually.

"Not really, but I'm sure it's a great deal. Each pair was made out of a different gemstone. One pair was made out of sapphires, one out of rubies, one out of diamonds, one out of opals and one out of pearls. The story is that Emelina Fleetwood knew she would never marry and she was determined to give herself the kind of jewels a rich husband would have given her. She wanted to prove she didn't need a man to shower her in luxury. She could do it all by herself."

"And you want to follow in her footsteps?"

Sarah frowned. "Not exactly. I don't think you understand. The Fleetwood Flowers are a piece of history, my personal history."

"You're really fixated on those earrings, aren't you?"

"They're family heirlooms. Naturally I'm interested in them."

"Sure. Family heirlooms. They hold no monetary interest for you at all, do they? Just pure historic value. I suppose you're going to tell me you're not going to sell them if you find them?"

Sarah put down her glass of wine with great care. The laughter had completely vanished from her eyes. "What is this?" she asked quietly. "You think I'm some sort of opportunist? A gold digger? A scheming little hussy trying to get rich quick?"

"I didn't say that."

"You don't have to say it." Her gaze narrowed. "Look at it this way, Gideon. Unlike most treasure hunters, I'm at least going after a fortune that belongs to me."

"You think that because those earrings belonged to someone in your family who lived way back in the late eighteen hundreds that you now have a claim on them?"

"More of a claim than anyone else."

"I've got news for you. Treasure that old belongs to whoever is clever enough to dig it up."

"I plan to be the one who's clever enough to dig it up."

"Take it from me. Amateurs never find real treasure. You'll be wasting your time, Sarah."

"I was right. You do have a tendency to harangue."

Gideon glanced up and saw Bernice heading toward the table. "Let's change the subject. Here comes our fish."

Sarah lifted her eyes ceilingward in an expression of utter disgust and snapped back in her chair. "Wouldn't want to spoil your appetite."

"You won't."

Five minutes of oppressive silence followed. Gideon decided he wasn't going to be the one to break it. The salmon was good, as usual. Mort really could cook.

"Gideon?"

"Yeah?"

"You don't really think me a cheap, scheming opportunist just because I want to find the Flowers, do you? Do you genuinely believe I'm just trying to use you?"

He put down his fork. "I'm not sure what to think. It's possible you've spent the past four months establishing a sort of relationship with me so that when you finally asked for help, I'd be more likely to say yes and work cheap."

"Damn. It never occurred to me you'd see things in that light. I was so sure…"

He picked up his fork again. "You're an unusual woman, Sarah. And that's putting it politely. I don't know what to make of you, yet."

"I really have got you terrorized," she said, her voice unnaturally flat.

"I wouldn't say that."

"Does this mean you truly aren't interested in helping me find the Flowers?"

"I didn't say that."

"Well, what are you trying to say, for heaven's sake?"

"Don't get mad."

"I'm not mad. I just want to know where I stand. Are you going to help me or not?"

"I'm still thinking about it."

"Was your ex-wife a gold digger?" Sarah demanded suddenly. "Is that why I'm making you nervous? Do I look like her or something?"

"No, you definitely do not look like her. Leanna liked success in whatever form it took and she liked flash. But I wouldn't call her a gold digger. She had too much class for that."

"Flash? What do you mean by flash?"

"Never mind. Eat your linguine."

"Gideon, are you going to help me with my treasure hunt or not? Tell me now. I don't take suspense well."

"You should, since you write it."

"That's different. What's your answer?"

"I don't know yet. I'll let you know later."

"Oh, yeah?" She glowered at him. "I'm not so sure I need or want your answer now or later."

"Okay."

"Don't be so bloody difficult, Gideon. Let's just forget the whole thing."

"Fine."

Her fingers clenched around her fork. "I can't believe I was so wrong about you. Can't we at least talk about this some more?"

"Not right now. I said I'd give you my answer later and I will. Let's talk about something else."

"Like what?"

He shrugged. "Pick a topic."

She paused. "All right. What kind of academic background do you have?"

"Does it matter?"

"I was just curious. You said to pick a topic. I picked a topic. If you don't like it, you're free to choose another."

"School of hard knocks. I graduated with honors." When she said nothing in response, Gideon began to feel guilty. He had only himself to blame for sabotaging her buoyant spirits. "What about you?"

"Does it matter?"

He winced. "No. Just trying to make conversation."

"I've got a better idea. Let's not try. I think it would be best if we both shut up for a while."

This time the silence that hung over the table stretched until Bernice arrived with the check.

Well, Trace, you've managed to dazzle her with your usual devastating charm, haven't you? You're hell on wheels with the female of the species, all right. You had to work real hard this time, didn't you? She didn't get discouraged easily. You had to really push. But now you've done it. You've managed to turn her off completely. Nice going. Even Machu had the sense not to screw up this badly when Ellora turned up on the doorstop.

Gideon was startled at the unexpected sense of loss he felt.

THE MAN MUST HAVE BEEN MAULED rather thoroughly at some point in the past, Sarah decided some time later. She sat quietly in the passenger seat of Gideon's car as he drove back to her motel. She no longer knew what to say. She couldn't believe she had been so wrong about him, but there was no doubt he didn't seem to want to have much to do with her.

Had she misjudged him completely?

It was possible. She had managed to fool herself once before.

Another curtain of fog was closing in from the sea as Gideon parked his car in front of Sarah's room. A yellow lamp illuminated the number on her door. She started to dig out her keys without much enthusiasm.

"Good night," Sarah made herself say without any emotion. "Sorry I took up so much of your time. Good luck with your magazine. Maybe I'll contact you again some day if I ever decide to do another treasure hunt story."

Gideon didn't move from behind the wheel. He just sat there, large and forbidding in the deep shadows. "Is the offer still open?"

Sarah's hand froze on the door handle. "Yes."

"I'll take the job."

"Gideon." All the doubts of a moment before dissolved in a second. Without a moment's hesitation she threw herself across the seat and into his arms.

Chapter Three

IT CAME AS A DISTINCT SHOCK TO SARAH when Gideon's arms abruptly tightened around her in a crushing grip. His mouth came down over hers with devastating swiftness as he pinned her against the back of the seat.

Belatedly she tried to pull away from the overwhelming embrace as she realized what she had initiated. She had been intending only a quick, impulsive, friendly hug. She should have known better than to let herself get this close to him. She was too vulnerable.

It had finally dawned on her over dinner that Gideon had not fallen for her during the past four months the way she had fallen for him. Her letters had meant nothing to him. He had not been thinking about her as anything more important than just another *Cache* subscriber asking for assistance. He was nowhere near ready for a relationship.

But now she found herself trapped in an embrace that was more shatteringly intimate than any she had ever known. It was only a kiss, her mind cried out. But she had never been kissed like this. It was, after all, her first kiss from Gideon. Gideon with whom she had slowly, surely fallen in love during the past few months.

Gideon, her own personal dream hero come to life.

Except that he didn't see himself in quite the same light. What's more, he saw her as a nuisance.

"Gideon?" She could barely speak his name. She gripped his shoulders with feverish intensity as four months of gathering desire welled up inside and threatened to swamp her.

"You're so delicate and fragile," Gideon muttered against her mouth. His hands moved over her with incredible sensitivity, learning the shape and feel of her. "I could crush you."

"You won't." She could not think clearly now that he had finally touched her. She clung to him even more tightly, her arms curving around his neck, her head tipped back against the seat. He was so wonderfully solid and substantial—so real. She'd known all along she couldn't have been wrong about him. Perhaps he was finally beginning to realize it, too.

His mouth moved against hers again. The kiss was far more satisfying than she had dared to dream it would be. There was an exciting, intoxicating hunger in him that she responded to instantly. She felt the edge of his teeth nibbling on her lower lip and she trembled.

He held her in a grip of iron, as if he was afraid she would evaporate. One of his hands slid down to her hip, squeezing gently. She splayed her fingers over his broad shoulders, savoring the strong, smoothly muscled contours. The masculine power in him drew her like a magnet. She moved beneath his crushing weight.

"Sarah?" His voice was ragged.

She murmured softly, a small, choked cry of delight and need.

"It's okay, Sarah," Gideon said harshly. "You don't have to fake it."

Sarah froze as if someone had just poured ice water over her. Frantically she tried to pull her scattered senses back into a coherent pattern of thought.

"Fake it?" she gasped. "What do you mean, fake it?"

"I've already said I'll help you look for the earrings. You don't have to pay me off with sex."

She struggled frantically to wriggle out of his arms. When he didn't release her, she managed to get one hand free. She swung wildly, aiming for the side of his face.

The blow never landed. Gideon caught her wrist when her palm was less than two inches from the target. "There are limits, lady. I'll be damned if I'll let you slap me."

"Let me go." She was frightened now, thoroughly aware for the first time of just how vulnerable she was.

"You started this, remember?"

"Get away from me, Gideon. Go back to your big, cold house and your cats. I don't need you to help me find those earrings. I'll do just fine on my own."

He looked down at her as she lay trapped and helpless in his arms. His eyes glittered with dangerous, unreadable emotions. Sarah held her breath.

Then, very slowly, he released her.

Sarah didn't hesitate. She scooted rapidly across the seat and yanked at the door handle.

"Wait." Gideon leaned across the seat and snagged her wrist, effectively chaining her when she tried to get out of the car.

"Let go of me."

His hard face tightened. "You're a temperamental little thing, aren't you? Simmer down. I've said I'll help you and I will. What did you expect me to think was going on a few minutes ago when you threw yourself into my arms?"

"You weren't supposed to think anything sordid or cheap or tacky about me, that's for sure." Sarah stared stonily ahead at the yellow light over her motel door. "I tend to be impulsive when it comes to things like affectionate little hugs."

"That was no affectionate little hug we had going there."

"You're the one who tried to turn it into something more. And then you had the nerve to throw it in my face when I...when I... Never mind."

He swore softly. "Would it help if I said I'm sorry?"

She slid a sidelong glance at him. "Are you?"

"Yeah."

"For kissing me or for what you said afterward?"

He was silent for a heartbeat. "Not for kissing you."

"How about for calling me an opportunist and a gold digger earlier?"

His mouth kicked up wryly at the corner. "I didn't call you those things."

"You implied them. Are you sorry for that, too?"

"I guess."

She wrinkled her nose. "You sound like a five-year-old. *I guess I'm sorry for that, too.* But you aren't. Not really. Because deep down you still wonder if I am just a cheap, hustling bimbo looking for a fast buck. You have sadly disappointed me, Gideon."

"I can see that," he said dryly. "Obviously I'm not turning out to be heroic material. Let's forget about the personal side of this for a minute. Do we still have a deal?"

She tried to tug her wrist out of his grasp and got nowhere. "I don't know. Now I'm the one who will have to think about it. Your attitude is changing everything. I'll give you my answer in the morning."

"You do that. And one other thing. If I go with you on this treasure hunt, it won't be as your employee. I don't work for anyone. We'll be partners. I won't be taking salary from you."

"What do you want?"

"I'll want a share of whatever treasure we find."

She scowled at him. "But you've already said we probably won't find anything."

"I'll take my chances. Are you willing to split the profits?"

"Well, I don't know. I hadn't actually planned to sell the earrings. I was going to keep them."

"Fine. You keep four pairs. I'll take the fifth. My choice of the lot."

"I'm not sure that's fair. What if one pair turns out to be far more valuable than the others in today's market? The diamond pair, for instance?"

"That's the risk you take."

"I don't have to take any risk at all, Gideon. I'm the one with the map, remember?"

"Expert advice doesn't come cheap."

"You've already told me you're not a professional treasure hunter. You just write about treasure hunting."

"I'm a lot more professional than you are."

Her resentment flared. "Too bad I can't get hold of the famous Jake Savage, isn't it? Then I wouldn't need you."

His mouth thinned. "You said you thought I'd do just fine, remember?"

She wrenched her wrist free of his grasp at last and shoved open the car door. "I'll make my decision in the morning."

He didn't try to stop her as she stalked toward her room, flexing her hand to see if her wrist still functioned. It did. He hadn't really hurt her. He was a powerful man but one who was very much in control of his own strength.

Just like one of her heroes.

She refused to give Gideon the satisfaction of glancing back over her shoulder as she opened the door of her room.

He didn't start the car until she was safely inside. Hurrying over to the window, she peeked through a small opening in the curtains to watch as he drove off into the night.

When the parking lot was silent again she switched on a light and sank down on the edge of the bed to think.

No doubt about it. Her impulsiveness and blind faith in her own intuition had gotten her in trouble again. She had moved too fast without taking the time to analyze just what she was dealing with.

Just because she had started to fall in love with Gideon Trace from the moment she had opened his first letter did not mean that she understood him. The man was turning out to be much more of an enigma than she had anticipated. The fact that he could even begin to suspect her motives was proof of that. She did not see how he could possibly doubt her.

Sarah twisted her hands in her lap, aware of a chilled feeling in the room that was not entirely a result of the gathering fog outside. She did not want to face the obvious, but she had to force herself to do so.

She had to wonder if she was making the same kind of mistake she'd made with Richard. She had to wonder if she was turning a blind eye to the obvious warnings.

Margaret was right. Impulsiveness was a dangerous quality.

With a wretched sigh, Sarah got to her feet and went about the business of getting ready for bed. There was nothing she could do tonight. She would wait and see if dawn brought a clearer notion of how to handle the situation.

GO BACK TO YOUR BIG, COLD HOUSE and your cats.

Hours later it occurred to Gideon that he had been sitting for a long time in the darkened living room. There was a half-empty glass of brandy on the table in front of him. Ellora was curled up against his thigh, purring contentedly. Machu Picchu was stretched full length across the back of the sofa.

Gideon hadn't bothered to turn on any lights. It was almost midnight. And the house was cold. He wondered if it was worth building a fire.

"The place was just fine until she arrived. It didn't seem cold at all until after she'd been in it and left," he told the cats.

Machu flicked his ears, not bothering to open his eyes. Ellora slithered around a bit until she was more comfortable.

"No offense, but you two aren't the world's greatest conversationalists."

Gideon got up off the sofa. He picked up the brandy glass and walked over to the table where the chess pieces had been set out. Idly he fingered the wooden figures for a moment and then he set them out in a slightly different pattern.

Machu rumbled inquiringly.

"Think she'd have made the deal with Jake Savage if the bastard was still around, Machu? Savage always had a way with women. He sure wouldn't have screwed up the way I did tonight. He'd have charmed her straight into bed."

Machu didn't answer but his gem-hard eyes watched Gideon intently.

"You and me, we're not exactly loaded with charm, are we, pal?" Gideon studied the new positions of the wooden figures. The balance of power had now shifted to his side of the board. "But Savage isn't here. I am. And she wants the Flowers. I can lead her to them. The question is, do I really want to get mixed up with her? We've been doing pretty well here on our own."

Ellora lifted her head and meowed silently.

"So why does the house seem cold, damn it? It's almost summer."

GIDEON TRACE WAS AT SARAH'S DOOR before she had even finished dressing for the day in a pair of white jeans and a lemon-yellow shirt. Deliberately she made him wait while she anchored her hair in an off-center twist over one ear. Then she went to open the door.

"Hi." She offered nothing further. He looked larger than ever standing there in the cold, gray light of a new day.

"Good morning." Gideon braced himself with one hand against the doorjamb. "Make up your mind, yet?"

"I had no idea you were waiting on pins and needles."

He gave her his faint, twisted smile. "I know I'm early. I was afraid if I left it too long, you'd sneak off to go after the Flowers without me."

"I was only going to sneak as far as the coffee shop." She turned to pick up her windbreaker, aware that he was scanning her room from the doorway. She was suddenly very conscious of her nightgown lying in a heap on the bed, the open suitcase with a sock trailing out of it and the collection of toilet articles littering the dresser. She closed the door very quickly.

"I'll join you for breakfast," Gideon said. "I didn't get a chance to eat before I left the house this morning."

"Your own fault." She locked the door behind her and started across the street to the small coffee shop. The lights were just coming on inside. To the right, the narrow, two-lane road vanished around a bend into the fog-shrouded trees.

"You hold a mean grudge, don't you?" Gideon paced beside her. His hands were thrust into the pockets of a sheepskin jacket.

Sarah said nothing more until they were seated in a booth in the corner of the coffee shop. She studied Gideon for a long moment, remembering all the fleeting thoughts, hopes and dreams that had come to her in the night. She fought back the sense of longing that threatened to over-whelm her and tried to make herself speak coolly and log-ically. There would be no more impulsiveness on her part, she vowed silently.

"Let me get this straight," she said. "You think I'm an opportunist who uses sex to get what she wants, but you're willing to help me search for the earrings if you get to keep one pair for yourself, right?"

His big hands folded around the mug in front of him and his eyes met hers in a level gaze. "I'll help you search for the earrings. Let's leave it at that."

"All right. I guess that makes us both opportunists, doesn't it? At last we have something in common."

He stared at her unblinkingly, the way Machu Picchu would stare at a mouse. "We're in this together? We've got a deal?"

"Sure. Why not? I came to you in the first place because I don't know anything about treasure hunting. You do. That makes you very useful to me and I'm willing to bar-gain with you for your talents. Since you claim it's unlikely we'll ever find the earrings, I'm getting a heck of a deal, aren't I? If there aren't any profits in this, I won't have to split anything with you."

"I see you've decided on the role of tough little cookie this morning. Just for the record, it doesn't suit you." Gideon took a swallow of his coffee.

"You like me better as a scheming little seductress?"

He grinned reluctantly. "I really ruffled your feathers, didn't I?"

She glared at him. "I made a serious mistake in dealing with you the way I did yesterday. I can see that now. I should have been restrained and businesslike right from the start. Unfortunately that's not my normal nature."

"I gathered that much."

"That does not mean, however, that I can't behave in a restrained and businesslike manner when I put my mind to it."

He looked frankly disbelieving. "Think so?"

"Of course. And a restrained, adult, businesslike manner is precisely what I will project from now on. No nonsense. I shall just think of you as a business partner and deal with you as I would with one." She put her hand across the table. "Very well, Mr. Trace, we have a deal."

He stared down at her extended palm and then slowly reached out to solemnly shake her hand. She allowed him to crush her fingers for about two seconds and then she quickly withdrew her hand to safety. "What about your cats?"

He shrugged. "They'll be fine for a week or so. I've left them on their own before. My neighbor will check their food and water."

"How long will you need to pack?"

"I packed last night."

"You're suddenly very eager for the hunt."

"When do you want to leave?"

She took a breath. "I'll be ready as soon as I settle the motel bill."

"Fine. We'll take my car. You can leave yours at my place."

Sarah looked at him and wondered if she was really intuitive or just plain crazy.

Half an hour later she signed the credit card slip in the motel office while Gideon waited out in the parking lot, leaning against the fender of his car.

"You a close friend of Trace's?" The inquisitive-eyed little clerk glanced out the window and back at Sarah. He was a thin, balding man in his sixties, dressed in brown polyester pants and an aging polo shirt. He had been pleasant enough, but it was clear he had a keen interest in local gossip.

"We're business associates," Sarah said crisply. She finished her scrawling signature with her usual flourish.

"Business associates, huh? Didn't know Gideon had any business associates. Thought he worked on that treasure-hunting magazine of his all by himself."

Sarah smiled loftily. "He's acting as a consultant for me. I'm doing some research on treasure hunting for a book."

"That right? Interestin'. Never met a real-life writer before. Except for Gideon, of course. And he don't exactly write books, just articles for that magazine of his. The two of you goin' somewhere together?"

"A business trip."

"Right. A business trip." The clerk chuckled knowingly. "Wished we'd had business trips like that in my day. Well, at least this time Trace won't be goin' off alone on one of his business trips."

That stopped Sarah just as she started to turn away toward the door. "He's gone off on trips before?"

"Well, sure. 'Bout once a year he just ups and disappears for a while. Sometimes as long as a month." The clerk winked. "I asked him once where he went and he said on vacation. You the one he's been vacationin' with all these years?"

"I don't really think that's any of your business." Sarah closed the door behind her on the sound of the desk clerk's cackling laughter.

Gideon straightened away from the fender and unfolded his arms. He scowled. "Old Jess give you a hard time?"

"Not really."

"Why's he falling all over himself laughing in there?"

"He thinks he's a stand-up comedian."

They drove both cars back to the big old house on the bluff. Machu Picchu sat placidly on the top step watching as Gideon transferred Sarah's luggage from her car to his. Ellora flitted about with an air of delicate concern. The silver-gray cat hung around Sarah, tangling herself up between Sarah's feet and asking to be picked up and held.

When Sarah obligingly lifted Ellora into her arms, the cat purred.

"I think she wants to come along," Sarah announced.

"That's all we'd need. A couple of cats to keep track of while we're traipsing around the Cascades. Forget it. The cats are just fine staying here by themselves."

Sarah held the cat up so she could look Ellora straight in the eye. "Hear that? You have to stay behind. But we'll miss you."

There was a low, grumbling cat roar from the top step. Sarah glanced over and saw Machu looking more cold-eyed than ever. "You, too, Machu. You take good care of Ellora while we're gone."

Machu Picchu looked away, his ears low on his broad head, tail moving in a slow, restless arc.

"He hasn't got the most charismatic personality in the world," Gideon said, "but you can count on old Machu. He'll do a good job of taking care of Ellora and watching over the place, won't you, pal?" Gideon scratched the oversized cat briefly behind the ears. Machu tolerated the caress in stony silence.

"When you're that big, you don't have to be charming, I suppose," Sarah said with a small smile.

"Does that logic apply to human males or just to cats?" Gideon asked.

"Just to cats." Sarah made a production out of checking the back seat of her car. "I guess that's everything," she said a little uneasily as she realized she was about to be cooped up with Gideon for several hours.

"Don't lose your nerve now." Gideon calmly locked his front door.

"I wasn't losing my nerve."

"Having second thoughts?"

"A few."

"Don't worry. Something tells me you're going to like the treasure-hunting business. It's tailor-made for bright-eyed, gullible types like you."

Sarah paid him no attention as she patted Ellora one last time. "Goodbye, Ellora. Don't let that beast push you around too much."

Ellora purred more loudly, looking not the least bit concerned about being bullied by Machu Picchu. When Sarah put her down she trotted over to the steps and bounded up to station herself beside the big cat. Machu unbent so far as to touch noses with her in greeting. Then his big tail curved around her neat hindquarters. Ellora looked shamelessly smug.

"Are you sure they'll be all right?"

"They'll be fine. Stop looking for an excuse to delay things. We've got a long drive ahead of us."

Sarah slid into the front seat and adjusted her seat belt. "I have to tell you, Gideon, that your sudden enthusiasm for this venture is making me nervous. What changed your mind? Did you decide the map and the legend are real, after all?"

"I figure it's worth a shot." He swung the car out onto the narrow highway. He was silent for a minute or two before he said, "Couple of things you ought to know about treasure hunting, Sarah."

"And you're going to tell me what I should know, right?"

"Right."

"I've told you, I don't like being lectured."

"You came to me for advice. I intend to earn my share of the loot."

"*If* we find it."

"I thought you were already sure we would." He gave her a fleeting, mildly derisive glance.

She ignored that. The truth was, she was almost certain they would find the Flowers. The problem now was what might happen when they did. "All right, expert. Tell me the couple of things I ought to know about the treasure-hunting business."

"The most important thing is that we don't make a public production out of it. The less attention we attract, the better, especially if we do get lucky."

"Why?"

"Use your head, Sarah. If we do find the Flowers, we're talking about a tidy little fortune in gemstones. People have killed for less, believe me."

That shocked her. "Good grief, I never thought of that."

"Somehow that doesn't surprise me."

"I can't believe we'd attract the attention of a killer."

"That's the worst possible case. It's far more likely we'd attract the interest of other treasure hunters, curious tourists and little kids who would want to follow us around and watch while we dig. There might also be legal complications. Do you know who owns the old Fleetwood property now?"

She smiled, vastly pleased with herself. "Yeah. Me."

"You do?" That obviously startled him.

"I bought it two months ago. It was incredibly cheap because it has no real value. It's lousy farmland by today's standards and it's not a good building site for a modern home. I'll sell it right after we find the Flowers."

Gideon whistled softly. "I'm impressed."

"About time."

"All right, you've taken care of the major complication, the legal ownership of the land. But I still recommend we keep our plans quiet. Nothing pulls attention like a hunt for real treasure and attention usually means trouble for small operations like ours. If this were a major salvage operation to find a sunken ship, that would be one thing. We'd want investment money and plenty of media hype. But the two of us operating alone are highly vulnerable. We go in and we get out without making waves."

Sarah debated briefly the wisdom of confiding that she'd mentioned the Flowers to one Jim Slaughter of Slaughter Enterprises and then decided not to say anything to Gideon. After all, she'd definitely told Slaughter she wasn't interested in either hiring him to help her find the earrings or in financing his downed-airplane-full-of-gold project. He was definitely out of the picture and if she mentioned him to her new consultant, Gideon might get nervous. Things were tricky enough at best right now.

"Okay," Sarah said easily. "Very low profile. I understand. I figure we'll just check into a couple of rooms at a motel in the little mountain town that's near the property. We'll make the motel our home base. Who's going to notice our coming and going?"

"Probably everyone in town," Gideon said.

Sarah thought about that. "You really think so?"

"Yes."

"Well, what do you suggest we do?" she asked, irritated. "Camp out? I warn you, I'm not big on roughing it."

"We don't need to go as far as setting up a tent."

"Thank heavens." Sarah shuddered.

"My suggestion is that we act like a couple of city folks on vacation in the mountains. You know, tourists who've come to take photographs of the spring wildflowers."

"I didn't bring my camera."

"I brought one."

"That was very clever of you," she said with genuine admiration.

His brows rose. "Thanks. Wait until you hear the rest of the cover story."

"Cover story." Sarah tasted the words, her excitement reawakening rapidly. "I've always wanted to have a cover story. What's ours?"

"As I said, a couple of people on vacation." He shot her a cool, assessing glance. "But it's going to look strange if we don't act like a real couple. A man and a woman traveling together are either lovers or business associates. Since we don't want anyone to know we're business associates, we have to look like lovers."

Sarah turned her head to stare at him in amazement. "What on earth are you trying to say, Gideon?"

His expression hardened. "We can't risk taking separate motel rooms the way you planned. Someone might notice and start asking why we always take off together during the day but don't sleep together at night."

"Oh." She tried to absorb that slowly.

"The legend of the Flowers is not unknown in the region where we're going. Someone with enough curiosity might put two and two together and decide to follow us. If they did, they'd see us head for the old Fleetwood property to dig every day and then we'd have problems."

"You're suggesting we pass ourselves off as a couple of lovers? You think I'm going to share a room with you? After the way you've been treating me? Forget it, Gideon."

"Don't get upset. This is business, remember? I'm not saying you have to sleep with me."

"How very accommodating of you." Sarah crossed her arms under her breasts. "I don't like this cover story. Come up with another one."

"It's the best one I can come up with at the moment." He glanced at her again. "Oh, hell, Sarah, don't act like I've just threatened your virtue. All I'm saying is that the best cover we can have is to look like two people involved in a relationship who are on vacation in the mountains. Nobody will pay any attention to us."

"You do this a lot?"

"Hell, no. What makes you say that?"

"Old Jess, the motel clerk, said you have a habit of disappearing on vacation at least once a year."

"A man's got a right to get away for a while."

Sarah eyed him thoughtfully. Gideon looked annoyed but otherwise innocent of any lecherous intentions. "You're sure that traveling as a couple is the only good way to handle this?"

"I think it's the best way under the circumstances." Gideon concentrated on watching a car in the side mirror. "Also the simplest. Simple explanations always work best."

"You sound very knowledgeable on the subject."

He shrugged. "Just using a little logic. Don't forget this is my field of expertise."

She chewed on that for a moment. "You guarantee separate beds?"

"For a woman who was convinced yesterday that I was the romantic hero of the century, you've sure changed your tune."

"Gideon, I'm warning you—"

"Sure. Separate beds. I've already taken care of it."

She sucked in her breath. "You have?"

"A friend of mine has a cabin up here that's not too far from your property. I called him last night. He said we could use it for a week."

Sarah felt dazed. She had the distinct feeling that she was somehow losing control of the situation. She tried to imagine what it would be like sleeping under the same roof with Gideon Trace and her mind reeled. If he'd been falling in love with her during the past four months the way she had with him, that would be one thing. But this business of a one-sided attraction was very dangerous.

On the other hand, the situation was fraught with tantalizing possibilities if she could just keep her head. She would have a chance to work on Gideon, a chance to let him get to know her.

"All right. I'll go along with your idea for the sake of our cover story," Sarah said with sudden decision.

He glanced at her and then shook his head in silent wonder. "You really are something, aren't you?"

"Why do you say that? Because I trust you enough to share a cabin with you?"

"Uh-huh."

"This is now a business relationship, right?"

"Right."

"Well, I've known you long enough to be quite certain you'll be an honest, dependable, reliable business partner."

"Amazing. As I said, you shouldn't be allowed out without a leash."

"Stop complaining. This is all your idea and you are the expert, aren't you?"

"I keep telling myself that."

Chapter Four

GIDEON RISKED A FEW GLANCES AT Sarah's face as he set the luggage on the bare floor of the rustic cabin. He closed the door carefully, unable to tell what she was thinking. He wondered if she was wrinkling her nose in that interesting fashion because she didn't like the looks of the old, run-down place or because she was starting to have a few additional reservations about sharing it with him.

Personally, he was still stunned by his own daring and astounded by the success of his small coup. He couldn't quite believe he'd pulled it off. *She was here with him under the same roof.* In fact, she'd hardly put up any argument at all.

He still didn't know whether to be insulted or delighted or irritated by her ready trust, though. It was possible she'd gone along with the idea of posing as a couple on vacation simply because she had written him off completely as a potential lover.

Or had she abandoned the notion of seduction as a tactic now that he'd agreed to go on the quest for a share of the profits? Either way, he had no reason to feel so euphoric. But he did.

The fact of the matter was that, after blundering in where an intelligent angel would fear to tread, Sarah had tried to pull back to safe territory and he had rather neatly prevented her from doing so. Gideon was quite pleased with himself. He had managed to salvage the situation after nearly wrecking it.

"Not much, is it?" He followed her glance around the cabin they had rented for a week. There was one bed in a small room off to the left and a sagging couch near the old brick hearth. The kitchen was tiny but it had a refrigerator and a stove and all the necessities. They wouldn't be forced to locate a restaurant every day.

"Actually it's quite picturesque." Sarah set down the bag of groceries she had bought en route to the cabin. She wandered over to the hearth, her hands thrust into the back pockets of her jeans. "Very atmospheric, in fact. A lonely cabin in the woods. Who knows what might have happened in a place like this in the past? Maybe one of these days I'll—"

"Use it in a book?"

She smiled briefly. "Yes."

"Think you'll ever use me in a book?"

"I already have. Several of them."

He wasn't sure how to take that, but it sounded positive. "The guy who rented this place to me said the couch pulled out into a bed. I'll take that."

"It doesn't look very comfortable."

"Is that an invitation to share the other bed with you?"

"Of course not," she snapped. "Don't tease, Gideon. This is a business relationship now, remember? That's the only kind of relationship you seem to want."

Sure. That's why I spent an hour on the phone last night trying to locate the owner of this place. That's why I agreed to pay him in-season rates even though it's not summer yet, Gideon thought. "Sorry about the cabin," he muttered gruffly. "I guess the motel rooms would have been more comfortable."

Sarah turned her head, her fey eyes registering surprise just before she stepped into the bedroom. "There's nothing wrong with the cabin. It's a perfect location for an adventure. This may be a business deal to you, Gideon, but for me finding the Flowers is still an exciting idea."

She closed the door before he could think of an adequate response.

Some time later, after a meal of ravioli with pesto sauce that Sarah had somehow magically produced in the kitchen amid incredible chaos, Gideon wandered around the cabin, checking the locks on the windows. They were about what he'd expected—not much better than paper clips.

Things seemed to have gotten off to a promising start. Of course there had been that one brief moment of panic on Sarah's part when she'd realized the kitchen didn't have a dishwasher but she'd calmed down when Gideon had made her an offer she couldn't refuse.

"You take care of the cooking and I'll handle the cleanup," he'd suggested.

"It's a deal. I told you that you had all the makings of a real hero," she'd retorted cheerfully.

He studied the decrepit sofa, wondering if it would fall apart completely when he pulled it out into a bed. He gave it a tentative yank.

It survived the jolt but the lumps did not look promising.

He stood looking down at it while he listened to Sarah rustling around in the bathroom. It had been a long time since he'd shared quarters with a woman. The realization of just how long it had been made him feel old.

On the other hand, the fact that he was getting aroused

just listening to Sarah undress behind the closed door had definite youthful implications. *You're only as old as you feel, Trace*. Right now he felt he could hold his own with any young stud of twenty. Too bad the lady was no longer throwing herself at him.

He had what he'd decided he wanted last night as he'd sat brooding in the shadows of his aging house. He'd set up this scene in his own heavy-handed way but now he wasn't certain how to play it. Sarah no longer showed any signs of wanting to be swept off her feet by him.

As usual, his timing was excellent with everything except women.

Gideon wondered if he'd lost his only shot at playing hero.

The door of the bathroom opened.

Sarah stood there enveloped in a green velour robe that she'd belted around her small waist. Her hair was loose around her shoulders and her face was freshly scrubbed. She looked touchingly vulnerable and at the same time incredibly sexy.

"It's all yours," she said as she headed toward the bedroom.

He figured she meant the bathroom, not the body in the velour robe. "Thanks." He knew he was staring. The bedroom door closed firmly.

Gideon sighed, picked up his shaving kit and headed for the bath. The small room was still warm and moist. He felt big and awkward standing in the middle of the tiny place, as if he had accidentally invaded a medieval maiden's private bower. A bright yellow toothbrush stood at attention in a glass on the sink and a hairbrush lay on the counter next to the toothpaste tube.

The top had been left off the toothpaste. Automatically Gideon replaced it.

Ten minutes later he went back out into the main room. No crack of light showed under the bedroom door. He stood for a moment, trying to think of something clever to do next. The only action that came readily to mind was to open the bedroom door and that was out of the question.

Business partners.

"Damn." So much for sweeping her off her feet. He wondered if she'd brought along any of her books that featured his doppelgänger as a hero. Maybe he could figure out how to proceed if he saw himself in action.

His mouth quirked ruefully as he undressed and slid into the cold, uncomfortable bed. It was disconcerting to think of himself as a hero in a novel of romantic suspense. *Be interesting to read the sex scenes.*

Half an hour later he was still awake, his hands folded behind his head, his mind playing with the image of Sarah wearing nothing but a pair of antique earrings, when the bedroom door opened softly. He went very still.

"Gideon?" Sarah's voice was low and hesitant.

"Yeah?"

"Are you asleep?"

"Not any more."

"Good. Because I've been thinking."

She came farther into the room. Gideon turned his head and looked at her in the shadows. He could just barely make out the fact that her feet were bare on the hardwood floor. Her hands were thrust into the sleeves of her robe.

"Something wrong?" he asked, wondering if she'd already seen through his flimsy excuse for sharing a cabin and had decided to complain.

"Yes." Her chin came up determinedly. "Yes, there is something wrong. Very wrong."

So much for his cleverness. "What is it, Sarah?"

"I have to know something." She started pacing the length of the room, looking more medieval than ever in the darkness as the robe floated around her small, bare ankles. "I realize that I should probably just let it go, but I can't. I have to find out what went wrong. I can't believe I was this mistaken a second time."

"Sarah..."

She stopped him with a raised hand. "Just tell me the truth and I promise I won't ask anything personal again." She went as far as she could in the small space available, swung around and started back in the other direction. "Why don't you trust me?"

That caught him off guard. "It's not a matter of trusting you," Gideon said cautiously.

"Yes, it is. You don't. Why?" She was still pacing. "I mean, is your inability to trust me based on some significant event in your past? Do you distrust all women? Did your marriage sour you on the female of the species? Or is it something about me, personally. Did I just come on too strong? Was that it? I know I'm not always subtle."

Gideon groaned. "Look, I'm not real good at conversations like this."

"Talk, Gideon. I've been your friend for four months. The least you can do is tell me why you still don't trust me."

"Damn it, why do you have to take it personally?"

"Because it is personal."

He began to get annoyed. "You're a demanding little thing, aren't you? Demanding and arrogant."

"Arrogant."

"Yeah, arrogant. Who do you think you are, Sarah Fleetwood? You just explode in my life like a firecracker. You tell me you think we're meant for each other on the basis of a handful of letters as if you're my mail-order bride or something and, oh, by the way, would I help you recover a fortune in lost jewels. And you wonder why I've got a few questions about your motives?"

She paused at the far end of the room again. He could see she was nibbling on her lower lip. "Put like that, it does sound a little strange, doesn't it?"

"Strange is right."

"I still think there's more to it than that." She resumed her pacing. "Are you sure there isn't something in your past that's making you extra cautious about trusting me?"

"Sarah, I'm forty years old. I'm not exactly a naive, trusting innocent. And if you had any sense, you wouldn't be, either. The world does not reward naïveté. I would have thought getting left at the altar would have taught you that much."

"I am not naive, damn it. And leave Richard out of this. You're evading the point."

"What do you want? A complete history of my life to date so you can psychoanalyze my reasons for being cautious about you? Don't hold your breath."

"What was your wife like?"

"Good Lord, you don't let go of something once you've glommed onto it, do you?"

"No. Was she pretty?"

"Yeah."

"Was she kind?"

That made Gideon flounder for a split second. He had never thought of Leanna as kind. She had been too wrapped up in her career and her own emotional problems to be kind to others. She had needed kindness, but she hadn't dispensed much of it. On the other hand she certainly hadn't been vicious, he reminded himself. Just a little mixed up about what she wanted.

"You think kindness is important in a beautiful, sexy woman?" he asked derisively.

"Of course, it is. It's important in anyone."

"What cloud have you been living on? Look, everyone liked Leanna and, as I recall, she was fond of small animals so she certainly couldn't have been unkind, right? She was also very intelligent, very attractive and very sophisticated."

"Oh."

Gideon smiled grimly in the darkness. Sarah sounded woefully disappointed. Obviously she'd been hoping to hear that Leanna was a bitch. But Leanna had not been a bitch, just an unhappy, confused young woman who'd turned to Gideon at a low point in her life and then realized her mistake.

"She was also published," he added, not knowing why he felt compelled to twist the knife. It was as though he had to find a way to rip through the iridescent veil of Sarah's bright-eyed optimism and discover what lay underneath.

"She wrote?" Sarah sounded more wretched than ever. "Like me?"

"No, not like you. She was an assistant professor at a small college in Oregon when I met her. She wrote articles on archaeology for academic journals."

"I see. Important, scholarly stuff." Sarah was obviously getting more depressed by the minute.

Gideon suddenly felt as if he'd been pulling wings off a fly. "The only problem Leanna and I had was that she wasn't in love with me. She just thought she was for a while. She tried, I'll give her credit for that."

"What happened, Gideon?"

"We split when she realized she loved someone else."

"Someone with flash, you said?"

"Did I?" Gideon frowned, remembering the brief conversation on previous marriages he'd had with Sarah yesterday. "I did say that, didn't I? Yeah. She found someone with flash and she went for it the way a trout goes for a bright, shiny lure."

"Did you try to stop her?"

"I tried to tell her she was making a mistake. The guy she fell for didn't have it in him to be faithful to any woman for long. I warned her she wasn't going to be happy with him. But she thought she could change him."

"She married him?"

"No. They got engaged as soon as our divorce was final, but he was killed before the marriage could take place."

"How sad. For all of you. But maybe that way Leanna never had a chance to find out what a louse he really was."

Gideon shrugged. "Maybe. I never saw her again after the divorce. I heard she remarried a couple of years ago. A college professor. With any luck she picked the right man this time."

"That's very generous of you," Sarah said with obvious admiration. Her voice glowed with approval.

"It is, isn't it?" He grinned briefly and was surprised by his own amusement. It was certainly the first time he'd ever found anything at all humorous about his divorce. Something about Sarah seeing him as benevolent, kind and generous was very entertaining, however.

"Does this mean you're not carrying a torch for her?" The hope in Sarah's voice was unmistakable.

"Carrying torches is a waste of time."

"Well, that's certainly true. Unless, of course, you're thinking of someday trying to fan the flames?"

"I'm not. I learned a long time ago never to look back."

There was silence from the far end of the room. Gideon could feel Sarah mulling over the information he had given her. Her head was bent in concentration.

"This man your ex-wife married," Sarah said at last, "the one with flash, was he a friend of yours, by any chance?"

Gideon didn't move. His momentary flare of amusement evaporated. "I knew him."

"Ah. So he was a friend of yours. A close friend?"

He didn't like the sound of that. "It's not what you think, Sarah."

"Sure it is." She obviously felt she had hold of something important now. She started pacing the floor again. "Your wife betrayed you with your best friend. Very simple. Tragic, but simple. It explains everything, especially your inability to trust me."

"What the hell are you talking about? Do you always leap to conclusions like this?"

"Sometimes. Gideon, having your wife betray you with your best friend is not a minor event. Wars have been fought over less."

"I'm not planning on starting any wars. Besides, I told you, the guy's dead and Leanna's remarried. There's nothing left to fight over even if I was so inclined."

"Which you're not. A very hopeful sign. Okay, now I think I've finally got a handle on our relationship. This is the curse from your past that needs lifting, isn't it? Just like in the story of 'Beauty and the Beast.'"

"What the hell are you talking about?"

"Relax, Gideon. I was just using a familiar metaphor from the old fairy tale. Put in modern terms, the fact is, I was missing some of this information from the beginning. That's why I botched up our initial meeting. It was all my fault. I rushed things."

Gideon was beginning to get that uneasy sense of being left behind in her dust again. "Sarah, don't go flying off on some new tangent, okay?"

She ignored him as she paced faster and faster. A fresh sense of anticipation was radiating from her in waves of energy Gideon could almost feel.

"I realize now you need plenty of time to get to know me so that you'll be able to see how totally different I am from both your best friend and your ex-wife," Sarah said.

"You've never even met either of them."

"That doesn't mean I can't figure out what their problems were."

"What is this? Instant psychoanalysis?"

"Common sense and a touch of intuition. I know a lot about you now, so I can make some good guesses about the other two people who were involved in this mess." Sarah spun around at the far end of the room and buzzed past Gideon, robe flying. "Let's take Leanna first: neurotic with problems of her own that she was trying to use a husband to resolve."

Gideon blinked owlishly, taken back by the accuracy of that comment. "Of all the idiotic conclusions," he growled. "You don't know what you're talking about. You don't know any of the people involved, except me."

"Knowing you is enough. Any woman who couldn't see what a terrific husband you'd make is immature, neurotic and probably trapped in her own emotional problems. I'm sorry to have to tell you that, Gideon, but I'm afraid it's the truth. How old was Leanna when you married her?"

He propped himself up on one elbow, scowling at her as she went whizzing past the bed again. "Twenty-five, I think, why?"

Sarah was nodding to herself. "Twenty-five going on seventeen. Some people, male and female, are still awfully immature at twenty-five. They often don't know what they really want. Some people go through their whole lives never knowing what they really want. Add to that immaturity a certain lack of brainpower or a lot of personal problems and you've got a powder keg of a marriage."

"I've already told you my ex was not exactly a dummy."

"I'm talking about common sense, not academic ability. There's a world of difference. It's common sense that makes people act intelligently, not education. All education does is give you a wider frame of reference to utilize when you're using your common sense to go over your options. A lot of people with Ph.D.'s make stupid decisions because they lack common sense. Now, then. Give me a minute to think this through."

"Take your time." Gideon was exasperated. He wondered how he'd ever gotten involved in this crazy discussion.

"Don't be sarcastic. This is important. Critical to our whole future together, in fact."

He shook his head, watching her in disbelief as she went to stand at the window. He was suddenly out of patience. If she came waltzing by the sofa one more time he was going to grab her and pull her down beside him. "Sarah, I don't know what's going through that weird brain of yours, but I think it would be best if you went back to bed."

She turned to face him. "Yes, you're probably right. I can finish thinking about this in my own room. No need to keep you awake while I go over all this information in detail. Good night, Gideon."

Anger surged through him. How dared she presume to analyze and dissect him like this? He made a grab for her as she glided past him on her way back to the bedroom.

He heard her soft gasp of surprise as his fingers locked around her wrist. "You think you know it all, don't you?" he muttered. He drew her inexorably toward him, playing seriously with the idea of dragging her down onto the bed. It would be so easy. She was so small and delicate.

"Gideon?" Her eyes were very wide now.

"Somebody ought to give you the lesson you need."

"You may be right," she agreed tremulously. "But, please, not tonight. I'm not sure I could handle it." She leaned down and gave him a quick, fleeting kiss on his cheek.

Gideon jerked back as if he'd been burned. Unthinkingly he released her. Sarah instantly sailed on past him into the safety of her bedroom. Gideon rubbed his cheek and scowled into the darkness as her door closed softly behind her.

Intent on inducing a little healthy fear in her, he had been expecting a struggle, not the small, gentle caress he had received. Her reaction had startled him and he'd let her go before he'd realized quite what he was doing, he told himself, thoroughly irritated.

He lay there for a moment, aware that he was breathing a little heavily and feeling baffled. Then he rolled onto his back and stared at the shadows on the ceiling. This must have been how poor old Machu Picchu had felt in the first days after Ellora's arrival.

SARAH ROSE AT DAWN THE NEXT MORNING, feeling very much her normal cheerful, optimistic self again. After several intense hours of close thought during the night, her mind was clear and serene once more. She was back on track at last and she knew what had to be done. Hurrying over to the wooden chair in the corner, she grabbed her robe, slipped into it and opened the bedroom door.

Gideon was still asleep, sprawled on the sofa bed, the sheets and blankets bunched at his waist. He was lying on his stomach and the sleek expanse of his well-muscled back was a riveting sight in the early light. Sarah longed to stroke him, the way she would have stroked one of his cats.

But she knew that would be a mistake. He would only assume she was still trying to seduce him for her own nefarious purposes. Which she was, of course, she thought with a grin. She was determined to make him fall in love with her. But the seduction was going to take a slightly different form than originally planned. This was not the time to be obvious.

She hurried through her morning routine in the bathroom, trying not to use up all the hot water. Gideon would not appreciate a cold shower. On the way back to her own room, she saw that he had not moved. She took one last, wistful look at his powerfully built shoulders and went to finish dressing.

A few minutes later, wearing jeans and a shirt, her hair tied up out of the way at the back of her head, she made her way into the kitchen. It didn't take long to locate the pans she needed. She opened the refrigerator.

Within minutes she had filled the cabin with the inviting aroma of fresh-brewed coffee. The counters were cluttered with utensils, plates and a frying pan she had set out.

She was humming to herself as she whisked pancake batter in a large bowl when she realized she was no longer alone in the kitchen. She glanced over her shoulder and saw Gideon standing in the doorway. He had put on his jeans and nothing else. He scanned the kitchen, rubbing absently at the dark shadow of his beard.

"Do you always make this much of a racket in the morning?" he asked.

"Uh-huh. Are you always this grouchy?" She put a pan of syrup on the stove to heat.

"One of the things about cats is that they don't complain about my mood in the mornings. What are you making? Pancakes?"

"Yep. With real maple syrup. None of that caramel-colored sugar water for us. Run along and take your shower. Everything will be ready as soon as you get out of the bathroom."

"Why?"

"Why what?"

"Why the fancy breakfast?"

She debated briefly how much to tell him and then decided he might as well know what he was facing. "Because it's the first step in the courtship, if you must know the truth."

"Courtship." He looked dumbfounded. "What the devil are you talking about now?"

She stopped whisking the pancake batter and turned around to face him. "I figure your problem is that I went too fast."

"My problem, huh?"

"Right. Thanks to our conversation last night and all the thinking I did afterward, I have a much better idea of how to handle you now."

His eyes flashed with something that might have been amusement. "That's certainly a relief to hear."

"Laugh if you must, but it's true." She pointed the dripping whisk straight at him. "I can see that when I arrived on your doorstep, I was already light-years ahead of you in terms of my position within our relationship."

"Hell. Are you still on that kick?"

"Of course. What we need to do is let you catch up with me. Your progress has been severely retarded by the fact that you've got a few unpleasant events in your past that have made you gun-shy when it comes to relationships. In short, you're afraid I might be as foolish and as uncertain of what I really want as your ex-wife was. You don't trust my judgment."

"I didn't say Leanna was foolish or uncertain."

"No, but it's obvious she was if she actually thought she wanted someone else instead of you."

"I don't know what makes you think I'm such a hell of a catch, but—"

"On top of having your wife desert you, you also had the traumatic experience of being betrayed by a close male friend. In short, you've got a legitimate fear of being betrayed by people you trust. You're carrying some serious scars. You've obviously learned to keep yourself aloof from people who try to get too close to you. You've gotten in the habit of questioning everyone's motives. It's entirely understandable."

Gideon stared at her. "No kidding?"

"Don't act so insulted. We're all shaped emotionally by our pasts even when our rational mind tells us we don't have to repeat our mistakes. If we're reasonably intelligent, we're afraid we might repeat those mistakes. If we're not too intelligent or self-aware we go on repeating them. Either way, it's hard to break the cycle."

Gideon propped one shoulder against the doorjamb. He looked fascinated. "What hang-ups have you got from your traumatic experience of being left at the altar?"

"Well, for one thing, you'd never find me waiting in a wedding dress in front of a church full of people again, that's for sure."

"You don't plan to marry?" he asked slowly.

"I didn't say that. I just wouldn't risk a big wedding with all the trimmings. Believe me, if I ever decide to try it again, it'll be a quick trip to Vegas or Reno." She grinned. "See? We all have our scars. Rationally I tell myself that I wouldn't screw up and make such a major error in judgment again. I'll be sure of what I'm doing the next time and it will be perfectly safe to plan a big wedding if that's what I wanted."

"But you won't plan one?"

She shook her head swiftly. "No, I won't. Emotionally I couldn't face it. I couldn't bear to risk that sort of humiliation again, no matter how sure I was of the man I was marrying. Just the prospect of addressing invitations to all the people who witnessed the first fiasco is enough to make me cringe." She shook off the old pain and smiled reassuringly. "You see? That's how our mistakes affect us. We try to learn from them, to protect ourselves and in doing so we sometimes err on the side of caution."

He watched her intently. "If I'd have been there, I'd have nailed the bastard's hide to the wall."

Sarah was instantly warmed by the unexpected words. She smiled mistily. "Gideon, that's about the nicest thing anyone's ever said to me. Thank you."

"Forget it." He came toward her.

Sarah felt the immediate tingle of sensual awareness ripple through her. She wasn't sure what the determination in Gideon's eyes meant, however. Instinctively she stepped back and found herself up against the kitchen counter. "Gideon?"

He didn't halt, just kept coming toward her until he was looming over her, crowding her against the counter. He was overwhelming when he was this close. Sarah was mesmerized by the pattern of crisp, curling hair on his broad chest. She gripped the whisk handle as if it were a lifeline to sanity.

Deliberately he reached out and removed the bowl of pancake batter and the whisk from her frozen fingers.

"Gideon, I don't think…"

"Sarah," he muttered, his voice lower and grittier than usual as his hands slid up her arms to her shoulders, "let's get something understood here. You don't have to go through a lot of crazy rationalization or try to see me through rose-colored glasses if all you really want is for me to take you to bed. I'll be glad to lay you down on that sofa over there right now."

Sarah panicked. "Don't you dare do this to me, Gideon Trace. This is a relationship we're building here. I'm not about to let you reduce it to nothing more than a roll in the hay."

"I wasn't going to do that."

"Yes, you were. That's exactly what you were going to do and I won't have it, do you hear me?"

He winced as her voice rose hysterically. "Believe me, I hear you."

"I mean it. Every word. This is very important to me. I gave it hours of thought last night and I know how I'm going to handle everything. Things are back on track now and I won't let you mess it all up with sex."

He smiled faintly, his mouth very close to hers. "I kind of like the thought of messing it up with sex. I'm not the knight in shining armor you seem to think I am, but I'll certainly do my best to give you what you want in bed."

"*No.*"

He kissed her before she could find a way to deflect him. Sarah struggled furiously for a moment and then capitulated with a small, trembling sigh as his mouth moved on hers. He was so real, this man who had filled her thoughts and her heart for the past four months. How could she resist his kiss?

It was no wonder she was vulnerable on this front, she thought fleetingly. Everything felt so *right* when he kissed her. She flexed her nails experimentally on his shoulders and he responded with a heavy groan.

She could feel his strong thighs pushing against her and there was no mistaking the solid evidence of his early morning desire. His beard scraped along her cheek in a way that was unbelievably sexy.

"Gideon." His name was torn from her in a breathless gasp. She could feel his teeth on her earlobe now. The sensation was driving her wild. Frantically she fought to hold on to her common sense. "Gideon, no. Not like this. Not until you're ready."

"I'm ready. Believe me, I'm ready."

"No, damn it, not yet. Please."

He broke the kiss at last, but he didn't release her. His eyes were as green as emeralds as he looked down into her upturned face. She knew she was trembling and she also knew the heat she felt was probably evident on her flushed cheeks.

"You really want me, don't you?" Beneath the blatant, masculine desire in his gaze was an odd, bemused look. "You really do want me. I've never had a woman look at me quite the way you're looking at me now."

"Of course, I want you." She glowered at him, trying to hide her flustered emotions. "I've never made any secret of that. But that's got nothing to do with it. You need time to realize you want me, too."

"I do want you."

"I mean, really want me."

"I really want you." Sexy amusement lit his eyes again.

Sarah grabbed the dripping whisk and threatened him with it. "Stop teasing me and go take a shower, you beast. And when you come back into this kitchen, you are going to behave yourself, is that clear?"

He grinned slowly, his eyes alight with a sensual promise that made her ache to throw herself back into his arms. "Real clear. Be interesting to see how you enforce your own rules." He turned and sauntered out of the kitchen.

Chapter Five

TWO DAYS LATER, SARAH AGAIN succumbed to serious self-doubts. Conducting the courtship of a man might be a feasible notion if the object of the effort was shy and retiring by nature but Gideon was definitely not shy or retiring.

What he was, was difficult and maddeningly unpredictable. He was also proving dangerous on a sensual level.

Having discovered just how vulnerable she was to his kisses, he tormented her with them. He seemed to delight in catching her off guard and pulling her into his arms for a quick, stolen caress that inevitably left her feeling giddy and breathless.

But whenever she tried to introduce a serious, personal topic or questioned him about his past, he became as silent and uncommunicative as a mountain.

She could not tell if she was making any progress at all.

And the courtship wasn't the only area that wasn't progressing with satisfying rapidity. They had not broken the code on the map and Sarah was getting frustrated. She had expected the actual treasure hunt to go smoothly.

"You're too impatient," Gideon remarked as they tromped back and forth across the heavily wooded acreage that had once been owned by Emelina Fleetwood.

There was very little left of Emelina Fleetwood's home, just a tumbledown cabin that was completely bare inside. Some distance away from where the house stood was the collapsed wall of what might have been the barn. A few feet from the back door of the cabin itself were several boards left from what might have been an outhouse. Rusty nails and a couple of pieces of metal from some old farm equipment were scattered around the ruins.

Almost everything had long since been reclaimed by the forest. The multitude of owners who had tried to farm the place since Emelina's time had not made any noticeable improvements.

"Two whole days, Gideon, and we've gotten nowhere."

"People spent most of the century looking for the *Titanic.* They're still looking for Kidd's and Laffite's gold. And they still haven't found Amelia Earhart's plane. Treasure hunting requires time and effort and plenty of patience."

"But we've got a map."

"You keep saying that. Your precious map isn't a magic talisman, you know. It's just a crude sketch that could have been made by almost anyone at any time and mean almost anything."

"I'm sure the map is genuine. It's a family heirloom."

"You got any idea of how many family heirlooms are nothing but junk?"

"This isn't junk. There shouldn't be any problem. Darn it, this is your area of expertise. Why can't you figure out what this code means?" She scanned the odd notes in front of her. "Sixty, ninety and a straight line connecting two dots with the number twenty-five beside it. Then the phrase, 'White rock at intersection of B and C. Ten paces due north.' I tell you, Gideon, we're overlooking something obvious here."

"Yeah. A white boulder."

"That, too. Where do you suppose it is?" She looked around as she had countless times during the past two days and saw nothing of a white rock.

"It probably got washed away or covered up with mud and debris years ago. People who bury treasure expect to dig it up again within a few months or years at the most. They often use transient points of reference like an out-house or a tree or something else that could easily be gone by the time the next generation comes looking for grandpa's gold."

Sarah wrinkled her nose. "An outhouse?"

"Sure. That was a favorite place to bank the retirement funds in the old days. Who would go looking for gold in an outhouse?"

"You, obviously." She laughed up at him. "Ever find any that way?"

"I refuse to respond to that on the grounds that it may make me look like an idiot."

Sarah giggled. "You did, didn't you?"

"It was a long time ago." Gideon came to a halt. "Isn't it time for lunch, yet?"

"You know, Gideon, there are times when I get the feeling you're only in this for the food. You've been showing an uncommon interest in mealtimes since I cooked that first dinner for you."

"Hey, how was I to know you could cook? And what are you complaining about, anyway? The way to a man's heart is through his stomach."

Sarah slid him a sidelong glance. "Is that true? Am I getting closer?"

He threw a heavy arm around her shoulders and pulled her against his side for a moment. His lips moved sensually in her sun-warmed hair. "You're welcome to get as close as you want, Sarah."

"Unfortunately your idea of close is not the same as mine. Not yet, at any rate."

"Are you sure of that?" He boldly let his hand glide over the curve of her breast.

"Positive." She pushed free of the tempting embrace and stalked across the small clearing in back of the old cabin to where she had left the picnic basket.

Gideon followed more slowly, his eyes thoughtful. "What happens if we find the earrings, Sarah?"

"*When*, not *if*, we find them." She knelt on the ground and spread out the red and white checked cloth she had brought along in the basket. "And what happens is that you get one pair and I get the other four. Just like we agreed."

"And then you go back to Seattle and I go home to my place on the coast?" He settled down on the ground, one leg drawn up.

She thought about that as she unwrapped tuna fish sandwiches. "No, of course not. This is a long-term plan I'm working on here. But I haven't made all the decisions. I'm not exactly sure how to handle our relationship after we find the earrings. I can't just move in with you, yet. You're not ready for that."

"I'm not?" He took a big bite out of his sandwich.

"No. So it looks like it'll be a long-distance commute for a while. Which won't be easy because I'm scheduled to start a new book next month. Once I start working on it I won't have a lot of free time."

"And I've got a magazine to get out by the first of every month."

"Things will get complicated, won't they? But we'll manage somehow."

"More likely once we find the earrings you'll go back to your real world and that'll be the end of my courtship," Gideon said flatly. He took another large bite of his sandwich.

"No, that's not the way it will be."

"I think it will be exactly that way, Sarah."

"Damn it, you really do think I just brought you along so you could help me find my treasure, don't you? You think that once we've found it, I'll give up courting you."

"I think I'd assign a high probability to that scenario."

"Is it so hard for you to develop a little faith in me?"

"I'm supposed to have faith in you after knowing you for all of three days?"

"Stop saying that. We've known each other for four whole months."

"We were pen pals for four months, not lovers."

Without any warning, Sarah found herself very close to losing her temper. "Pen pals. Yes, that's what we were and you liked it that way, didn't you? In fact, I'll bet you preferred it that way because you didn't have to take any risks or make any commitments. Letter writing is a very safe way to conduct an affair, isn't it?"

"It has a few advantages," he agreed, obviously satisfied at having provoked her. "But it also has a few distinct disadvantages." He leered cheerfully at her. "Now that I've met you in the flesh, I can see what I was missing when all I was getting were recipes."

With a supreme act of willpower, Sarah pulled herself back from the brink. She had been on the verge of flying into a genuine rage, she realized, shaken. Gideon had done this deliberately.

"Stop teasing me, Gideon."

"I'm not teasing you. I mean every word. What do you say we make a deal? You've had your four months of letters. Let me have four months of you in bed, regardless of whether or not we find your earrings. Then we'll decide what sort of relationship we've got."

Sarah refolded the sandwich wrapper with shaking fingers. "Don't talk like that, Gideon."

"You don't like the terms?" he asked, voice hardening. "That doesn't surprise me. You don't get much out of it under those conditions, do you? All right, I'll make the deal contingent on finding the earrings. If we do turn them up, I get my four months."

"I said stop it damn you." She threw the unfinished portion of her sandwich back into the basket and leaped to her feet. The sunlight still poured into the clearing but the warmth had gone out of the day. She was suddenly feeling very cold.

There was a long silence during which Sarah stood with her back to Gideon, her hands thrust into the pockets of her jeans. A lazy breeze ruffled the delicate wildflowers scattered around her feet. She could not bring herself to turn around for fear Gideon would see the hint of tears in her eyes.

The sound of another sandwich being unwrapped behind her finally broke the spell.

"Sorry," Gideon growled. "I was pushing it, wasn't I?"

"Yes, you were." Sarah turned back to watch as he wolfed down another of her sandwiches. "Why?"

"Why?" He looked momentarily blank. "Because I want to take you to bed. Why else?"

"You're going about it the wrong way."

"Yeah, I got that feeling. Sit down and eat the rest of your lunch, Sarah. I'll work on keeping my mouth shut."

Moodily she dropped back down onto the ground, folding her legs tailor-fashion. Her appetite was gone. "I was so sure this was going to work, but I'm not getting anywhere."

"You've only been looking for the earrings for two days. There's a lot of territory left to cover around here."

"I didn't mean the treasure hunt."

"I see. You meant our famous relationship. Well, don't get impatient about that, either. You haven't given it any more time than you've given the treasure hunt."

"I've given it four whole months."

"More like three whole days."

She dropped her forehead down onto her updrawn knees and took ten deep breaths. When she raised her head again, her emotions were calmer once more. "Let's talk about the treasure, since we don't seem to be able to discuss our relationship."

"That'a girl. Stick to the real stuff. The stuff you can count on. Nothing like knowing you're sitting somewhere near a cache of jewels to take your mind off a courtship, is there?"

Sarah lost it then. All the self-control she had been practicing for the past few minutes disintegrated in a flash. "You sarcastic, hateful, son of a…. Don't you dare talk to me like that. Do you hear me? Not ever. I won't tolerate it. I'm trying to give you a proper courtship—trying to give you time to catch up with me in this relationship. The least you could do is be polite."

Gideon narrowed his eyes, his expression suddenly fierce. He reached for her, caught her arm and dragged her across his lap to cradle her in a grip of steel.

"I'm sorry," he muttered over and over again as his big hands stroked her. "I'm sorry. You're right. I'm not used to trusting people and I'm not any good at dealing with women. If you want gallantry and charm and trust, you're going to have to look somewhere else."

She huddled against him, aware of the tension that was tightening his whole body. Her fury evaporated. "You really are a beast, aren't you? Your first instinct is to bite that hand that's trying to feed you."

"I said I'm sorry," he said again. His fingers moved in her hair.

"I don't know if I can believe that."

"It's the truth. I shouldn't have pushed you like that." He drew his head back to look down into her glistening eyes. "But I can't guarantee you it won't happen again."

"You have a long way to go to catch up with me, don't you? A lot further than I thought at first."

"So? Are you going to give up on me?"

She shook her head slowly. "No."

"Sarah…"

She put her fingers over his lips. "And don't, I warn you, make any cracks about me not giving up on you until you've helped me find the Flowers. If you say anything even close to that, I swear I won't be responsible for my actions."

He shut his mouth and squeezed her so tightly she thought her ribs would crack.

THE NEXT MORNING SARAH AWOKE WITH more doubts. The gentling of Gideon Trace was proving to be a formidable task.

The man was like a wild animal that had once been wounded. The bleeding had stopped long ago and he had recovered physically, but the scars would forever make him cautious about trusting anyone.

The coffee was brewing and the biscuits were in the oven. In a few minutes she and Gideon would sit down to breakfast just like two people who were involved in a real relationship.

She was deliberately trying to give Gideon a taste of what living with her would be like but she couldn't tell yet if she was having any impact.

Perhaps the treasure hunt had been a bad idea. She considered that thought very seriously as she slipped outside to taste the morning air while she waited for Gideon to finish shaving.

It was beginning to dawn on her that she might have made a drastic mistake in using the treasure hunt as an opening for contacting Gideon Trace.

Perhaps the truth was, she had only herself to blame for some of his wariness.

How would she have felt if some stranger with whom she had conducted only a casual correspondence suddenly showed up on her doorstep and said he wanted to have a relationship while they searched for a fortune in jewels?

Sarah grimaced and dug her toe into the ground. Perhaps she should call a halt to the treasure hunt for now and go back to square one. She had been convinced somehow that the Fleetwood Flowers and Gideon were linked and it had seemed natural to pursue the two of them together. But she might have been wrong about that part of things.

Certainly her relationship with Gideon was the most important part of the equation. Perhaps she should give it her full attention for now.

Equation.

Sarah blinked in the morning light, inhaling the sweet scent of the evergreens. *Equation.*

She stood staring a moment longer at the stand of trees that edged the clearing. Then, moving slowly, she turned and went back into the cabin.

Gideon was just emerging from the bathroom, tucking his shirt into his jeans in an intimate, somehow very sexy gesture. But, then, Sarah reminded herself, everything about Gideon was sexy to her. He took one look at her face and his brows rose questioningly.

"What's wrong?"

"Nothing. I just thought of something."

"What?"

"Emelina Fleetwood was a schoolteacher."

"So?"

"So in those days a good schoolteacher emphasized the basics, reading, writing and arithmetic."

"And?" He went into the kitchen to help himself to a cup of coffee.

"Gideon, it just hit me that one very logical way for a retired schoolteacher to make the directions to her treasure was with a classic mathematical equation. One she was never likely to forget. The most likely sort of equation to choose for that kind of thing would be one from geometry. You know, triangles."

"Triangles?"

"You can make all sorts of measurements if you know just a little bit of information about a particular triangle. Heck, the Egyptians built whole pyramids based on stuff they knew about triangles."

Gideon regarded her for a moment as he sipped his coffee. His eyes were very green. "It wouldn't be the first time someone used that technique. It requires that whoever hid the treasure be familiar with geometry, but you're right, a schoolteacher would have been."

"We're sitting here with a map that's just loaded with info that could be elements of an equation." Excitement flowed through Sarah as she moved over to the kitchen table to look down at the map in the plastic envelope.

"Look at these numbers. Sixty and Ninety and twenty-five. A ninety-degree triangle is a right triangle. Right?"

"Right."

Sarah frowned. "So maybe what we've got here is a right triangle. Maybe the sixty refers to the size of one of the other angles. Right triangles with sixty-degree angles in them are common in geometry."

"What about the number twenty-five? My geometry is rusty but I seem to recall that the angles of a triangle have to add up to 180 degrees. Sixty, ninety and twenty-five don't add up to that."

"Maybe twenty-five is the length of one of the sides of the triangle. The distance between the two small squares on the map, perhaps." Sarah was getting more excited by the minute as she examined the markings on the copy of the Fleetwood map. "Given a couple of angles and the length of one side, you could solve for the remaining two sides, right?"

"Sounds like we're talking your basic Pythagorean theorem here."

"Yes, of course. The square of the length of the hypotenuse of a right triangle is equal to the sum of the squares of the lengths of the other two sides."

"Congratulations to your memory."

"Don't congratulate me, congratulate Mrs. Simpson. Math was not my strong point in high school," Sarah said as she continued to study the map. "But Mrs. Simpson drilled some of the basics into me. Little did she know I was going to become a writer and never need the stuff. Until now, that is. I guess you never know. Now, if we assume twenty-five is the length of one side…Gideon, we're going to need a calculator. I'm not *that* good at the basics. Got one?"

"Not on me, but we can pick up a cheap one in town this afternoon. We're almost out of milk, anyway."

"Let's go now."

"Sarah, it's only seven o'clock. The stores won't be open until nine or ten."

She sat back, disgusted with the delay. "This is it, Gideon. I know it. I have a feeling."

"Uh-huh. I have a feeling there's something getting very close to being done in the oven."

Sarah's eyes widened. She leaped to her feet. "My biscuits."

"First things first," Gideon said. "The Flowers can wait. I'll get the honey."

LATER THAT MORNING, WITH THE HELP of a five-dollar calculator, they ran the numbers. Sarah was beside herself with excitement. She practically danced around the table as they drew triangles and labeled the sides.

"We've got the length of all three sides and we know there's supposed to be a white rock at the point where B and C intersect," she said, delighted with the results.

"None of this does any good unless we can figure out what points Emelina used to measure her triangle," Gideon noted.

"Well, she gave us the length of one side of the triangle, twenty-five feet. She must have been using familiar points of reference. You said yourself, people tended to do that. Gideon, this is so thrilling. I've never done anything like this before." She looked up when there was no response from his side of the table. "But you have, haven't you?"

"Once or twice." He sat watching her with an unreadable expression in his eyes.

"Like once or twice a year when you go off on one or your mysterious vacations?" Sarah asked shrewdly.

He exhaled heavily. "Magazines are expensive to run. *Cache* needs an infusion of cash periodically."

"So you go out and dig some up. Wonderful."

"It's not quite that easy, Sarah. More often than not, you don't get lucky."

"Still, you know more about second-guessing someone like Emelina Fleetwood than I do. What do you think she used as points of her triangle?"

He hesitated for a long time. Then, as if he had reached a decision, he pulled the map closer. "We're assuming that all these figures apply to a right triangle. We could be totally off base with all this. The numbers might mean something else entirely."

Sarah shook her head. "No, I don't think so."

His mouth curved faintly at her air of certainty. "Yeah, I know. You've got a feeling. All right, we'll assume your intuition is valid and go from there." Gideon leaned over the map. "My first hunch is that she was using the distance between the outhouse door and the back door of her cabin. Twenty-five feet sounds about right for that. But she might also have used a clothesline or a tree as a marker."

"No, no, I think you're right. Brilliant idea. Lucky you've had experience with outhouses, isn't it?"

He gave her a warning glance. "One more outhouse joke and I'm through as a consultant."

She grinned, undaunted. "Let's go see if we can find enough left of that old outhouse to tell us where the door was."

"It probably faced the main house." Gideon glanced wistfully toward the kitchen counter. "What about lunch?"

Sarah started to protest any further delay and then thought better of it. There was something in Gideon's expression that made her think another picnic lunch was important today. "I'll make us some sandwiches."

Forty minutes later they paced off the distance between the toppled outhouse and the sagging back door of the cabin. Sarah held a tape measure in one hand and Gideon took the other end.

"Twenty-five feet," he called from the back door of the cabin.

"All right," Sarah sang out. "I'm sure this is it, Gideon. Now, if we assume that the right angle was at her back door, then the one at the outhouse door was the sixty-degree angle."

"She could have drawn the triangle to either the right or the left of her base line," Gideon remarked.

"We may have to measure it twice and see which point is near a white rock." Sarah glanced to the side. "Let's try it off to the right, first. The woods on that side of the house look promising. Got the measuring tape?"

"I've got it."

Five minutes later they came to a halt in a grove of pine and fir.

"I only hope we're walking a reasonably straight line," Sarah said as they started to pace off the remaining side of the imaginary triangle.

"I think we can gauge it fairly accurately this way. You getting hungry yet?" Gideon was carrying the picnic basket and seemed more interested in its contents than he did in locating the white rock.

"No. I'm too excited. Aren't you feeling any thrill at all? We're so close."

"Ninety-nine times out of a hundred you end up with nothing but a pile of dirt at the end of this kind of hunt."

"Don't be so pessimistic."

"Sarah, we walked all over this section of ground yesterday and found nothing."

"We'll get lucky today. Today we know what we're doing."

"I'm glad one of us does."

But when they finished, there was no white rock at the point where the B and C of the triangle supposedly intersected. Sarah looked around, utterly baffled.

"I don't understand it. I was so sure we'd find it using the triangle formula. Maybe we should try the other side of the clearing."

"Maybe." Gideon glanced up at the sky. "Lunchtime."

"Is it?"

"Yes, it is. I vote we take a break and eat right here." Gideon settled down on the ground right at the point where the intersecting lines of the triangle should have revealed a large white boulder. He spread the checkered cloth on the thick carpet of dried pine needles and started unwrapping sandwiches.

Reluctantly Sarah plopped down beside him. "Do you think maybe this really is a wild-goose chase, Gideon?"

"How should I know? You're the one with the map and the sense of intuition. Here. Have some carrot sticks."

She took a carrot and munched absently. "I wonder if I've blown this whole thing out of all proportion. This morning I was wondering if I'd been mistaken in thinking that you and the earrings are linked."

He slanted her a glance. "Which is more important? Me or finding the earrings?"

"You, naturally." She wrapped her arms around her knees and gazed straight ahead into the forest. "But I can't quite figure out why meeting you seemed so bound up with my finding the earrings. It's kind of weird when you think about it."

"It was *Cache* that put the idea into your head. The coincidence of the fact that I publish a treasure-hunting magazine is probably what made you connect me to the idea of hunting down the earrings. It's logical."

"Yes, but I don't usually operate on logic."

"I've noticed. Have some lemonade." He poured her a cupful from the Thermos.

"Things are getting confusing, Gideon."

"I can see your problem. It always gets confusing when you mix a fortune in gems with the great romance of the century."

She took that seriously. "Yes, it does. I'm worried that if we do find the jewels, you'll think I used you. How am I going to convince you that you're more important?"

Gideon leaned over her and brushed his mouth against hers. "You are one wacky female."

"*Interesting*. I'm an interesting female. Not wacky."

"If you say so." He kissed her again. "You taste like lemonade."

"So do you."

He rolled onto his back. "What do you say we take a nap?"

She shook her head automatically. "I never take naps."

"I do. When I'm lying out in the middle of the woods on a warm afternoon, that is."

She smiled. "Do you do that a lot?"

"No." Gideon folded his arms behind his head and closed his eyes. In a moment he was sound asleep.

Sarah watched him for a while, the sweet longing deep inside making her feel unaccountably sad. She wished he belonged to her so that she could touch him; make love to him.

A few minutes later she pillowed her head on his strong shoulder and fell asleep.

When she awoke a long while later, Gideon's fingers were on the buttons of her shirt and he was leaning over her with a compelling passion blazing in his gemlike eyes.

"You want to prove to me that I'm more important than finding the earrings?" he challenged softly. "Let me make love to you. Here. Now."

Dazed with sleep, sunlight and a sudden, searing sense of longing, Sarah reached up to put her arms around his neck.

Chapter Six

AN ALMOST UNBEARABLE SENSE OF excitement washed through Gideon as he watched Sarah awaken with a smile of sensual welcome in her eyes. It suddenly occurred to him that he had been waiting all of his life to see just that look in a woman's gaze. The feel of her arms stealing around him was more satisfying than finding hidden treasure. His hand trembled from anticipation and desire as he touched her.

"Gideon? What is it?"

"I want you. So bad I can taste it."

He winced inwardly at the sound of his own voice. It was harsh and raspy in his throat. He wanted to murmur in her ear; he wanted to charm her; coax her into making love with him; persuade her into sensual surrender. He longed to reassure her—to tell her he would be careful with her, infinitely careful. He would do everything he could to make it good for her.

But the only words he could get out were the ones that

told her he was starving for her. He wondered if he'd frightened her.

"I'm glad you want me," Sarah said. "So glad."

She wasn't trying to pull away from him, he realized. She still wanted him as much as she had seemed to want him whenever he had kissed her during the past few days.

Gideon relaxed slightly. He touched her throat, inhaling the scent of her, and felt her fingers move in his hair. The gentle caress sent passionate chills down his spine.

When he finally got her shirt open he thought he would lose what remained of his self-control. He lifted his head to stare down at the curves of her small, full breasts. His whole body was tight, hot and heavy now.

"So sweet." He bent his head to kiss the soft, inviting fullness of her. "Soft. Hot." He caught her nipple gently between his teeth. It grew taut and firm almost instantly and his whole body clenched in response.

"Oh, Gideon."

Her leg shifted, sliding alongside his, and Gideon was suddenly impatient with the clothing. He splayed his fingers over her warm belly and slid his hand down to the fastening of her jeans. He hesitated, waiting to see if she would resist this next step.

She didn't. She simply lifted her hips so that he could push the jeans off entirely. When he saw the scrap of red lace she wore as panties, he thought he would go out of his mind.

"I've never seen anything sexier in my life," he whispered as he slipped one finger beneath the elastic edge of the delightfully shameless undergarment.

She laughed softly and buried her flushed face in his shoulder. "Good. I wore them just for you."

"Does that mean you intended to let me make love to you today?"

"I've got six other pairs just like these with me. I bought them in Seattle before I came to meet you. I've worn one of the pairs every day since I found you. I never knew when this was going to happen, you see. I wanted to be prepared."

He was torn between laughter and a frustrated groan. "What about your famous intuition? Didn't that warn you when this would happen?"

"My intuition is always at war with my common sense when I'm around you," she complained softly. "You make it hard for me to think straight. Things aren't always clear for some reason."

"I'm glad. And I can't wait to see the other six pairs." He covered her mouth with his own, his tongue surging intimately between her lips. He knew he was seeking advance knowledge of what it would be like when he claimed her completely. The sample he got was enough to make his head whirl.

His fingers found the hot, flowing warmth of her and he almost came unraveled.

"I love the feel of you," Sarah said, her eyes narrowing with desire. "Your hands. Yes, please, touch me, Gideon. Such wonderful hands." She sucked in her breath. "That feels incredible."

Gideon watched her hair spill over his arm, the soft, thick strands turning to honeyed gold in the splintered light. He was enthralled with her response, mesmerized by it. He'd never had a woman come alive like this under his touch. She was literally melting for him. He could see the heat in her cheeks and feel her racing pulse.

A glittering host of emotions rocked him as she twisted and lifted herself against his probing hand. He was at once filled with a sense of raw, masculine power and great tenderness. He wanted to bury himself in her and find his own release before the gathering pressure drove him out of his mind. But at the same time he longed to bring her such pleasure that she would never even want to look at another man.

"My jeans," he muttered abruptly. "Give me a second, honey." He released her to fumble with his own clothing. All his actions seemed unbelievably awkward suddenly. She was so sleek and sinuous and delicate. He felt like a great, rutting male animal next to her.

But Sarah didn't seem to mind. In fact, she seemed to find him endlessly fascinating. Her eyes were glowing with a shimmering heat as she helped him tug off his pants. When she saw him reach into one pocket for a little plastic packet she grinned teasingly.

"Obviously I'm not the only one who's been running around prepared for this," she said.

He felt himself redden as he busied himself for a few seconds but he merely shook his head. "No, you're not. But I wasn't relying on intuition, just hope." He took a deep breath and tugged off the red panties. For a long moment he could only stare at the tangled triangle of hair that was revealed. He was held in thrall by the promise of what awaited him.

Sarah seemed equally enchanted. She touched him, wonderingly at first and then more boldly, stroking him as if he were a big cat. Under her fingers Gideon began to feel like one. A sense of his own fluid grace and power filled him, washing out the awkwardness.

She did this to him, he thought. She made him feel this way, made him glory in his own manhood.

"I don't know if I can wait very long for you," he warned her. "I'm going up in flames. You have a hell of an effect on me."

"That's only fair. Because you have the same effect on me."

She kissed his throat and shoulder. He felt first her tongue and then her small teeth on his skin and he shuddered.

She seemed to sense when he was at the end of his tether. When he grasped the ripe curve of her thigh and pushed tentatively, she went easily onto her back, reaching up to draw him down to her.

Gideon fought for control as he watched her part her legs for him. Her silent invitation was the most compelling action he'd ever witnessed. It said without words that she was giving herself to him—that she was his.

He could no more have resisted the siren call of her in that moment than he could have flown into the sun.

With a short, muttered exclamation of need he slid between her thighs, astounded at the silky feel of them. He hesitated an instant, afraid once more that he was going too fast, that he might hurt her.

But she was beckoning him into her with that ancient summons in her hazel eyes.

He pushed slowly against her hot, damp opening, seeking an easy, gentle entry. But she was small and tight, in spite of her obvious willingness.

"Sarah?"

"It's all right." She stroked him gently when she felt his hesitation. "You're just right for me."

She lifted her hips, urging him to complete the union. Gideon groaned as the last of his control left him. He surged into her, pushing through the brief resistance of small, tight muscles and on into the clinging warmth that awaited him.

He went still for a few seconds, savoring the sensation of being inside Sarah. It was like nothing else he'd ever experienced.

"Buried treasure." He kissed her breast.

"What?" She was breathing quickly through her parted lips, her eyes glittering as she adjusted to him.

"Nothing. Never mind."

He began to move in her, slowly, powerfully. He got his hand down between their bodies and found the tiny nub hidden in her soft thatch of hair. She went wild when he touched her then.

"Gideon."

Suddenly she was clutching at him, her eyes widening briefly with distinct surprise before they squeezed shut. Gideon held her as she shivered in his arms. The emotions that flooded through him in that moment were chaotic and indescribable.

Before he could even begin to sort out his feelings, the full force of his own release roared through him. The power of it drove out all other sensation.

He heard himself call Sarah's name and then there was only a sweet, blissful exhaustion.

SARAH DRIFTED SLOWLY UP OUT OF THE dreamy web of satisfaction that had held her for several minutes. She was aware of the great weight of Gideon Trace on top of her. The deliciously crushed sensation made her smile. Her hands moved slowly on his smoothly muscled back, exploring the powerful, lean contours. He felt so right.

There had never been any real doubt. Gideon was her knight in shining armor, her moody, taciturn, difficult hero whose grim facade hid a passionate, loyal heart.

She had been wrong to worry about letting the lovemaking happen too soon. There had been no reason to hold off until she was sure of him. She was already sure of him. She had been since the beginning. Her intuition had not failed her.

And even if it had, it was too late to worry about it. She was head over heels in love with the man. She had been in love with him for months.

Sarah looked up into the trees, aware that it was now midafternoon. Branches rustled overhead. The sun that filtered through the leaves was still warm. The rock digging into her back was getting very hard.

Gideon exhaled heavily and raised his head to gaze down into her eyes. Satisfaction and an amusing, rather arrogant, vaguely leonine contentment gleamed in his eyes.

"You look a little like Machu Picchu," Sarah said.

Gideon smiled slowly. "Fair enough. You look like Ellora." He kissed her lightly on the mouth. "Any regrets?"

"None."

"That's good because I don't think I could go back to playing your courtship game."

"It wasn't a game. I just wanted to be sure you knew what you were doing."

He kissed her shoulder. "How'd I do?"

"Beast. You knew what you were doing, all right."

He raised his head again, laughing down at her with his eyes. "Thanks. I'll assume that's a compliment."

"The resemblance to Machu Picchu is getting stronger by the minute."

"How's that?"

"Well, you're getting quite heavy, for one thing." She wriggled her shoulders, trying to find a more comfortable spot on the ground.

"And you're such a delicate little thing, aren't you? Wouldn't want to squash you." Gideon moved, rolling over onto his back and dragging her with him so that she sprawled on top of him. "Now about this treasure hunt we're on...."

She shook her head, framing his hard face between her palms. Frowning with serious intent, she looked deep into his eyes. "Forget the treasure hunt. As of this afternoon, the earrings are no longer important. I'm still not sure why searching for them was so linked to finding you, but everything is much clearer now than it has been for the past few days."

His brows rose in silent laughter. "Sex has made it clearer?"

She smiled. "I suppose so. The point is, you're my important discovery, Gideon. I don't need the earrings now. They can wait." She brushed her mouth against his.

His arms closed around her, hard and tight and strong. Sarah was sure that his kiss was saying everything he did not yet seem able to say with words. He wanted her, needed her, loved her. It was enough, more than enough for the present.

When he freed her mouth, she was breathless again. She saw the look in his eyes and laughingly shook her head. "Oh, no. Not a second time on the ground. Not unless you're on the bottom."

"Not that comfortable, huh?"

"Like being trapped between a rock and a hard place."

He grinned wolfishly. "So how did I compare to one of your heroes?"

"Bigger." She kissed the tip of his nose. "Harder." She kissed his cheek. "Stronger." She kissed the strong line of his jaw. "Sexier." She kissed his mouth. "Much sexier. To sum it up, the reality was much better than the fantasy version, but I like to think that creating you over and over again in my books prepared me for the real thing when you walked into my life."

"I didn't exactly walk into your life. You walked into mine."

"Details, details. Same result. A happy ending."

The wicked satisfaction in his eyes was echoed in his laughter. "Are all romance writers experts at happy endings?"

"It's our stock and trade. You only get two fundamental choices in the world when it comes to philosophies: optimism or pessimism. Romance writers are basically optimists at heart, just like treasure hunters."

He gave her an odd look. "I've never thought of myself as an optimist. God knows, I'm no Pollyanna."

"Nonsense. Under that gruff, grouchy, bristly exterior beats the heart of a man who secretly believes in the same things I do. You're just too macho to admit it."

"You think you know me so well, don't you?"

She smiled serenely. "Naturally. I've been studying you since I was old enough to figure out the basic differences between men and women. That's how long you've been in my head."

He touched her hand. "You were studying a fantasy creation, not a real man."

"I know the difference between fantasy and reality," she assured him as she sat up and reached for her shirt and jeans.

"And you're convinced I'm real?"

She paused in the act of buttoning her shirt, aware already of the faint soreness in her thighs. She flashed him a rueful grin. "Very real. I can still feel the effects."

His gaze grew serious. "Did I hurt you?"

"No, of course not. I was just teasing." She patted his cheek and began struggling into her jeans.

"Sarah?"

"Umm?"

"Never mind." Gideon got slowly to his feet, pulling on his own clothing with quick, efficient movements.

She watched him out of the corner of her eye as she began to pack up the picnic basket. Something important was going through that inscrutable mind of his but she couldn't begin to guess what it was. Perhaps he was searching for a way to tell her he loved her, she thought happily.

Gideon leaned over to catch hold of one corner of the red-checked cloth. He pulled it back slowly, as if not sure how to refold it.

"Here, I'll do that," Sarah offered, taking the corner of the cloth out of his hand. She shook out the old tablecloth as Gideon walked around, kicking at pine needles. "What are you doing?" she asked finally.

"Just making sure we don't leave any sandwich wrappers behind." He used the toe of his boot to sweep back another layer of needles.

Sarah glanced down and saw the tip of moss covered rock thrusting up out of the earth. "That's what was digging into my back when you were making love to me. No wonder I felt as if I were trapped between a rock and a—" She broke off. "Oh, my God. A rock. Gideon, it's a *white* rock. Look at it."

He glanced down. "It looks like a green rock to me."

"Rocks aren't green. It's just got a lot of moss growing on it." Sarah dropped the red cloth and knelt on the ground for a closer look. Experimentally she scraped off some of the moss with her fingernail. "It is white."

Gideon crouched beside her. "Think so?"

"I'm sure of it." She looked up at him with growing delight. "Gideon, this is so exciting. Maybe we've found the jewels after all. Help me dig away some of the dirt."

Obediently he reached out and pulled away a few clods of dirt. More of the white boulder was revealed. "If this is your famous rock, it's no wonder we didn't see it when we went looking for it. It got covered up long ago in a mud slide."

"Yes, that's exactly what must have happened." Sarah sat back on her heels, frowning. "We'll never be able to uncover it with our bare hands. We'll need tools."

"An excellent observation." The distant sound of an engine shattered the stillness of the forest. Gideon was on his feet instantly, tugging Sarah up beside him.

"What's wrong?" she asked, taking the picnic basket as he thrust it into her hands.

"Nothing. But it sounds like we may have company coming. The cardinal rule of treasure-hunting expeditions is you don't reveal the location of the treasure to strangers."

Sarah hugged the basket to her and hurried to follow him out of the woods, past the old Fleetwood homestead and on to the cabin they were renting. The sound of the engine in the distance grew louder. "Do you really think we might have found the white rock that marks one of the points on Emelina Fleetwood's triangle?"

He threw her an amused glance over his shoulder. "What does your famous intuition tell you?"

She frowned, trying to sort out the jumbled impressions in her head. "I'm not sure," she said slowly. "I think that white rock is the one we've been looking for, but..."

"But what?" The engine roar was closer now.

"But I just don't feel much urgency about the whole thing." She grinned. "Not that finding a fortune in gems is totally uninteresting, of course. I'm not that laid back about it all."

"I'd wonder at your sanity if you were."

"Well, it certainly would be great fun to turn them up. But like I said, they're not as important as they once were." Sarah abandoned the effort to explain. "Never mind. Here comes our visitor and you're right about one thing—I don't want some stranger to get his hands on them. Those earrings are Fleetwood earrings."

A black Jeep roared around the bend in the road. Instead of going on past the isolated cabin, it turned into the long, winding drive as if whoever was behind the wheel knew exactly where he was going.

"You tell anyone else you were coming up here?" Gideon asked, his gaze on the Jeep as it drew closer to the cabin.

"Sure, a couple of people, including my friend Margaret Lark. But she doesn't own a Jeep and neither does anyone else I know. Maybe it's our landlord."

"No, I don't think so." Gideon reached the front step of the cabin and drew her to a halt beside him as the Jeep entered the yard. His gaze never left the vehicle.

The Jeep came to a halt in a cloud of dust. Sunlight glinted on the windshield, obscuring the view of the driver. Sarah experienced a sudden shaft of deep uneasiness.

"Gideon?"

He didn't respond. His whole attention was on the Jeep. She sensed the tension in him.

The door of the Jeep cracked open with a flourish. A black boot, so brilliantly polished that it caught the sun, hit the ground. Something silver glinted at the heel.

"Hell," Gideon said.

The man who got slowly out of the Jeep was as spectacular as his boots. He moved with laconic grace, well aware he was making an entrance and obviously enjoying it. His hair was as black and gleaming as his footwear. His eyes were blue, a bright, devilish sapphire blue.

There was no doubt the stranger had been ruggedly good-looking at one time. He still was, to be perfectly honest. The chin and nose and cheekbones were all well chiseled. But Sarah could see that there had always been an underlying weakness and the years were starting to reveal it.

He wore khaki pants tucked into the tops of the high, dashing boots and a shirt that had a large number of pockets, epaulets and flaps on it. The clothes fit him so precisely they might have been hand-tailored.

"He looks like something out of a men's fashion magazine," Sarah whispered.

"Plenty of flash, all right. But, then, he always had that."

She frowned up at Gideon but he was still watching the newcomer. The stranger smiled, an easy, knowing, charming grin that revealed sparkling white teeth. Sarah's sense of unease grew a hundredfold. She knew she was not going to like this man, whoever he was.

"Hello, Gideon. I hear the last name is Trace now, is that right? Nice touch. That's all you left behind when you changed your identity, wasn't it? Just a trace. It's taken me a while to find you but it looks like I finally did it with the help of Ms. Fleetwood here. Long time, no see, Gid. How's it going, buddy?"

"Sarah," Gideon said, "meet Jake Savage."

"My pleasure, Ms. Fleetwood. But I believe we already know each other."

She stared at him. "We do?" But her intuition was already giving her the answer. Something about this man was awfully familiar even though she knew she had never met him. That voice…

"Jim Slaughter, owner and operator of Slaughter Enterprises, at your service. We had the pleasure of exchanging a few letters and a couple of calls regarding an expedition to find a downed plane full of gold, remember? You declined to invest. I'm still hoping to change your mind on that subject, by the way. I think we could do a lot for each other, Ms. Fleetwood."

"You're Slaughter?" She was horrified. It was beginning to dawn on her that she was the one who had led him to this place. She'd mentioned the Fleetwood Flowers to him. "Why did you change your name? I don't understand any of this."

"I had to change my name about the same time as

Gideon here changed his, ma'am. But that's all in the past now."

"I thought you were dead, Mr. Savage," she said.

Savage chuckled. "So did a lot of people, including my old partner, here, right, Gid?"

Partner. Sarah looked at Gideon. "You were his partner? The partner you said disappeared in the jungle along with Mr. Savage?"

Gideon didn't bother to reply. His eyes were still on the swashbuckling figure of his former associate. "What brings you back to life after all this time, Jake?"

"Got some big plans, Gid, old pal. Thought you might be interested in going back into partnership. Like I said, I've been looking for you for a while. I had a hunch you weren't any more dead than I was. You're a hard man to kill. Who'd have guessed I'd have found you through the charming Ms. Fleetwood? Piece of luck, huh?"

Gideon's brows rose sardonically. He slid a speculative glance toward Sarah. "How *did* you find me through the charming Ms. Fleetwood?"

"Simple enough," Jake said easily. He grinned his engaging grin at Sarah. "The little lady contacted me five months ago wanting to know if I'd be interested in helping her do some research. I did a little research myself and decided Sarah and I could be very useful to each other. So I offered her a chance to participate in a real-life search for lost gold."

"At a price," Sarah muttered.

"Well, naturally," Jake said, still smiling. "A fine investment opportunity. And just picture the publicity we could get: romance writer and one of her heroes go hunting for a fortune in the South Pacific. We could have drawn money and media like crazy. We'd have had people lined up for blocks wanting in on the deal."

"I take it you declined the offer, Sarah?" Gideon glanced at her.

"Yes." She clutched the picnic basket more tightly to her chest.

"I was pretty sure I could talk her into it, given a little time," Jake said with irrepressible self-confidence. "I mean, it's easy money, right? Hey, we take the investment cash but we don't actually have to *find* anything. How many treasure-hunting expeditions get lucky? Almost none. None of the investors squawk too loudly because they all know the odds going in."

"Easy money," Gideon agreed dryly.

"But in the meantime, she's led me to you, Gid. And that changes everything. I've got a deal for both of you."

"Forget it. I changed my name for a reason, Jake. I'm out of the business."

"I don't believe it for a minute. If you're out of the business, what are you doing here looking for the Fleetwood Flowers?"

"This is personal," Gideon said softly.

Sarah risked a quick glance at Gideon. He was grim-faced, his eyes very cold.

"Hey," said Jake, "so it's personal." He winked at Sarah. "I can understand that. But that doesn't mean the three of us can't do a little business. I've been thinking this through and I've got it all planned out."

"I'll bet," Gideon said.

"Now just listen, pal. Here's how it shapes up. Slaughter Enterprises gets a nice splash of publicity by turning up the Fleetwood Flowers for a pretty little romance writer, see? Lots of press on that. Then, when we're riding the wave of that announcement, we let it be known that Sarah is going to join us on an expedition to the South Pacific to find a plane full of gold. Like I said, money and media will pour in. It's dynamite, Gid. Dynamite. Better than the old days, huh? No risking our necks in some godforsaken South American jungle this time. First class, all the way. And get this—with you along, we'll probably find the damned gold."

"No thanks," Gideon said.

"Think it through," Jake urged. "Give it a chance to sink in, that's all I ask. We made a hell of a team in the old days. You know it and I know it."

"What makes you think we're going to find the Fleetwood Flowers?" Gideon asked.

Jake Savage looked at him in astonishment and then to Sarah's surprise, he burst out laughing. "Hey, Gid, this is me, your old buddy, Jake, remember? I know you, pal. You never go after anything but a sure thing. If you've agreed to help Ms. Fleetwood here, it's because you've cut yourself in for a slice of the action and you're damned sure there's going to be some action. Neither of us ever worked for free, even when it was *personal*."

Chapter Seven

"I DESERVE A FEW ANSWERS, GIDEON." Sarah took the tops off several stalks of fresh broccoli with a few ferocious strokes of her knife. She dropped the broccoli into a colander and picked up a carrot and a peeler.

There had been a taut silence in the small cabin after Jake Savage had driven off to find a motel in the nearby town. He'd seemed unoffended by Gideon's failure to offer him a bed for the night. Sarah had the feeling that it took a lot to offend Jake. He was so accustomed to wowing people that it would never occur to him that he was being insulted.

"What do you want to know first?" Gideon was sitting at the kitchen table, a cold beer in front of him. He looked remote and austere, the way he had the day she'd arrived on his doorstep.

"Well, we could start with your real name, I suppose," Sarah said tartly as she whacked strips off the carrot.

"My real name is Gideon."

"Gideon what?"

"Does it matter?"

"It matters, damn it. What's your legal name?"

"My legal name is Trace. I've got a bunch of credit cards, a social security number and a driver's license under that name. How much more legal does it get?"

"What was it before it was Trace?" she asked through set teeth. "Back when you were the partner of the famous Jake Savage?"

He ran a hand through his hair. "Carson."

"Carson." She tasted that for a minute. "Not bad. But I like Trace better. Maybe it's because I met you under that name." *Maybe because you made love to me under that name.* "All right, let's go on to the next question. What really happened back in that jungle where the two of you were supposed to have disappeared? What jungle was it, anyway?"

Gideon was quiet for a moment. "It doesn't really matter now. I told you Savage and Company occasionally did odd jobs all over South America."

"And?"

"And this was one of the odder ones. The kind where you don't ask a lot of unnecessary questions and you take your pay in cash. On delivery. Savage and Company never got involved in anything illegal on general principle, but there were times when it walked a fine line."

"You would never do anything illegal," Sarah declared.

Gideon's mouth twisted faintly. "The problem is that the definition of legal varies a lot once you get south of Tijuana."

"I can imagine. Okay, go on."

"As I said, it was a job. For which Savage and Company was supposed to be paid a great deal of money. We were to take a shipment of supplies to a group of archaeologists excavating an old Indian ruin deep in the jungle. But it

turned out the folks waiting for the supplies weren't legitimate researchers. They were in the business of smuggling
antiquities. We saw more than we should have seen and
they didn't want any witnesses."

"Dear heaven," Sarah breathed. "What happened?"

"We were ambushed on the way back out of the jungle."

"By the so-called archaeologists?"

Gideon nodded. "It had to be them, although I didn't
stick around to take a close look."

Sarah stared at him in shock. "How did you escape?"

"With a little luck and the usual advance research on
the terrain that I had done before we went in. That was
my speciality, Sarah. My contribution to Savage and Company. I did all the research on a job, made all the prepa-
rations, checked out all the people involved. I went over
every detail ahead of time, envisioned all the worst case
scenarios and planned for them. Getting stiffed by the
client is one of the worst case possibilities. I always allowed
for it."

"What did Jake Savage contribute to the company?"
Sarah asked dryly.

Gideon gave her a derisive look. "Flash. What else?
You've seen him. He brought image and style to the team.
A natural salesman. He was everything people wanted to
see when they hired a professional adventurer of any kind.
He made people think we could handle anything. And we
did. We had a hell of a reputation down south. We always
got the job done."

"And you always took a cut of the action," Sarah concluded quietly.

Gideon shrugged. "It was business. At least for me. Jake
liked the money, too, of course. He needed a lot of it because he tended to go through it like water. But the truth
was, he got most of his kicks from being a living legend.

He was addicted to his own image. He could walk into any bar from Mexico City to Buenos Aires and the women would fall all over him. And the men all wanted to be able to say they'd met him and bought him a beer."

"But you were the one who really made Savage and Company work, weren't you?" Sarah said, knowing she was right. "You were the strategist, the planner, the one who knew the terrain."

"Jake had his uses as an image. He drew business and investors like flies. But the truth is, he couldn't find candy on Halloween night without help."

Sarah started to giggle before she could stop herself. When she realized Gideon was watching her curiously, she took a swallow of wine to give herself time to regain her firm demeanor. She was not going to stop grilling Gideon until she got all the answers.

"So Savage and Company wouldn't have lasted a week without you behind the scenes."

"It was a partnership. And for the most part it worked well for both of us. We made a lot of money. Did a lot of fast living. You can get addicted to adrenaline just like you can to anything else."

Sarah eyed him sharply. "Do you still crave the excitement?"

Gideon smiled slightly. "Nothing more than what I can get once a year when I go on vacation and do a little treasure hunting."

"All right," Sarah continued forcefully, determined not to be sidetracked, "what happened at the scene of the ambush? Why did you and Jake get separated and each think the other might be dead? What went wrong?"

Gideon took a mouthful of beer and thought about the question. "I don't know."

"What do you mean, you don't know? You were there."

"I was there, all right. But that doesn't mean I know what went wrong. All I know is that one minute we were alone in a Jeep on the trail. We were carrying the cash the so-called archaeologists had paid for their supplies. The next minute I just sort of knew we weren't alone."

"You *knew* it?" Sarah's attention was caught by the odd phrasing. "What does that mean?"

Gideon moved his hand impatiently. "Just what it sounds like. There was no one in sight ahead or behind us, but I had a feeling we were in deep trouble. I told Jake I thought we'd better get out of the Jeep and get into some cover. I knew a place we could disappear to until the coast was clear. Usually he trusted my instincts. In fact he always did. This time he insisted I was crazy. But I was driving. I stopped, picked up the suitcase full of cash and headed into the jungle. Jake didn't have any choice but to follow."

"But he didn't want to go with you?"

"No." Gideon was quiet for a moment, reflecting on some private vision. "About two minutes after we had left the Jeep we heard gunfire back on the trail. Then a lot of noise in the undergrowth. Whoever had attacked the Jeep had realized it was empty and was looking for the principal stockholders of Savage and company. I took off in the direction of a cave I had found on one of the maps. Jake kept stalling. I couldn't figure out why he was having such a hard time keeping up with me, why he kept arguing."

"He was probably disoriented and scared."

"Hell, I was scared, too, but at least I wasn't disoriented. I never get disoriented."

"Instinct again?"

"Whatever. At any rate, I got Jake and the money into the cave and we found the cavern tunnel that an old guide had told me about. It led through the heart of a small mountain and out the other side. The perfect escape route. I'd earmarked it for just that kind of emergency."

Sarah momentarily forgot about her need to stay firm. She was enthralled with Gideon's story. "That was brilliant of you."

His mouth quirked. "Well, it was the best I could come up with under the circumstances. Unfortunately there was a narrow ledge over a gorge on the other side of the cave. Only room for one man at a time to cross it. I went first with the money and Jake started to follow. Then he seemed to lose his nerve. He told me he'd take his chances hiding in the cave. I yelled back that he was a fool and I tried to throw him a vine to use to steady himself. But he panicked and raced back into the cave."

"And you never saw him again," Sarah concluded.

"Not until today. When I walked out of the jungle a few days later, I discovered we were both supposed to be dead. The local gossip, though, was that there was a price on our heads if we did happen to show up. The smugglers wanted us to stay dead. I obliged. I got off the island on a fishing boat and that was the end of it."

"Why did you change your name and create a whole new identity for yourself?"

Gideon turned the beer can in his hands. "It's hard to explain. The truth is, I saw it as an opportunity to start over. I wanted out of the kind of business Savage and Company did. Twelve years is long enough in that line. Thirteen years in it could get a man killed. But it's not always easy to walk away. I wasn't famous like Jake, but a lot of people knew me, knew the kind of work I'd done in the past. Some held a few grudges, like those smugglers who had tried to get rid of us after the last trip. All in all, it was simpler to just start fresh."

Just like one of my heroes, Sarah thought with a surge of empathy. Gideon had turned his back on the past in search of another life. "What about Jake?"

"I wasn't sure Jake was dead. In fact, I figured there was a good chance he wasn't. It took several months and a lot of research but I eventually found out he was very much alive and doing business under the name of Slaughter."

"You've known who he was and where he was all this time?"

"I told you, I like to cover all possible contingencies," Gideon explained quietly.

Sarah picked up her wine and sat down across from him, thinking quickly. "You didn't want him to find you again, did you?"

"No."

"Because you were afraid he'd pressure you into going back into business with him and you wanted out of that kind of work?"

Gideon hesitated. "That was part of it, I guess, but not all of it. I could have resisted the pressure easily enough. But the truth is, I just didn't want to deal with him ever again. Or any of the people from that old life." He searched her face. "Does that make sense?"

"Of course. You had a right to try a new path. What better way to do it than under a new name? But why did Jake change his name when he came out of the jungle? Oh!" Sarah clapped her hand over her mouth as the realization hit.

"What is it, Sarah?"

"Yes, I see now. He had to change his name, didn't he? He thought you were either dead or determined to stay missing and he knew that with you gone Savage and Company was effectively out of business. He knew he couldn't run it without you. Better to go out a legend than to go on as a has-been who can't hack it on his own. He had his image to think of and from what you've said, his image was everything to him. He couldn't bear to destroy it by proving how incompetent he was to run Savage and Company without you."

Gideon studied her. "You really think that was the reason he changed his name?"

"It makes perfect sense when you think about it."

"I always figured he used a new name because he was afraid of running into those smugglers again," Gideon said slowly. "Or someone like them. Who knows what other deals he had cooking behind my back?"

"That may have had something to do with his decision to change his name, but I doubt that's the reason he made it permanent." Sarah leaned forward. "Tell me something. You say you've been keeping tabs on him. What's he been doing in the past five years?"

"Small-time stuff for the most part. Nickle and dime guide jobs for tourists who want to picnic in the jungle near an old ruin. That kind of thing," Gideon said vaguely. "I haven't paid close attention. All I cared about was having him stay out of my way."

Sarah bit her lip. "But now he's very much in your way, isn't he? And it's all my fault. I led him straight to you."

Gideon gave her a wry look. "Just how many so-called treasure hunters, salvage operators, amateur adventurers and assorted riffraff did you contact when you first started doing research on *Glitter Quest?*"

"A couple of dozen, at least," she admitted. "I wasn't sure what I was looking for at first, you see."

"A couple of dozen. Hell."

"Don't worry," Sarah assured him hastily, "I only mentioned the Flowers to you and Slaughter, or Savage, or whatever his name is."

"That's something to be grateful for, I guess." Gideon gave her a direct look. "Two dozen. What made you pick me out of the pack?"

"Two reasons. First of all, I knew as soon as your letter arrived that I wanted you and no one else to help me in my research."

"The famous Fleetwood intuition strikes again."

"Don't laugh. It was true. But there was a second reason I picked you. You didn't ask for money. In fact, after I mentioned the Fleetwood Flowers, you actually tried to talk me out of wasting my time, remember?"

"I remember. For all the good it did me."

"All of the others turned out to be screwballs or outright frauds who wanted me to invest in their various schemes. I was invited to pour money into every lost gold mine from here to Australia. Jim Slaughter, I mean, Jake, turned out to be more persistent than the rest, though. He liked the idea of teaming up with a writer. I got the feeling that, in addition to wanting me to finance him, he had visions of me doing a book on him or something."

"Or something," Gideon agreed coldly.

She ignored that, frowning intently. "What did your family think about you changing your name?"

"That wasn't a problem."

"No family?"

Gideon shook his head. "No."

"And no wife," Sarah said as she put the rest of it together for herself. "Because Leanna had already divorced you by that time, hadn't she?"

"Yeah."

"And she was waiting for Jake Savage, wasn't she?"

Gideon was silent for a long moment. "That's about the size of it."

"Savage and Leanna. Those were the two people who betrayed you."

"Don't make it sound so melodramatic. Leanna fell in love with Jake and I was in the way. That was all there was to it."

"Hah." Sarah was incensed all over again. "It was an outright betrayal. The worst kind. How dare they do that to you? Your wife and your best friend. Impossible to forgive or forget."

"I wouldn't put it that way."

Sarah glared at him. "Have you forgotten?"

"No, but that doesn't mean I'm still holding a grudge."

"You've got every right to hold one. No wonder you never wanted to see Jake Savage again."

"If you say so. Look, could we change the subject?"

"To what?" Sarah asked.

"How about we discuss the little matter of Emelina Fleetwood's earrings? We've got some decisions to make now that we've located that white rock."

Sarah scowled and got up to go back to peeling carrots. "Good point. What are we going to do about Jake? I don't want him hanging around the Flowers."

"I agree. He's got his eye on those earrings, all right. And on you."

"You mean because he thinks he can use me for publicity purposes? You may be right. In any event, he's definitely the type who will step in at the last minute to claim all the credit. I can see him having a photographer and a couple of reporters waiting in the bushes to cover his big discovery of the Fleetwood Flowers."

"Yeah, that's Savage, all right. He always liked to have a photographer or a reporter around."

"So what should we do?"

"Leave."

"Leave? After finding the white rock? We can't just walk away and let Jake Savage dig up my earrings. It's not fair."

"I've told you, he won't find them on his own. They're as safe now as they've been for the past few years."

"You really think so?" Sarah asked doubtfully.

Gideon watched her, his legs stretched out in front of him. "Trust me on this. I know Jake Savage."

"I'm not so sure he's as incompetent as you say he is."

"Those earrings are getting more important again, aren't they?" Gideon asked softly. "This afternoon you said you weren't very concerned about them at all, but now you're getting downright agitated on the subject."

"It's the principle of the thing. This afternoon I didn't know Jake Savage was going to pop up. He has no right to get his hands on those earrings."

"He won't."

"You sound awfully confident," Sarah said resentfully. "But I have a funny feeling about him. I know he's going to try to claim the Flowers, Gideon." She shivered as her intuition conjured up an image of Jake Savage reaching for the earrings. "I just know it. He has no right."

"I was his partner for a long time," Gideon said. "I know his limitations."

"One of his limitations is that he has no scruples. A man with scruples does not steal his best friend's wife."

"He didn't steal her. She fell in love with him. It wasn't anyone's fault."

"The heck it wasn't. Neither one of them had any scruples if you ask me. How did you get mixed up with a couple of bozos like those two, Gideon?"

"The same way you got mixed up with Richard Whatshisface and managed to get yourself left at the altar. These things happen."

She sighed. "I guess."

There was silence for a moment as the vegetables cooked on the stove. Sarah drummed her fingers on the countertop and stared at the cloud of steam that drifted up from the pot.

"Sarah?"

"Yes, Gideon?"

"About what happened this afternoon...."

She glanced over her shoulder and met Gideon's intent eyes. "What about it?"

"I know I sort of pushed you into it."

"You didn't push me into it."

"Yes, I did. You'd been trying to resist for the past few days."

She smiled. "Not very successfully."

"Are you sure you don't have any regrets?"

"I'm sure. What about you?"

He looked surprised at the question. "Hell, no. Why would I have any regrets?"

"Why, indeed?" she muttered as she dished up the vegetables.

Three hours later Gideon won another hand of gin rummy. He had been winning steadily since they'd begun the game shortly after dinner. "You're not concentrating," he accused.

"I know." Sarah propped her elbows on the table and rested her chin on her folded hands.

"Thinking about the earrings again?"

"No."

"Savage?"

"No."

Gideon leaned back in his chair. "Then what were you thinking about?"

"Us."

His eyes narrowed. "What about us?"

"I'm wondering what to do next, if you must know. Nothing has gone quite the way I thought it would since I met you."

"I knew it," Gideon said swiftly, "you are having regrets."

"I am not having regrets," she snapped. "I'm just feeling confused about a few things."

"Such as?" he challenged roughly.

"Such as what to do with this courtship."

"The courtship's over," Gideon announced, getting to his feet.

Sarah looked up in astonishment. "It is?"

"That's right. We're no longer involved in a courtship. It ended this afternoon when I seduced you on that white rock. We are now involved in an affair."

He came around the table, bent down and scooped her up out of her chair.

"What do you think you're doing?" But her pulse was already racing with anticipation.

"What does it look like I'm doing?" He stalked out of the kitchen, carrying her weight easily. "I'm taking you to bed."

"Oh."

"Is that all you can say—*oh?*" He carried her through the bedroom door and dropped her lightly down onto the bed.

She smiled in the shadows. "The truth is, it's so terribly romantic, I'm left speechless."

He grinned as he began stripping off his clothing. "You're bound and determined to think of me as a romantic hero, aren't you?"

"It's not a fantasy, you know. You are a fascinating, romantic man and I—" She broke off abruptly as he came down beside her on the quilt. It was not yet time to tell him how passionately in love she was. He was not yet ready to let himself believe in love even though she was certain he was in love with her.

"You what?" Gideon gathered her close, nuzzling the delicate curve of her shoulder.

"I think you're also the sexiest man I've ever met." She leaned over him, tasting him with her tongue, tangling her legs with his.

"I don't know about that," Gideon said as he began unfastening her jeans, "but I do know for a fact that you're the most exciting thing that's ever walked into my life." He stopped working on her jeans and framed her face between his big hands. "Sarah?"

"Yes?"

"Promise me you won't walk out again for a long time."

"Never, Gideon. I swear it."

"Don't make impossible promises," he advised. "Just swear you'll give me a little time."

"All the time in the world." She brushed his hard mouth with her own.

He took the silent offer of reassurance, his arms closing fiercely around her and then there was no more talk.

SARAH WAS MIXING THE BATTER FOR BLUE CORN griddlecakes the next morning, listening to the sound of the shower so she could gauge when to start cooking when she heard the roar of the black Jeep in the drive.

"Damn him, anyway," she said beneath her breath as she went to the window and watched Jake Savage step out of the vehicle. The man looked as rakishly handsome as ever. She wondered if he traveled with a valet. No normal man could keep such a perfect crease in his khakis or such a polish on his boots.

As he walked to the steps, Sarah saw that Savage had something in his hand. It was a bunch of flowers. She groaned as she went to open the door.

"Good morning. Ms. Fleetwood." Savage held up the

flowers with a flourish. "I thought these might brighten up the place a bit. This cabin Gid rented isn't exactly the Ritz, is it?"

Automatically Sarah took the flowers. "The cabin suited us perfectly." Behind her the shower was still going strong. She wished Gideon would hurry and get dressed. She did not like being alone with Jake Savage. "What can I do for you, Mr. Savage?"

"Invite me in for breakfast? I can't remember when I last had a real home-cooked meal. Is that coffee I smell?"

Sarah wondered if there was any civilized way to refuse him a cup. But it was difficult to think of an excuse while she was holding the flowers he had brought. "I'll get you some. Gideon should be out of the shower in a minute."

"Thanks." Jake's smile had just the right touch of boyish masculine charm and gratitude as he followed her into the kitchen. "I guess I make you a little nervous, don't I?"

"Yes, you do."

"Relax. I'm not after the earrings, if that's what's worrying you," Jake said as he took Gideon's seat at the table. "But I can arrange some great publicity for you as well as myself when you find them. A little PR never hurt a writer, did it?"

Sarah felt chilled. Very carefully she put the flowers into a pan of water. "How did you find me up here in the mountains?"

"One of your neighbors told me you'd gone over to the coast to meet the publisher of a magazine called *Cache*. After that, one thing led to another. I talked to a few of Gid's neighbors, including the one who was letting you use this cabin. It finally hit me just who Gideon Trace really was. When I showed an old picture of him to the guy who runs the motel where you stayed, I knew for certain. Hell of a coincidence, huh? Turning up Gid along with you?"

"Amazing."

Jake looked briefly contrite. "Hey, I didn't mean to scare you."

"You didn't scare me." She poured a cup of coffee and put it on the table in front of Jake. "Where have you been living since you got out of that jungle?"

"Gid told you the story, huh? Did he tell you about me getting trapped in that cave while he escaped?"

"He told me you didn't make it out with him," Sarah said cautiously.

Jake shrugged. "No hard feelings. I don't blame Gid for leaving me behind. That's the way it goes. Sometimes you've got to look out for number one and let your partner take his chances. Who knows? If I'd been in his place, maybe I'd have done the same." But his wry smile and clear blue eyes said he'd never abandon a partner in a million years. A man could count on a guy like Jake Savage.

Sarah watched him with increasing fascination. She poured herself some tea and sat down. "That's very broadminded of you, Mr. Savage."

"Call me Jake. Or Jim. Doesn't matter. Hey, this coffee's terrific. Trust old Gid to find himself a woman who could cook this time around. He never makes the same mistake twice. You and Gid been together long?"

"We've known each other for over four months," Sarah said.

Jake nodded. "When did you tell him about the Fleetwood Flowers?"

"Why?"

"Just curious. Wondered if Gid was still doing business in the usual way. Did he ask for up-front money and a cut of the action? That was the usual policy."

Sarah stirred her tea, thinking of Gideon's demand for one pair of earrings—his choice. "I haven't paid him a dime."

Jake grinned, showing an expanse of sparkling white teeth. "Fair warning, little lady, Gid never works for free. If he didn't take any up-front money from you, then that means he really does believe in the treasure and it means he's got his eye on a chunk of it. You sure you don't have a contract guaranteeing him a slice of the pie?"

"We have a verbal understanding," Sarah said stiffly.

"Hell. That's too bad." Jake gave her a pitying look. "Then my advice is to be very careful, Sarah. Very, very careful. Gid and I had a verbal understanding before we went into that jungle five years ago. I not only didn't get my cut, I nearly died in that damned cave."

Sarah heard the shower stop but her entire attention was on Jake Savage. "You're trying to frighten me, aren't you? Trying to make me distrust Gideon."

"All I'm saying is, watch your back. And your treasure. If you don't know how to do either, hire me. I'll do it for you. I've had experience in both departments."

"*Hire* you?"

"Why not? Call me a consultant. I'll handle the media and Gideon for you. Gideon's useful but you've got to keep your eye on him."

"And in return all you'll take is a nominal fee and full credit for finding the Flowers?"

"I think you'll realize that I'm worth every penny, Sarah. Just ask any of my old clients." Jake reached across the table and covered her hand with his own. His blue eyes were serious and full of understanding. "All you want is the Flowers. All I want is the publicity so I can attract some really big investors. This downed-airplane-full-of-gold thing is going to be a major score. You and me, we can work together, even without Gideon. Like I said, we don't actually have to find the treasure."

"What about Gideon?" Sarah removed her hand from under Jake's.

"Yeah," said Gideon from the doorway. "What about me?"

Sarah jumped and turned her head to see him buttoning his shirt as he walked into the room. She saw the cold expression in his eyes and knew he'd seen her hand under Jake's. She wanted to go to him and reassure him that everything was all right, but he was already helping himself to the coffee.

"If you join us you'll get your cut, as usual," Jake said easily. "I'm just trying to convince Sarah here to let me handle the press for her."

"We don't need any attention from the media," Sarah said, her eyes on Gideon.

"Right," said Gideon. "The last thing we need is an orchestrated media blitz. It's time for you to leave, Jake."

"We can do each other a lot of favors, Gid. We were big once. We can be again."

"No."

"Think about it, Gid. And don't tell me you don't miss the old days. Or the money."

"Get lost, Jake."

"Come on, Gid, this is me, your old buddy talking."

"Get out of here," Gideon said very softly. "Now."

Sarah froze at the steel in Gideon's voice. She looked at Jake and saw frustrated rage flash for an instant in his blue eyes.

But the anger was gone almost immediately as the self-assured gleam came back into Jake's gaze. He got to his feet. "Okay, okay. Take it easy. Hey, I'm gone already, right? So much for old times. You've changed, Gid." He turned to Sarah. "Listen, if you change your mind, Sarah, let me know. You can leave a message at this number any time of the day or night."

Jake scrawled a phone number on the back of a business card and reached across the table to press it into Sarah's hand. He folded her fingers around it with an intimate gesture and then he got to his feet and sauntered out of the room. A moment later the Jeep roared off down the drive.

Sarah looked down at the card in her hand. *Slaughter & Co. James Slaughter, President.* There was no address, just a box number in Anaheim, California. That made a certain sense. Anaheim was the home of Disneyland. She looked up and saw Gideon watching her over the rim of his cup.

"The two of you got involved in a nice, cozy little chat while I was in the shower, didn't you?"

"Don't get defensive. It's not my fault he showed up this morning."

"Is that right?"

"It certainly is. Now stop trying to bully me."

"Let's eat breakfast and get packed, Sarah."

"Packed?" Sarah frowned. "Gideon, I did a lot of thinking last night and I still feel we shouldn't leave the Flowers behind. Not now that Jake Savage is hanging around. Something tells me he's going to try to find the Flowers, that he'll come close, maybe even get his grubby hands on them. I've got this feeling…"

"I've told you he won't find them. Damn it, Sarah, don't argue with me. We don't have the time. The Flowers are safe enough for now. We're getting out of here."

"Not without the Flowers, Gideon."

"Forget the Flowers. We'll come back for them. Eventually."

"But, Gideon…"

"I want to be out of here by eight o'clock."

Sarah shot to her feet, exasperated. She planted both palms on the table and glared at him. "I'm in charge of this little expedition, remember? I say we stay and dig up the earrings so Jake Savage won't get his hands on them."

"No." Gideon sipped his coffee. "You're not in charge. We're partners."

"Oh, yes, that's right. You're in this for a cut of the action, aren't you? I almost forgot."

"I'm sure Savage reminded you."

"He did say something about the fact that you never work for free," Sarah retorted. "But I was beginning to think our partnership was a little more than a mere business arrangement."

"Did you think I'd give up my claim to one of the Flowers just because we're having an affair? Is that why you're sleeping with me? You figure you can persuade me not to take my cut when this is all over?"

He might just as well have slapped her across the face. Sarah gasped with shock. She took a step back from the table, her eyes widening in hurt and anger.

"You're right," she whispered, aware that she was trembling from head to foot. "The sooner we get away from here, the better. I'll go and pack."

Chapter Eight

SARAH STARED AT THE MOUNTAIN SCENERY through the car window. "You can drop me off in Seattle." They were the first words she had spoken since they had left the cabin.

"I'm taking you back to the coast with me." Gideon's refusal was quiet but resolute.

Sarah shot him a seething, sidelong glance. "What are you going to do? Kidnap me until you can figure out a way to get your hands on all of the Fleetwood Flowers?"

"I'm not kidnapping you. I'm giving you a lift back to where you left your car. It's still at my place, remember?"

"I remember." She sank down low in her seat, her arms folded tightly beneath her breasts. He had a point. "You're right. I'll need my car." She looked at her watch. "We'll be at your place shortly after noon. I'll drive back to Seattle this afternoon. I'll be home in plenty of time."

"Plenty of time for what?"

"For whatever I want to do."

"Planning on going after the Flowers by yourself?"

"It's none of your business what I do about the Flowers. Our partnership is hereby dissolved. Finished. Terminated. Liquidated."

"I'm not ready yet to be fired."

"Oh, yes, you are. You and Jake Savage had both better stay out of my life from now on. If I catch either one of you anywhere near my property, I'll have you both arrested for trespassing."

"Sarah, you're not being rational about this. How are you going to catch Savage or anyone else hanging around your property when you're in Seattle?"

"I'm heading back up here just as soon as I can," Sarah vowed. "This time I'll bring my own shovel and a shotgun."

"Have you got a shotgun?" Gideon asked.

"No, but I expect I can get one. Guns are readily available these days."

"You don't need a shotgun or anything else to protect your damned Flowers," Gideon said wearily. "I've told you a hundred times, Savage won't find them."

"Is that right? Well, what about you?"

"If you want to make certain I don't dig them up on my own, all you have to do is stick around and keep an eye on me."

"I'm a busy woman, Trace. I've got more important things to do than try to keep tabs on you. No, the fastest solution to this problem is for me to dig up my earrings before either you or your old buddy gets to them."

"I don't think that would be a good idea."

"I don't care what you think any more," Sarah said. "I've told you, you're fired as a treasure-hunting consultant and as my partner."

There was a long silence from the driver's side of the car. Gideon concentrated on the narrow, twisting road that was taking them down out of the rugged terrain to where the main freeway sliced through the mountain pass.

"Does it occur to you that you might be overreacting a bit?" Gideon said eventually.

Sarah gritted her teeth. "Overreacting to what, pray tell? Do you think it's possible I've gone a bit overboard in my response to your insults? Perhaps I should have just laughed off the accusation that I slept with you in order to get you to help me find my treasure. Maybe I overreacted to being accused of trying to use sex to stiff you out of your cut of the action."

"Sarah…"

"Or perhaps I'm being just a tad irrational now that I've come to my senses and realized I've been deluding myself about you right from the start. The famous Fleetwood intuition screws up again. I can't say I wasn't warned. Hell, you warned me, yourself."

"Sarah…"

"Then again, maybe I'm being a bit petty and overly defensive now that I've discovered I've got to protect the Fleetwood Flowers from not one, but two professional opportunists. Yes, I can see where I might be overreacting. I'll have to watch that, won't I?"

"Do you get worked up like this a lot?"

"What do you care? I won't be around you long enough for it to be of any great concern to you." Sarah continued to scowl out the window for a minute. "I wonder if I should just turn around and drive straight back up here this afternoon instead of going back to Seattle for the night. I know you don't think Savage can find the jewels on his own, but my intuition tells me he can and will. And now there's you to worry about, too, of course. Yes, I think I'd better get right back up here today."

"Forget it, Sarah. You're not coming back into these mountains to dig up the Flowers on your own."

"Who's going to stop me?"

"Me."

"I knew it, you *are* kidnapping me. Well, you won't get away with it. If you think you can just lock me away in your cellar or something and have no one notice I'm missing, you're crazy. My best friends in the whole world know I went to find you and if I turn up missing, Margaret and Kate won't rest until they've found out what you did to me. And Kate's husband will probably help them look."

"I'm beginning to see why you're successful at writing novels of romantic suspense. You have a very unique imagination, don't you?"

"And that's another thing. Better not forget what I do for a living. I've got an outstanding contract to complete. If I don't finish the last book on it, my publisher and my agent will come looking for you, too."

His mouth flickered suspiciously, but all Gideon said was, "I'll keep that in mind before I do anything rash."

Satisfied she'd made all the threats she could for the moment, Sarah lapsed back into a brooding silence. She needed her anger. At the moment it was all that was keeping her from tears.

"Sarah, I know you're in no mood to listen to explanations."

"You're right."

"But I'd like to point out that it's not entirely fair to blame me for wondering about your motives. You landed on my doorstep like a small tornado and I feel as though I've been swept up and carried along in a high wind ever since. From the first day you acted as though we were long-lost lovers—as if we'd known each other for ages. You practically begged me to make love to you every time I kissed you. You told me you were going to court me, which is another way of saying seduce me. You went wild when I did finally make love to you, as if I was some irresistible, private fantasy of yours that had come to life. It was crazy, Sarah."

"So I made a teensy little mistake."

"That was one explanation," Gideon said dryly. "But the other, more likely one is that you had a few private motives for wanting to ensure you had me tied up in knots. I don't blame you. You figured you needed some expert help finding the Flowers."

"Shut up, Gideon."

"I'm not saying you were faking your response in bed. I don't think any woman could give that convincing a performance, although that may just reflect my own lack of experience. I haven't been involved with that many women and none of them ever had sufficient reason to want to—"

"I said shut up and meant it," Sarah hissed. "If you dig that hole any deeper, you may never be able to crawl out of it."

"I'm just trying to point out my side of this."

"You've made your point. Damn. When I think of all the excuses I made for you based on the trauma you'd been through with your ex-wife and Jake Savage, I could just spit. You don't need any excuses for the way you've been acting, do you? You come by it naturally. Let's change the subject."

"To what?"

Sarah chewed thoughtfully on her lower lip. "Why didn't you want us to dig up the Flowers before we left this morning? Jake was gone. If we'd hurried, we could have gotten them without him ever knowing. Are you planning to come back on your own and take all of them for yourself?"

He didn't rise to the bait. "I didn't want to start digging for them knowing Savage was still in the neighborhood."

She caught her breath. "You mean you think he might wait until we've dug them up and then try to steal them from us? I never thought of that."

"I know."

"But he was your *partner.*"

"I'm aware of that."

"Of course, he did steal your wife. I can see where you might wonder a bit about his trustworthiness in other matters."

"It's not because of what happened with Leanna that I'm worried."

"It's because of what happened on that last trip you two made into the jungle, isn't it?"

Gideon concentrated on the slow-moving truck ahead of them. "I can't help but wonder how he survived."

"You survived."

"I'm better at it than Savage." There was no arrogance or ego in his voice. It was just a simple statement of fact.

"So you're wondering how he got out of that jungle?"

"I'm wondering how he managed to get out of that cave alive, let alone find his way out of the jungle."

"How do you think he managed?" Sarah asked slowly.

"I think it's possible he had help."

"But the only help around from what you've said would have been the smugglers and they were the ones who staged the ambush."

"You've got it."

Sarah was shaken by the implications. "You think it was a conspiracy? That Jake was part of it?"

"I think it's a possibility."

"That would mean he deliberately set you up that day. That he intended to get you killed. But the plan failed because you sensed trouble."

"Savage was never very good at the planning side of things. Believe me, it would be totally in character for him to have screwed up the timing on the ambush."

"I don't get it. Why would he want to kill the goose that lays the golden eggs?"

"A goose, hmm? I never thought of myself that way, but I guess that's one point of view. To answer your question, all I can say is, there was a lot of cash involved."

"How much of it did you get out of the country?"

"All of it except what I spent bribing the captain of the fishing boat. I used the remainder to set myself up in business with *Cache*."

"Good heavens. You did lead an adventurous life, didn't you? I see what you mean about adrenaline. So what this all boils down to is you're afraid we'll be standing there plucking the Fleetwood Flowers from the ground and your old buddy Jake might show up to take them away from us at gunpoint."

"I'd just as soon not take any risks."

"I can understand that. You've got a lot to lose. Just one pair of those earrings will be worth a lot of money. I've got an even bigger problem, though, don't I? I have to figure out a way to protect the Flowers from you and Savage."

"Sarah, if you continued to make not-so-veiled accusations about my trustworthiness, I'm eventually going to lose my temper."

"The way I lost mine when you started making nasty cracks about my reasons for sleeping with you?"

Gideon shook his head ruefully. "Something like that. For the record, and not that you've bothered to ask, I give you my word I'll abide by our original bargain."

"We don't have a bargain. I fired you, remember?"

"I warned you that I don't fire that easily."

"Which, translated, means you're not going to give up your claim to the jewels."

"I don't suppose it's occurred to you that I'm more worried about you than I am the Flowers?"

"No."

"Sarah, be reasonable. As long as Savage is hanging around, it's dangerous for you to even think about digging up the earrings. Leave them where they are until he gets bored and leaves the vicinity."

"What makes you think he'll get bored?"

"I know him. If he believes I've really given up on the Flowers, myself, he'll give up on them, too. He got used to trusting my instincts. And he never hangs around too long if there's no percentage in it. One of these days he'll disappear and leave us in peace. When he does, we'll go back and get the Flowers."

"It might interest you to know," Sarah said slowly, "that Jake doesn't trust you any farther than you trust him."

"What the hell does that mean?"

"We had quite an interesting conversation this morning while you were in the shower. Jake tells a slightly different version of what happened that day in the jungle. According to him, you more or less abandoned him to his fate."

Gideon's head snapped around, his eyes blazing. "He said I cut out on him?"

"Yup."

"And you believed him?"

Sarah was feeling resentful enough not to respond immediately to that.

"*Sarah*. Of all the... You didn't believe him, did you?"

"What is this? I'm supposed to have complete, unswerving faith in you even though you can have serious doubts about my integrity?"

"For God's sake, just tell me if you actually believed him."

Sarah blinked, startled at the intensity of Gideon's reaction. "Calm down. I didn't believe him. Although I have to say I think it's entirely possible that in the stress of the moment each of you could have misinterpreted the other's actions."

"Thanks for that much, at any rate."

"You're welcome. How long do I have to wait for my apology this time?"

"Until hell freezes over."

"Never mind. I can see your heart's not in it. Getting back to how we deal with Jake Savage. I'm supposed to just twiddle my thumbs until the coast is clear?"

"Patience is a virtue."

"I was patient for four long months until I decided it was time to look you up. It turned out to be a futile exercise in virtue from every viewpoint."

"Give me some credit. I found your white rock for you, didn't I?"

"After seducing me on top of it."

He smiled briefly. "It was kind of symbolic, wasn't it?"

"Of what?" She felt goaded now.

He shrugged. "Making love to you was a lot like finding buried treasure."

She shot him a suspicious glance, trying to see if he was making fun of her. But he looked perfectly serious. Sarah couldn't help it. She tried to ignore what he'd said, but she wound up hugging his incredibly romantic words to herself even though she tried not to read too much into them.

MACHU PICCHU AND ELLORA WERE WAITING on the front porch when Gideon pulled into the drive. Machu stayed posed regally on the top step, waiting for Gideon to get out of the car and come over to be recognized. But Ellora glided happily down the steps and trotted over to greet Sarah.

"Hello, sweetheart," Sarah murmured as she bent to pick up the cat. "Did you miss us? Did that big, old Machu bully you while we were gone the way Gideon bullied me?"

Ellora purred and butted her head against Sarah's chin. Then she wriggled free, leaped onto the roof of the car and padded over to welcome Gideon. He gave her an affectionate pat on the head and went back to unloading the luggage.

"Hold it," Sarah called out as she saw him start toward the front steps with her bags. "You can put those right into my car."

Gideon was already on the top step. He put down one suitcase and bent to scratch Machu behind the ears. "I think it would be better if you stayed here with me for a few more days, Sarah."

"No."

"We already went over this in the car. I don't trust Savage and I don't want you having to deal with him on your own. You told me yourself, you've got two weeks to play with. You'll stay here where I know you're safe and when the time is right, we'll go dig up the Flowers together."

"I didn't agree to anything in the car. I'm leaving. I'll be perfectly safe in Seattle."

"Savage knows where you live," Gideon said patiently. "He's liable to come calling on the old divide-and-conquer theory. If he decides you can lead him to the earrings on your own, he won't hesitate to try to talk you into doing just that."

"Don't worry, he can't talk me into doing anything I don't want to do. Furthermore, I'm not about to cut you out of the deal and then turn around and let him in, instead."

"Savage can be very convincing. Especially with women," Gideon said. "I've seen him in action."

Especially with women. Sarah opened her mouth to protest the idiotic assumption that she could be swayed by someone like Jake Savage, but something stopped her. She was getting a familiar, faint tingling sense of awareness. Her intuition was kicking in again. She stood there, hands on her hips and contemplated Gideon and his big cat.

All this emphasis on Jake Savage's untrustworthiness was beginning to sound like overkill. Obviously Gideon was not physically afraid of the man. She couldn't imagine Gideon being afraid of anyone. Furthermore, she wasn't at all sure there was anything to Gideon's vague, farfetched theories about Jake having somehow set his partner up with the smugglers.

But the one thing about Jake Savage that Gideon had genuine reason to worry about was the man's effect on women.

It was true Gideon had said some terrible, hurtful things back there in the mountains, but for the first time Sarah was calm enough to realize he might have been lashing out from the depths of his own uncertainty. She remembered the look on his face when he'd walked into the kitchen that morning and seen Jake's flowers sitting in the pan of water.

And Jake's hand covering her own on the table.

And Jake looking intently into her eyes, telling her they'd make a great team.

Maybe what Gideon had really seen in his mind's eye was his ex-wife, Leanna, falling so easily for Jake's good looks and easy charm. Gideon should know by now that she, Sarah, was not at all the same sort of woman Leanna had been. But men could be awfully thick-headed about things, especially men like him who had been savaged in the past by people they had trusted.

"You have nothing to worry about," she told him finally.

"Nevertheless, I will worry. You're staying here, Sarah."

"Stop telling me what to do, damn you." Sarah whirled around and raced toward her car, fumbling in her bag for the keys.

She wasn't even halfway there when Gideon's arm caught her around the waist and jerked her to an abrupt stop. The breath was driven out of her lungs.

"I said, you're staying."

Sarah gasped for air as he turned and hauled her back toward the porch. "Gideon, you can't do this."

"Watch me." He took the keys from her hand and dropped them into his pocket. "We can do this hard or we can do it easy, Sarah, but one way or another, you're staying."

He meant it. Sarah slanted him a speculative glance out of the corner of her eye and read the implacable determination in Gideon's face. In that moment he looked more than ever like one of her dangerous heroes.

"If I do decide to stay," she said in her most imperious tones, just as if she had a choice, "it will be for only a few more days and it has to be understood that we're not going back to our old relationship. Is that very clear?"

Gideon's brows rose as he cautiously released her. "Old relationship? It seems like a fairly new relationship to me. We've barely gotten started."

"You know damn well what I mean." Sarah started toward the steps. "No sex."

"You said that once before but you changed your mind."

"That was different. This time I won't be changing my mind." Her chin was high as she swept past him into the gloomy old house. "I'll pick out my bedroom right now. You can leave my luggage in it."

Gideon muttered something under his breath. Then he looked down at Machu Picchu. "How the mighty are fallen, huh, pal? Yesterday I was a legendary lover. This afternoon I've been demoted to bellhop."

"I heard that," Sarah yelled from inside the house. "And you're absolutely right. Furthermore, if I were you, I wouldn't expect much of a tip. Where's the thermostat in this place? It's freezing in here."

Gideon hoisted the luggage again and followed her into the living room. He glanced around at the familiar bleak, faded, excessively neat interior. It didn't seem all that chilly to him. But he knew that was because Sarah was already running around inside, opening the old drapes to let in the light, putting hot water on the stove for tea and generally warming things up with her effortless, effervescent vitality.

SEVERAL HOURS LATER GIDEON SAT ALONE on the sofa, Machu draped in his usual position along the back. Ellora was nowhere in sight and Gideon suspected she had accompanied Sarah to bed.

"Just us guys left out here," Gideon muttered to the big cat. "But at least she stayed without too much of a fight."

He was damned lucky she had given in as easily as she had and he knew it. He'd thought for a while there that he'd ruined all his chances when he'd asked her if she'd played sensual games with him in an effort to get him to give up any claim on the Flowers.

Nearly done in again by his own mouth.

One of these days Gideon hoped he would learn not to fire from the hip. He was getting too good at shooting himself in the foot.

But the sight of Savage's flowers sitting in that pan in the cabin's kitchen had rendered him cold with rage. He'd been furious, not only with Jake who was, after all, only acting in character, but with Sarah who'd accepted the flowers. Furthermore, she'd let the bastard put his hand over hers. He'd *touched* her.

Gideon knew now she hadn't meant anything by accepting the flowers or letting Jake get close. She seemed to be able to see right through the facade in a way no other woman ever had. Sarah's problem was that she just didn't understand how dangerous Savage could be when it came to women. She was too naive, too trusting.

Just look how quick she'd been to trust one Gideon Trace, he reminded himself morosely as he took a large swallow of brandy. The little fool had come skipping cheerfully into his life just as if he really were one of the heroes out of her books.

No common sense, Gideon told himself. That was Sarah's whole problem. She was good-hearted and sweet and fascinating in many ways, but she obviously needed a strong-willed man to take care of her. She needed someone to keep her from getting into trouble. Someone to protect her from the likes of Jake Savage.

Jake Savage. Why the hell did he have to show up after all this time? Why couldn't he have done one decent thing in his life and stayed dead?

But it was typical of Jake to come back now, Gideon thought.

Just when things had been starting to fall into place between himself and Sarah. Just when he'd figured he was getting a handle on her. Just when he'd started an affair with her and he'd begun to realize how important she was to him.

Gideon got to his feet, brandy glass in one hand, and went up the stairs and down the dark hall to the room Sarah had chosen. She'd picked the bedroom at the far end, the one that would catch the first rays of morning sunshine.

He tried the antique glass doorknob. It twisted easily in his hand. He wanted to take that as an invitation but he knew it was more likely Sarah simply hadn't found the key in the bottom bureau drawer.

Gideon cracked the door a few inches and peered into the shadows. Ellora stirred, meowing silently as she watched him from the depths of the big, old four-poster. The cat was curled up against Sarah's leg. Sarah, herself, was a small, curved shape under the quilt. Her hair spilled out in a dark fan across the pillow. She was sound asleep, one hand curled near her chin.

Gideon wondered what she would do if he got into bed beside her. He stood there for a long while, sipping his brandy while he studied her in the dim light that filtered through the partially opened door.

Every time he had taken her into his arms, she'd melted for him, even when she'd claimed she didn't think he was ready for a sexual relationship. She'd always responded when he touched her.

In fact, she couldn't really resist him, Gideon told himself.

He opened the door a little farther and stepped into the room. She didn't move. He put the brandy glass down on the bureau and began to undress slowly.

A few minutes later, naked, he started toward the bed.

"Take one more step and I'll scream the house down," Sarah said from the shadows.

Gideon halted, feeling like an idiot. The sensation made him angry and fueled his sense of outraged frustration. "Why? You like it when I make love to you in my arms. Don't try to deny it."

"If you think I'm going to let you sleep with me after some of the things you said this morning, you're out of your mind. Go to bed, Gideon. Your own bed."

Gideon didn't move. "What do you want from me? Damn it, Sarah, I don't understand you."

"That's obvious. The answer to your question is that I don't want anything from you tonight. Go to bed."

"Sarah." He hesitated, some deep, primitive part of him urging him to ignore her protests. He was certain that if he just climbed into bed with her and took her into his arms, she would cling to him the way she always did. "Give it a chance. You want to communicate? This is one way we communicate just fine."

"Not tonight, Gideon. I mean it."

"Damn it, you want me to say I'm sorry? To apologize for what I said at the cabin? Is that it? All right, I'm sorry."

"That's not enough. Not this time."

"What more can you ask?"

"I want you to admit why you did it."

"Why I did it?" he asked blankly.

"Yes. Why you did all of it. Why you said those things about the reasons I was sleeping with you, why you whisked us away from the cabin and why you're so determined to keep me here instead of letting me go back to Seattle."

He stared at her, wishing he could see her face. "But I told you why I did all those things."

"You gave me a fine song and dance about having legitimate reasons to question my motives and how you were going to protect me from Jake Savage in spite of myself, but that's not the real reason."

"It's not?"

"No, it's not. I've been doing a lot of thinking and I've finally figured out what's going on inside that thick skull of yours. It's time you admitted to me and to yourself the real reason you've been acting the way you have today."

"All right, I give up. What is the real reason?"

Sarah sat up against the pillows, her eyes glinting in the shadows. "Actually, there are two reasons. First, you're afraid to admit how much you've come to care for me, and second, you're jealous of Jake Savage."

"Jealous?"

"You're afraid he's going to steal me, not the Flowers, aren't you? Isn't that the truth? Isn't it? Come on, Gideon, say it. You've finally started to realize you're in love with me and you're afraid I'm going to get swept off my feet by Jake Savage. That's the real motivation behind your actions, isn't it?"

Gideon felt as if he'd been sandbagged. "Is that why you didn't put up much of a fight about staying here with me?"

"Of course it is. If I didn't think there was hope for you, I'd have gone straight back to Seattle. But I finally realized the real reason you were acting like a lion with a thorn in its paw and I decided to give you a little time to understand your own actions. But I'm not about to sleep with you again until you finally acknowledge how you really feel about me. Then we'll discuss your little problem with jealousy. Don't worry. It's nothing we can't work out."

For once Gideon managed to keep his mouth shut, although how he managed it, he never knew. Jealous? Jealous of Savage? The blood was pounding in his veins, but not from desire. He hadn't been this furious in a long time. He turned on his heel, picked up his discarded clothes and stormed out of the room. He slammed the door so hard the wall trembled.

He was damned if he would admit he was jealous of Savage. He would not give Sarah that much power. Never in a million years. He would never again give any woman that kind of power over him.

Besides, she was a hundred miles wide of the mark. He wasn't jealous, he was just cautious. He was keeping her out of Savage's reach only because he was trying to protect her from her own naïveté. If she couldn't see that, she was a fool and a manipulative one at that.

If she wanted to think she was in love with him, that was fine, Gideon told himself. But it would be a cold day in Hades before he set himself up to be betrayed again by his woman and his ex-partner. This time around he was going to stay in charge of the situation.

He'd learned a long time ago that the only safe way to exist was to keep his emotions under rigid control. Sarah Fleetwood was not going to force him to break the rules under which he had been living successfully for the past five years.

Chapter Nine

SARAH TRIED HER BEST TO IGNORE GIDEON'S foul mood for the next two days. She pursued a variety of activities as if she were on vacation, experimenting with new recipes in the kitchen, taking long walks on the beach, reading books from Gideon's extensive library.

She was unfailingly good-natured and upbeat, even though she had to grit her teeth on more than one occasion when Gideon turned on her like a cornered cat. In truth, there were some very discouraging moments.

But Sarah was determined that one way or another Gideon was going to learn that this relationship worked on trust, not good sex.

"How long do you think you can keep this up?" Gideon demanded as he washed dishes on the second night.

"Keep what up?" Sarah reclined at the kitchen table, her feet propped on a chair as she recovered from her labors. Dinner had been a particularly spectacular affair, one of her best efforts yet. The Thai-style noodles, hot-

and-sour soup and raspberries in filo had been a culinary triumph as far as she was concerned. Gideon had made no comment as he'd worked his way steadily through the meal. He'd risen to do the dishes without a word.

"You know what I'm talking about." Gideon rinsed the dishes under a spray of hot water. "How long are you going to flit around here acting like you're my roommate or a boarder I've taken in for the summer?"

"Oh, that. As long as it takes, I guess."

A pan clattered loudly in the sink. "As long as it takes to do what, damn it?"

"As long as it takes for you to realize that we're supposed to be building a relationship."

He swung her a brief, angry glance. "If your crazy intuition is telling you this is the way to create a good relationship, you've got bigger problems than I thought."

"What do you want me to do, Gideon?" Sarah asked as Ellora plopped into her lap. "Sleep with you on demand even though you don't trust me and won't admit you love me? What's in it for me?"

"What the hell do you want from me?"

"You know what I want."

He snagged a dishtowel and began drying plates with swift, violent motions. "You started throwing yourself at me the minute I met you. I thought for a while you wanted me."

"I do."

"You don't seem to be having much of a problem pretending I'm just the landlord lately."

"That's not true," Sarah said. "This is as hard on me as it is on you. I'm suffering, too, you know."

"Not as far as I can see." He slung the dishes into the cupboard. "How does this new tactic work? If I go down on my knees and swear I love you and will trust blindly in you forever, do I get to go to bed with you?"

Sarah held her breath. "That would certainly be a promising start."

He shot her a scowling look as he put the rest of the dishes away. "Don't press your luck, Sarah."

She sighed. "It's all Savage's fault. If he hadn't shown up out of the blue when he did, you'd have made much more progress by now. I just know you would have. I wish he'd stayed gone."

"You and me both." Gideon closed the cupboard door and stalked over to stand in front of her. "Come here." He reached down to grab her hand.

She looked up warily. "Where are we going?"

"If you're going to act like a roommate or a summer boarder, you might as well give me a few of the benefits I'd expect from one."

"Gideon, I told you…"

Ellora squawked in annoyance as she was dumped unceremoniously from Sarah's lap. It wasn't Sarah's fault. Gideon had yanked her to her feet and was pulling her through the doorway into the living room.

"Sit." Gideon used a hand on her shoulder to propel her into a chair in front of the chess table. He took the seat across from her and studied her as she sat scowling at him.

"You ever play chess?" Gideon asked.

"Nope."

"Somehow I thought that might be the case. Well, if you're going to hang around here, you'd better learn. I need a regular partner. My neighbor obliges once in a while but he's not always around when I feel like a game."

Sarah felt a sudden glow of pleasure at his words. Her expression softened instantly. "You want me to play chess with you? Gideon, I'm touched. It's wonderful that you're starting to see me as something more than a convenient sex object."

"You were never that."

"Never a sex object?"

"Never very convenient. In fact, you've been nothing but inconvenient since the day you arrived." Gideon began setting out the chess pieces. "Pay attention. The first thing you're going to have to learn about chess is that you can't rely solely on your famous intuition."

"Why not?" She surveyed the pieces with deep interest.

"Because you'll lose if you do. Chess demands foresight, planning and strategy."

"That's the sort of thing you're supposed to be so good at."

Gideon smiled grimly. "Right. You're going to have to work hard if you want to beat me."

"I don't mind learning to play, but I should tell you I don't have the killer instinct when it comes to games. Somehow it's just never seemed all that important to win." Sarah was increasingly fascinated by the carved wooden chess figures. She picked up a knight. It felt good in her palm. "Did you make these?"

"Yes." He eyed her as she fingered the knight. "One winter when I had a lot of spare time. Why?"

Sarah shrugged and put the knight back down on the board. "Oh, I don't know. They're just interesting. Unusual. Maybe you have heretofore undiscovered talents as a sculptor."

"I doubt it. All right, we're all set. You ready?"

"That depends. Are you going to yell at me a lot if I don't learn fast enough to suit you?"

"Probably. I'm not feeling real patient at the moment."

Sarah glared at him. "If you start yelling, I'm outta here. Understand?"

"Don't bother issuing threats, Sarah. You've already got me tied up in knots. There's not a whole lot more you can do to me."

She reached across the table and impulsively put her hand on his. "Gideon, I'm sorry. Please believe me, I'm only trying to do what's best for both of us."

He eyed her laconically. "Sorry's not good enough, remember? You told me that, yourself."

She flushed and took her hand off his. She stared unseeingly down at the chess pieces. "I get the feeling this is going to be a perfectly miserable experience."

"Must be your intuition at work again."

But it really wasn't all that bad, Sarah decided two hours later. Gideon proved to be a surprisingly patient instructor, in spite of his veiled threats. At one point Machu Picchu lumbered over to take up a position in a nearby armchair and Ellora curled up beside him. The two cats supervised Sarah's progress with placid expressions.

"Not bad for a sex object," Gideon said finally. "I think you've got possibilities as a chess partner."

Sarah's head came up swiftly, unsure if he was teasing her. Gideon's eyes held a rare spark of humor, however, so she gave him a saucy smile. "Does that mean I have some practical uses, after all?"

"I could think of ways in which you'd be infinitely more useful."

Sarah got to her feet and went around the table to kiss him lightly on the cheek. "Good night, Gideon."

"Sarah?"

"Yes?" She halted at the foot of the stairs, her attention caught by something in his tone. She looked back and saw that he was toying with one of the chess figures.

"Never mind." Gideon put down the chess piece and reached for the brandy decanter. "Go to bed."

She went on up the stairs, Ellora trotting at her heels. Machu Picchu stayed behind, apparently feeling obliged to offer silent masculine support to the other male in the household.

Sarah lay awake a long time waiting for the sound of Gideon's footsteps in the hall. She did not go to sleep until after she heard him climb the stairs and go past her room to his own.

THE FOLLOWING DAY SARAH AWOKE to a world of infinite gray. The morning fog blanketed everything just as a strange feeling of uneasiness shrouded her normally exuberant emotions.

She looked out the window and realized she could not even see the beach. She was not usually depressed by fog. In fact, as a writer, she generally found it curiously exciting and even inspiring. But this morning was different.

She felt moody and restless. It was as if she sensed something ominous hovering out there in the fog.

But it made no sense to feel this way, she told herself as she showered and dressed in jeans and a sweater. Last night had gone rather well, all things considered. Gideon had seemed content to teach her chess and she had taken his interest in doing so as a good sign. He was trying to find other avenues of communication.

So why was she feeling so strange this morning?

Out in the hall she saw that the door to Gideon's room was half-open but all was quiet inside. Machu Picchu appeared in the opening and Ellora skipped forward to greet him. He touched noses with her and then stalked past Sarah as if she didn't exist. Sarah had the unsettling feeling that the big cat had somehow adopted Gideon's attitude toward her. When Ellora offered a silent apology for her companion's behavior, Sarah smiled.

"Don't worry about it," she told the small cat. "I understand. Men are very stubborn at times, aren't they?"

She followed the cats downstairs and went into the kitchen. The old Victorian lacked any semblance of cheerfulness today, even after she got the drapes open. Everything was dark, cold and depressed-looking. None of her plans for sprucing things up appealed this morning. Sarah tried to come up with some interesting ideas for breakfast but failed.

The fog hung heavily outside the window, drawing her in some strange way. Part of her longed to lose herself in the physical manifestation of the moodiness that seemed to have engulfed her during the night.

Intuition was sometimes a curse, especially when one didn't know how to interpret the vague warnings it was giving out. Sarah realized she wanted to go for a walk.

Without questioning the impulse, she found her windbreaker and let herself out into the chilled morning air. A few minutes later she was on the long, craggy beach below Gideon's house. She started walking, her hands thrust deeply into her pockets. The fog ebbed and swirled around her. She felt alone in the world and at the same time, threatened by something she did not yet understand.

One by one the doubts began to creep in and take root.

Maybe she was handling everything all wrong, she thought. What did she really know about dealing with a man like Gideon? It was true that in some mysterious way he was the personification of the heroes in her books, but she was also discovering that there was a lot she did not know or fully comprehend about those heroes. They were a part of her and yet they were strangers—alien lovers about whom she understood certain aspects but not others.

She had the ability to fashion exciting stories around such male characters but the raw truth was that she could not make real life turn out as neatly as a novel of romantic suspense. She had landed on Gideon's doorstep fully prepared to live out the fantasy of "Beauty and the Beast."

But in real life a man like Gideon Trace was not so easy to rescue from the curse of his past, not so easy to gentle and tame. He was more complex, more unpredictable and far more powerful than any fictional hero.

Sarah came to an abrupt halt near a small tide pool as a familiar sense of tingling awareness went through her. She definitely was not alone on the beach. She stood very still, waiting.

A moment later Jake Savage materialized out of the fog, not more than ten feet in front of her. He was dressed with his usual flair, polished boots and khakis and a leather jacket that, although it appeared to be brand new, was designed to look well worn and extremely macho. His black hair was damp from the fog and his bright blue eyes were alive with an almost feverish anticipation. Sarah suddenly wished that Gideon was not sound asleep in the house.

"Hello, Sarah. I'm surprised Gid let you out of his sight. Or did you slip the leash?"

"I just felt like taking a morning walk. What are you doing here, Jake?"

"What do you think I'm doing here? I came to find you. I've been keeping an eye on the house since yesterday, waiting for a chance to talk to you alone for a few minutes. I caught a glimpse of someone coming down the path through the fog a while ago and decided to see if it might be you."

"You've been spying on us?"

"Like I said, just waiting to talk to you. I knew Gid wouldn't let me anywhere near you if he had anything to say about it."

"Why did you want to talk to me?"

Jake smiled wryly. "I know it's none of my business, but I thought you ought to be told a few facts. Call me sentimental, but I didn't want to see you go through what Gid's wife went through."

"Oh, yes, Leanna. She cheated on him with you, didn't she?"

"Is that what Gid told you?"

"Isn't that what happened?"

Jake ran a hand through his hair, tousling it rakishly. "She was a very unhappy woman, Sarah. She turned to me for comfort. I guess I felt sorry for her."

"But not sorry enough to marry her after she left Gideon for you, right?"

Jake frowned. "Leanna wanted rescuing and I'm not much into the role of knight in shining armor."

"You prefer the role of seducer and betrayer."

Jake's eyes narrowed. "Gid really told you a story, didn't he?"

"No. I've managed to piece a lot of it together for myself, thought. It's pretty obvious what happened. Leanna was an immature, unhappy woman who was probably initially attracted to Gideon's strength but later dazzled by your flash. I suppose one could say she got what she deserved, which was nothing, but that doesn't make you any less guilty of betraying your partner. Why did you do it? Surely one woman more or less wasn't that important. A man like you can probably have his pick of women."

"Is that supposed to be a compliment?"

"No. An observation. Why, Jake?"

"That's none of your damned business. I took what was being offered on a silver platter, that's all. Hell, Leanna was a beautiful woman. If Gid couldn't keep her satisfied, that wasn't my problem."

Sarah shook her head thoughtfully. "No, I think there was more to it than that. You were jealous of Gideon, weren't you? Sleeping with Leanna was a way of getting even with him."

"Are you nuts, lady? Why in hell would I be jealous of Gid?"

"Because you were nothing except a hustler without him and deep down inside, you knew it. He was the one who made the partnership work. He was the one who had the skill and the talent to find whatever you two went looking for."

"The hell he was."

"You knew that you were totally dependent on him and eventually you must have come to hate him. All you brought to the partnership was image and flash. Did you really scheme with those smugglers to betray him? What did you think was going to happen if you did get him killed? Savage and Company couldn't have survived very long without him. But maybe your jealousy was too strong at that point for you to see reason. Or maybe there was enough money involved to make it worth the risk of dumping your partner."

"You little bitch, I'll tell you what happened that day. Gid left me behind while he escaped with a suitcase full of cash, that's what happened. You think Carson, or Trace, or whatever he calls himself now is the nice, honest, up-front type? You think he's some kind of good guy, a hero out of one of your books who's going to help you find those earrings? Wise up, little girl. He's using you. When he does find your treasure for you, he'll also find a way to keep it for himself. That's his real specialty, you see, looking out for himself. And he's real good at it."

"You're lying."

"You think so? Just remember what I told you. When Gid goes out on a job, he never comes back empty-handed. And people who get in the way can get killed."

"You look very much alive to me."

"I was damned lucky. You better hope you're equally lucky, hadn't you?"

Jake swung around and vanished into the swirling fog.

Sarah waited a couple of minutes, but the tingling feeling of awareness did not ease. Frowning, she turned around to head back toward the bluff path.

And walked full-tilt into a large, solid object that had been shrouded in fog.

"Gideon."

His gemlike eyes were the only sparks of color in the swirling world of gray. "Do you believe him?"

Sarah took a step back. The depressed, moody feeling she had awakened with closed in upon her more heavily than the fog. "Does it matter?"

"Yes, damn it, it matters."

"Why?"

"Don't play games with me, Sarah."

"I'm not playing games. I have, however, finally come to the conclusion that I don't owe you anything more than what you're willing to give me in exchange. And I haven't gotten much trust from you, have I, Gideon?"

He caught hold of her arm as she made to step around him. "Where are you going?"

"Home."

"Seattle, you mean?"

"Yes."

"He got to you, didn't he? Just like he got to Leanna."

Sarah's eyes stung with tears. She dashed the back of her hand across them. "No, he didn't get to me the way he got to Leanna. You can't even give me credit for having more sense than your ex-wife had, can you? I've told you once and I'll tell you again. Leanna was a brainless little floozy without an ounce of common sense. Any woman should be able to tell at a glance that Jake Savage is a mirage of a man. All image and no substance. Amusing, perhaps, on occasion and definitely a sharp dresser. The kind who might look good escorting a woman to a fancy party. But that's about the end of it." She pulled her arm free of Gideon's grasp.

"Damn it, Sarah, you can't just walk away like this."

"Don't worry, I'm not running off with Jake Savage."

"You're not running off with anyone."

"Right. I'm going all by myself."

"Savage will try to use you," Gideon warned roughly. "Especially if he thinks we've split up. Remember what I said about him using the divide-and-conquer technique."

"I'm not going to lead him to that white rock."

"He'll find a way to make you." Gideon's voice was raw. "Tell me, Sarah, is it easy to walk away from me?"

She paused and looked back at him. His face was harsh in the gray mist. He stood there on the beach, a stark, bleak figure—a man who'd learned the trick of withdrawing completely into himself while he told the rest of the world to keep its distance.

"I was a fool to think you needed rescuing."

"Rescuing? What the devil do you mean by that?"

"Never mind. You like being alone, don't you? You like not having to take the risk of trusting anyone. No, Gideon, it's not easy to walk away from you. But I don't have much choice. Maybe you and my friends were right all along. I really shouldn't rely so heavily on my intuition." She smiled faintly. "At least this time I didn't get left at the altar, though, did I? Maybe things are looking up after all. Or else I'm getting smarter."

He made no move to stop her as she turned and started up the path toward the house.

GIDEON HUNCHED HIS SHOULDERS AGAINST the chilled fog, his hands thrust into his jacket pockets, and listened to the sound of Sarah's car pulling out of his driveway.

She had done it. She had left him. A part of him could not accept it and he wondered if he would ever be able to fully accept it.

He could not believe how much he had grown accustomed to her foolish conviction that they belonged together. She had been so positive that they were made for each other, so convinced he was the hero of her dreams.

But he hadn't known how to deal with her at first. She had knocked him off balance right from the moment she had descended out of the blue onto his doorstep. And she had moved much too quickly for him. He was, by nature, not the type who could take the risks of real intimacy easily and he knew it. So he tried to resist Sarah at every step along the way, always looking for hidden motives, always searching for the cold reality that he knew had to lie beneath her warm, affectionate surface.

When they had become lovers that day in the mountains he had relaxed somewhat because he'd finally found a way in which he could trust her, a way in which he could feel sure of her. From the beginning he'd never really doubted the genuineness of her physical response.

Now, thanks to Savage, he was right back where he'd started. Alone.

But this time it hurt. He felt as if something inside him was cracking open, exposing him to the kind of pain he had protected himself from for years.

The worst of it was that even as he began to climb slowly along the path toward the house, Gideon knew he couldn't blame Jake for this latest disaster. He had no one to blame but himself.

Machu Picchu was sitting at the top of the bluff, tail coiled around his paws. He watched with idle interest as Gideon climbed the last few steps.

"She's gone, isn't she, Machu? I didn't even get breakfast."

The big cat followed him into the kitchen where Ellora sat in Sarah's chair. The silver-gray cat glared at Gideon with accusing eyes.

"Hey, don't blame me. She's the type who appears out of thin air and vanishes the same way. Here today, gone tomorrow. Flighty. Know what I mean?" Gideon put the kettle on the stove for instant coffee. *No, not gone tomorrow—gone today. Now. This minute.*

The cats continued to regard him in profound silence. Gideon poured hot water over the coffee and stirred absently. "I shouldn't have let her drive off in this fog," he announced after a minute. "The roads could be real bad."

The cats licked their paws.

Gideon climbed the stairs with his mug of coffee in one hand and went to see if Sarah had packed absolutely everything or if she'd left in such an all-fired hurry she'd forgotten a few items.

In her room he found no trace she'd ever been there. In a totally uncharacteristic gesture, she'd even made the bed up neatly.

Gideon went back downstairs wondering why the house felt so damned cold again.

The cats were sitting at the bottom of the staircase, watching him with their otherworldly gaze.

"I know, I know," Gideon said. "I shouldn't have let her leave alone. Not in this fog. Too dangerous. If she's got any sense she'll stop at a café and have a cup of tea or something until the fog lifts. I'll bet she's at one of the coffee shops in town. On the other hand, common sense is not her strong point. I probably ought to check on her. Make sure she waits awhile before heading for Seattle."

Ellora started to purr.

Gideon picked up his car keys and walked to the door. Behind him Machu rumbled plaintively. "You've got enough food and water to last for a couple of days," he told the big cat. "Don't worry. I'll only be gone for an hour or less."

But there was no sign of Sarah's car at either the coffee shops or the local gas station. The fog was not nearly as bad now as it had been a while ago. Sarah had probably not encountered any great trouble at all in getting to the main highway.

Gideon stopped at the edge of town and thought about going back to the big, cold, empty house.

He could not bear the thought. He started driving.

A few hours later he found himself in Seattle.

There was no great difficulty in locating Sarah's apartment building downtown. After four months of corresponding with her, he'd long since memorized the address.

HER WARM, CHEERFUL, SUNNY APARTMENT wasn't nearly as inviting as it ought to have been. Sarah halted just inside the front door, her hastily packed suitcases in her hands. She glanced around uneasily. Something didn't feel right. She stood there a moment longer and then put down the luggage.

With a gathering sense of disquiet, she wandered around the living room. Everything seemed pretty much as she'd left it.

Until she got to her desk. It took her a minute or two to realize that the normal, exuberant clutter didn't look quite right. The desk was still a mess, of course, but it looked different somehow.

Someone had been through her things.

The maps.

On a hunch, Sarah gasped and yanked open the filing cabinet drawer where she had carefully stored the ten photocopies of her precious map. They were gone. All of them.

"Oh, you're back, are you, Sarah? Have a nice trip, dear?" Mrs. Reynolds from across the hall paused for a moment in the open doorway. "There was the nicest man inquiring about you after you left. A real charmer. Did he find you?"

"Yes, Mrs. Reynolds. He found me." Sarah slowly closed the cabinet door. Jake Savage had stolen the maps.

"Excuse me. I'm looking for Sarah Fleetwood's apartment." Gideon's gritty tones came down the hall from behind Mrs. Reynolds.

"Well, bless my soul, it's another one. Never rains but it pours, eh, Sarah, dear?" The elderly woman winked conspiratorially at Sarah. "Right this way, sir. Never knew our Sarah had such an active social life. Call me if you need help entertaining all these interesting young men, Sarah, dear." Still chuckling, Mrs. Reynolds disappeared into her own apartment and closed the door.

Sarah stared at Gideon as he came to a halt in the doorway. "What are you doing here?" she whispered.

"What the hell does it look like I'm doing? I followed you. I should have caught up with you long before you got to Seattle. The fact that I didn't means you drive too damned fast, Sarah."

She ignored that, feeling strangely weak. The stolen maps were forgotten. All the anger and hurt and frustration she'd been feeling since she'd left the coast were forgotten. All that mattered was that Gideon was here, glowering at her in his familiar, lovable, beastly manner.

"You *followed* me? All this way? You actually came after me?"

"Well, I didn't drive this far just to see the Space Needle."

"You came after me," she breathed, giddy with relief and euphoria. "You tracked me down to the ends of the earth so that you could drag me back to the coast, didn't you?"

Something warm and tender that was tinged with amusement flickered in Gideon's eyes, softening the grimness that had been there a moment ago. "I never really thought of Seattle as the ends of the earth, but I guess it's all relative, isn't it?"

"Gideon." She flew across the room and into his arms. When he caught her close, holding her in a grip of iron, she breathed a deep sigh of relief. "I was so afraid. I thought you just couldn't care enough, after all, that I didn't mean enough to you even though in the beginning I was so sure..."

"Sarah, honey, it's all right."

She clutched at him. "I don't mind telling you I was scared to death that it really was hopeless. You never seemed to be able to bring yourself to trust me. I couldn't believe I'd been so wrong about us, but you never know for sure. I've been wrong before and all the way back from your place I've been terrified that I'd made another mistake."

"Sarah, hush."

"Gideon, I love you so much and I've been so miserable. All those lonely hours on the road. It was the longest drive of my life, I swear. I just wanted to get home so that I could cry in the privacy of my own apartment."

"Sarah—"

"I've been telling myself I was a fool. I almost had myself believing it, too. But now here you are. You've come after me just like one of the heroes in my books and everything's going to be all right. I wasn't wrong about you, after all."

"Sarah, I'm here. Let's leave it at that for a while, all right?"

She raised her glowing face to his but before she could say anything else, he was kissing her. She parted her lips for him, pressing herself close into the comfort and strength of his big frame.

Gideon groaned, kicked the door shut with the heel of his boot, and picked Sarah up in his arms. Without breaking the kiss, he carried her over to the black leather Italian sofa.

Chapter Ten

SHE WAS CLINGING TO HIM, HOLDING onto him as if she'd never let him go. Gideon staggered a couple of steps and then fell onto the sofa, dragging Sarah down on top of him. He still couldn't believe the depths of the welcome he'd seen in her eyes when he'd stepped through the apartment doorway. He didn't think he'd ever forget it as long as he lived. He'd been right to follow her. *She'd wanted him to come after her.*

The thing inside him that had cracked open and caused so much pain was healing with miraculous speed.

"I'm no hero," he warned one last time, wondering why he felt compelled to try to set the record straight. It was getting hard to think. Her mouth was so warm and sweet and spicy as she persisted in raining kisses over him.

"Yes, you are," Sarah whispered passionately. "You're a perfect hero. I always knew it. It just took you a while to figure it out, too, that's all."

"Hell, who am I to argue? You're the expert." He tugged at her sweater, pulling it off and tossing it down onto the carpet. Her fine, gently rounded breasts tumbled into his waiting hands and he inhaled sharply as his whole body tightened.

When she wriggled against him, sliding her hips across his, Gideon gave a husky, choked laugh and tugged at the fastening of her jeans. Her small, gentle hands were already fumbling with the buttons of his shirt. As soon as the garment fell open he felt her fingers trailing through the hair on his chest. Waves of anticipation rolled through him.

He looked down at the scrap of turquoise she wore beneath her jeans. He knew he was looking at one of the seven pairs of brightly colored, sexy panties she had bought especially to wear for him.

"You knew I'd come after you, didn't you?"

"No. I just hoped you would."

"Come here," Gideon whispered, urging her down so that her breasts brushed against his bare skin. He could feel her taut little nipples against him. "That feels so good, sweetheart."

"I love you, Gideon." She kissed his shoulder and then his own flat nipple. "I've been feeling so awful for the past few hours. I could hardly stand it."

"You should never have left."

"Maybe not. But I couldn't bear to stay, either. Not with you refusing to admit that we have something special together. Not when you couldn't let yourself trust me. But now you're here and everything's the way it should be."

He slid his hands down the length of her back to the sensual curve of her buttocks. He began coaxing the jeans over her lushly rounded derriere, allowing his fingers to stray into all the secret places. She moved delightfully against him once more and he lifted his lips against hers, seeking the sweetness of her. There was still far too much denim in the way.

"Easy, honey, easy," he breathed, holding her gently away from him so that he could slide off the sofa and stand up long enough to get out of his own clothes. When he finished with the boots and the jeans and all the rest of it he sat down and reached for Sarah.

She came to him willingly enough as he finished undressing her but when she started to lie down and pull him to her he shook his head.

"This way," he mouthed in her ear, as he half-sat, half-sprawled against the leather cushions. Hands on her thighs, he parted her legs and eased her down so that she sat astride him. He felt her tremble.

"Gideon." She braced herself, kneeling on the cushions. Her fingers entwined in his hair. Her eyes glowed with excitement.

"Yeah. Like that." He took one nipple gently into his mouth and simultaneously touched her intimately. He found her warm and damp and ready for him. When he eased one finger into her she clenched almost violently. Gideon caught his breath.

"So sexy, baby. That feels so good," he muttered. He drew the tip of his finger across the small pearl hidden in the delicate nest and had the satisfaction of feeling her shiver again in his arms.

"Gideon, my wonderful, fabulous, Gideon." She nibbled on his ear, moving against his head. "I love it when you touch me."

He guided himself slowly into her, feeling her open to him and then close tightly around him. She gasped and began to slide up and down as he indicated with his hands on her waist. Then she began to set the rhythm, growing more confident and more forceful until Gideon could think of nothing except the powerful hunger that was sweeping through him.

When he could stand the ravening forces no longer, he surged into her one last time seeking the full satisfaction that he knew was waiting. Gideon felt Sarah shudder and cry out and then he was lost in the thrill of her release as it mingled with his own.

SARAH SMILED TO HERSELF AS SHE languorously stroked Gideon's shoulders. "I like this position," she murmured.

"So do I. But, then, I like any position with you." His eyes were closed. He continued to sprawl against the cushions, his well-muscled legs relaxed, his hands moving absently on her thighs. "Sarah, promise me you won't run off like that again."

Her leaving had shaken him, she realized. He really did care for her. But, then, she had been certain of that the moment she saw him standing in her doorway.

"What made you come after me?" she asked softly. "You must have left shortly after I did." She was consumed with curiosity now, needing to hear every detail of what he had been thinking when he made the decision to pursue her. "When did you finally realize you couldn't let me go?"

"Sarah?"

"Yes, Gideon?"

"Just promise me you won't do that again. Please."

She sighed, resigned to the fact that Gideon was never going to find it easy to talk about his emotions. "All right. I promise."

"I could sure use a cup of coffee."

She collapsed against him in a fit of giggles. "What a romantic."

"I try." His smile was slightly lopsided, his eyes bemused as he played with her hair. "But I'd better warn you, there are probably going to be times when I'll mess up."

"You think so?"

"I keep telling you, I'm no hero. But you won't run off again if I do occasionally fail to live up to your expectations, will you? Sarah, I don't want to have to be afraid that every time I screw up, you'll leave."

Sarah's amusement slipped away in an instant as she saw the seriousness in his steady gaze. She shook her head vigorously. "No, never. I won't run off."

"You did this morning."

"That was different."

"How?"

"This morning I was feeling depressed. I knew somehow that I'd gone as far as I could. It was up to you to make an effort or give me some sign. If you were never going to be able to let yourself love me or trust me I had to find out now. I knew I had to leave." Sarah smiled. "And you came after me."

Gideon moved his head slightly on the cushions, his eyes warm. "I think you're a little crazy, but that's all right." His gaze shifted to the room around them. "So this is your place? It looks like you. I knew there'd be unwashed cups on the coffee table."

"Thanks a lot." She rose reluctantly from his thighs and reached for her clothing. "Look at the bright side. Now that I've got you, I'll be able to let my weekly cleaning service go, won't I? I'll make you some coffee while you get dressed. The bathroom's down the hall. Give me a minute and then you can have it." She clutched her shirt and looked down at him. "Gideon, I'm so happy."

He smiled slightly, his eyes very intent. "The cats will be pleased. They didn't approve of your running off the way you did this morning."

"You'll all just have to understand that I had my reasons."

Gideon's eyes hardened. "It was more than depression, wasn't it? We could have talked about that. And more than wanting me to give you some sign that I cared. It was Savage finding you on the beach that made you give up on me."

"I didn't give up on you."

"He upset everything. You were all right until he showed up again. You were adjusting to being with me. Getting used to it. But then he cornered you on the beach and it was all over. He always had a knack for being able to throw a spanner into the works."

"That's not the way it was at all. My feelings had nothing to do with Savage. I left because I wasn't sure I was getting through to you. It was time to give you a strong nudge."

"You'd have gotten through to me a lot faster if you'd let me make love to you instead of trying to build a relationship without sex," Gideon muttered. "It wasn't natural, Sarah. I felt you were trying to manipulate me by withholding yourself and then when Savage popped up again, I—"

"*Savage.*" Sarah's eyes widened in belated anger as reality came back with a thud. "Good grief, I almost forgot. How could I? The man's a thief."

"I'm in agreement with you on that point. But you didn't really believe all those things he was saying about me, did you?"

"Of course, I didn't believe him. But that's not why I'm furious with him now. I'm mad because he broke in here and stole all my extra copies of the map, Gideon."

Gideon's eyes hardened. He reached slowly for his shirt. "The bastard."

"He's going to dig up the earrings," Sarah said with a sigh. "I know he is."

"He won't find them."

"Gideon, I keep telling you, I can almost feel him finding them. My intuition tells me he's very close to getting his hands on them. Maybe he couldn't get close without the map, but now that he's got all ten copies of the thing he's bound to figure it out."

"Sarah, be reasonable. Ten photocopies won't do him any more good than one. They're all the same. I guarantee you he won't get the earrings."

She gave him a speculative glance. "You're very certain of Jake Savage's incompetence."

Gideon grinned briefly. "As I've always said, he's got his talents, but finding treasure isn't one of them." His grin vanished as quickly as it had come. "But he's gone too far with this business of breaking into your place."

"That's certainly the truth. I won't have it. What are we going to do, Gideon? Call the cops? How will we be able to prove it was Jake who broke in?"

"We probably won't be able to prove it." Gideon shrugged into his shirt. "But I think it's time I had a private chat with my ex-partner. I've had it with him."

"What are you going to do?" Sarah asked anxiously.

"I'm not sure yet, but one thing's for certain, I liked him a lot better when he was supposed to be dead."

"Gideon, you wouldn't, would you? You can't be serious. I mean, you can't actually, uh, that is…."

"See that he goes back to being dead? Permanently this time? It's an interesting possibility. As a solution, it definitely has its merits."

"Gideon."

"Weren't you going to fix me some coffee?"

Sarah wasn't certain what to make of the blandly innocent expression in his cool green eyes. It occurred to her that on some level she had always understood that Gideon Trace was dangerous. She just hadn't ever expected to see that side of him. She still wasn't sure she was seeing it. There were definitely parts of this man she did not completely know or understand yet. The knowledge was disconcerting.

"I'll be right out," Sarah mumbled. Clutching the remainder of her clothing, she hurried off to the bathroom.

Gideon watched her until she disappeared down the short hall. He felt a lot better now than he had when he'd first arrived, he realized. Everything was going to be okay again. He could relax. Sarah had just succumbed to a brief storm of feminine emotion, that was all. She hadn't done anything drastic like change her mind about him.

She still thought he was some sort of romantic hero and apparently he had only reconfirmed her belief by chasing after her.

As if he'd had any alternative, he thought as he got to his feet and pulled on his jeans. He would never tell her, of course, but the truth was, it hadn't been any grand, romantic impulse that had brought him to Seattle. He'd been operating on instinct and his instincts had told him that he could not let her disappear from his life.

Gideon fastened his jeans and began wandering around Sarah's colorful, modern living room. The place fascinated him. It was so completely different from his own home. Everything was bright, breezy and exuberantly chaotic. Magazines that ran the gamut from *Cache* to *Vogue* were piled willy-nilly on the second level of a two-tier glass coffee table. A collection of bizarre paperweights occupied the top of the table. An unwashed mug or two stood proudly amid the clutter.

The furniture all looked as if it had been designed in an art studio, with more emphasis on abstract lines than functionality.

The walls were filled with posters of the Pike Place Market, photos of Sarah with two other women and framed book covers. He paused in front of one, studying it more closely.

The cover of *Dangerous Talent* showed a rugged-looking, dark-haired man braced at the edge of a jungle cliff. The man had apparently forgotten to button his rakish, khaki shirt that morning, Gideon noted. It hung open, revealing a lot of chest.

In addition to his unbuttoned shirt the guy in the picture was wearing boots and a wide leather belt. There was a knife strapped to his leg. In one hand he held a large revolver aimed at some unseen menace and with the other he embraced a beautiful woman.

Gideon wondered idly why the heroine had worn a sleek, sophisticated designer gown and high heels into the jungle. The glittering dress was already badly ripped and was probably going to get even more severely torn in the near future. Both characters looked far more concerned with how they were going to make love on the edge of a cliff than they were with whatever threatened them.

Gideon shook his head in mild amazement and then spotted an open box with a publisher's return address on it. Inside the box were several copies of *Dangerous Talent*. Unable to resist, Gideon lifted one paperback out of the box, opened it and turned to the first page.

Hilary sat frozen behind the wheel of the broken-down Jeep and watched helplessly as the man with the gun sauntered toward her. Around her the jungle was alive with brooding menace. But nothing it offered seemed even as remotely threatening at that moment as the cold, deadly expression in the eyes of the human predator in front of her.

Green, Hilary thought fleetingly as she stared, mesmerized through the windshield. She could see that his eyes were emerald-green like those of a jungle cat and just as chilling.

Her friends had told her Jed McIntyre was dangerous—a man who made his own rules out here in the wilds of Rio Pasqual. But Hilary, as usual, had refused to listen to good advice.

She had insisted on setting out to find McIntyre and now she was very much afraid that she had done exactly that. The man coming toward her with such casual, graceful menace certainly fit the description Kathy had given her.

Dangerous.

Jed McIntyre was perhaps ten paces away from the Jeep when Hilary came to her senses and remembered the pistol she had stuck in the glove box.

Jerking herself out of her momentary trance, she lunged across the seat for it.

She never made it.

Gideon closed the book and put it back in the stack as he heard Sarah's light footsteps behind him.

"See what I mean?" Sarah asked as she went on into the kitchen. "All my heroes are like you."

"Other than the color of Jed McIntyre's eyes, I didn't see much resemblance."

"Then you didn't read far enough." Sarah switched on the coffee maker and put a kettle of water on the stove.

Gideon shrugged. If she wanted to see him as dark, dangerous and sexy, who was he to complain? "Just tell me one thing. Do I have to start carrying a gun and wear a knife strapped to my leg?"

"Good heavens, no. You don't need one. In that sense, you're a lot more interesting than Jed. Jed, I'm afraid, tended to rely a bit too much on brawn instead of brain. But brawn works nicely in a romance novel."

Gideon smiled at that. "Well, that's a relief. I've never liked guns or knives. Or khaki, for that matter. Stuff wrinkles like crazy." He went down the hall to the bathroom, which smelled of lemon-scented soap. Automatically he plucked the used towel that was hanging askew off the rack and tossed it into the hamper. He located a fresh one in a small closet.

A few minutes later when he got back to the kitchen he found Sarah pouring freshly brewed coffee. The stuff really was a lot better than instant, he decided. He was getting used to it. He sat down in a high-backed stool at the counter and picked up the red mug.

In front of him on the counter lay an assortment of odds and ends including a couple of large yellow notepads, a glass jar holding a dozen pens and a stack of romance novels.

"All right," Sarah said as she plunked herself down on the seat beside Gideon. "What are we going to do about your pal, Jake?"

"As I said, I'll have a talk with him." Gideon sipped his coffee thoughtfully.

"But how will you convince him to stop pestering us about the earrings? This little matter of going through my files is more than I can tolerate, Gideon."

"I agree and I'll deal with it."

She looked skeptical. "If you say so."

"Don't tell me you're losing faith now?"

"No, it's not that." She broke off, her thoughts clearly taking her in other directions. "But I can't help worrying about those earrings. I don't like leaving them buried up there in the mountains. I don't have as much confidence in Jake Savage's lack of competence as you do, I guess."

"Okay," Gideon said, coming to a decision. This had gone on long enough. Time to end it. "We'll go get them."

Sarah swung around on her stool and stared at him in surprise. "We will?"

"I want you to be able to relax and stop worrying about them. Obviously the only way to do that is to dig them up and put them in a safe place. We'll go see if we can find them in the morning."

"What about Jake Savage?"

"With any luck, he's still over at the coast, looking for an angle or contacting a talk-show producer. If he saw me leave, he probably assumed I followed you to Seattle."

"Gideon, this is wonderful. Do you know what this means? Do you realize what you're saying?"

He eyed her warily. "I'm saying we're going to dig up the earrings. If we can find them."

"No, no, no." She shook her head with obvious impatience. "That's not what you're saying at all."

"It's not?"

She smiled, her bright eyes triumphant. "What you're really saying is that you finally realize it's all right to help me dig up the earrings because you no longer think I'm just using you to get them."

Gideon absorbed the statement slowly, struggling with the convoluted feminine logic. "You really do have a talent for leaping to conclusions, don't you?"

"Go ahead. Tell me I'm wrong. Tell me you haven't decided to trust me at last," she challenged happily.

Gideon studied her for a long moment, enthralled by the warmth and delight in her vivid gaze.

"You win. I trust you."

He became aware, even as he said it, that it was the truth. He wondered if he'd known it all along on some instinctive level or if it was some grand realization that had just hit him. He decided not to worry about it. How and when he had come to trust her was no longer important.

What he couldn't explain to her was that this business of going back into the mountains to dig up the Fleetwood Flowers proved nothing at all about his trust in her.

GIDEON'S SHOVEL HIT METAL AND CLANGED loudly in the morning stillness.

"Oh, my God, that's it," Sarah exclaimed. "You've found them. You've found the earrings. Gideon, this is so exciting. I can hardly believe it."

She leaned closer to examine the small pit they had dug precisely ten paces due north of the white rock. She had dragged Gideon out of bed very early so that they could get to Emelina Fleetwood's old cabin by midmorning. Gideon had hardly complained at all.

"Stand back and let me get a little more of the dirt out of the way. It might not be the earrings, Sarah. It could be nothing more than an old tin can that was covered by mud years ago. Or a hubcap. Or a hunter's trap. Anything."

"It's the earrings. I know it is." Sarah used her own shovel to pry out more dirt. Slowly but surely an old metal box came into view. "Look at that, Gideon. It's a locked chest."

Gideon studied the rusted metal lid of the box. "An old strongbox. And you can bet Emelina didn't bury the key along with it."

"Maybe it's not locked."

"If it's not, then I doubt there's anything valuable inside," Gideon said reasonably.

Sarah knelt in the freshly turned earth to reach down into the pit and drag out the heavy box. She studied it intently. "Darn it, you're right. It is locked." She brightened. "But, as you said, I guess that means the earrings are still inside."

"We'll get it open."

"But how?" Sarah shook the box but it was impossible to tell if there was anything inside. She could hardly stand the suspense. "This is killing me. I can't wait to get it open. This is such an incredible experience. I've never done anything like this before in my life. Imagine. We've actually dug up buried treasure. We decoded the map and found the cache. Just like in a book."

Gideon leaned on his shovel and watched her with a curiously enigmatic smile. "Don't tell me, let me guess. You're going to use the experience in a romance novel, right?"

"Probably, but first I'm going to savor every minute of it for myself. I have to get a picture of this." She dug her small camera out of her bag. "Good thing I thought to bring this along, isn't it? Here, you stand next to the box."

Gideon shook his head and put down the shovel. "No, you're the one who should be in the picture. This is your treasure hunt. I just came along to consult, remember?" He took the camera from her and went to stand a few paces away.

Sarah hesitated for an instant, wanting him in the shot with her. But that was impossible. She scooped up the old strongbox and held it in front of her. Laughing with delight at her trophy, she stood posing for the shot. Gideon raised the camera to his eye, smiled again and pressed the shutter release.

"Now all we have to do is figure out how to open this strongbox," Sarah said, examining the rusty container.

"It will take a little time but we'll find a way," Gideon said, putting down the camera and picking up the shovel. "I've had some experience with that kind of thing."

"Somehow that doesn't surprise me." Sarah glanced up from the locked box. "What are you doing?" she asked as she saw him lift a spadeful of dirt and toss it back into the hole he had just finished digging.

"Filling in the hole."

"Why?"

He gave her an odd glance. "I don't see any point in advertising the fact that we've been here and dug up something valuable."

Sarah smiled with sudden appreciation. "Good idea. Why leave tracks for someone who might want to steal our treasure from us? I told you that you were smarter than Jed McIntyre."

"As long as I'm a little smarter than Jake Savage, we'll be okay," Gideon muttered.

"What did you say?" Sarah asked, uncertain she'd heard him correctly.

"I said, it's going to be a long drive back to the coast this afternoon."

"We could stay here or in Seattle tonight," she suggested.

"No," said Gideon. "We'll go back to my place. I didn't have a chance to ask my neighbor to take care of the cats."

"We'd better get back there, then. Poor things. They'll be starving."

"Not likely. Machu can still hunt when he has to, although he doesn't much care for the effort involved. He'll see that Ellora eats if it's necessary but he'd much prefer someone opened a can for both of them."

Sarah grinned. "He's a lot like you, isn't he?"

Gideon cocked a brow. "Because he doesn't mind eating canned food?"

"No, because he can still hunt if it becomes necessary."

SHORTLY AFTER MIDNIGHT MACHU PICCHU landed on Gideon's bare back with a heavy, near-silent thud. Gideon stifled a soft groan. The cat stepped off his back and sat on the edge of the bed, tail moving restlessly as he waited for a response.

Gideon rolled over slowly so that he wouldn't waken Sarah who was curled up beside him. He eyed Machu's implacable face for a few seconds and then he slid carefully out of bed.

Machu leaped soundlessly down onto the floor and started toward the bedroom door. Gideon paused long enough to collect the revolver he always kept in a shoebox under the bed and quickly put on his jeans. Barefoot, he went down the stairs as silently as Machu had.

At the bottom of the staircase, Gideon turned right and went down the hall to his study. He stopped outside the open door and peered into the shadows. He was not unduly surprised to see the figure of a man hunched over the locked file cabinet where the strongbox had been stored earlier. Keeping the revolver hidden behind the half-open door, Gideon reached just inside the room and flicked on the light switch.

The intruder jumped and whirled around to face him, his mouth open in shock and alarm.

"Forget it, Jake," Gideon said calmly. "Even if you managed to get the file open, you'd only find an empty, rusted out strongbox with nothing in it. The Fleetwood Flowers are long gone. Somebody got to them years ago."

Jake's hands fell away from the file cabinet. "Damn it, Gid, you always did have a way of sneaking up on people."

"Sarah kept saying she was afraid you'd get close to the earrings. I guess this was what she anticipated, wasn't it? That you'd break in and find the old strongbox. Looks like I've got to start paying more attention to that woman's intuition."

Jake hesitated, relaxing slightly when Gideon didn't move or say anything else. Then his brashness returned in a rush. With a cocky grin he stalked across the room and threw himself down in Gideon's desk chair. Legs stuck out in front of him, hands behind his head, Jake continued to smile the rakish smile that had never failed to charm.

"Tell me the truth, Gid. This is your old partner here so you can be honest with me. I know you went back into the mountains this morning. I followed you. And I know you did some digging. I saw where you'd filled in the hole. You really didn't find the earrings?"

"Just an old strongbox. The earrings might have been stored in it at one time, but the box is empty now."

"Why keep it in a locked cabinet?"

"Sarah doesn't know yet that the strongbox is empty," Gideon explained patiently. "She's looking forward to opening it in the morning. I didn't want to spoil the surprise."

"But you couldn't resist taking a quick look for yourself, is that it?"

"That's it. You know me. I get curious about locked boxes."

"And you're telling me there was nothing inside, huh?"

"Right."

"I don't believe you." Jake Savage shook his head slowly. "You never came back empty-handed from a job."

"This wasn't my treasure hunt. It was Sarah's. I just went along as a paid consultant."

"Bull." Savage suddenly sat up straight in the chair, his eyes glittering with frustrated anger. "I think you found the earrings. I think you found them the same way you always find what you go looking for, you bastard."

"No. There's nothing inside. Take a look." Gideon opened the file cabinet and removed the strong box. Then he twisted a strip of metal in the old lock until something clicked. Then he raised the lid to expose the empty interior. He waited a few seconds while Jake stared into the box and then Gideon closed and relocked it.

Jake eyed him uneasily. "Come on, Gid. We can do a deal. Just like old times. All I want is the publicity and a chance to draw in some big bucks. I need a big score."

"Be content with staying a dead legend."

Savage slapped his hand on the desk. "Why the hell should I do that? I'm not dead and I've discovered during the past five years that I don't like being a nobody. They don't know who I am any more, Gid. I walk into a bar and no one even knows me."

Gideon exhaled thoughtfully. "That's not surprising, I guess. You did a good job of disappearing five years ago."

"As good a job as you did."

"Tell me something, Jake. What really did happen that day we both supposedly got killed in that damned jungle? Did you set up an ambush with those smugglers? Were you working with them all along and finally decide I'd become a handicap? I was the one who saw too much that day we made the delivery, wasn't I? You already knew what was going on. You were in on it."

Jake's eyes flickered. He sat very still behind the desk. "You figured it all out, didn't you?"

"I've had a lot of time to think about it."

Jake's hand tightened into a fist. "You want to know why I did it? I'll tell you. There was big money involved. Enough to set me up for a long, long time. Enough to ensure that I wouldn't need to rely on you any longer, you bastard."

"I thought we were supposed to be partners, Jake," Gideon mocked softly.

"Yeah, but we both knew you were the one with the magic, the one who made Savage and Company a legend. And I was sick of knowing I had to depend on you. Sick of trusting you. Sick of relying on you."

"So you saw your big chance and decided to end the partnership. Except it didn't quite work out the way you'd planned, did it?"

"No, you son of a bitch, it didn't. But it will." Jake's hand shot under the desk and Gideon knew he was reaching for the small pistol he'd always carried strapped to his leg beneath his pants.

"Forget it." Gideon moved his own hand from behind the door and aimed the revolver almost absently at Jake. Savage froze, one hand still under the desk. "You were never that fast or that lucky and we both know it. The truth is, Jake, you were always better as a legend than you were as a reality."

Chapter Eleven

GIDEON WATCHED, FIGHTING TO HIDE HIS amusement, as Sarah paced up and down the living room. The cats had long since grown bored with her diatribe against Jake Savage. Machu Picchu was sprawled in his usual position across the back of the couch, his ears flat against his head and Ellora was curled up, sound asleep, alongside Gideon.

"We should have turned him over to the police. He was guilty of everything from breaking and entering to being a damned nuisance. And the man lied through his teeth. How could you just let him go like that, Gideon?" Sarah turned and stalked back across the living room, robe flapping around her ankles. Her hair was anchored in a topknot that was coming adrift from it's moorings.

"He won't bother us again, Sarah."

"We don't know that for certain. We should have had him arrested. Why didn't you?"

"Jake would never have survived prison," Gideon said, thinking about it. "Assuming we could have actually gotten him convicted and sent up, which is highly doubtful. We'd have been lucky to make the charges stick. He didn't actually steal anything and he doesn't have a record. The most he would have gotten would have been a few months."

Sarah reached the far end of the room, spun around and headed back the other way. "I don't think that's all of it. I think you went easy on him for old times' sake."

"Old times sake?" Gideon cocked one brow.

"Sure. After all, he was your partner for several years. You'd been through a lot together. And you're the loyal type."

"I am?"

"Certainly. Don't laugh at me. It's your nature. I suppose it's one of the things I admire about you. But that still leaves us with a problem. What if he comes after the Flowers again?"

"He won't."

"I don't see what's to stop him this time."

"I told him that if anything happened to that strongbox, I'd destroy the legend I helped him build. That's all he's got left, Sarah. His own legend. It's the most important thing in the world to him."

Sarah paused and nibbled on her lip. "And you could do it? Through your magazine?"

"I could do it by sending letters to certain collectors and dealers telling them to take a second look at some of the South American artifacts they've acquired lately through Slaughter Enterprises."

Sarah's eyes widened. "You said you'd kept tabs on him. That's what he's been doing for the past five years? Selling antiquities?"

"Uh-huh."

"And some of them were fraudulent?"

"Right. Smuggling the real stuff is a better bet. Dedicated collectors and dealers won't ask too many questions about sources so long as the pieces are real, but they'll be mad as hell if they think they've been taken in by a fake."

"So Jake has been reduced to selling fake South American antiquities. What a comedown for him." Sarah shook her head. "That must have grated. No wonder he was looking for a way back to fame and fortune."

Gideon stroked Ellora. "Some people would say that publishing a small treasure-hunting magazine like *Cache* is even more of a comedown."

Sarah glared at him. "It certainly is not. You're in publishing, the same as I am. You're an author. Just like me. You write for people who can still dream, the same way I do. We perform a very valuable function for a very important group of people, Gideon Trace, and don't you forget it. As this world of ours gets more high-tech and more endangered, it needs its dreamers more desperately than ever."

"I never thought of it quite that way," Gideon murmured, amazed as usual by her highly biased view of him. It was very heartwarming.

Sarah turned away again. "I suppose somehow Jake is a dreamer, too, isn't he? Unfortunately he's just kind of screwed up in general."

"Unfortunately." Gideon yawned. "You were right, by the way, about why he set up that ambush five years ago. He was trying to prove something to himself. Trying to get free of his dependence on me."

Sarah nodded. "Trying to prove he didn't need you to be a success. You're sure he'll stay out of our lives from now on?"

"Reasonably sure."

"What about the Fleetwood Flowers? He wanted those very badly."

Gideon felt Ellora stretch languidly beneath his hand. "I told him the Flowers didn't exist."

Sarah stared at him, clearly startled. "But he knew we had the strongbox."

"I told him there was nothing in it."

Sarah smiled slowly, with obvious satisfaction. "That was very clever of you, Gideon. Did he believe you?"

"Not entirely, but I think that after a while he'll convince himself I was telling the truth. He'd rather believe there were no Flowers than that he failed to get hold of them."

"Yes, exactly. He'll convince himself there was no treasure. And since we have no reason to advertise the fact that we found the earrings, Jake will never know the difference."

Gideon leaned his head back against the cushions and watched her through narrowed lids. "It's possible that when we get the strongbox open tomorrow it really will be empty. You probably shouldn't get too excited about finding anything inside, Sarah."

"They'll be in there." She hugged herself happily. "I can't wait to go to work on that old lock tomorrow. It's going to be such a perfect ending to this whole adventure."

"What about us, Sarah? Does finding the Flowers mean the end of that, too?" Gideon asked quietly.

She smiled serenely. "Don't be an idiot, Gideon. You and I are just starting our adventure."

"You really mean that, don't you?"

She paused and gazed out into the night. "I've told you before, Gideon. In some way I've never been able to explain, the Flowers are linked to you, but they have nothing to do with our relationship. Do you see the difference?"

"I think I'm finally beginning to understand." Gideon glanced toward the stairs. "It's nearly two in the morning, Sarah. Let's get some sleep. Knowing you, you'll be up at the crack of dawn trying to jam a hairpin into that old lock."

She chuckled, reaching for his hand. "I don't have a hair-pin with me. But that's all right. We'll rely on your pro-fessional skills."

Gideon rose from the sofa and put his arm around her shoulder. With his other hand he lifted her chin. When his mouth closed over hers, she parted her lips for him and wrapped her arms around his neck.

Gideon picked her up and started toward the stairs.

"I love it when you do this kind of thing," Sarah said, her eyes cloudy with desire as Gideon carried her into his bedroom. "You're so good at it."

"You think so?" He put her down on the bed and came down beside her. Slowly he untied her robe and opened it. She was so lovely, he thought as he bent his head to kiss her breast. And she wanted him. *Him*, not Jake Savage or anyone else. Just him.

"Yes. Perfect." She caught his head and held him to her, lifting herself invitingly against him. "Absolutely perfect."

"Perfect," Gideon agreed softly. His hand slid down to her thighs. Gently he parted her legs and made a place for himself near her warmth.

This was what he wanted out of life, Gideon realized; it was all he asked for of the Fates. He had been cold for far too long. Now he knew he would be content if he could spend the rest of his days warming himself at Sarah's hearth.

SARAH AWOKE SHORTLY AFTER FOUR O'CLOCK when Ellora shifted slightly against her leg. Automatically she turned to find Gideon on the other side of the bed.

He was gone.

Sarah listened to the silence of the big old house for a moment or two and then she pushed back the covers and got to her feet. Her robe was on the back of a chair. She put it on, tied the sash and went very quietly out the door. Ellora followed at her heels.

Sarah crept down the stairs, avoiding the ones that creaked. At the foot of the staircase she hesitated and then turned down the hall toward Gideon's study. There was a thin wedge of light showing through the opening in the doorway.

Sarah tiptoed to the door and peered through the crack. Gideon was sitting at his desk dressed in only his jeans. Emelina Fleetwood's strongbox was open in front of him. Nearby sat five of the carved wooden chess pieces.

As Sarah watched, fascinated, Gideon picked up one of the chess pieces, removed the base and pulled out a small object wrapped in black velvet. He put the object into the strongbox and reached for the next chess piece.

Machu rumbled from somewhere inside the study and Ellora brushed past Sarah's bare feet. The little cat pushed through the crack of the doorway and trotted into the room. Gideon glanced up. He saw Ellora first and then he saw Sarah standing in the shadows of the hall.

A curious stillness gripped him. He sat as if made of stone, his green eyes glittering with an unreadable expression.

"Well, well, well," Sarah murmured. She pushed the door open wider, crossed her arms and leaned against the doorframe. She wanted to shout her happiness to the world.

"Couldn't sleep?" Gideon asked.

"Something woke me up."

"Probably your world-famous intuition."

"Probably." Sarah couldn't stop the smile that she knew was starting to light up her whole face.

Gideon sighed wearily and leaned back in his chair. "I guess you want an explanation."

She shook her head violently. "Not necessary."

"It's not?"

"No. Gideon, this is the most romantic thing that has ever happened to me in my entire life."

He glanced at the open strongbox. "It is?"

"Definitely. It proves you love me. Proves it beyond a shadow of a doubt."

"It does?"

"Oh, yes." She walked into the room and came to a halt on the other side of the desk. She planted both hands on its polished wooden surface.

"Sarah..."

"Admit it," Sarah said, wanting to laugh out loud at his wary expression. "Go on, admit it. Tell me you love me. Tell me that you're doing this—" she waved a hand to include the array of chess pieces and the open strongbox "—because you're wildly, madly, passionately, head-over-heels in love with me."

"Well..."

"Gideon, this is the sweetest, most romantic gift I've ever had. You knew how much I was enjoying my treasure hunt. You know how excited I was about opening that strongbox. And you couldn't bear for me to find it empty, could you? You wanted to give me a gift and letting me find the Fleetwood Flowers at the end of my big adventure was your present to me. Gideon, I am so thrilled, so incredibly touched. *You love me.*"

Gideon gazed down at the knight still in his hand. "You're amazing, you know that? Some women would look at a scene like this and assume right off the bat that they had been or were about to be robbed, cheated or otherwise swindled out of a fortune. You look at it and assume it's evidence that I'm in love with you."

Sarah grinned. "It is and you are. Aren't you?"

Gideon's answering smile was slow. His eyes lost their wariness. A deep, aching tenderness took its place. His hard face seemed to gentle in the lamplight. "I must be to have gotten myself into a situation like this."

Sarah laughed, her delight bubbling up inside like champagne. She darted around the edge of the desk and threw herself into Gideon's lap. "Tell me," she demanded. "Say the words."

He touched the side of her face wonderingly. "I love you, Sarah."

"Since when?" she pressed.

"I don't know. Does it matter?"

"No." She put her fingertips on his lips. "It doesn't really matter. The only thing that matters is that you're sure now."

"I'm sure."

She put her head down on his shoulder, nestling close. "I figured you must or you wouldn't be putting the Fleetwood Flowers back into that strongbox for me to find in the morning. When did you dig them up?"

"About four years ago. I needed the money to expand *Cache* and since I was now supposed to be an expert in treasure hunting I decided to do some. I went through a file I had put together on old treasure stories that sounded promising—the real stuff, you understand, the kind of tales I never print in *Cache.*"

"The kind you pursue yourself when you go on vacation?"

Gideon nodded. "The Flowers was a story that had possibilities and it was fairly close to my home here on the coast. So I did a little research, scraped together enough for a down payment on the land and bought the old Fleetwood property for a few months. As soon as I found the Flowers, I sold the land again."

"Just the way I had planned to do it. I guess this proves that great minds really do run in the same track, doesn't it? Why didn't you sell the earrings if you needed the money?"

"Believe me, I was going to sell them. It was the reason I'd dug them up in the first place. They'd definitely bring a nice chunk of change. Take a look."

Gideon unwrapped one of the black velvet packages. A pair of glittering sapphire earrings set in an old-fashioned design tumbled out onto the desk. They lay there like brilliant blue flowers. He opened another velvet bundle and a set of beautifully matched pearl earrings cascaded onto the desk. Then he unwrapped the next three sets of Flowers. Rubies, opals and diamonds winked in the light.

"Emelina Fleetwood's buried treasure," Sarah breathed. "They're beautiful."

Gideon gazed down as the small fortune lying in front of him. "I intended to sell them off quietly, a stone at a time, but I kept making excuses not to do it. Then one day I realized I wasn't going to be able to ever sell them at all. For some insane reason, I felt I had to hang on to them."

"Of course you did. You were waiting for me to come and claim them. It all fits together now. I always knew the Flowers were linked to you. I just didn't understand quite how. But now it's perfectly clear. You were holding them, waiting for me to show up in your life, weren't you? You just didn't know it. You've got intuition, too, Gideon."

"You think so?" Gideon wrapped his arm around her waist, holding her tightly to him.

"Definitely. Why do you think you were the one who made Savage and Company a legend? Why did you sense that ambush five years ago? Why do you think you found the Fleetwood Flowers without even a map?"

He gave her a wry look. "Why did I marry the wrong woman the first time around? Why did I trust Jake Savage to be my partner and friend?"

Sarah waved that aside. "I guess your intuition works better with treasure and danger and that sort of thing. Mine seems to work mostly with people. We'll make a great team."

"I think we will." He kissed her throat.

"You let me go through the whole treasure hunt from start to finish so I'd have the thrill of actually finding the Flowers on my own, didn't you?"

"I don't know if that was my initial plan," Gideon said. "I wasn't thinking that clearly in the beginning. I just knew I had to keep you around for a while and hiring on as your consultant and partner was a way to do that."

"And naturally you stipulated that you'd get to keep at least one pair of the earrings. After all, you'd already found the whole bunch. You had some rights in the matter."

"That's very understanding of you. It's also exactly what I told myself at the start."

Sarah giggled. "When I think of how you let me tramp all over the Fleetwood property and struggle with that darned map... Oh, Gideon, it's too much. You must have been laughing yourself silly."

"Treasure hunting is fun. I wanted you to have the thrill." Gideon's eyes turned serious. "And I didn't want the adventure to end too soon. I wanted time with you. I couldn't figure out what was going on between us, but I didn't want to let you go out of my life too quickly. The treasure hunt was a way of stalling you for a while."

"What about arranging for us to have to share that cabin? That was a deliberate ploy to try to get me into bed, wasn't it?"

"I guess it could be viewed in that light," Gideon said modestly.

"And virtually kidnapping me and forcing me to come back here instead of going home to Seattle? That was a ploy to try to keep me around, too, right? Protecting me from Jake Savage was just a convenient excuse."

"For all the good it did me."

"They were all terribly romantic gestures, Gideon, worthy of any true romance hero, but I would have to say that seducing me right on top of the white rock was the pièce de résistance."

"I was rather proud of that move myself."

She kissed him. "You were going to have great fun watching me discover the earrings in the strongbox in the morning, weren't you? And now I've gone and spoiled your surprise. Sorry about that." She kissed him again. "Gideon, you are so wonderful."

His eyes held hers. "So are you. What did I ever do without you?"

"We were bound to connect eventually. After all, you're the man of my dreams. How many times do I have to tell you?"

Gideon's fingers tightened in her hair was sudden fierceness as he held her still for his kiss. "You can keep on telling me that for the rest of my life. I like being your hero. I like it very, very much."

"Good. And you won't mind if I continue to use you in my books? After all, I've built a whole career based on you."

Gideon looked down into her warm, loving eyes. And for the first time since Sarah had known him, he laughed out loud. The cats, sitting side by side on the couch, flicked their ears at the unusual sound.

"Just so long as you change my name," Gideon said.

"No problem. I always change your name in each new book."

Gideon caught hold of her hand and kissed her fingers. "Now, about the wedding…"

"Yes," said Sarah. "I was thinking of a quick trip to Reno or Las Vegas. What do you think?"

"I was thinking of something a little different."

MARGARET LARK RECEIVED THE TELEGRAM at ten in the morning. Without stopping to calculate the time difference between Seattle and Amethyst Island, she dialed the phone. Kate Inskip Hawthorne answered at once.

"You got one, too, I take it?" Margaret asked without preamble.

"Reminds me of the one I sent," Kate said cheerfully. "Looks like we've got a tradition going here. I guess Sarah's intuition was right again, as usual."

"She was sure of him from the first letter, wasn't she? A Beast waiting to be saved with Beauty's love." Margaret smiled to herself. "The poor man didn't stand a chance."

"Neither did Sarah, if you ask me. That treasure hunter of hers must be very extraordinary."

"Why do you say that?"

"Are you kidding? I would have bet good money that there wasn't a man left on the face of the earth who could have convinced Sarah to go for a big wedding. Not after what happened the last time."

"Good point. That settles it. It must be love on both sides. Will you be flying to Seattle for the festivities?" Margaret asked.

"I wouldn't miss this wedding for the world."

Margaret laughed. "We'll get to be bridal attendants. That should be fun. I've never been one." She hung up the phone a few minutes later and picked up the telegram on

the kitchen counter. She reread it with a gathering sense
of happiness for her friend, Sarah.

Pleased to report that my adventurer is even better
in real life than he is in my books. He's got everything, including a couple of cats. Wedding set for one
month from today. Will need lots of help as Gideon
insists on the works. Will return to Seattle on Monday to start interviewing caterers and shop for gown.
Wait until you see the earrings I'm going to wear.

Love,
Sarah

THE COWBOY

Prologue

"MARGARET, PROMISE ME YOU'LL BE careful." Sarah Fleetwood Trace, struggling to get out of her frothy wedding gown with the help of her two best friends, paused and frowned. For an instant the joyous glow that had infused her all day vanished. She looked at Margaret Lark, her fey hazel eyes clouded with sudden concern.

Margaret smiled reassuringly as she carefully lifted Sarah's veil and set it aside. "Don't worry about me, Sarah, I'll be fine. I promise to look both ways before crossing the street, count calories and not talk to strange men."

Katherine Inskip Hawthorne, concentrating on the row of tiny buttons that followed Sarah's spine, flashed a brief grin. "Don't get carried away, Margaret. You're allowed to talk to a few strange men. Just exercise some discretion."

Sarah groaned, her golden-brown hair moving in a heavy wave. Diamonds set in an old-fashioned gold design glittered in her ears. "This isn't a joke, you two. Margaret,

I have a feeling…" She nibbled her lip in concentration. "I just want you to be careful for a while, all right?"

"Careful?" Margaret arched her brows in amusement. "Sarah, you know I'm always careful. What could possibly happen to me while you're on your honeymoon?"

"I don't know, that's the whole problem," Sarah said in exasperation. "I told you, I just have this feeling."

"Forget your feeling. This is your wedding day." Kate undid the last of the buttons, green eyes sparkling with laughter. "Your famous intuition probably isn't functioning normally at the moment. All the excitement, champagne and rampaging hormones have undoubtedly gotten it temporarily off track."

Margaret grinned as she hung up the wedding gown. "I don't know about Sarah's hormones, but I think it's a good bet Gideon's are rampaging. The last time I saw him, he was looking very impatient. We'd better get you changed and on your way, Sarah, before your husband comes looking for you. He's very good at finding things."

Sarah hesitated, her worried gaze still on Margaret, and then she relaxed back into the glorious smile she had worn for the past few hours. "Having a big wedding was Gideon's idea. He'll just have to put up with the necessary delays."

"Gideon doesn't strike me as the type to put up with anything he doesn't want to put up with." Margaret handed a quince-colored shirt to Sarah along with a pair of jeans.

Kate chuckled as she reached for a brush. "I had the same impression. He's a lot like Jared in that respect. Are you really going to spend your honeymoon on a treasure hunt, Sarah? I can think of better things to do."

"I can't," Sarah said blithely as she slipped into the jeans. She leaned toward the mirror to touch up her lipstick.

Margaret met her eyes in the mirror, warmed by her friend's evident happiness. "Hoping to find another treasure like the Fleetwood Flowers?"

Sarah touched the diamond earrings she was still wearing. "There will never be another treasure like the Flowers. After all, when I went looking for them, I found Gideon."

"What did you do with the other four sets of earrings?" Kate asked.

"Gideon has them safely hidden. He chose this pair for me to wear today." Sarah turned away from the mirror and buttoned the bright-colored shirt. "Okay, I'm ready." She hugged Kate and then Margaret. "Thank you both so much. I don't know what I would do without either of you. You're more important to me than I can ever say."

Margaret felt herself grow a little misty. She quickly blinked away the moisture. "You don't have to say it. We all understand."

Kate smiled tremulously. "That's right. You don't have to say it. Friends for life, right?"

"Right. Nothing will ever change that." Sarah pulled back, her expressive face full of emotion. "There's something very special about a woman's friends, isn't there?"

"Very special," Margaret agreed. She picked up Sarah's shoulder bag and handed it to her. "Something very special about a husband like Gideon Trace, too. Don't keep him waiting any longer."

Sarah's eyes danced. "Don't worry, I won't."

Margaret followed her friends into the elevator and across the hotel lobby to the large room where the wedding reception was still in full swing. A crowd composed chiefly of other writers, bookstore people and their families milled about inside, sipping champagne and dancing to the music of a small band.

As the three women stepped through the open doorway, two big, lean men moved into their path. One of them reached for Sarah's hand, a look of proud satisfaction on his face. The other flashed a wicked pirate's grin and took Kate's arm.

Margaret stood quietly to the side, studying the two males who had claimed her best friends as brides. On the surface there was no great similarity between Gideon Trace and Jared Hawthorne, other than the fact that they were both large and both moved with the kind of fluid grace that came from strength.

But although they looked nothing alike there was something about them that stamped them both as being of the same mold. They were men in the old-fashioned sense of the word—men with an inner core of steel, a bit arrogant, perhaps, a bit larger than life, but the kind of men who could be relied upon when the chips were down. They were men who lived by their own codes.

Margaret had met only one other man who was in the same league. That momentous event had occurred last year and the fallout from the explosive encounter had destroyed her career in the business world and left her bruised emotionally for a very long while. A part of her would never completely recover.

Dressed in black and white formal attire, both Jared and Gideon were devastating although neither was particularly handsome. There was an edge to them, Margaret realized—a hardness that commanded an unconscious respect.

Jared was the more outgoing of the two. He had an easy, assured manner that bordered on the sardonic. Gideon, on the other hand, had a dour, almost grim look about him that altered only when he looked at Sarah.

"About time you got down here," Gideon said to his new wife. "I've had enough wedding party to last me a lifetime."

"This was all your idea," Sarah reminded him, standing on tiptoe to brush her lips against the hard line of his jaw. "I would have been happy to run off to Las Vegas."

"I wanted to do it right," he told her. "But now it's been done right. So let's get going."

"Fine with me. When are you going to tell me where, exactly, we're going to?"

Gideon smiled faintly. "As soon as we're in the car. You've already said goodbye to your family?"

"Yes."

"Right." Gideon looked at Jared. "We're going to slide out of here. Thanks for playing best man."

"No problem." Jared held out his hand. His eyes met Gideon's in a man-to-man exchange. "See you on Amethyst Island one of these days. We'll go looking for that cache of gold coins I told you about."

Gideon nodded as he shook hands. "Sounds good. Let's go, Sarah."

"Yes, Gideon," Sarah spoke with mock demureness, her love as bright in her eyes as the diamonds in her ears. Gideon took her hand and led her swiftly out the door and into the Seattle night.

Margaret, Kate and Jared watched them go and then Kate rounded on her husband. "What cache of gold coins?"

"Didn't I ever tell you about that chest of gold my ancestor is supposed to have buried somewhere on the island?" Jared looked surprised by his own oversight.

"No, you did not."

Jared shrugged. "Must have slipped my mind. But unfortunately that old pirate didn't leave any solid clues behind so I've never bothered trying to find his treasure. Trace said he might be able to help. I took him up on the offer."

Kate smiled, pleased. "Well, at least it's a good excuse to get Gideon and Sarah out to the island soon. You'll come, too, won't you, Margaret?"

"Of course," Margaret agreed. "Wouldn't miss it for the world. Now, if you'll excuse me, I promised one more dance to a certain gentleman."

Kate's eyes widened. "You mean, an *interesting* gentleman?"

"Very interesting," Margaret said, laughing. "But unfortunately, a bit young for me." She waved at Jared's son, David, as the boy zigzagged toward them through the crowd. The youngster, who was ten years old, was an attractive miniature of his father, right down to the slashing grin. He even wore his formal clothes with the same confident ease.

"You ready to dance yet, Ms. Lark?" David asked as he came to a halt in front of her.

"I'm ready, Mr. Hawthorne."

THREE HOURS LATER, MARGARET GOT OUT of the cab in front of her First Avenue apartment building and walked briskly toward the entrance. The cool Seattle summer evening closed in around her bringing with it the scent of Elliott Bay.

A middle-aged woman with a small dog bouncing at her heels came through the plate-glass doors. She smiled benignly at Margaret.

"Lovely evening, isn't it, Ms. Lark?"

"Very lovely, Mrs. Walters. Have a nice walk with Gretchen." The little dog yapped and hopped about even more energetically at the sound of her name. Margaret smiled briefly and found it something of an effort. She realized that she was suddenly feeling tired and curiously let down.

There was more to it than that, she acknowledged as she crossed the well-appointed lobby and stepped into the elevator. An unusual sense of loneliness had descended on her after the wedding reception had ended. The excitement of planning the event and the fun of seeing her two best friends again was over.

Her friends were both gone now, Sarah on her mysterious honeymoon, Kate back to Amethyst Island. It would be a long time before Margaret saw either of them again and when she did things would be a little different.

In the past they had all shared the freedom of their singlehood together. Late evening calls suggesting a stroll to the Pike Place Market for ice cream, Saturday morning coffee together at an espresso bar downtown while they bounced plot ideas off each other, the feeling of being able to telephone one another at any hour of the day or night; all that had been changed in the twinkling of two wedding rings. Sarah had found her adventurer and Kate had found her pirate.

Sarah and Kate were still her closest friends in the world, Margaret told herself. Nothing, not even marriage, could ever change that. The bond between them that had been built initially on the fact that they all wrote romance novels, had grown too strong and solid to ever be fractured by time or distance. But the practicalities of the friendship had definitely been altered.

Marriage had a way of doing that, Margaret reflected wryly. A year ago she herself had come very close to being snared in the bonds of matrimony. A part of her still won-

dered what her life would be like now if she had married
Rafe Cassidy.

The answer to that question was easy. She would have
been miserable. The only way she would have been happy
with Rafe was by changing him and no woman could ever
change Rafe Cassidy. Everyone who knew him recognized
that Cassidy was a law unto himself.

Now what on earth had brought back the painful memories of Rafe?

She was getting maudlin. Probably a symptom of post-
wedding party letdown. She thought she had successfully
exorcised that damned cowboy from her mind.

Margaret stepped out of the elevator into the hushed,
gray-carpeted hall. Near her door a soft light glowed from
a glass fixture set above a small wooden table that held an
elegant bouquet of flowers. The flowers were shades of
palest mauve and pink.

Margaret halted to fish her key out of her small gilded
purse. Then she slid the key into the lock and turned
the handle. She thought fleetingly of bed and knew that,
tired though she was, she was not yet ready to sleep.
Perhaps she would go over the last chapter of her current manuscript. There were a few changes she wanted
to make.

It was as she pushed open the door and stepped into the
small foyer that she realized something was wrong. Margaret froze and peered into the shadows of her living room.
For a moment she saw nothing but deeper shadow and
then her vision adjusted to the darkness and she saw the
long legs clad in gray trousers.

They ended in hand-tooled Western boots that were arrogantly propped on her coffee table. The boots were fashioned of very supple, very expensive, pearl gray leather

into which had been worked an intricate design of desert flowers beautifully detailed in rich tones of gold and blue.

A pearl gray Stetson had been carelessly tossed onto the table beside the boots.

The hair on the back of Margaret's neck suddenly lifted as a sense of impending danger washed over her.

Sarah's words came back in a searing flash. *Promise me you'll be careful.*

She should have heeded her friend's intuitive warning, Margaret thought. Instinctively she took a step back toward the safety of the hall.

"Don't run from me, Maggie. This time I'll come after you."

Margaret stopped, riveted at the sound of the deep, rough-textured voice. It was a terrifyingly familiar voice— a voice that a year ago had been capable of sending chills of anticipation through her—a voice that had ultimately driven her away from the man she loved with words so cruel they still scalded her heart.

For one wild moment Margaret wondered if her thoughts had somehow managed to conjure reality out of thin air. Then again, perhaps she was hallucinating.

But the boots and the hat did not disappear when she briefly closed her eyes and reopened them.

"What on earth are you doing here?" Margaret whispered.

Rafe Cassidy's faint smile was cold in the pale gleam of the city lights that shone through the windows. "You know the answer to that, Maggie. There's only one reason I would be here, isn't there? I've come for you."

Chapter One

"HOW DID YOU GET IN HERE, RAFE?" Not the brightest of questions under the circumstances, but the only coherent one Margaret could come up with in that moment. She was so stunned, she could barely think at all.

"Your neighbor across the hall took pity on me when she found out I'd come all this way just to see you and you weren't here. It seems the two of you exchanged keys in case one of you got locked out. She let me in."

"It looks like I'd better start leaving my spare key with one of the other neighbors. Someone who has a little more common sense."

"Come on in and close the door, Maggie. We have a lot to talk about."

"You're wrong, Rafe. We have nothing to talk about." She stood where she was, refusing to leave the uncertain safety of the lighted hall.

"Are you afraid of me, Maggie?" Rafe's voice was cut

glass and black velvet in the darkness. There was a soft, Southwestern drawl in it that only served to heighten the sense of danger. It was the voice of a gunfighter inviting some hapless soul to his doom in front of the saloon at high noon.

Margaret said nothing. She'd already been involved in one showdown with Rafe and she'd lost.

Rafe's smile grew slightly more menacing as he reached out and flicked on the light beside his chair. It gleamed off his dark brown hair and threw the harsh, aggressive lines of his face into stark relief. His gray, Western-cut jacket was slung over a convenient chair and his long-sleeved white shirt was open at the throat. Silver and turquoise gleamed in the elaborate buckle of the leather belt that circled his lean waist.

"There's no need to be afraid of me, Maggie. Not now."

The not so subtle taunt had the effect Margaret knew Rafe intended it to have. She moved slowly into the foyer and closed the door behind her. For an instant she was angry with herself for obeying him. Then she reminded herself that this was her apartment.

"I suppose there's not much point in telling you I don't want you here?" she asked as she tossed her small golden purse down onto a white lacquer table.

"You can kick me out later. After we've talked. Why don't you pour yourself a brandy for your nerves and we'll continue this conversation in a civilized manner."

She glanced at the glass he held in one hand and realized he'd found her Scotch. The bottle had been left over from last year. No one she knew drank Scotch except Rafe Cassidy and her father. "You were never particularly civilized."

"I've changed."

"I doubt it."

"Pour the brandy, Maggie, love," he advised a little too gently.

She thought about refusing and knew it wouldn't do much good. Short of calling the police there was no way to get Rafe out of her apartment until he was ready to leave. Pouring brandy would at least give her something to do with her hands. Perhaps the liquor would stop the tiny shivers that seemed to be coursing through her.

Rafe's hard mouth twisted with faint satisfaction as he realized she was going to follow orders. With laconic grace he took his booted feet off the coffee table, got up and followed her into the gray and white kitchen.

"I never did like this picture," he said idly as he passed the framed painting on the wall. "Always looked like recycled junk stuck in paint to me."

"Our taste in art was one of several areas in which we had no common ground, wasn't it, Rafe?"

"Oh, we had a lot in common, Maggie. Especially in the middle of the night." He stood lounging in the doorway as she rummaged in the cupboard for a glass. She could feel his golden-brown eyes on her, the eyes that had always made her think of one of the larger species of hunting cat.

"Then again, the middle of the night was about the only time you had available to devote to our relationship," she reminded him bitterly. "And I recall a lot of nights when I didn't even get that much time. There were plenty of nights when I awoke and discovered you were out in the living room going through more papers, working on more ways to take some poor unsuspecting company by surprise."

"So maybe I worked a little too much in those days."

"That's putting it mildly, Rafe. You're obsessed with Cassidy and Company. A mere woman never stood a chance of competing."

"Things are different now. You look good, Maggie. Real good."

Her hand shook a little at the controlled hunger in his voice. The brandy bottle clinked awkwardly on the rim of the glass. "You look very much the same, Rafe." *Overwhelming, fierce, dangerous. Still a cowboy.*

He shrugged. "It's only been a little over a year."

"Not nearly long enough."

"You're wrong. It's been too damn long. But we'll get to that in a minute." He picked up her brandy glass as soon as she finished pouring and handed it to her with mock gallantry. His big hand brushed against her fingers in a deliberate movement designed to force physical contact.

Margaret snatched her glass out of his hand and turned her back on him. She led the way into the living room. Beyond the wide expanse of windows the lights of Seattle glimmered in the night. Normally she found the view relaxing but tonight it offered no comfort.

She sat down in one of the white leather chairs. It was something of a relief not to have to support her own weight any longer. She felt weak. "Don't play games with me, Rafe. You played enough of them a year ago. Just say whatever it is you feel you have to say and then get out."

Rafe's eyes raked her face as he sat down across from her. He gave her his thin smile. It was the only sort of smile he had. "Let's not get into the subject of who was playing games a year ago. It's a matter of opinion."

"Not *opinion.* Fact. And as far as I'm concerned, the facts are very clear."

He shook his head, refusing to be drawn. "We can sort it all out some other time, if ever. Personally, I think it's best to just forget most of what happened a year ago."

"Easy for you to say. It wasn't your career and your professional reputation that were ruined."

Rafe's eyes darkened. "You could have weathered the storm. You chose to walk away from your career and take up writing full-time."

Margaret allowed herself a small, negligent shrug. "You may be right. As it happens I had a better career to walk to. Best professional move I could have made. I love my writing and I can assure you I don't miss the business jungle one bit. I wouldn't go back for anything." Her writing, which had been part-time until last year, had become full-time after the disaster and she didn't regret it for a moment.

"You dropped out of sight. Found a new apartment. Took your listing out of the phone book." Rafe leaned back in his chair and crossed his ankles once more on the coffee table. He sipped reflectively at his Scotch. "Took me a while to find you when I started looking. Your publisher refused to give out your address and your father was not what you'd call cooperative."

"I should hope not. I told him I never wanted to see you again as long as I lived. I assumed the feeling was mutual."

"It was. For a while."

"When did you start looking for me?"

"A few months ago."

"Why?" she demanded bluntly.

"I thought I made that clear. I want you back."

Her stomach tightened and her pulse thrummed as it went into a primitive fight-or-flight rhythm. "No. Never. You don't want me, Rafe. You never wanted me. You just used me."

His fingers clenched the glass but his face betrayed no change of expression. "That's a lie, Maggie, love. Our relationship had nothing to do with what happened between Cassidy and Company and Moorcroft's firm."

"The hell it didn't. You used me to get inside information. Worse, you wanted to taunt Jack Moorcroft with the news that you were sleeping with his trusted manager, didn't you? Don't bother to deny it, Rafe, because we both know it's the truth. You told me so yourself, remember?"

Rafe's jaw tightened. "I was mad as hell that morning when I found you warning Moorcroft about my plans. As far as I was concerned, you'd betrayed me."

The injustice of that seared her soul. "I worked for Jack Moorcroft and I discovered you were after the company he was trying to buy out; that you'd used me to help you try to outmaneuver him. What did you expect me to do?"

"I expected you to stay out of it. It had nothing to do with you."

"I was just your pawn in the game, is that it? Did you think I'd be content with that kind of role?"

Rafe drew a deep breath, obviously fighting for his self-control. "I've thought about it a lot during the past year. Every damn day, as a matter of fact, although I told myself at the time that I wasn't going to waste a minute looking for excuses for you. It took me months to calm down enough to start assessing the mess from your point of view."

"Since when did you ever bother to examine anything from my point of view?"

"Take it easy, Maggie, love. I realize now that you felt you had some legitimate reason to do what you did. Yes, sir, I've given it a lot of thought and the way I see it, the whole thing was basically a problem of confused loyalties. You were mixed up, that's all." His mouth curved ruefully.

"And a multimillion-dollar deal went down the drain because of it, but I'm willing to let bygones be bygones."

"Oh, gee, thanks. Very magnanimous of you. Rafe, let's get one thing straight. I never asked you to make excuses for me. I don't want you making excuses for me. I don't need your forgiveness because I didn't do anything wrong."

"I'm trying to explain that I don't feel the same way about what happened as I did last year," he said, his voice edged with impatience.

"If you're feeling a twinge or two of guilt about the way you used me and the way you treated me afterward, I hereby absolve you. Believe me, if I were in the same situation again, I'd act exactly the same way. I'd still warn Moorcroft. There. Does that make you feel justified in treating me the way you did?"

He stared at her, his leonine eyes brilliant with some undefined emotion. "You weren't his mistress, were you? Not before or afterward."

She wanted to strike him. It took everything she had to maintain her self-control. "Why should I confirm or deny that?"

"Moorecroft said you'd been sleeping with him up until he realized I was interested in you. He saw a golden opportunity and decided to take advantage of it. He told you to go to me, let me seduce you, see what you could learn."

Margaret shuddered. "You and Moorcroft are both outright bastards."

"He lied to me that morning, didn't he? You were never his."

"I was never any man's."

"You were mine for a while." Rafe took another swallow of his Scotch. "And you're going to be mine again."

"Not a chance. Never in a million years. Not if you were the last man on earth."

Rafe ignored each carefully enunciated word. He frowned thoughtfully as he stared into the darkness. "From what I can tell, you never even saw Moorcroft again after you handed in your resignation. Why was that, Maggie? Did he kick you out because you'd become a liability? Was that it? He didn't want you working for him once the scandal broke? Did he force you to resign?"

"Wouldn't you have asked for my resignation in the same circumstances? If you found out one of your top management people was sleeping with your chief competitor, wouldn't you have demanded she leave?"

"Hell, yes. Everyone who works for me knows that in exchange for a paycheck the one thing I demand is loyalty."

Margaret sighed. "Well, at least you're honest about it. As it happens, Jack didn't have to ask me to turn in my resignation. I was very anxious to go by then. I'd been planning to quit my job in another couple of years to pursue my writing full-time, anyway. The scandal last year just speeded up the process a bit."

Rafe swore softly. "I didn't come here to argue with you. I've told you, as far as I'm concerned, the past is behind us and it's going to stay there."

"Why did you come here? You still haven't made your reasons clear. I'm out of the business world these days, Rafe. I have no secrets to spill that might help you force some company into an unwilling merger or enable you to buy out some poor firm that's gotten itself into a financial mess. I can't help you in any way."

"Stop making it sound as if I only used you for inside information," Rafe said through gritted teeth.

"You knew who I was before you approached me at that charity function where we met, didn't you?"

"So what? That doesn't mean I plotted to use you."

"Oh, come on, now, Rafe. I'm not a complete fool. Do you swear it never crossed your mind that it might be useful to talk to someone who was as close to Jack Moorcroft as I was? Wasn't that why you introduced yourself in the first place?"

"What the hell does it matter why I approached you that first time? Within five minutes of meeting you I knew that what we were going to have together had nothing to do with business. I asked you to marry me, damn it."

She nearly choked on her brandy. "Yes, you did, didn't you? The first week I met you. And I was actually considering it even though every instinct I possessed was screaming at me to run." That was not quite the truth. A few of her more primitive instincts had shouted at her to stay and take the risk.

"I'm going to ask you again, Maggie."

She was suddenly so light-headed she thought she might faint. "What did you say?"

"You heard me." Rafe got to his feet and paced soundlessly across the white carpet to the window. He stood looking out into the night. "I'm prepared to give you a little time to get accustomed to the notion again. I know this is coming out of the blue for you. But I want you, Maggie. I've never stopped wanting you."

"Is that right? I distinctly recall you telling me you never wanted to see me again."

"I lied. To myself and to you."

She shook her head in disbelief. "I saw the rage in you that morning. You hated me."

"No. Never that. But I was in a rage. I admit it. I couldn't believe you'd gone straight to Moorcroft to warn him about my plans. When you didn't even bother to defend yourself, I decided I'd been had. Moorcroft was more than willing to reinforce the idea."

"I did go straight to Moorcroft," Margaret agreed grimly. "But I was the one who'd been had. As far as I'm concerned you and Moorcroft both took advantage of me. It's one of the reasons I left the business world, Rafe. I realized I didn't have the guts for it. I couldn't handle the level of warfare. It made me sick."

"You were too soft for that world, Maggie, love. I knew that from the first day I met you. If you'd married me, you would have been out of it."

"Let's be honest with each other, Rafe. If I'd married you a year ago, we'd have been divorced by now."

"No."

"It's the truth, whether you want to admit it or not. I couldn't have tolerated your idea of marriage for long. I knew that at the time. That's why I put off giving you my answer during those two months we were together." She also knew that if the blow-up hadn't occurred, she probably would have succumbed to Rafe's pressure tactics and married him. She would have found a proposal from Rafe impossible to resist. She had been in love with him.

Rafe glanced over his shoulder, his mouth gentling. "It might have been a little rough at times but it would have worked. I'd have made it work. This time it will work."

Margaret squeezed her eyes shut on hot tears. Determinedly she blinked them back. When she looked at Rafe again, she saw him through a damp mist but she was fairly certain she wouldn't actually break down and cry. She must not do that. This man homed in on weakness the way a predator homed in on prey.

"I'm surprised at you, Rafe. If you felt this strongly about the matter, why did you wait an entire year to come after me?" Margaret thought with fleeting anguish of the months she had spent hoping he would do just that before she had finally accepted reality and gotten on with her life. "It's not like you to be so slow about going after what you want."

"I know. But in this case things were different." His shoulders moved in an uneasy, uncharacteristic gesture. "I'd never been in a situation like that before." He turned toward her and swirled the Scotch in his glass. His eyes were thoughtful when he finally raised them to meet hers. "For the first few months I couldn't even think clearly. I was a menace to everyone during the day and stayed up most of the nights trying to work myself into a state of exhaustion so I could get a couple of hours' sleep. Ask Hatcher or my mother if you want to know what I was like during that period. They all refer to it as the Dark Ages."

"I can imagine you were a little upset at having your business plans ruined," Margaret said ironically. "There was a lot of money on the line and Moorcroft's firm cleaned up thanks to my advance warning. You lost that time around and we all know how you feel about losing."

Rafe's gaze sparked dangerously but the flare of anger was quickly dampened. "I can handle losing. It happens. Occasionally. But I couldn't handle the fact that you'd turned traitor and I couldn't deal with the way you'd walked out without a backward glance."

"What did you expect me to do after you told me to get out of your sight?"

Rafe smiled bleakly. "I know. You were hardly the type to cry and tell me you were sorry or to grovel on your knees and beg me to forgive you and take you back, were you?"

"Not bloody likely," Margaret muttered. "Not when I was the innocent victim in that mess."

"I used to fantasize about it, you know."

"Fantasize about what? Me pleading for your forgiveness?"

He nodded. "I was going to let you suffer for a while; let you show me how truly sorry you were for what you'd done and then I was going to be real generous and take you back."

"On your terms, of course."

"Naturally."

"It's a good thing you didn't hold your breath, isn't it?"

"Yeah, I'd have passed out real quick because you sure as hell never came running back to me. At first I assumed that was because you'd gone back to your affair with Moorcroft."

"Damn you, there never was any affair with Moorcroft."

"I know, I know." He held up a hand to cut off her angry protest. "But I couldn't be certain at the time and I could hardly call up Moorcroft and ask, could I? He'd have laughed himself sick."

"It would have served you right."

"My pride was already in shreds. I wasn't about to let Jack Moorcroft stomp all over it."

"Of course not. Your pride had been a lot more important than whatever it was we had together, hadn't it?"

He turned to face her. "I'm here tonight, aren't I? Doesn't that say something about my priorities?"

She eyed him warily. "It says you're up to something. That's all it says. And I don't want any part of it. I learned my lesson a year ago, Rafe. Only a fool gets burned twice."

"Give me a chance to win you back, Maggie. That's all I'm asking."

"No," she said, not even pausing to think about her response. There was only one safe answer.

He watched her for a moment and Margaret didn't like the look in his eyes. She'd seen it before and she knew what it meant. Rafe was running through his options, picking and choosing his weapons, analyzing the best way to stage his next assault. When he moved casually back to the white chair and sat down, Margaret instinctively tensed.

"You really are afraid of me, aren't you, Maggie, love?"

"Yes," she admitted starkly. "You can be an extremely ruthless man and I don't know what you've got up your sleeve."

"Well, it's true there are a few things you don't know yet," Rafe said softly.

"I don't want to know them."

"You will."

"All I want is for you to leave."

"I told you when you opened the door tonight that you don't have to be afraid of me."

"I'm not afraid of you. But I have some common sense and I will admit I'm extremely cautious around you. I definitely do not intend to get involved with you again, Rafe."

He turned the glass in his hands. "What I had in mind was a little vacation for you."

That alarmed her. "A *vacation*? I don't need or want a vacation."

"At the ranch," he continued, just as if she hadn't spoken.

"Your ranch in Arizona?"

"You never had a chance to see it. You'll like it, Maggie."

"No, absolutely not. I don't want to go to any ranch. I hate ranches. If I wanted to go on a vacation, I'd choose a luxury resort on a South Sea island, not a ranch."

"You'll like this one." Rafe swallowed the last of the Scotch. "It's just outside of Tucson. I grew up there. Inherited it when Dad died."

"No."

"You don't have to worry," Rafe said gently. "You won't be alone with me. My mother will be there."

"I thought she lived in Scottsdale."

"She does. But she's paying me a visit. My sister, Julie, is going to drop in on us, too. She lives in Tucson, you know. I thought you'd feel more comfortable about going down there if you knew you weren't going to be completely alone with me."

"Look, I don't care who's going to be down there. Rafe, stop stalking me like this. I mean it."

"There'll be someone else there, too, honey."

"I just told you, I don't care who's there. In case you didn't realize it, knowing your mother will be around is not much of an incentive for me to go to Tucson. She undoubtedly hates my guts. She thinks the sun rises and sets on you. She made her opinion of me clear that one time I met her last year and I'm sure she thinks even less of me after what happened between us. I'm sure she blames me for your losing Spencer Homes to Moorcroft. I wouldn't be surprised if your sister feels exactly the same."

"Now, Maggie, love, you've got to allow for the fact that people change. My mother is looking forward to seeing you again."

"I don't believe that for a minute and even if it's true, I'm not particularly anxious to see her."

"You'd better get used to the idea of seeing her," Rafe said. "She's going to marry your father."

"She's *what?*" Margaret felt as if the world had just fallen away beneath her feet. She clutched at her brandy glass.

"You heard me."

"I don't believe you. You're lying. My father would have said something."

"He hasn't said anything because I asked him not to. I wanted to handle this my own way. He's the other person who will be at the ranch while you're there, by the way."

"Oh, my God." She felt physically sick as she put the untouched brandy down on the table.

"Are you all right?" Rafe frowned in concern.

"No."

"It's not as bad as all that. They make a great couple, as a matter of fact."

"When...where...how did they meet?"

"I introduced them about four months ago."

"For God's sake, why?"

"Because I had a hunch they'd hit it off. Your father wasn't too keen on the idea at first, I'll admit. He was more inclined to string me up from the nearest tree. Seems he was under the impression I was the bad guy in that mess last year. When I straightened him out on a few details, including the fact that I still wanted to marry you, he settled down and saw the light of sweet reason. Then he met Mom and fell like a ton of bricks."

Margaret stared at Rafe in bewildered horror. "I don't understand any of this. What's behind it? You never do anything unless the bottom line is worth it. *What is going on here?*"

He smiled his thin smile. "If you want to find out you'll have to take a couple of weeks off and come down to the ranch." He reached inside the jacket he'd slung over the back of the chair and removed an airline ticket folder. "I've made the reservations for you. You're scheduled on the eight o'clock flight to Tucson next Monday."

"You're out of your mind if you think you can just walk in here and take control of my life like this. I'm not going anywhere."

"Suit yourself, but I think you'll want to find out what's happening and the only way to do it is to come down to Arizona."

"If my father is crazy enough to get involved with your mother, that's his affair. I'll give him my opinion when he asks for it, but until then, I'm staying out of it."

"It isn't just their relationship that's at stake," Rafe said calmly.

Margaret dug her fuchsia-colored nails into the white leather upholstery. "I knew it," she bit out. "With you there's always a business reason. Tell me the rest, damn you."

"Well, it's true your father and I are thinking of doing a little business together."

"Good Lord. What kind of business?"

"I'm going to buy Lark Engineering."

It was the final bombshell as far as Margaret was concerned. She leaped to her feet. She wanted to call him a liar again, but even as the words crossed her mind, she was terribly, coldly afraid. "My father would never sell the firm to you. He built it from the ground up. It's his whole life. If he's thinking of selling out, it's because you're forcing his hand. What have you done, Rafe? What kind of leverage are you using against him?"

Rafe rose slowly to his feet, looming over her. He dominated the elegant room—a dark, dangerous intruder who threatened Margaret's hard-won peace of mind as nothing else ever had. She looked up at him, feeling small and very vulnerable. But she refused to step back out of reach. She would not give him the satisfaction.

"You really don't think very much of me, do you?" Rafe's mouth was taut with his rigidly controlled anger. "It's a good thing I learned something about handling my own pride this past year because the look in your eyes right now is enough to make a man feel about two inches tall."

"Really?" Her voice was scathing. "And do you feel two inches tall?"

"No, ma'am," he admitted. "But I probably would if I were guilty of whatever it is you think I'm doing to your father. Lucky for me I'm as innocent as a new foal."

"Are you saying you're not forcing him to sell out to you?"

"Nope. Ask him."

"I will, damn you."

"You'll have to come down to the ranch to do that," Rafe said. "Because that's where he is and he won't reassure you on the phone."

"Why not?"

"Because he knows I want some time with you down there and he's agreed to act as the bait. You'll have to fly to Arizona if you want to convince yourself that I'm not pulling a fast one."

"And if I don't go?"

"Then I reckon you'll sit here in Seattle and worry a lot."

She shook her head, dazed. "I don't believe any of this. Why are you doing it?"

"I've told you why I'm doing it. I want another chance with you. This is the only way I know to get it."

"Even if that disaster last year didn't stand between us, we have no business thinking about getting involved again. I've told you that. I could never marry you, Rafe. Not for long, at any rate."

"I'll make you change your mind."

"Impossible. I know you too well now. The truth is, I knew you too well last year. That's the reason I didn't give you an answer the first time you asked. Or the second or the third. Your first love is business and your overriding passion in life is for making money, not making love."

Rafe contrived to look hurt. "I don't recall you complaining too loud in bed."

Margaret clenched her fists. "On the rare occasions you managed to find time to take me to bed you performed just fine."

"Why, thank you, honey. It's real sweet of you to remember."

"You're missing the point," she hissed.

"Yeah?"

"The point is, you don't have a lot of time in your life for a relationship of any kind. During the two months we were dating you were always flying into Seattle for a weekend and then flying out again Monday morning. Or you would show up on my doorstep at midnight on a Wednesday, take me to bed and then disappear at six the next day to get to a business conference in L.A."

"I admit I used to do a fair amount of traveling, but I've cut back lately."

"And when you weren't traveling, you were tied up at the office. Remember all those times you called from Tucson and told me you wouldn't be able to make it up here to Seattle? I was expected to rearrange all my plans to accommodate you. Or else you'd arrive with a briefcase full of work and Doug Hatcher in tow and the two of you would take over my living room for a full day."

"Now, honey, there was a lot going on at the time."

"With you there always will be a lot going on. It's your nature. Your mother was kind enough to point that out to me. Said you were just like your father. You thrive on your work. Beating the competition to the draw is the most important thing in your life."

"You're getting carried away now, Maggie, love. Just take it easy, honey. I'm dead serious about this. I want to get married."

"Oh, I believe you. You'd find a wife useful. You want a wife who will be a convenience for you—someone to handle your entertaining, your home, your social life. Someone who will warm your bed when you want it warmed and stay out of your way when you've got other things to do. Someone who knows how to live in your world and who will accommodate her entire life to yours. In short, you want the perfect corporate wife."

"Give me the next couple of weeks to prove that I'm willing to make a few accommodations of my own."

Margaret's head came up sharply. "You're hardly starting out on a promising foot, are you? You're trying to blackmail me into going down to your ranch."

He sighed. "Only because I know it's a sure-fire way to get you there. Maggie, listen to me…"

She glared at him. "Don't call me Maggie. I never did like the way you called me that. No one else ever calls me Maggie."

Rafe's brows rose. "Your dad does."

"That changes nothing. I dislike being called Maggie."

"You never said anything about it before."

"It didn't seem worth arguing about last year. Good grief, there wasn't time to argue about it. This year is different, however. I'm not putting up with anything from you this year."

"I see. That's too bad. I always kind'a liked Maggie."

"I don't."

"All right," he said soothingly, "I'll try to remember to call you Margaret."

"You don't have to try to remember anything. You won't be around long enough to make the mistake very often."

"You're not going to give an inch, are you?"

"No." Margaret eyed him defiantly.

Rafe's mouth curved faintly. "I had a feeling you were going to be like that. Which is why I went to so much effort to set this whole thing up the way I did. I need you to give me a chance to prove that I've changed. I'm only asking for two weeks."

"You're not asking, you're demanding. That's the way you always did things, Rafe. You haven't changed at all."

Temper flashed briefly in his eyes and was almost immediately overlaid with something far more dangerous: frustrated desire. Rafe lifted a hand to slide around the nape of Margaret's neck beneath the neat chignon of her hair. She froze.

"How much have you changed, Maggie?" he asked softly, his mouth only inches from hers. "Do you still remember this?" He brushed his lips across hers in the lightest of caresses. "Do you still go all hot and trembly when I do this?" He caught her lower lip gently between his teeth and then released it.

Margaret flinched from the jolt of deep longing that knifed through her. She did not move. She was not sure she could have moved if she'd tried. She was paralyzed– a rabbit confronted by a mountain lion.

Rafe's mouth slanted across hers again and she was thoroughly confused by the unexpected tenderness of his kiss. His fingers stroked her nape, feather-light against her sensitive skin. A tremor sizzled along her nerve endings. She shivered.

"Yeah, you still do, don't you? I've been thinking about this for the past year," Rafe muttered. "One whole year, damn you. Every night and every day. There were times when I thought I'd go clear out of my mind with wanting you. How could you do that to me, Maggie?"

She was shaken by the bleak depths in his voice. "If it was the sex you missed, I'm sure there must have been someone around to give you what you wanted."

"No," he stated harshly. "There was no one. There hasn't been anyone since you, Maggie."

She stared up at him in shock. When he finally had found time for bed, Rafe had proved himself to be a deeply sensual man. She remembered that much quite vividly. "I don't believe you."

"Believe it," he growled as his mouth grazed hers one more time. "God knows I do. I had to live through every night alone and it nearly drove me crazy."

"Rafe, you can't walk back in here after a whole year and do this to me," Margaret said desperately. "I won't let you."

"Let me stay tonight."

"No."

He drew back slightly, releasing her. "I had a hunch you'd say that but I had to ask. Don't worry about it, I've waited this long, I can wait a little longer."

"You'll wait until hell freezes over," she said crisply. "You've said what you had to say, Rafe. Now leave."

He hesitated briefly. Then he nodded and picked up his hat. He jammed it down low over his glittering eyes. As he reached for his jacket, he glanced at the airline ticket he'd left on the table. "Next Monday. The eight o'clock flight."

"I won't be on it."

"Please."

Margaret's mouth fell open in amazement. "What did you say?"

"I said *please*. Please be on the eight o'clock flight. Come to Arizona to talk to the woman who will probably be marrying your father. Come to Arizona to find out what kind of evil deal I've cooked up to get your dad to sell his company to me. Come to Arizona to see if I really have changed. Come to Arizona to give us both a second chance."

"I'd be a fool to do it."

"There hasn't been anyone else for either of us for the past year, Maggie. That should tell us both something." He hooked the jacket over his shoulder and strode to the door.

"Rafe, wait, I'm not going to do it, do you hear me? I won't be on that plane." Margaret managed to unstick herself from the carpet and go after him, but she was too late.

The door closed softly behind him before she could ask him how he knew there had been no one else for her during the past year.

Chapter Two

IT HAD BEEN THE LONGEST YEAR OF HIS LIFE, Rafe thought savagely, and Maggie looked as if she'd spent it sleeping on rose petals and sipping tea. It was almost more than he could take to see her looking so serene and untouched by the past twelve months.

He clung to the knowledge that she had been as celibate as he had. It was the only thing that gave him any real hope. On some level she had been waiting for him, he told himself. On some level she was still his and knew it.

Outside on the street in front of her apartment building he managed to find a cab for the ride back to his hotel. Knowing he was heading toward a lonely hotel room when he should have been spending the night in Maggie's bed did nothing for Rafe's temper. Still, the players in the game were finally in position at last and the first moves had all been made. The action was ready to start.

She was as striking as ever, he admitted to himself as he sprawled back against the seat in the cab. More so. She was a little more sure of herself now than she had been a year ago. *And a hell of a lot less willing to accommodate herself to his schedule,* he thought with grim humor.

The sight of her tonight had nearly shattered his carefully honed self-control. He had promised himself he would remain in command of the situation, but when she had walked through the door his first instinct had been to pull her down onto the carpet of her elegant living room and make love to her until she was wild. He needed desperately to feel her respond to him the way she had the last time on that memorable night before everything had gone up in smoke. Lord, he was starving for her.

He had never been so hungry in his life and he had to be patient. He stared moodily at the cheerfully garish lights of the public market as the cab driver turned east on Pike Street. It had been a year since he had seen Seattle at night.

The cab halted in front of the lobby of the expensive hotel and Rafe got out. He reached for his wallet.

"Nice boots," the cabbie remarked as he pocketed the excessive tip.

"Thanks." Rafe turned toward the lobby.

"Hey, if you've got nothin' else to do this evenin'," the cabbie called after him, "I can give you a couple of suggestions. I know where the action is here in town. No sense spendin' the night alone."

"Why not? It's the way I spend all of my nights lately."

Rafe went on into the marble and wood-paneled lobby. He couldn't stop picturing Maggie as she had looked tonight standing framed in the doorway of her apartment. Her sleek black hair had been pulled back to accent the delicate lines of her face. Her aquamarine eyes were even larger and more compelling than they had been in his dreams.

The sophisticated silk dress she wore glided over subtle, alluring curves. She looked as if she'd put on a couple of pounds but they had gone to the right places. She still moved with the grace of a queen.

Maggie had obviously found her footing in her new career as a writer. In fact, she looked depressingly content. Rafe felt like chewing nails. It seemed only fair that she should have suffered as much as he had. But apparently she hadn't.

He reminded himself once more of the report from the discreet investigative agency he had employed. Maggie dated only rarely and never seriously. Until recently she had spent a lot of her free time with two other women who had been friends of hers for the past couple of years.

Rafe had never met Sarah Fleetwood and Katherine Inskip but their names showed up so often in the reports that he had come to think of the unknown women as duennas for his lady. Somewhere along the line he had unconsciously started depending on them to keep Maggie out of trouble.

Trouble meant another man in Maggie's life, as far as Rafe was concerned. But as luck would have it, Sarah and Katherine had been the ones who had found the other men. He wasn't making his move any too soon, Rafe told himself. No sense leaving a woman like Maggie at loose ends for very long.

Rafe went into the hotel bar and found a secluded booth. He ordered a Scotch and sat brooding over it, analyzing the scene in Maggie's living room, searching for flaws in the way he'd handled the delicate negotiations, wondering if he'd applied just the right amount of pressure.

He'd spent months putting the plan together and he'd used every lever he could find. He would have bargained with the devil himself to get Maggie back. But tonight he'd played the last cards in his hand. Now he could only pray Maggie would be on that Monday morning flight to Tucson. His whole future was hanging in the balance and Rafe knew it. The knowledge made his insides grow cold.

THE BOOK SIGNING SESSION ON SATURDAY morning went well. Margaret thoroughly enjoyed talking to the readers and other writers in the area who had made their way by car, bus and monorail into downtown Seattle to meet the author of *Ruthless*. She was especially grateful for the enthusiastic crowd this morning because it took her mind off the difficult decision that had to be made by Monday. For a while, at least, she did not have to think about Rafe Cassidy.

"I just loved *Ruthless*." A happily pregnant woman with a toddler clinging to her skirts handed her copy of the book to Margaret to sign. "I always feel good after I've read one of your books. I really love your heroes. They're great. Oh, Christine is the name, by the way."

"Thanks, Christine. I'm glad you liked the book. I appreciate your coming downtown today." Margaret wrote Christine's name on the title page, a brief message and then signed her own name with a flourish.

"No problem. Wouldn't have missed it for the world. I was an account executive at a brokerage house here in Seattle before I quit to raise kids for a while. I really identify with the business settings in your stories. When's your next book due out?"

"In about six months."

"Can't wait. Another hero like Roarke, I hope?"

Margaret smiled. "Of course." Roarke was the name of the hero in *Ruthless*, but the truth was all her heroes were similar. They all bore a striking resemblance to Rafe Cassidy. That had been true from her first book, which had been written long before she had ever met Rafe. It was probably why she had fallen so hard and so fast for him when he'd exploded into her life last year, she thought.

At first sight she had been certain Rafe was the man of her dreams.

Except for the boots, of course. Looking back on the disaster Margaret knew she ought to have been warned when her dream man showed up in a Stetson, fancy boots and a silver belt buckle. In her books her heroes always wore European-styled suits and Italian leather shoes.

Hard, savvy and successful businessmen for the most part, her male characters always had a ruthless edge that made them a real challenge for the heroines. But in the end, unlike Rafe, they all succumbed to love.

A stylish-looking woman in a crisp suit who was standing directly behind Christine extended her copy of *Ruthless*. "Christine's right. Give us another hero like Roarke. He was great. I love the tough-guy-who-can-be-taught-to-love type. I think of them as cowboys in business suits."

Margaret stared at her. "Cowboys? Good heavens, what makes you call them that? I like the sophisticated urban type. That's the kind I always write about."

The woman shook her head with a knowing look in her eye. "But your heroes are all cowboys in disguise, didn't you know that?"

Margaret eyed her thoughtfully. She had long ago learned to appreciate some of the insights her readers had into her books but this one took her back. "You really think so?"

"Trust me. I know cowboys when I see them, even if they are wearing two hundred dollar silk shirts."

"She's right, you know," another woman in line announced with a grin. "When I'm reading one of your books, I always visualize a cowboy."

"What on earth makes you do that?" Margaret asked in utter amazement.

The woman paused, considering her answer. "I think it's got something to do with their basic philosophies of life—the way they think and act. They've got a lot of old-fashioned attitudes about women and honor and that kind of thing. The sort of attitudes we all associate with the Old West."

"It's true," someone else in line agreed. "The shoot-outs take place in corporate boardrooms instead of in front of the saloon, but the feeling is the same." She leaned forward to extend her copy of *Ruthless*. "The name is Rachel."

"Rachel." Margaret hurriedly signed the book and handed it back. "Thank you."

"Thank you." Rachel winked mischievously. "Speaking of cowboys," she said, exchanging a smile with the other woman, "maybe one of these days you can give us the real thing, horse and all."

"We'll look forward to it," the first woman declared as she collected her signed book.

Margaret managed a laugh and shook her head, feeling slightly dazed. "We'll see," she temporized, not wanting to offend the readers by telling them she'd once run into a real corporate gunslinger who was very much a cowboy and the result had been something other than a happy ending.

She turned, smiling, to greet the next person in line and nearly dropped her pen when she caught sight of the familiar figure standing in front of her. It never rained but it poured, she thought ironically.

"Hello, Jack. What are you doing here? I didn't know you read romance."

Jack Moorcroft smiled down at her, his light hazel eyes full of genuine curiosity. "So you really made it work, did you?"

"Made what work? My writing? Yes, I've been fortunate."

"I didn't think you could turn it into a full-fledged career."

"Neither did anyone else."

"Can I buy you a coffee or a drink when you're finished here? I'd like to talk to you."

"Let me guess what this is all about. I haven't seen you since the day I resigned. You moved the headquarters of Moorcroft Industries to San Diego nearly a year ago, according to the papers. And now, out of a clear blue sky you suddenly show up again in Seattle two days after Rafe Cassidy magically reappears. Can I assume there's a connection or is this one of those incredible coincidences that makes life so interesting?"

"You always were one smart lady. That's why I hired you in the first place."

"Forget the flattery, Jack. I'm immune."

"I get the feeling you're not enjoying old ties with your former business associates?"

"You're very perceptive for a businessman."

Jack nodded, accepting the rebuff. "I think I can understand. You got a little mauled there at the end, didn't you? Cassidy can play rough. But I do have to talk to you. It's important, Margaret. Coffee? For old times' sake?"

She sighed, wishing she could think of a polite way out of the invitation. But the truth was Jack had been a reasonably good boss. And he'd never actually asked for her resignation. It had been her idea to leave the firm. "All right. Coffee. I'll be finished here in another fifteen minutes or so."

"I'll wait."

Twenty minutes later Margaret bid goodbye to the bookstore manager and the last of the readers who had dropped by the store to say hello. Slinging her stylish leather shoulder bag over her arm, she went to join Jack Moorcroft who was waiting patiently at the entrance of the store near the magazine racks.

He smiled when he saw her and put back the copy of *Forbes* he had been perusing. She studied him objectively as he held the door for her. Moorcroft was five years older than Rafe, which made him forty-three. On the surface he fit her mental image of a hero better than Rafe ever did. For one thing, there wasn't a trace of the cowboy in Moorcroft's attire or his accent. He was pure corporate polish.

Moorcroft was also a genuinely good-looking man. He kept himself trim by daily workouts at an exclusive health club and he dressed with impeccable finesse. His light brown hair was streaked with silver and thinning a bit, but that only served to give him a distinguished look. His suit was European in cut and the tie was silk.

By right Moorcroft should have been a living, breathing replica of one of her heroes but Margaret had never once thought of him that way.

In addition to his beautifully cut suits, Jack Moorcroft also wore a wedding ring. He was married and that fact had made him off-limits from the day she had met him.

But even if he had not been married Margaret knew deep down she could never have fallen for him the way she had fallen for Rafe. What she couldn't quite explain was why Moorcroft could never have been the man of her dreams.

"All right, Jack, let's get the cards on the table." Margaret sat down across from her former boss at a small espresso bar table. "We both know you're not in Seattle to rehash old times."

Jack toyed with the plastic stir stick that had come with his latte. He eyed Margaret thoughtfully for a long moment. "You've changed," he said finally.

She cocked a brow, amused. "Everyone does."

"I suppose. You like the writing business?"

"Love it. But that's not what you're here to talk about, is it?"

"No." Moorcroft took a sip of the latte and set the cup down on the small table. "My information says Cassidy came to see you this week."

Margaret shrugged. "Your information is good. He was here Thursday night. What does that matter to you?"

"He wants revenge, Margaret. You know him as well, if not better than I do. You know he always gets even."

"He's already had his revenge against me. You were there that morning. You heard him tell me to get out of his life."

"But now he's back, isn't he?" Jack's mouth twisted. "Because he never got his revenge against me. He kicked you out of his bed but there wasn't much he could do to me."

Margaret felt her cheeks burn at the blunt reference to her relationship with Rafe. "Why should he want revenge against you? I was the one he thought betrayed him."

Moorcroft's eyes narrowed. "Ah, but you betrayed him to me, remember?"

"Damn it, I didn't betray anyone. I was caught in the middle and I did what I had to do."

"The way he saw it, when the chips were down, I was the one who owned your loyalty. He was right in a way, wasn't he? But he didn't like that one bit, Margaret. I think he saw me as the other man in your life."

"You were my employer, nothing more. Rafe knew that. Tell me something, Jack, did you really lie to him about us?"

Moorcroft shrugged apologetically. "Cassidy was out of control that morning. He thought what he wanted to think, which was that you felt loyal to me not only because you worked for me but because we'd been involved in an affair."

Margaret shook her head in sheer disgust. "You did lie to him."

"Does it matter if I let him think what he was already thinking? The damage had been done. He'd already thrown you out and he knew he'd lost Spencer to me."

"So you decided to take advantage of the situation and gloat over your victory."

Moorcroft smiled cryptically. "I'll admit I couldn't resist the chance to sink the knife in a little deeper. Two years ago Cassidy cost me a bundle when he wrecked a merger I had set up. I owed him."

"And I just happened to get caught in the middle this time."

"You probably don't believe this, but I'm sorry about what happened, Margaret."

"Sure. Look, let's just forget this, all right? I've got better things to do than talk over old times."

"Unfortunately I can't forget it." Moorcroft leaned forward intently. "I can't forget it because Cassidy hasn't forgotten it. He's after me."

"What are you talking about?"

"This isn't just a business rivalry between that damned cowboy and me any longer. Because of you it's turned into some kind of personal vendetta for him. A hundred years ago he would have challenged me to a showdown at high noon or some such nonsense. But we live in a civilized age now, don't we? Cassidy's going to be a bit more subtle about his vengeance."

Margaret stared at him. "What in the world are you talking about, Jack?"

Moorcroft sat hunched over his latte, his hazel eyes intent. "He's up to something, Margaret. My sources tell me he's got a deal going, a deal that could directly affect Moorcroft Industries. I need to find out what's going on before it's too late. I need inside information."

"Sound like you've already got information."

"Some. I don't know how much I can trust it."

"That's your problem, Jack."

"Look, Cassidy always plays his cards close to his chest but after what happened with you last year, he's more cautious than ever. Whatever he's working on is being kept under very tight security. I have to find out what he's up to, Margaret, before it's too late."

"Why are you coming to me about this? I don't work for you any longer, remember? I don't work for anyone except myself now. And I like it that way, Jack. I like it very much."

Moorcroft smiled. "Yes, I can see that. You look good, Margaret. Very good. I know you're out of the scene and you want to keep it that way, but I'm desperate and I need help. That business between me and Cassidy last year?"

"What about it?"

"That's all it was until you got involved. Business as usual. Cassidy and I have tangled before. Bound to happen. We're natural competitors. But after you came into the picture all that changed. Cassidy's out for blood now. Lately I've had the feeling I'm being hunted and I don't like it. I'm asking you to help me."

"You're out of your mind. I can't help you. I wouldn't even if I were in a position to do so. As you said, I'm out of this."

Moorcroft shook his head. "It's not your fault, Margaret, but the truth is, unwittingly or not, you started it. And now Cassidy is involving you again."

Margaret sat very still in her chair. "What makes you say that?"

"He's invited you down to that spread of his in Arizona, hasn't he?"

"How do you know that?"

Moorcroft sighed. "I told you, I don't have totally reliable inside information, but I have some. I've also heard your father has been seeing Beverly Cassidy."

Margaret grimaced. "Your information is better than mine, Jack. I didn't know that myself until Thursday night. My own father. I didn't even believe it at first. How could Dad…" She bit her lip. "Never mind."

She had spent most of Thursday night trying to convince herself that Rafe had lied to her. But several phone calls on Friday had failed to elicit any response from her father's home in California. His housekeeper had told her he had gone to Arizona.

When Margaret had angrily dialed the Cassidy ranch she had been told by another housekeeper that her father was unable to come to the phone but was looking forward to seeing her on Monday.

The unfortunate reality was that Rafe Cassidy rarely bluffed—so rarely, in fact, that when he did, he usually got away with it. Connor Lark probably was involved with Mrs. Cassidy and if that much was true, the part about selling Lark Engineering to Rafe was probably also true.

That knowledge gave Margaret a sick feeling. What was Rafe up to? she wondered.

"We're on the same side this time, Margaret." Jack's tone was soft and cajoling. "We're natural allies. Last time you were caught in the crunch. You were in love with Cassidy but you felt loyal to me. A real mess. But that's not true this time, is it? You don't owe Cassidy anything. It's payback time."

"What are you talking about? I don't want revenge, I just want out of the whole thing."

"You can't get out of it. Your father is involved. If he marries Beverly Cassidy, you're going to spend the rest of your life connected by family ties to Rafe Cassidy."

"That notion is certainly enough to kill what's left of my appetite," Margaret said morosely. The thought of being related by marriage to Rafe was mind-boggling.

Moorcroft picked up his latte and took a swallow. "You'll be going to Arizona, won't you?"

She groaned. "Probably." She had been facing that reality since Rafe had walked out the door on Thursday night. She had to find out what, exactly, was going on.

"All I'm asking is that you keep your eyes and ears open while you're down there. You may pick up something interesting, something we can both use. Maybe something that could save my hide. I'd make it worth your while, Margaret."

She looked up sharply. "Forget it, Jack. If I go down there, it won't be as your spy. I have my own reasons."

He exhaled slowly. "I understand. It was worth a shot. I'm a desperate man, Margaret. There's an outlaw on my trail and I'll do anything to survive."

"You're that afraid of Rafe?" she asked in genuine surprise.

"Like I said—before we were just business rivals. Win some, lose some. No problem. That's the name of the game. But this time things are different. This time I have a feeling I may be fighting for my life."

"Good luck."

Moorcroft turned his cup of latte carefully in his hands. He studied Margaret's face for a long moment. "You're not going to help me, are you?"

"No."

"Because you love him?"

"How I feel about Rafe has nothing to do with it. I just don't want any part of this mess, whatever it is."

"I guess I can understand that."

"Terrific," she murmured. "I'm so glad."

"Margaret, there's something I want to ask you."

She waited uneasily. "Yes?"

"If Cassidy hadn't ridden up when he did and swept you off your feet, do you think you could ever have been interested in what I had to offer?"

"You didn't have anything to offer, Jack. You're a married man, remember?"

"But if I hadn't been married?"

"My best guess is no."

"Mind telling me why not?"

"First, when I was in the business world I had a policy of never getting involved with my employers, even if they did happen to be single. From what I saw, it's almost always a bad career move for a woman to sleep with her boss. Sooner or later, she finds herself looking for another job."

"And second?"

"Let's just say you're not exactly the man of my dreams," she said dryly.

RAFE WAS WAITING AT THE AIRPORT GATE. Margaret didn't see him at first. She was struggling with her carry-on luggage and scanning the crowd for her father. She was annoyed when she couldn't spot him. The least Connor Lark could do after causing all this commotion in her life was meet her at the airport, she told herself. When someone moved up behind her and took the travel bag from her arm, she spun around in shock.

"I'll take that for you, Maggie, love. Car's out front."

She glared up at Rafe, who was smiling down at her, a look of pure satisfaction in his gaze. He was dressed in jeans and boots and a white shirt that had the sleeves rolled up on his forearms. His hat was pulled down low over his eyes. The boots were truly spectacular—maroon leather with a beautiful turquoise and black design worked into them.

"I thought my father would have had the courtesy to meet me," she muttered.

"Don't blame Connor. I told him I'd take care of it." Rafe wrapped his hand around the nape of her neck, bent his head briefly and kissed her soundly. He did it hard and fast and allowed her no time in which to resist.

Margaret had barely registered his intentions before the whole thing was over. Scowling more furiously than ever, she stepped back quickly. She longed to slap the expression of triumph off his hard face. But at the last instant she reminded herself it would be dangerous to show any sign of a loss of self-control.

"I would appreciate it if you would not do that again," she bit out in a tight voice.

"Have a good flight?" Rafe smiled his thin, faint smile as he started down the corridor.

Margaret recalled belatedly that Rafe was very good at ignoring things he didn't care to deal with at the moment. He was already several feet away, moving in a long, rangy, ground-eating stride. She swore silently as she hurried to catch up with him. Following him was not an easy task dressed as she was in high heels and a turquoise silk suit that had an extremely narrow skirt.

"Good Lord, it's like an oven out here." Margaret gasped as she stepped through the doors of the Tucson airport terminal and into the full, humid warmth of a July day. She pulled a pair of sunglasses from her purse and glanced around at her surroundings.

The unrelenting blue of a vast desert sky arched overhead. There wasn't a cloud in sight to offer any relief from the blazing sun. Heat welled up off the pavement and poured down from above. Around her the desert stretched out in all directions, meeting the purple mountains in the distance.

"It's summer in the desert," Rafe pointed out. "What did you expect? You'll get used to it."

"Never in a million years."

"I know it's not Seattle." Rafe led the way to a silver-gray Mercedes parked in the short-term parking lot. "Gets a little warm down here in the summer. But as I said, you get used to it."

"You might be able to get accustomed to it, but I certainly never would." It was a challenge and she knew it.

"Try, Maggie," he advised laconically. "Try real hard. You're going to be here awhile. Might as well learn to enjoy it."

"Threats already, Rafe?"

"No, ma'am. Just a little good advice." He unlocked the passenger door of the Mercedes and held it open for her.

She glared up at him as she slid into the seat. The glare turned to a wince of pain as the sun-heated leather burned through her thin silk suit.

"I'll have the air conditioner going in a minute," Rafe promised. He tossed her bags into the trunk and then got in beside her to start the Mercedes. When the car purred to life he paused for a moment with his big, capable hands on the wheel and looked at Margaret. There was a dark hunger in his eyes but it was overlaid with a cold self-control.

Margaret was grateful for the protection of her sunglasses. "How far is it to your ranch?"

"It's a few miles out of town," he said carelessly, his attention clearly on other things. "You know something? It's hard to believe you're really here. It's about time, lady."

She didn't like the way he said that. "You didn't give me much choice, did you?"

"No."

"I should have known I wasn't going to get an apology out of you."

"For what?"

"For your high-handed, arrogant, overbearing tactics," she snapped, goaded.

"Oh, those. No, you shouldn't expect an apology. I did what I had to do." He put the Mercedes in gear and pulled smoothly out of the lot. "I had to get you down here, Maggie. There wasn't any other way to do it."

"You're wasting your time, Rafe. And please stop calling me Maggie. You gave me your word you'd remember to call me Margaret."

"I said I'd try to remember."

"Try, Rafe," she murmured, mimicking his earlier words. "Try real hard."

Rafe gave her an amused look as he stopped to hand some cash to the gate attendant. "But I've got a lot on my mind these days and the small stuff tends to slip through the cracks."

Her hands clenched in her lap. "That's all I ever was to you, wasn't it, Rafe? Small stuff. Unimportant stuff."

"You're small, all right." His voice had an affectionate, teasing edge to it now as he pulled away from the gate. "But no way are you going to slip through the cracks. Not this time."

"You don't want me back, Rafe."

"No? Why would I go to all the bother of blackmail to get you here if I didn't want you back?"

She frowned. "I've been thinking about that. The only conclusion I can come up with is that in your mind I'm the one who got away. It's true you kicked me out of your life, but when I went without a backward glance and stayed out, your ego took a beating, didn't it?"

"You did a number on my ego, all right," he agreed dryly. "It hasn't been the same since."

"Is that what this is all about? Revenge?" She shivered, remembering what Jack Moorcroft had said. *Cassidy is out for blood.*

"I would do a lot of things for revenge under certain circumstances," Rafe said, "but getting married isn't one of them. I'm not masochistic. Don't make any mistake about it, Maggie. I brought you down here to give myself some time to undue the damage that got done last year."

"The damage is irreparable."

"No, it's not. We're going to put that mess behind us and get on with our lives."

"I have been getting on with my life," she pointed out. "Very nicely, thank you. I've been quite happy this past year."

"Lucky you. I've been to hell and back."

She sucked in her breath. "Rafe, please, don't say things like that. We both know you're not the type to pine for a woman, especially one you think betrayed you. You're far more likely to look for a way to reap some vengeance against her. And I suspect that's exactly what you're doing by going after my father's firm."

"I'm not going after it. Your dad wants to sell to me. It's a profitable operation that will fit in well with the other businesses Cassidy and Company runs, so I'm taking a serious look at it. That's all there is to it."

"I don't believe that."

"I know. That's why you're here, isn't it? To rescue Connor from my clutches. You might be able to do that, Maggie, but I doubt you'll get him out of my mother's hands. Wait until you see them together. They're made for each other."

"It's all part of some plot you've cooked up, Rafe. Why don't you tell me what you're really after?"

"You're beginning to sound paranoid, honey."

"I'm not paranoid, I'm careful."

He smiled fleetingly at that. "No, Maggie, you're not careful. If you were careful, you wouldn't be here."

Margaret took refuge in silence for the next several miles. She folded her arms beneath her breasts and stared out the window at the arid landscape as she tried desperately to think. She had been struggling to put together some sort of battle plan ever since she had accepted the inevitability of this trip. But she was still very uncertain of what to do now that she was here. Part of the problem was that she could not be sure of what Rafe was really up to.

She did not believe for a moment that he wanted to marry her. But it was entirely possible he wanted to seduce her so that he could have the satisfaction of punishing her for her so-called betrayal.

Then, too, there was Moorcroft to consider. She didn't care what happened to Jack or his firm but she had to wonder if Rafe intended to use her in some scheme to get even with his rival.

Finally there was the business of her father getting involved with Beverly Cassidy and planning to sell Lark Engineering to Rafe.

No doubt about it, the situation was complicated and potentially dangerous.

A typical Rafe Cassidy operation, Margaret thought.

Chapter Three

"THIS IS YOUR HOME, RAFE?" MARGARET watched in amazement as the main buildings of the Cassidy Ranch came into view.

Set in the foothills with a sweeping view of Tucson in the distance, the ranch was an impressive sight. At the end of a long, winding drive was a graceful house done in the classic Spanish Colonial style. The walls had the look of warm, earth-toned adobe and the roof was red tile. Lush greenery surrounded the place, a welcome antidote to the rugged desert landscape. Low, white, modern-looking barns, white fences and green pastures spread out from the house. Margaret could see horses in the fields.

"Things were a little rushed during that two-month period after we met," Rafe reminded her coolly. "There wasn't time to get you down here to see the place before you...left me."

"You mean before you threw me out of your life."

Rafe drew a breath. "It was an argument, Maggie. A bad one. I lost my temper and said a lot of things I didn't mean."

"Oh, you meant them, all right. Where are the cows?" Margaret added in mild curiosity. "Shouldn't there be cows on a ranch like this?"

"This time of year the cattle are scattered all to hell and gone up in the foothills," Rafe said impatiently.

"Why so many horses? They don't look like quarter horses."

"They aren't. They're Arabians. We breed them. Some of the best in the world. The profit margin is a lot more reliable than cattle. In fact, I'm thinking of getting out of the cattle business altogether."

"Well, that figures. I don't see you getting involved in anything that doesn't show an excellent profit margin. Have you considered chickens?"

"*Chickens?*" His expression was a mask of outrage, the sort of outrage only a true cattleman could manage.

"Sure. Red meat is out, Rafe. Haven't you been following the latest health advice? Chicken, fish and vegetables are in. Oh, and turkeys. You might try raising turkeys. I understand they're not real bright so you should be able to figure out a way to round them up and brand them if you feel you must maintain the old traditions."

"Forget chickens and forget turkeys," he growled.

"All right. I imagine the real basis for the family fortune is Cassidy and Company anyway, isn't it? You rustle companies now instead of cattle."

Rafe slanted her a brief, annoyed glance as he parked the Mercedes. "You're determined to make this difficult, aren't you?"

"As difficult as I can," she assured him as she opened her own car door and got out. "Where is my father?"

"Probably out by the pool. That's where I left him when I went to get you." Rafe got out of the Mercedes just as a young man wearing a striped shirt and black jeans came around the corner of the house. "Tom, this is Maggie Lark. Maggie, this is Tom. He takes care of the house gardens and a lot of other odds and ends around here. Tom, grab the lady's luggage, will you? It goes into the south guest bedroom."

"Sure thing, Rafe. Afternoon, Miss Lark. We've been expecting you. Have a good trip?"

"Fine, thank you, Tom." Margaret smiled coolly at him. "Where is the pool?"

Tom looked surprised. "The pool? Out in the patio. Straight through the house. But don't you want to settle into your room first? Maybe change your clothes?" He eyed her silk suit dubiously.

"I want to see my father first. This is a business trip as far as I'm concerned."

"Oh, yeah. Sure. Business." Tom was obviously baffled by that statement. "Like I said, right through the middle of the house."

Margaret did not wait for Rafe to do the honors. She felt his sardonic gaze on her as she turned and strode straight toward the wide, dark wooden door of the Spanish-style home. She opened it and found herself in a cool, tiled hall. The air-conditioning felt wonderful. She took off her sunglasses and glanced around with unwilling curiosity.

This was Rafe's hideaway, she knew, the Cassidy family ranch. He had mentioned it once or twice during the brief time she had been dating him. It was the place he came to when the pressure of his fast-track life-style occasionally caught up with him. That wasn't often. Rafe's stamina was legendary.

The Southwestern style of the outside of Rafe's home had been carried on inside. Soft earthtones, terra cotta, peach and pale turquoise dominated. Here and there was a shot of black in the form of a vase or a lamp. Heavily beamed ceilings and rugs with geometric Indian designs woven into them gave a rustic effect that was also surprisingly gracious.

Through the floor-to-ceiling windows that lined one entire wall of the long living room Margaret could see the pool. It occupied the center of a beautifully landscaped courtyard that was enclosed by the four wings of the house. Two figures were seated under an umbrella, a pitcher of tea on the table between them. Connor Lark and Beverly Cassidy were laughing in delight over some private joke.

Margaret watched the couple for a moment, uncertainty seizing her insides. Her father looked happy—happier than she had ever seen him since her mother died several years ago. She sensed suddenly that her mission to rescue him was going to be difficult to carry out.

"What's the matter, Maggie? Afraid it's not going to be so simple after all?" Rafe asked as he walked into the hall behind her. "I told you they were made for each other."

She glanced back at him, her eyes narrowing. "Hard to imagine you as a matchmaker, Rafe."

"You think I arranged for them to fall for each other just to make it easier to get my hands on Lark Engineering?" He sounded amused. "I'm good, Maggie, but I'm not that good. I take full responsibility for introducing them. After that, they did it all by themselves."

"You think you're very clever, don't you?"

"If I were really clever, we wouldn't have wasted a year of our lives apart. Look, Maggie, do everyone a favor and don't take your father's relationship with my mother as a personal threat, okay? The fact that he fell in love with her doesn't translate directly into a betrayal of you. It's not like your father has gone over to the enemy camp."

Her fingers tightened on the strap of her purse as the shot went home. A part of her had been viewing the situation in exactly that light, she acknowledged privately. It was irrational but the feeling was there on some level. "My father was already halfway into the enemy camp before he met your mother. He took to you right from the start, didn't he?"

"He thought I'd make you a good husband. He was right."

"Oh, yes, he thought you were the ideal husband for me. A genuine cowboy. The son he'd never had, or something along those lines I imagine. I swear, if he'd had the power to arrange the marriage, I think he would have done it. Lark Engineering would have been my dowry."

"There is something to be said for arranged marriages, isn't there?"

"This is not a joke, Rafe."

"So Connor and I get along." Rafe leaned against the wall and folded his arms. "So what?"

Margaret smiled grimly. "Well, at least I've got one person on my side."

"Who?" His eyes were taunting.

"Your mother. She must have been enormously relieved when you threw me out of your life last year."

The lines of his face hardened. "Don't count on it. And stop saying I threw you out."

"That's what happened."

"It was your damn pride that screwed everything up, and you know it. If you'd had the grace to admit you were wrong a year ago, we could have worked things out."

"I wasn't wrong. I did what I had to do. If you'd had the decency not to use me in your campaign to beat Moorcroft to Spencer in the first place, the entire situation would never have developed."

Rafe swore softly and then straightened away from the wall as Tom approached with the luggage. "Go say hello to your father, Maggie."

Feeling a little more cheerful because it seemed like she'd just won that round, Maggie crossed the living room and opened one of the glass doors. Her father looked up as she stepped onto the patio.

"Maggie, my girl, you're here. It's about time. Come on over and have some tea. Bev and I've been waitin' for you to come rescue me from Cassidy's clutches. Good to see you, girl, good to see you. Been a while since we talked."

"We could have had a nice long talk if you'd bothered to answer the phone when I called down here to see what was going on."

"Now, Maggie, girl, don't go gettin' on your high horse. I only did what I thought was best. You know that."

It was impossible to hold on to her anger when her father looked at her with such delight. Margaret saw the relaxed good humor in his eyes and she sighed inwardly. No question about it, her father was here of his own free will.

Connor Lark was a big man, almost as big as Rafe, and he was built like a mountain. There was a hint of a belly cantilevered out over the waistband of his swimming trunks, but he still looked very solid. His black hair had long since turned silver and his aqua eyes, so like her own, were as lively as ever.

Margaret's mother had always claimed he was a diamond in the rough whom she'd had to spend a great deal of time polishing. Connor always claimed she'd enjoyed every minute of the task and Margaret knew she had. From a desperately poor background as a rancher, Connor had risen to become a self-made entrepreneur who had built Lark Engineering into a thriving modern business.

"Well, Dad. Looks like you're enjoying the process of selling out." Margaret smiled affectionately at her father and then turned a slightly wary smile on the attractive woman who sat on the other side of the table. "Hello, Bev. Nice to see you again."

Rafe's mother was a trim, energetic-looking woman who was approximately the same age as Connor, although she looked younger. Her short, well-styled hair was the color of fine champagne. She was wearing a black-and-white swimsuit cover-up and a pair of leather sandals that projected an image of subtle elegance, even though they constituted sportswear. Bev's expression was gracious but her pale gray eyes held the same hint of wariness Margaret knew were in her own.

"Hello, Margaret. I'm pleased to see you again."

Margaret leaned down to kiss her father's cheek, thinking that she and Bev were both good at social lies. She was well aware she had not made a particularly good impression on Beverly Cassidy on the one occasion they had met last year. There was an excellent reason for that. Bev Cassidy had not considered Margaret a good candidate as a wife for her one and only son. Margaret tended to agree with her.

"Do sit down, Margaret," Bev said, reaching for the pitcher of iced tea and pouring her guest a glass. "You must be exhausted from your trip. Your father and I just finished a swim. After you've said hello you must go and put on your suit. I'm sure a dip in the pool will feel good." She turned her welcoming smile on her son as Rafe came through the glass doors and followed Margaret to the shaded loungers. "Oh, there you are, Rafe. Iced tea?"

"Thanks."

He held out his hand for the glass as he sat down beside Margaret on one of the loungers. His powerfully muscled thigh brushed her leg and Margaret promptly shifted to put a few more inches between them. He ignored the small retreat.

Margaret took a long, fortifying sip of iced tea and studied the three people who surrounded her. Her father and Bev appeared to be waiting for her to make the next move. Rafe didn't look particularly concerned one way or the other. To look at him one would have thought this was a perfectly normal family gathering. Margaret frowned over her glass.

"Why don't we all stop playing games," she suggested in a voice that she hoped hid her own inner tension. "We all know this isn't a happy little poolside party."

"Speak for yourself," Connor suggested easily. "I'm happy." He reached across the table and caught Bev's hand, smiling at the older woman. "And I think Bev is, too. Did Rafe tell you the good news?"

"That you and Bev are involved? Yes, he did."

Connor scowled slightly. "I don't know about *involved.* I'm not up on all the new terminology. Is that what they call plannin' to get married nowadays?"

Margaret swallowed. Rafe had been right. This was serious. "You're planning marriage?"

"Yes, we are." Bev looked at Margaret with a faint air of challenge. "I hope you approve."

"I wish you both the best," Margaret made herself say politely. "You'll understand that the news has come as something of a shock. I had no idea you two had even met until Rafe mentioned it."

"Take it easy, Maggie, girl," Connor said gently. "There were reasons I didn't want to talk about it until now."

"Reasons?" She pinned him with her gaze.

"Now, Maggie, lass, you know what I'm talkin' about. The situation 'tween you and Rafe here has been a mite tense for some time."

Margaret arched her brows and slid a long, assessing glance at Rafe. "Tense? I wouldn't say that. I wasn't particularly tense at all during the past year. Were you tense, Rafe?"

"I had my moments," he muttered.

She nodded. "Well, I did try to warn you about stress, didn't I? As I recall, I gave you several pithy little lectures about your long hours, non-existent vacations and general tendency to put your work first."

"I believe you did mention the subject. Several times, in fact."

Margaret smiled coldly. "Come now, Rafe, you can be honest in front of Dad and your mother. Admit the full truth. Toward the end there I was starting to turn into a full-blown nag when it came to the matter of your total devotion to work, wasn't I? I think I was even beginning to threaten you that if our relationship didn't get equal time there wouldn't be a relationship."

Bev shifted uneasily in her chair, her eyes swinging to Connor.

Margaret's father whistled soundlessly. "Oh, ho. So that's the way of it, is it?"

Rafe gave Margaret a repressive stare. "I had my hands full last year when we met, if you'll recall. I was juggling a couple of companies that were valued in the millions.

Things are different now. I'm making some changes in my life."

"Such as?"

"I've cut way back on the juggling, for one thing." He flashed her a quick grin.

Margaret was not amused. "I find that hard to believe."

"Hey, I'm down here in Arizona with you, aren't I?" He smiled again. "Two full weeks, maybe three if I get lucky. You have my full attention, Maggie, love."

"Not quite. You're in the middle of negotiating a deal with my father, remember?"

Connor chuckled. "She's got you there, Rafe. We are supposed to be talking business off and on, aren't we?"

"Speaking of this little matter of selling the company you built with the sweat of your brow, Dad, just what is going on?" Margaret pinned her father with a quelling glare.

"What can I tell you?" Connor shrugged massively. "It's the truth. If I can get a decent offer out of Cassidy, here, Lark Engineering is his."

"But, Dad, you never told me you were thinking of selling."

"The time has come to enjoy some of the money I made with all that brow sweat. Bev and I plan to do a lot of traveling and a fair amount of just plain fooling around. I'm even looking at a nifty little yacht. Can't you just see me in that fancy yachting getup?"

"But the company has always been so important to you, Dad."

"It's still important. Maggie, girl, I'll be perfectly truthful with you. If you'd stayed in the business world, shown a real interest in it, I'd probably have turned it over to you one of these days. But let's face it, girl, you aren't cut out for that world. And now you've got yourself a fine new career, one you've taken to like a duck to water. I'm glad for you, but it leaves me with a problem. I've got to do something with the firm."

"So you're just going to hand it over to Rafe?"

"He's not exactly handing it over," Rafe muttered. "Your father is holding me at gunpoint. You ought to hear what he's asking for Lark."

"I see." Margaret felt some of the righteous determination seep out of her. Everything was already beyond her control. Rafe was in command, as usual. Things would go his way. A curious sense of inevitability began to come over her. Determinedly she fought back. "Where's the ubiquitous Hatcher?" Margaret asked, glancing meaningfully around the pool. "Surely you haven't dismissed your faithful, loyal, ever-present assistant for two solid weeks?"

Rafe took a swallow of tea. "Hatcher is going to drop by occasionally to brief me on how things are going at the main office. But that's all. I've delegated almost everything else. I'm only available for world-class emergencies. Satisfied?"

"You don't have to worry about my feelings on the subject," Margaret said. "Not anymore. You're free to run your life any way you choose."

"Ouch." Connor winced.

"I know what you mean," Rafe remarked. "She's been sniping at me like that every chance she gets. But I've promised myself I'll be tolerant, patient and understanding. She can't keep it up forever."

"Don't bet on it." Margaret got to her feet. "I believe I will have that swim now. If you'll excuse me, Bev?"

"Of course, dear. The water is lovely."

Bev looked relieved to see her go. But there was an unexpected trace of unhappiness in her gaze, too, Margaret noticed. She wondered about that as she turned to walk back into the house. Surely after the things Bev Cassidy had said to her last year, she couldn't be hoping for a reconciliation between her son and his errant mistress.

Mistress. The old-fashioned word still burned in Margaret's ears whenever she remembered Bev's last words to her. *You'd make him a better mistress than you would a wife.*

"Cocktails at six out here by the pool, dear," Bev called after her. "We'll be eating around seven-thirty. Connor and Rafe have promised to grill us some steaks."

"Right," Connor said cheerfully. "Got us some of the biggest, juiciest, thickest steaks on the face of the planet."

Margaret laughed for the first time since Thursday night. She looked back at the small group gathered under the umbrella. "I almost forgot to mention that I've made a few life-style changes myself during the past year."

"Such as?" Rafe asked, lion's eyes watchful.

"I never touch red meat." Margaret walked on into the cool house, paying no attention to her father's bellow of astonishment.

SHORTLY AFTER ONE O'CLOCK IN THE MORNING, Margaret eased open the patio door of her bedroom and slipped out into the silent courtyard. She had changed into her bathing suit a few minutes earlier, finally admitting that she was not going to be able to sleep.

The balmy desert air was still amazingly warm. It carried a myriad of soft scents from the gardens. Overhead, the star-studded sky stretched into a dark infinity. Margaret had the feeling that if she listened closely she might actually be able to hear a coyote howl from some nearby hilltop.

The underwater lights of the swimming pool glowed invitingly. Margaret slipped off her sandals and slid into the water. She hovered weightlessly for a long moment and then began to swim the length of the pool. The tension in her muscles slowly dissolved.

It had been a difficult evening.

If she had any sense she would leave tomorrow, she told herself as she reached the far end of the pool and started back. It was the only thing to do. Her father was happy. It was obvious he was not being bamboozled out of Lark Engineering. He truly wanted to sell out to Rafe so there was nothing she could say or do. It was his business, after all.

Yes, she should definitely leave tomorrow. But every time she felt Rafe's eyes on her she found herself looking for an excuse to stay. The excuse of doing battle with him was the only one she had.

There was no sound behind her on the flagstone but something made Margaret pause in the water and look back toward the far side of the pool. Rafe stood there in the shadows clad in only a snug-fitting pair of swim trunks. Moonlight gleamed on his broad shoulders and in the darkness his eyes were watchful and mysterious.

"Couldn't sleep?" he asked softly.

"No." She treaded water wondering if she should flee back to the safety of her bedroom. But she seemed to lack the strength of will to get out of the pool.

"Neither could I. I've been lying in bed wondering what kind of reception I'd get if I went to your bedroom."

"A very cold reception."

"You think so? I'm not so sure. That's what was keeping me awake, you know. The uncertainty." He lowered himself silently into the water and stroked quietly toward her.

Margaret instinctively edged back until her shoulders were against the side of the pool. She gripped the tiled edge with one hand as Rafe came to a halt in front of her. "Rafe,

I don't think this is a good idea. I came out here to swim alone."

"You're not alone any longer." He put his hands on either side of her, gripping the tile and effectively caging her against the side of the pool. But he made no move to bring his body against hers.

"Are you trying to intimidate me?" Margaret asked, shockingly aware of the brush of his leg against hers under water. Old memories, never far from the surface, welled up swiftly, bringing with them the jolt of desire.

"My goal isn't to intimidate you, honey, it's to remind you of a few things," Rafe said gently. "A few very good things." He came closer, causing the water to lap softly at her throat and shoulders. "Maggie, I've wanted you back in my bed every night since you left. Every damned night. Doesn't that mean anything to you?"

She shivered, although the water was warm. "Did you mean what you said last Thursday? There hasn't been anyone else since you and I...since we've been apart?"

"I meant it. The only thing that kept me sane was knowing you weren't sleeping with anyone else, either."

She scowled. "How did you know that, anyway?"

His mouth thinned. "It's not important."

"You aren't just guessing about my love life during the past year, are you? You know for a fact I haven't been serious about anyone else. Damn it, Rafe, there's only one way you could be so certain. You hired someone to spy on me, didn't you?"

"Maggie, honey, I told you, it's not important."

"Well, it's very important to me. Rafe, how could you?"

"Hush, love." His hand wrapped around her nape and he kissed her lightly. "I said it's not important. Not any longer."

"You should be ashamed of yourself."

"Have pity on me, love. I was a desperate man."

"Rafe, the last thing I will ever have for you is pity. Just what did you think you were going to do if I got involved with someone else?" she demanded.

"Could we discuss something else? Your voice is rising. If you're not careful, you'll wake Mom and Connor. Their bedrooms open onto this courtyard, too."

The last thing she wanted was for anyone to overhear this particular conversation. Margaret reluctantly lowered her tone to a fierce whisper. "What did you think you were going to do, Rafe?"

"Move our thrilling reconciliation up a few months," he told her wryly.

"You're impossible." She didn't believe for a moment that was all he would have done. It was becoming very clear that Rafe had never stopped thinking of her as belonging to him during the past year. Only the knowledge that he'd been celibate during that entire time himself kept her from going up in flames over the matter.

"Tell me you missed me, Maggie. Just a little?"

She shook her head mutely.

"Admit it," Rafe urged, moving a little closer in the water. "Give me that much, honey."

"No." The single word was a soft gasp of dismay. He was only inches from her now. His hands were on either side of her, trapping her.

"You remember how good it was, don't you, love?" He kissed her fleetingly again, closing the distance between them until there wasn't any at all. "I didn't go looking for anyone else because I knew it would be useless. You knew there wasn't anyone else for you, either, didn't you?"

"Oh, Rafe." She muttered his name in a soft cry that was part protest, part acceptance of a truth that could not be denied.

"Yeah, Maggie, love. You do remember, don't you? A whole year, sweetheart. A year of pure hell."

Margaret felt his leg slide between hers as his mouth came down to claim her lips. She felt her breasts being softly crushed against his chest. The hot, sweet rain of passion too long denied swept through her, pooling just below her stomach. Rafe was the only man who had ever been able to do this to her, the only one who could bring her to such shockingly intense arousal with only a look and a kiss and a touch.

Nothing had changed.

"Maggie, love, this time we'll make things work between us." Rafe's mouth moved on hers, gliding along the line of her jaw up to the lobe of her ear. He bit gently, tantalizing her with a pleasure that was not quite pain. "Just give me a chance, sweetheart. I'm going to prove it. Everything is going to be different this time around. Except for this part. No need to fix this, is there?"

He was right about one thing, Margaret thought. This part was still very, very good. Slowly, with a growing sense of inevitability, she felt herself sliding back into the magic world of sensuality that she had shared all too briefly with Rafe.

"Let me love you, Maggie. Let me hold you the way I used to hold you."

"Back when I was your mistress?"

He shook his head, his gaze suddenly fierce. "I never thought of you as a mistress. You were the woman I was going to marry. I knew that from the first day I met you."

"Your mother said I would make a better mistress for you than I would a wife and I think she may have been right."

Rafe's head came up abruptly. "What the devil are you talking about?"

"Never mind. As you said a minute ago, it's not important."

"Maggie, stop talking in riddles."

"I've got a better idea," she suggested softly. "Let's not talk at all." She put her arms around his neck as she made her decision. Heaven help her, she did not have the power to deny herself a night in Rafe's arms. "You were right, Rafe. This part was always very good." She brushed her lips lightly across his and felt his shudder of response.

"Maggie, love." Rafe's voice was a husky groan. "Are you telling me the waiting is over?"

"I want you, Rafe. I never stopped wanting you."

Rafe's mouth closed over hers once more, hard and passionate and filled with a year's worth of pent-up need. Margaret felt his hands moving on her under the water, relearning the shape and feel of her.

His tongue surged between her lips as his fingers slipped under the edge of her swimming suit bra. She gasped as she felt his thumbs slide over her nipples.

"Rafe?"

"Not here," he muttered. "Too much chance of an audience. I'm taking you back to my room."

He hauled himself up onto the tiled edge of the pool with easy strength, then reached down and lifted her up beside him. Margaret looked up into his dark eyes and saw the undiluted hunger there. She felt the answering ache of desire within herself and knew she was still in love with Rafe Cassidy.

You'd make him a better mistress than a wife.

Bev Cassidy's words rang in Margaret's ears once more as Rafe swept her up into his arms and started toward the open door of his bedroom.

Chapter Four

THE BEDROOM WAS FILLED WITH THE inviting mysteries of the night. The woman in Rafe's arms was intoxicating and seemed a part of that glittering darkness.

He was only half conscious of the dark, cool shadows and the pooling white sheets on the wide bed. All Rafe could think of now was the warm, sensual weight of the woman he held. *His woman.* She was finally back where she belonged.

"It's been so long," he muttered thickly as he set her down beside the bed and reached for a towel. "Too damn long."

He used the towel carefully, tenderly, lovingly. He squeezed the moisture out of her hair and then combed the damp strands back from her forehead with his fingers. She had a misty look on her face. She smiled at him and kissed him gently.

He stroked the water droplets off her arms and knelt to sleek it from her long, curving legs. As he worked he touched her, aware of a surging sense of pure delight as he trailed his fingers along her smooth skin.

When he was finished he quickly dried himself and tossed the towel aside. Then he reached for her.

"Maggie, love. My sweet, sexy Maggie." He pulled her against his chest until her head was resting on his shoulder and then he undid the fastening of her swimsuit bra. Carefully he pulled it free, sliding the straps off her shoulders. He looked down and saw the hardened tips of her breasts and for an instant he thought the desire would overcome him then and there.

It took all his self-control not to rush. He stroked her the way he would one of his beautiful, sensitive mares— gently and slowly. She responded at once, vividly, the way she always had to his touch. Her reaction only served to enhance his own. When her lips moved against his bare skin and her arms went around his waist, he shuddered.

"I missed you so, Rafe."

The soft admission nearly sent him over the edge. "Oh, babe." His fingers trembled as he slid them under the edge of her bikini and pushed the scrap of material down over her hips. It fell to the floor and she stepped daintily away from the damp fabric.

Rafe took a deep breath as he looked down at her. "You're more lovely than you were even in my dreams. And believe me I had a few that were so hot I'm amazed you didn't feel the flames all the way up there in Seattle."

"I had a few of my own." Her eyes were luminous in the shadows as she slid her fingers through the hair on his chest. She traced the shape of his shoulders and then her palm shaped the muscles of his upper arms.

Rafe couldn't wait any longer. He picked her up and set her down on the bed. He felt heavy, his body taut with arousal. His mind whirled with it. He stripped off his swim trunks and lowered himself down beside her. Then he flattened his palm on her stomach and moved his fingers into the triangle of curls at the junction of her thighs. Suddenly his hand was still.

"Rafe, what's wrong?" Margaret asked softly.

"Nothing. Nothing's wrong." He bent his head and tasted one full nipple. The sensation was exquisite. "I'm just half out of my mind with wanting you now that I've finally got you back in my bed. But I want to do this right. I intended to take it slow. I've waited this long to make it perfect for you."

She laughed, a soft, throaty sound that made him want to hug her. "Rafe, it was always so good, no matter how we did it—fast, slow or in between. You don't have to worry about how we do it tonight."

He groaned and kissed her throat. "Touch me, baby. Feel how much I want you."

Her gentle fingers closed around him and Rafe sucked in his breath, his eyes slitting in reaction to the caress. "You're right. It was good any way we did it and there's no way I can take it slow tonight." He reached over and yanked open the drawer in the nightstand, groping for the small box he had optimistically put there earlier. He used one hand and his teeth to open the packet so he could keep the other hand on Maggie's thigh. He didn't want to let go of her for a second.

A moment later he moved again, rolling on top of Maggie with the wild eagerness of a stallion. He tried to control himself but she was reaching up to clasp him to her and her willingness was his undoing. He parted her legs with his own.

"Yes, Rafe. Please."

He felt her silken thighs alongside his hips and a near-violent wave of desire surged through him. When he probed her carefully he met the damp, welcoming heat and that was all he could stand. He guided himself into her, driving forward into her core. She was so tight. He wondered if he should stop and give her time to adjust to him. After all, it had been a whole year.

But he couldn't stop. Not now. He needed to bury himself within her. Rafe moaned as he slid fully into her depths. He heard her soft cry in his ear and her nails dug into his shoulders.

"Am I hurting you?" he asked, his breathing turning ragged.

"No. No, it feels wonderful. It's just…been a while, that's all."

"Too damn long for both of us."

"Yes." She lifted her hips against him, telling him she was ready now, urging him into the ancient rhythm.

Rafe needed no additional coaxing. He held her so tightly he was half afraid of crushing her. But she clung to him just as fiercely. He sank himself again and again into her heat until he felt her tightening around him in the old, familiar way.

"*Rafe.*"

"That's it, Maggie, love," he muttered against her mouth. "Come on, honey. Go wild for me."

She shivered and cried out again. He opened his mouth over hers and swallowed the soft, sweet sound. She bucked beneath him and he groaned heavily. Nothing had ever been as shatteringly sexy to Rafe as the feel of Maggie climaxing beneath him.

He waited until the last of the tremors were fading and

then he slammed into her one more time and felt himself explode.

Rafe rode the storm for what seemed like forever, the passion in him apparently limitless. And then it was over. He relaxed heavily on top of Maggie, squashing her into the damp sheets.

His last coherent thought was that the waiting and planning were finally finished. He had his Maggie back. No one had ever made him feel the way Maggie did.

It was a long time before Rafe reluctantly stirred. He only did so because he felt Maggie pushing experimentally against his shoulder.

"What's wrong?" he mumbled, half asleep.

"You're getting very heavy."

"Nag, nag, nag." He levered himself slowly away from her and rolled onto his back. He cradled her close to his side and yawned. "Better?"

"Umm-hmm." She kissed his jaw and then his shoulder, her lips incredibly soft against his skin. "I'd better get back to my own room before I fall asleep."

"No," he muttered instantly. He opened one eye to glare at her. "You sleep here."

She smiled. "I think it would be better if I went back to my own room."

"Why?" He was beginning to feel belligerent.

"Because we aren't alone in the house, remember?"

"My mother and your father both know we've had an affair in the not so distant past and they both know why you're here now. They're not going to ask any questions about why you spent the night in my room. They've taken more than one weekend trip together, you know. Hell, I wouldn't be surprised if your father is paying a late night visit to my mother even as we speak."

"Even if he is, you can bet he'll be back in his own room by dawn. That's the way their generation does things. It's a matter of propriety."

"Yeah? Well, our generation is different."

She chuckled softly. "I'm not so sure about that." Her eyes sobered. "Please, Rafe. I think it would be better if I go back to my own room. It would be embarrassing for me in the morning if..." Her voice trailed off abruptly.

Rafe grinned knowingly and ran his fingers through her hair. "You mean if everyone in the house finds out you surrendered after only one night back under my roof? Yeah, I can see where that would be a little embarrassing for you."

She poked him in the ribs and scowled. "I did not surrender."

Her eyes searched his face. She looked as if she was about to say something and changed her mind. "Good night, Rafe."

He didn't like it but he didn't want to argue with her. Not now that things were finally all right again. "You always were a little shy about this kind of thing, weren't you?"

"I prefer to think of it as circumspect."

"Downright prudish if you ask me. You know what? You're just an old-fashioned girl at heart. But I guess I can put up with your modesty until we make things official." He dragged her head down for another slow, deep kiss and then he forced himself to his feet. He stretched broadly, flexing his muscles for the sheer physical pleasure of it. He hadn't felt this good in a long, long time. A year, to be exact.

"You don't have to walk me back to my room. It's just across the patio. Won't take me ten seconds to get there." Margaret was already reaching for her swimsuit and a towel. He watched her fasten the bra of the suit and wrap the towel around her waist.

"Hey, you're not the only old-fashioned one around here. I'm a little old-fashioned myself. I always walk my dates home, if I can't persuade them to stay until morning." He spoke lightly but when she gave him a strange, searching glance, he frowned. "Something wrong?"

She shook her head quickly, her still damp hair clinging beguilingly to her throat. "No. I was just remembering something someone had said to me a couple of days ago at a book signing session. Something about cowboys being old-fashioned when it came to things like women."

"Yeah, well, that's what I am when you come right down to it, Maggie, love. A cowboy."

"But you're a very modern sort of cowboy," she said, as if trying to convince herself of something. "You run a large corporation and you routinely make multimillion-dollar deals."

"I can also work cattle and break a horse."

"You can order good wine when the occasion calls for it."

"Yeah, but I don't drink it unless somebody's holding a gun to my head."

"You know the best hotels to stay in when you travel."

"I can also build a fire and skin a rabbit."

"Rafe, I'm trying to make a point here."

"So? What's the fact that I can move in two different worlds got to do with anything? Once a cowboy, always a cowboy. Take a look at your father. He was born and raised on a ranch. He may have gotten an engineering degree but that doesn't change what he is deep down inside. That's one of the reasons he and I get along. We understand each other."

"Oh, what's the use. You may be right. I have to tell you the truth, Rafe. I never wanted to get involved with a cowboy, modern or otherwise."

"Too bad, Maggie, love, because you are involved with one. For your own sake, don't go trying to convince yourself you've gotten hooked up with one of those new, sensitive, right-thinking males you read about in ladies' magazines."

Margaret wrinkled her nose. "What would you know about the new, sensitive, right-thinking man? You don't read women's magazines."

"I heard all about 'em from Julie once when she was trying to convince me to approve of some damned psychologist she was dating."

"Rafe, did you ruin that relationship for her?"

"I didn't have to. The guy ruined it for himself. She found out he was seeing someone else on the side and when she confronted him he told her he needed a relationship in which he could be free to explore his full potential as a human being."

Margaret eyed him curiously. "What happened?"

"What do you think happened? Julie's a Cassidy, too. Cassidys don't believe in open relationships. She gave him a swift kick in his new, sensitive, right-thinking rear."

"Good for her," Margaret said automatically and then frowned darkly. "Still, you shouldn't judge the new, sensitive, right-thinking man by one bad apple, Rafe."

"I'm not going to judge the new, sensitive, right-thinking man at all. I'm going to ignore him and so are you." He bent his head and brushed her lips with his own.

Her mouth was still full and soft from the aftereffects of their recent lovemaking. The scent of her hung in the room and would be clinging to his sheets. Rafe felt himself getting hard all over again just thinking about what was going to happen to him when he climbed back into those sheets.

"Rafe?"

"You're sure you want to go?"

"Yes."

"As I said, I can wait. I'm one hell of a patient man, Maggie, love." He pulled on his trunks, took her hand and led her out into the starlit patio.

MARGARET ROSE VERY EARLY THE NEXT MORNING after a restless night's sleep. Her thoughts, confused and chaotic, had tumbled about in her head after Rafe had left her to return to his own room. She could not regret their lovemaking or the resumption of their precarious relationship, but she knew there was trouble on the horizon.

There were too many unresolved issues, too many things from the past that had not changed. Rafe was still Rafe. And that meant there would be problems.

Still, this morning she could allow herself to think more positively about the possibilities of an affair with the man she loved. She would never find anyone else like him, Margaret knew.

She chose a pair of designer jeans that were cut to show off her small waist and emphasize the flare of her hips. She added a rakish red shirt and sandals and went out into the patio to savor the short cool hours of early morning in the desert. Soon the temperature would start climbing rapidly.

"Good morning, Margaret. Come and join me in a cup of coffee."

Margaret glanced in surprise at Bev Cassidy who was sitting alone under the umbrella. A stout-looking woman in her fifties had just finished putting a silver pot of coffee and a tray of fresh breakfast pastries and fruit down on the table. The woman smiled at Margaret and nodded a greeting. Margaret smiled back.

"Margaret, this is Ellen. Ellen comes in during the days to take care of the house for Rafe."

"Ellen."

"Nice to meet you, Miss Lark. Hope you enjoy your stay. By the way, I love your books."

"Thank you very much."

"Sit down," Bev urged as the housekeeper disappeared.

"You're up bright and early, Bev." Margaret summoned up a smile and walked over to take a seat opposite her hostess. She had known when she had boarded the plane that there would be no way to avoid Rafe's mother. She braced herself for this first one-on-one confrontation.

"I love the early hours in the desert." Bev poured a cup of coffee and handed it to Margaret. "Did you sleep well, dear?"

Margaret took refuge in a social white lie. "Very well, thank you."

Bev smiled gently. "I'm sorry you had to learn about your father's engagement the way you did. Rafe was very insistent on keeping the full truth from you until…" She let the words slide away into nothingness.

"Until he was ready to close his trap?" Margaret nodded as she sipped her coffee. "That's Rafe, all right. Sneaky." She reached for a slice of melon.

Bev let out a small sigh. "He cares very deeply about you, Margaret. I hadn't fully realized just how much until you left him last year."

"I would like to clear up a major misconception around here, Bev. I didn't leave Rafe. He told me to get out of his life."

"And you went."

"Yes."

Bev slowly shook her head. "I won't deny that at the time I thought it was for the best."

"I can imagine your feelings on the matter. I know exactly how you felt about me as a wife for your son." Margaret smiled to cancel any bitterness that might have tinged the words. "If it makes you feel any better, I've come to agree with you."

Bev's eyes widened with sudden shock. "What are you saying?"

"That you were right when you told me I would make a lousy wife for Rafe."

"I only said that because I was afraid you would try to change him—make him into something he was not. Margaret, please believe me when I tell you that I never had anything at all against you personally. The truth is, I like you very much. I admire you." Bev smiled. "I've even started reading your books. I'm enjoying *Ruthless* enormously."

Margaret grinned. "As any author will tell you, flattery will get you anywhere. We're suckers for people who say they like our books."

"Good. Then perhaps you'll forgive me for some of the things I said to you last year?"

"We both know they were true, Bev. I would probably make Rafe very unhappy, frustrated and eventually blazingly angry if I were to marry him."

"I used to think so but I'm not so sure about that anymore, Margaret."

"I am. For starters, I would insist on our relationship getting equal billing with his business interests. Truth be known, I'd go farther than that. If the chips were down, I'd insist that our marriage come first. I would make every effort to force him to live a more balanced life. I would make him work regular hours and take vacations. And I would not play the role of the self-sacrificing executive's wife who always puts her husband's career first."

Bev sighed. "I sensed that when I met you. I think I reacted so strongly to you because I had played exactly that role for Rafe's father. I was certain Rafe needed a wife who would do the same."

"I think you're right. He does need a wife like that. But I couldn't live that life, Bev. It would turn me bitter and unhappy within a very short period of time. I want a husband who loves me more than he loves his corporation. I want a man who puts me first. I want to be the most important thing in his life. And we both know that for Rafe, business is the most important thing in the world. For him, a wife will be only a convenience."

"Margaret, listen to me. Last year I believed that every bit as much as you did. But now I no longer think that's true. Rafe has changed during the past year. Your walking out on him did that."

"I did not walk out on him."

"All right, all right, I didn't mean to put it that way." Bev held up one hand in a placating fashion. "Losing you did change him, though. I wouldn't have believed it possible if I hadn't seen it with my own eyes. Until you were gone, he was as driven to succeed as his father had been—more so because the stakes were higher after John died."

Margaret frowned. "Rafe was trying to show that he could be as successful as his father?"

"No, he was trying to rescue us from the financial disaster in which John left us." Bev's mouth tightened. "My husband was a good man in many respects, but his business was everything to him. He ate, slept and breathed

Cassidy and Company. But shortly before he was killed in a plane accident, he suffered some enormous financial losses. You'll have to ask Rafe for the details. It had to do with some risky investments that went bad."

"Was Rafe involved?"

Bev shook her head. "No. Rafe had gone off on his own. He was too much like John in many ways and he knew it. He realized from the time he was in high school that he could never work for his father. They would have been constantly at each other's throats. They were both stubborn, both smart and both insisted on being in charge. An impossible working situation."

"Did your husband accept that?"

"To his credit, John did understand. He wished Rafe well when Rafe started his own business. But John always assumed that when he retired, Rafe would take over Cassidy and Company and then John was killed."

Margaret watched Bev toy with her coffee cup. "Rafe did come back to take over Cassidy and Company, then, didn't he? Just as your husband would have wanted."

"Oh, yes. Rafe took the reins. And that's when we discovered that John had been on the brink of bankruptcy. Rafe worked night and day to save the business and he did save it. Against all odds. You can be certain the financial community had already written off Cassidy and Company. We survived and the company is flourishing now, but the experience did something to Rafe."

"What do you mean?"

Bev poured more coffee. "Watching Rafe work to salvage Cassidy and Company was like watching steel being forged in fire. He went into the whole thing as a strong man or he wouldn't have survived. But he came out of it much harder, more ruthless and a lot stronger than he'd been before his experience. Too hard, too ruthless and too strong in some ways. His sister Julie calls him a gunslinger because he's made a habit of taking on all challengers."

Margaret had never met Julie. There had been no opportunity. But it sounded as if the woman had her brother pegged. She looked down into the depths of her coffee. "He didn't like losing to Moorcroft's firm last year."

"No, he did not." Bev smiled briefly. "And you can be certain that one of these days he'll find a way to even the score."

Margaret felt a frisson of uneasiness go down her spine. She thought about her conversation with Jack Moorcroft shortly before leaving Seattle. "I'm glad I'm out of it."

"What Rafe does about Moorcroft is neither here nor there. It's your relationship with my son that concerns me. Rafe put a lot of his life on hold while he worked to save Cassidy and Company. One of the things he avoided was marriage. Now he's nearly forty years old and time is running out. I think he realizes that. I want him to be happy, Margaret. I have come to realize during the past year that you are probably the one woman who can make him happy."

Margaret stared at her helplessly. "But that's just it, Bev. I can't make him happy. Not as his wife, at any rate. I simply can't be the kind of wife he wants or needs. So I'm going to take your advice."

Bev looked at her with worried eyes. "What advice?"

"I'm going to try having an affair with him."

"You mean you're not going to marry him?" Bev looked stunned.

Before Margaret could respond, her father's voice bellowed over the patio. "What the hell do you mean, you're not marrying him? Cassidy swore he was offering marriage. That's the only reason I agreed to get involved in this tomfool plan to get you down here. What the blazes does he think he's trying to pull around here?"

"Dad, hang on a minute." Margaret turned in her chair to see her father bearing down on her. "Let me explain."

"What's to explain? I'll have Cassidy's hide, by God. I'll take a horsewhip to that boy if he thinks he can lead my little girl down the garden path."

"Sit down, Dad."

Bev tried a pacifying smile. "Yes, Connor. Do sit down and let your daughter explain. You didn't hear the whole story."

"I don't need to hear anything more than the fact that Cassidy isn't proposing. That's enough for me." Connor glowered at both women, but accepted the cup Bev pushed toward him. "Don't you worry, Maggie. I'll set him straight fast enough. He'll do the right thing by you if I have to tie him up and use a branding iron on him."

Rafe came out of his bedroom at that moment, striding across the patio with his usual unconscious arrogance. Margaret watched him, memories of the night flaring again in her mind. He looked so lithe, sensual and supremely confident in a pair of jeans and a shirt that was unbuttoned at the throat. His dark hair was still damp from a shower and his eyes told her he, too, was remembering what had happened out here between them last night. When he saw he had her full attention, a slight smile edged his mouth and his left eye narrowed in a small, sexy wink.

"Morning, everyone," he said as he came to a halt beside the table. He bent his head to kiss Margaret full on the mouth and then he reached for the coffeepot. He seemed unaware of the fact that his mother was looking uneasy and that Connor was glowering at him. "Beautiful day, isn't it? When we're finished here, Maggie, love, I'll take you out to the barns and show you some of the most spectacular horseflesh you've seen in your entire life."

"Hold on there, Cassidy." Connor's bushy brows formed a solid line above his narrowed eyes. "You aren't going anywhere with my girl until we sort out a few details."

Rafe lounged back in his chair, cup in hand. "What's with you this morning, Connor? Got a problem?"

"You're the one with the problem. A big one."

"Yeah? What would that be?"

"You told me you intended to marry my Maggie. That's the only reason I overlooked the way you treated her last year and agreed to help you get her down here."

Rafe shrugged, munching on a breakfast pastry. "So?"

"So she just said you two weren't gettin' married after all."

Rafe stopped munching. His eyes slammed into Margaret's. A great deal of the indulgent good humor he had been exhibiting a minute ago had vanished from the depths of his gaze.

"The hell she did," Rafe said, his eyes still locked with Margaret's.

"Heard her myself, Cassidy, and I want some answers. Now." Connor's fist struck the table to emphasize his demand.

"You're not the only one." Rafe was still staring grimly at Margaret.

Margaret groaned and traded glances with a sympathetic-looking Bev. "You shouldn't have eavesdropped, Dad. You got it all wrong."

"I did?" Connor stared at her in confusion. "But I heard you tell Bev you and Cassidy weren't going to get married. You said something about settling for a damned affair."

"Is that right?" Rafe asked darkly. "Is that what you said, Maggie?"

Margaret got to her feet, aware of the other three watching her with unrelenting intensity. She felt cornered. "I said that I would not make a good wife for Rafe. That does not mean, however, that he and I can't enjoy an affair. I've decided to pick up where we left off last year."

"We were engaged last year," Rafe reminded her coldly.

"No, Rafe. You might have felt you were engaged because you had asked me to marry you several times, but the truth is I was still considering your proposal when everything blew up in my face. I had doubts about the wisdom of marrying you then and after having had a full year to think about it, I have even more doubts about it now. Therefore, I'm only willing to go as far as having an affair with you. Take it or leave it."

"The hell I will."

"Rafe, your mother was right. I'll make you a much better mistress than I would a wife." Without waiting for a response, Margaret turned and started toward the sanctuary of her bedroom.

She never made it. Rafe came silently up out of his chair and swooped across the patio in a few long strides. He caught her up in his arms and tossed her over his shoulder before she knew quite what had happened.

Rafe didn't pause. He didn't say a word. He simply carried her through one of the open glass doors, across the living room and out into the hot sunshine.

Chapter Five

"WHAT DO YOU THINK YOU'RE DOING, Rafe? This is inexcusable behavior, absolutely inexcusable. I will not tolerate it."

"It's cowboy behavior and I'm just a cowboy at heart, remember?" He strode swiftly toward one of the long, low white barns.

"You're an arrogant, high-handed bastard at heart, that's what you are." Margaret was suddenly acutely aware of an audience. Tom and another man in work clothes and boots glanced toward Rafe and grinned broadly. "Rafe, people are watching. For heaven's sake, put me down."

"I don't take orders from a mistress."

"Damn it, Rafe."

"Now, I might listen to an engaged lady or a wife, maybe, but not a mistress. No, ma'am."

"*Put me down.*"

"In a minute. I want to find us some privacy first."

"Privacy. Rafe, you're creating an embarrassing public spectacle. And you have the nerve to wonder why I never came crawling back to you on my hands and knees this past year begging you to forgive me. This sort of behavior is exactly why I considered I'd had a very lucky escape."

"Let's not bring up past history. We're supposed to be making a fresh start, remember? If I can let bygones be bygones, so can you."

"You are unbelievably arrogant."

"Yeah, but even better, I usually get what I want."

He carried her into the soft shadows of a long barn. Hanging upside-down as she was, Margaret had an excellent view of a straw-littered floor. The earthy scents of horses and hay wafted up around her. A row of equine heads with pricked ears appeared above the open stall doors.

Margaret gasped as Rafe swung her off his shoulder and onto her feet. As she regained her balance she glared at her tormentor and fumbled to readjust the clip that held her hair at her nape.

"Honestly, Rafe, that was an absolutely outrageous thing to do. I'd demand an apology but I know I won't get one. I doubt if you've ever apologized in your entire life."

"Maggie, love, we'd better have a long talk. There appears to be a slight misunderstanding here."

"Stop calling me Maggie. I've told you a hundred times I don't like it. That's another thing. You never really listen to me, do you? You think everything has to be done your way and the rest of us should just learn to like it that way, no matter what. Your mother tried to tell me this morning that you'd changed during the past year but I knew better and I was right, wasn't I? You just proved it. You're still a thickheaded, domineering, bossy, overbearing cowboy who rides roughshod over everyone else."

"*That's enough.*" Rafe stood with his booted feet braced, his hands on his hips, his eyes narrowed dangerously.

"Good Lord, you are a real cowboy, aren't you?" Her voice was scathing. "You look right at home here in this barn with that...that *stuff* on your boots."

He glanced down automatically and saw the stuff to which she referred with such disdain. There was a small pile of it near his left boot. Prudently he moved the elaborately tooled black leather boot with its red and yellow star design a few inches to the right.

"Goes with the territory," Rafe said. He looked up again. "And you can quit playing the sophisticated city girl who's never seen the inside of a barn. I know the truth about you, lady. Connor and I have had a few long talks."

"Is that right?" she sniffed.

"Damned right. I know for a fact you were born on your dad's ranch in California and you were raised on it until you were thirteen. You didn't start picking up your fancy airs until Connor sold the place and your family went to live in San Francisco."

"I prefer to forget my rustic background," she retorted. "And for your information, my standards have changed since I was thirteen. For all intents and purposes, I'm very much a city girl now and I expect a certain level of appropriate behavior from the male of the species."

"You'll take the behavior you get. Furthermore, I think I've had all the squawking I want to hear from you, *city girl.* You're not the only one who expects a certain level of appropriate social behavior. You're acting like a sharp-tongued, temperamental prima donna who thinks she can play games with me."

"That's not true."

"Yeah? Then what was all that nonsense by the pool a few minutes ago? What do you think you're doing telling our folks you don't intend to marry me?"

"It's the truth. I don't intend to marry you. I've never said I would marry you. Marrying you would be an extremely dumb thing for me to do."

The glittering outrage in his eyes was unnerving. Rafe took a single step closer. Margaret took a prudent step backward. A horse in a nearby stall wickered inquiringly.

"I didn't bring you down here to set you up as a mistress and you know it," Rafe said between his teeth.

"Don't use that word."

"What word? Mistress? That's what you're suggesting we call you, isn't it?"

"No, it's not." Margaret scowled angrily. "That's your mother's word. I explained to you last night, people like her and my father come from another generation."

"You also said that deep down you didn't think we were all that different from them," Rafe shot back. "What the hell did you think you were doing last night if you weren't agreeing to come back to me?"

She lifted her chin. "Last night I decided that we might try resuming our affair."

"That's real generous of you. The only problem is that we don't happen to have an affair to resume."

She glared at him in open challenge. "Is that right? What do you call us sleeping together for nearly two months last year?"

"Anticipating our wedding vows."

Margaret stared at him, open-mouthed. She did not know whether to laugh or cry. Rafe looked perfectly serious, totally self-righteous. "You're joking. That's what you called our affair? How quaint. But there never was a wedding, so what does that make the whole business? Besides a big mistake, I mean?"

"There's damn well going to be a wedding."

"Why?" she asked bluntly.

"Because you and I belong together, that's why. And you know it, Maggie. Or have you forgotten last night already?"

"No, I haven't forgotten it, but just because we're good together in bed does not mean we should get married. Rafe, listen to me. I've tried to explain to everyone that I would make you a lousy wife. Why won't anyone pay any attention to what I'm saying?"

"Because you're talking garbage, that's why."

Margaret sighed heavily. "This is impossible. We're getting nowhere. Talk about a communication problem. I'd better leave—the sooner the better."

Rafe reached out and caught her arm as she would have turned away. A fierce determination blazed in his eyes and his voice had a raw edge to it. "You can't leave. Not now. I spent six months in hell trying to pretend you didn't exist and another six months figuring out ways to get you back. I'm not going to let you go this time."

"You can't stop me, Rafe. Oh, I know I let you coerce me into coming down here. But we both know you can't make me stay against my will. And the truth is, there's nothing I can do here, anyway. I've seen for myself that my father is happy with your mother. I would hurt him by trying to interfere. And if he wants to sell Lark Engineering to you, that's his business. It's clear you're not trying to cheat him out of the firm."

"I didn't bring you down here so that you could protect your father. We both know he can take care of himself. I got you down here so that we could start over again, Maggie, and you know it. Furthermore, if you're honest with yourself for once, you'll admit that's why you used that ticket so damn fast once I'd given you a good enough excuse."

He was right and that jolted her. She had known all along that her father could take care of himself, even against the likes of Rafe Cassidy. Everyone involved had politely let her pretend that she had rushed down here to rescue Connor but everyone knew the truth.

"This is extremely humiliating," Margaret said.

"If it makes you feel any better, take it from me you don't know what I was going through yesterday morning at the airport waiting to see if you were on that flight. I was afraid to even call your apartment in Seattle in case you answered the phone. How's that for proof that you have an equal ability to make me feel like an idiot?"

The intensity of his words shook her. She bit her lip and then reached out hesitantly to touch his hand. When he glanced down she withdrew her fingers immediately. "Rafe, it won't work. We might have managed a long-distance affair. For a while. But we'll never manage a marriage. Your mother was right all along."

"Stop saying that, damn it. She was wrong and she admits it. Why do you keep quoting something she said a year ago as if it were carved in stone?"

"Because she was right a year ago. You're a driven man when it comes to business or anything else you decide you want. This morning she told me more about why you're driven but that doesn't change anything. It just helps explain why you are the way you are."

Rafe swore in disgust. "She gave you some tripe about me being somewhat, uh, aggressive in business because I had to work so hard to rescue Cassidy and Company, didn't she? Julie says that's her current theory on my behavior."

"Well, yes. And you're not *somewhat* aggressive, Rafe, you're a real predator. What's more, you get downright hostile when someone steals your prey the way you think I helped Moorcroft do last year."

"Look, maybe I'd better make one thing clear here. My mother likes to think I'm the way I am—I mean, was—because of what happened after Dad was killed. But the truth is, I was like that long before I took over Cassidy and Company. Dad knew it. Hell, I was born that way, according to my father. Same as he was."

Margaret nodded sadly. "You didn't change so that you could salvage the company, you managed to salvage the company because you were already strong enough and aggressive enough to do it."

"But things are different now. I've changed. I keep telling you that. Give me a chance, Maggie."

"Last night I thought I could."

"You call having an affair with me giving me a chance?" he demanded incredulously.

She nodded. "It was a way to try again. A way that left us both free to change our minds without breaking any promises. It would have given us time to observe each other and reassess the situation."

"Hell." He ran his hand through his hair in a gesture of pure frustration. "I don't need any more time, Maggie. I've been reassessing this damned situation for months."

"Well, I do need time."

"This isn't just a question of my work habits, is it?" he asked shrewdly. "The truth is you aren't going to forgive me for what happened between us last year, are you?"

"You've never asked me to forgive you, Rafe." She smiled bleakly. "You're much too proud for that, aren't you? Oh, you very generously forgave me, but you don't think you need to be forgiven. It's all black and white to you. You were right and I was clearly in the wrong."

"You made a mistake. Conflicting sets of loyalties, as I said. You were under a lot of pressure at the time and you got confused."

"So confused I'd do it again if I had to. I didn't like being used, Rafe."

His jaw tightened. "I did not use you."

"That's not the way I saw it. You knew I was working for Jack Moorcroft when you started dating me, didn't you?"

"Yeah, but damn it…"

"I, on the other hand, did not have the advantage of knowing you were a business rival of his. I didn't even realize you two knew each other, let alone were fierce competitors. You kept that information from me, Rafe."

"Only because I knew you'd have a problem dating me in the beginning if you knew the whole truth. I didn't want to lose you by telling you Moorcroft and I were after the same prize. You'd have felt guilty going out with me. And if you'll recall, I never tried to pump you for inside information."

"You let me talk about my job," she accused. "You let me tell you about the projects I was working on. You showed so much interest in me. I was so terribly flattered by that interest. It makes me sick to think how flattered I was."

"What was I supposed to do? Tell you not to talk about your work?"

"Yes. That's exactly what you should have told me."

"Be reasonable, Maggie. If I had tried to explain just why you shouldn't talk to me about your job, you'd have very quickly figured out who I was. I couldn't let that happen."

"Because you needed the inside information in order to beat Moorcroft to Spencer."

"That's a lot of horse manure," he told her roughly. "I didn't tell you to shut up about your work because I'd have lost you if I had. If it makes you feel any better, you can rest assured I had all the information I needed to beat Moorcroft to the punch from other sources. Nothing you told me made any difference in my plans."

"Oh, Rafe."

"You want the flat honest truth? Moorcroft's the one who got the advantage out of our relationship. You ran to him that morning and warned him I was after Spencer. Thanks to you, he was able to move his timetable ahead fast enough to knock me out of the running. I was the one who lost out because I was sleeping with a woman who felt her first loyalty belonged to another man."

Margaret looked up at him appealingly, longing to believe him and knowing she should not. "Rafe, is that the full truth? Really? You didn't use any of the information I accidently gave you?"

His mouth twisted ruefully. "It's the truth, all right. If you'd known everything in the beginning, you'd have assumed I'd started dating you because of your connection to Moorcroft and you'd have backed right off. Don't try to deny it. I know you. That's exactly how your brain would have worked—exactly how it did work when you finally discovered who I was."

Margaret felt cornered again. He was right. She would have been instantly suspicious of his motives if she'd known who he was back at the beginning. "And you really didn't need inside information from me?"

"I already had most of it. Nothing you told me was particularly crucial one way or the other. In fact, if you'll stop and think about it, you'll recall that you didn't talk all that much about your job. You mostly talked about the career in writing that you were working on. I heard all your big plans to work two more years in the business world and then quit to write full-time."

"I wish I could believe that." She clasped her hands in front of her, remembering her terrible feeling of guilt at the time. "I felt like such a fool. I felt so used. I went over and over every conversation we'd had, trying to recall exactly what I'd told you. I knew I had to go straight to Moorcroft, of course. He had trusted me. I had to make up for what I'd done to him."

"You didn't do one blasted thing to him," Rafe roared. "I was the one you screwed."

She frowned in annoyance. "You don't have to be quite so crude about it."

He spread his hands in a disgusted movement and made an obvious grab for his self-control. "Forget it. I'm sorry I mentioned my side of the story. I know you aren't particularly interested in it. You're only concerned with your side."

Tears welled in Margaret's eyes. She blinked them back as she sank down onto a bale of hay and tried to think. "It was such an awful mess at the time," she whispered. "And when I tried to do the right thing by warning Moorcroft about you, you turned on me like a…a lion or something. All teeth and claws. The things you said to me… You ripped me to shreds, Rafe. I wasn't certain for a while if I was ever going to recover."

"You weren't the only one who felt ripped up." Rafe sat down beside her, elbows resting on his knees, his big hands loosely clasped. He stared straight ahead at a pretty little gray mare who was watching the proceedings with grave curiosity. "I wasn't sure I was going to make it, either." He paused for a moment. "My mother says it was probably the best thing that ever happened to me."

"She said *what?*"

"She said I needed a jolt like that to make me pay attention to something else in life besides business." His smile was ironic. "Believe me, after what happened last year, you had my full attention. I couldn't stop thinking about you no matter how hard I tried. I've put more energy into getting you back than I've ever put into a merger or a buy-out."

Margaret thought she really would cry now. "Rafe, I don't know what to say."

He turned his head, his eyes glittering with intensity. "Say you'll give me a chance, a real chance. Let's start over, Maggie. For good this time. Give me the next two weeks and be honest about it. Don't spend the time looking for excuses and a way out."

The love for him that she had been forced to acknowledge to herself last night made Margaret light-headed. She looked into his tawny eyes and felt herself falling back into the whirlpool in which she had nearly drowned last year. "You are a very dangerous man for me, Rafe. I can't go through what I went through last time. I can't."

He caught her chin on the edge of his hand. "You're not the only one who wouldn't survive it a second time. So there won't be a second time."

She searched his eyes. "How can you be so certain?"

"Two reasons. The first is that we learned something from that fiasco. We've both changed. We aren't quite the same people we were last year."

"And the second reason?"

He smiled faintly. "You aren't working for Moorcroft or anyone else, so the pressures you had on you last time don't exist."

"But if they did exist?"

Rafe's smile hardened briefly. "This time around your commitments are clearer, aren't they? This time around you'd know your first loyalty belongs to me."

"What about *your* loyalty?" she challenged softly, knowing she was sliding deeper into the whirlpool. In another moment she would be caught and trapped.

Rafe cradled her face between two rough palms. "You are the most important person in my life, Maggie, love. My first loyalty is to you."

"Business has absolutely nothing to do with this?"

"Hell, no."

"If there were to be a conflict between our relationship and your business interests, would our relationship win?"

"Hands down."

Her fingers tightened around his wrists. Everything in her wanted to believe him. Margaret knew her future was at stake. If she had any sense she would get out while she still could.

"Rafe…"

"Say it, Maggie. Say you'll stay here and give me a real chance."

She closed her eyes and took a deep breath. "All right."

He groaned and pulled her close against him, his arms locking around her. His mouth moved against her sleekly knotted hair. "You won't regret it, Maggie. This time it will work. You'll see. I'll make it work. I've missed you so much, sweetheart. Last night…"

"What about last night?" she asked softly.

"Last night was like taking the first glass of cool water after walking out of the desert. Except that you're never cool in bed. You're hotter than the sun in August. Lord, Maggie, last night was good."

She hugged him, her head resting on his chest. "Yes."

"Maggie?"

"Um?"

"You said a few minutes ago that I'd never asked for forgiveness because I was too arrogant to think I needed it. But I'm asking for it now. I'm sorry I was so rough with you last year."

She took a breath. It was probably as much of an apology as she was likely to get. "All right, Rafe. And I'm sorry I assumed you'd been using me to beat Moorcroft. I should have known better."

"Hush, love. It's all right." His hands stroked her back soothingly. "We'll make this a fresh start. No more talk about the past."

"Agreed."

For a long while they sat on the bale of hay, saying nothing. If anyone came or went in the barn, Margaret didn't notice. She was conscious only of the feel of Rafe's hands moving gently on her. With a deep sigh of newly found peace, she gave herself up to the luxury of once more being able to nestle in Rafe's strong arms. *A fresh start.*

For the first time in a year something that had felt twisted and broken deep inside her relaxed and became whole again.

"Boss?" Tom's shout from the far end of the barn had a trace of embarrassed hesitation in it. "Hatcher's here. Says he needs to talk to you."

Rafe slowly released Margaret. "Tell him I'll be there in a minute."

"Right."

Rafe looked down at Margaret, his expression rueful. "Sorry about this. Hatcher's timing isn't always the best. Want to come say hello to him?"

"Okay. But he probably doesn't want to say hello to me."

"Maggie, love, you're getting paranoid. You thought my mother wouldn't want to see you again, either, but she could hardly wait for you to get down here, right? Don't worry about Hatcher's opinion. He works for me and he does what I say."

Shaking her head, Margaret let Rafe tug her to her feet. He draped an arm possessively around her shoulders and guided her out of the barn. She blinked as she stepped out into the hot sunlight. There was an unfamiliar car in the drive.

Doug Hatcher was already standing in the doorway of Rafe's home, a briefcase in one hand. Rafe's chief executive assistant looked very much as Margaret remembered him from the occasions he had accompanied his fast-moving boss to Seattle.

Hatcher was in his early thirties, a thin, sharp-faced man with pale eyes. He was dressed in a light-colored business suit, his tie knotted crisply in defiance of the heat. He did not seem surprised to see Margaret coming out of the barn with his boss.

"Good morning, Miss Lark." Hatcher inclined his head politely. "Nice to see you again."

"Thank you, Doug." She knew he was lying through his teeth. The poor man was no doubt struggling mightily to maintain a polite facade. There was little chance he was actually glad to see her. Hatcher was fiercely loyal to Rafe and he probably blamed her for the collapse of the Spencer deal last year. She was not at all certain his opinion of her would have changed just because Rafe ordered him to change it.

Then, again, when Rafe gave orders, people tended to obey.

"What's up, Hatcher?" Rafe asked easily. "I'm on vacation, remember?"

"Yes, sir." Hatcher indicated the briefcase. "I just need to update you on a couple of things. You said you wanted to keep close track of the Ellington deal. There have been a couple of recent developments I felt you should know about. I also have some figures to show you."

Rafe released Maggie abruptly. His good mood seemed to have suddenly evaporated. She recognized the signs instantly. She could almost feel him shifting gears into what she always thought of as his "business alert" mode. He was fully capable of remaining in it for hours, even days, on end. When he was caught up in it nothing else mattered to him. He brooked no distractions, not even from the woman he was currently bedding.

"Right," Rafe said. "Let's go inside and take care of it. Maggie, why don't you take a swim or something?"

Her first reaction was a rush of anger. Same old Rafe. As soon as business reared its ugly head, he was like a hunter who had caught the scent of prey. He was already dismissing her while he took care of more important things.

Then she looked at his face and saw the tension in him. He knew what she was thinking. The fact that her incipient disapproval had gotten through to him was something, she told herself. Last year he wouldn't have even noticed.

"I don't really feel like a swim, Rafe."

"Honey, this won't take long, I swear it. I guarantee I've developed some new ways of working lately but I can't just let go of everything, you know that. I'm still responsible for my family, the ranch and a heck of a lot of jobs at Cassidy and Company. Be reasonable."

She relaxed slightly as she saw the expression in his eyes. "I know, Rafe. It's all right. I understand. I think I will have that swim, after all." Of course he couldn't let go of everything. She didn't expect him to abandon his business altogether. She just wanted him to learn to put things in perspective. He was trying, she realized. And that was the first step.

Rafe nodded once, looking vastly relieved. "Thanks. Let's go, Hatcher. I want to get this over with as fast as possible. I've got other things to do today. More interesting things."

"Yes, sir."

Margaret preceded both men into the house and was turning to go down the hall to her bedroom when Bev Cassidy came through the patio doors. Connor Lark was right behind her. They both looked anxiously first at Margaret and then at Rafe.

"You two get this marriage business settled?" Connor demanded aggressively. "Bev and I aren't takin' off for Sedona day after tomorrow the way we planned if you two haven't worked this out."

"Don't worry, Connor. Everything's under control," Rafe said mildly.

"You sure?"

"I'm sure," Rafe said.

"About time."

"Yeah. You can say that again." Rafe started toward the study he used as an office. "I need to spend a few minutes with Hatcher. Maggie's going swimming, aren't you, Maggie?"

"Looks like it," said Maggie.

Bev brightened. "I've got another idea, if you're interested, Margaret?"

"What's that?" Margaret smiled.

"How would you like to go shopping? I thought you might want to buy something to wear to the engagement party tomorrow evening."

Margaret reeled. Her eyes widened in shock as she whirled to glare at Rafe. "*Engagement party.* Now, just hold on one minute, here, I've never said anything about getting officially engaged. Don't you dare try to rush me like this, Rafe. Do you hear me? I won't stand for it."

Hatcher, Conner and Bev looked at each other in obvious embarrassment. But there was a suspiciously humorous glint in Rafe's eyes when he said very gently, "Mom is talking about the engagement party she and Connor are giving tomorrow night to celebrate their engagement. Not ours."

"I'm so sorry, dear," Bev said quickly. "In all the excitement of your arrival yesterday, I forgot to mention it. We're having a few friends over to celebrate tomorrow evening. The next day Connor and I are going to take a little trip."

Margaret learned the meaning of wishing the floor would open up and swallow her whole. "Oh," she said, flushing a bright pink. She turned to Bev. "Shopping sounds like a wonderful idea. I haven't a thing to wear."

Chapter Six

MARGARET PAUSED AT THE EDGE OF THE POOL, glanced around quickly at the patio full of well-dressed guests and realized she was alone at last. When she spotted her father disappearing into the house by himself she decided to take advantage of the situation. She put down her empty hors d'oeuvres plate and hurried after him.

"Caught you, Dad." She grinned triumphantly at a startled Connor as he headed toward the kitchen.

"Maggie, my girl." Connor made an effort to look genuinely pleased to see her. "I was wonderin' how you were gettin' along. Enjoyin' yourself, girl? Bev sure knows how to throw a mighty fine party, doesn't she? One of the things I love about her. She knows how to have a good time. Wouldn't think it to look at her, but she's not a bit stuffy or prissy. Great sense of humor."

Margaret folded her arms and regarded her father with a sense of amusement mixed with exasperation. "Bev Cassidy appears to be an all-around wonderful person and I'm delighted the two of you are so happy together, but I didn't corner you in here to listen to a glowing litany of her attributes. You've been avoiding me since I got here, Dad. Admit it."

Connor appeared shocked and horrified at the accusation. "Avoidin' you? Not a chance, girl. How could you think such a thing? You're my own little Maggie, my only child, the fruit of my loins."

"Hold it, Dad."

"It's nothin' less than the truth. Hell's bells, girl, why would I want to avoid you? I'm delighted you got down here for my engagement shindig. A man's one and only child should definitely be present when he takes the great leap into marriage."

"That's arguable, depending on when the leap is made," Margaret said dryly. "But your impending nuptials, exciting as they may be, are not what I wanted to discuss."

"Maggie, girl, you know I'm always available to you. I'm your father. Your own flesh and blood. You can talk to me about anything."

"Terrific. That's just what I'd like to do. I have a little matter I've been wanting to discuss with you ever since I got here."

Connor brightened. "Wonderful. We'll have us a nice father-daugther chat one of these days just as soon as we both have a spare minute."

"I've got a spare minute right now."

"Well, shoot, too bad I don't." Connor's face twisted into a parody of sincere regret. "Promised Bev I'd get on the kitchen staff's tails. We're runnin' out of ice. Maybe sometime in the mornin'?"

"Rafe is going to take me riding in the morning, if you'll recall."

"Hey, that's right. I remember him sayin' somethin' about that earlier today. You haven't been ridin' for quite a while, have you? You used to be darn good at it. Don't worry about bein' out of practice. It's like bicyclin'. Once you get the hang of it, you never forget. Rafe's got some fine horses, doesn't he?"

"I'm sure Rafe's horses are all first class. They're a business investment and Rafe has excellent instincts when it comes to business investments. Dad, stop trying to sidetrack me. I want to talk to you."

Connor exhaled heavily, surrendering to the inevitable. He eyed Margaret warily. "More likely you want to chew me out for my part in Rafe's little plot. You still mad about that? I thought you and Rafe had settled things."

"Rafe and I have an ongoing dialogue about certain matters."

Conner wrinkled his nose. "Is that a fancy way of sayin' everything's settled?"

"It's a way of saying we're both reevaluating the situation and waiting to see how things develop."

"You know, Maggie, girl, for a woman who's made a career out of writin' romance novels, you sure do have an unexcitin' turn of phrase when it comes to describin' your own love life. *Reevaluatin' the situation?*"

Margaret smiled ruefully. "I guess it does sound a little tame. But the truth is, Dad, after last year I'm inclined to be cautious."

Connor nodded, his eyes hardening slightly. "Yeah, I can understand that. Hell, I was inclined toward a few things, myself, after I got wind of what happened."

"Like what?"

"Like murder. Damn near killed Cassidy at our first meetin' a few months back. Raked that boy over the coals somethin' fierce, I can tell you that."

"You did?" Margaret was startled. But, then, no one had seen fit to inform her of that meeting.

"Sure. You hadn't told me all that much about what had happened, remember? You just said it was over and Cassidy had said some nasty things there at the end. But I was mad as hell because I knew how much he'd hurt my girl."

Margaret drummed her fingers thoughtfully on her forearms. "Just what did Rafe say at that first meeting?"

Connor shrugged. "Not much to start. Just let me rant and rave at him and call him every name in the book. Then, when I'd calmed down, he poured me a glass of Scotch and gave me his side of the story."

"And you instantly forgave him? Figured he was the innocent party, after all?"

"Hell, no." Connor glowered at her. "You're still my daughter, Maggie. You know I'd defend you to the last ditch, no matter what."

"Thanks, Dad."

"But," Connor continued deliberately, "I was extremely interested in the other side of the story. I'd taken to Cassidy right off when you introduced us last year. You know that. Figured he was just the man for you. Don't mind sayin' I was real upset with myself to think I'd misjudged the man that badly. I was relieved to find out the situation wasn't exactly what you'd call black and white. There was a lot of gray area and after a couple of Scotches and some rational conversation I could sort of see Cassidy's point of view."

"Rafe can be very persuasive," Margaret murmured.

"And you, Maggie, girl, can be a bit high in the instep when it suits you."

"So it was all my fault, after all? Is that what you decided?"

"No, it wasn't. Don't put words in my mouth, girl. All I'm sayin' is that when I heard Cassidy's side of the tale, I did some thinkin'."

Margaret couldn't help but grin. "You mean you reevaluated the situation?"

Connor chuckled. "Somethin' like that. At any rate, when I realized Cassidy was dead serious about gettin' you back, I figured I might lend him a hand." Connor's smile broadened conspiratorially. "Then he introduced me to Bev and I knew for certain I'd help him out."

"Your father," Rafe announced from the open doorway behind Margaret, "is a man who has his priorities straight. He just wanted you and me to get ours straightened out, too."

Margaret jumped and turned her head to glance over her shoulder. Rafe sauntered into the room, a drink in his hand. He was dressed for the party in a pair of gray, Western-cut trousers, a black shirt and a bolo tie made of white leather. His boots were also made of white leather with an elaborate floral design picked out in silver and black.

"How long have you been standing there?" Margaret asked, thinking that there were times when she felt distinctly underdressed around Rafe.

"Not long." He put his arm around her waist and grinned at Connor. "I wondered when she'd cut you out of the herd and demand a few private explanations, Connor. Need any help?"

"Nope. Maggie and I got it all sorted out, didn't we, girl?"

"If you say so, Dad."

Rafe grinned. "Good. Now that you two have that settled maybe you can give me some advice on what to do about Julie's artist friend. Did you meet him yet?" He shook his head. "I knew when she went to work managing that art supply store she'd be mixing with a bad crowd."

Margaret glared at him. "I met Sean Winters earlier this evening when I was first introduced to your sister. I like him. He seems very nice and he treats Julie like a queen. Where's the problem?"

Rafe gave her a sidelong glance as he took a swallow out of his glass. "Weren't you listening? The problem is that the guy's an artist."

"So?" Margaret arched her brows. "I'm a writer. You got something against people who make their living in the creative fields, Cassidy?"

Rafe winced. "Now, Maggie, love, don't take what I said as a personal comment, okay? I just can't see my sister marrying some guy who makes a living painting pictures."

"Why not?"

"Well, for one thing, it's not exactly a stable profession, is it? No regular salary, no benefits, no pension plan, no telling how long the career will last."

"Same with writing," Margaret assured him cheerfully. "And what's so all-fired safe about other professions? A person is always at risk of getting fired or being laid off or of being forced to resign. Look at my situation last year."

"Let's not get into that," Rafe said tersely.

"Nevertheless, you have to admit no job is really guaranteed for life. How many times have you seen a so-called friendly merger result in a purge of management that cost dozens of jobs?"

"Yeah, but…"

"I wouldn't be surprised if some of the mergers and buyouts you've instigated have resulted in exactly that kind of purge."

"We're not talking about me, here, remember? We're discussing Julie's artist friend. Hell, he's from a whole different world. They've got nothing in common. Julie's got a degree in business administration, although she has yet to do much with it. She's not the artsy-craftsy type. What does she see in Winters?"

"You're just looking for excuses, Rafe. You've got a typical redneck macho male's built-in prejudice against men in the creative arts and you're using the insecurity of the business as a reason to disapprove of Sean as a boyfriend for your sister."

"Damn." Rafe looked appealingly at Connor. "Wish I'd kept my mouth shut."

"Don't look to me for backup on this one." Connor gave his host a wide grin. "I learned my lesson a few years back when Maggie here was dating an artist. I tried to give her the same lecture. Couldn't see my girl getting involved with some weirdo who hung out with the art crowd. You should have seen his stuff, Cassidy. Little bits of aluminum cans stuck all over his canvasses."

That got a quick scowl out of Rafe. He glanced at Maggie. "How long did you date the weirdo?"

"Jon was not a weirdo. He was a very successful multimedia artist who has since gone on to make more from a single painting than I make from a single book. I've got one of his early works hanging in my living room, if you will recall."

Rafe's eyes narrowed. "That thing on your wall that looks like a collection of recycled junk?"

"I'll have you know that if I ever get desperate financially I'll be able to hock that collection of recycled junk for enough money to live on for a couple of years. It was a terrific investment."

"How long did you date him?" Rafe demanded again.

"Jealous?"

"Damn right."

Margaret grinned. "Don't be. Jon was a wonderful man in many respects but it was obvious from the start we weren't meant for each other."

"Yeah? How was it so obvious?"

"He was a night person. I'm a morning person. And never the twain shall meet. At least not for long."

"Glad to hear it."

"The point is, our incompatibility had nothing to do with his profession. And you shouldn't judge your sister's boyfriend on his choice of careers. Besides, Julie's old enough to make her own decisions when it comes to men."

"That's another point. He's too old for her."

"He is not. He's thirty-five. The difference between their ages isn't much more than the difference between our ages, Rafe."

"Okay, okay, let's drop this discussion. We're supposed to be celebrating an engagement here tonight." Rafe looked at Connor with a hint of desperation. "Need some help with the ice?"

"Appreciate it," Connor said.

Rafe gave Margaret a quick, hard kiss. "See you outside in a few minutes, honey."

"Go ahead. Make your escape. But keep in mind what I said about giving Sean Winters a chance." Margaret fixed both men with a meaningful glance before she turned and headed for the door.

"Whew." Rafe exhaled on a sigh of relief as he watched her leave the room. He stared after her departing figure for a moment, enjoying the sight of her neatly rounded derriere moving gently under her elegant cream silk skirt.

"I know what you mean," Connor said. "Women get funny notions sometimes. Maggie tends to be real opinionated."

Rafe took another sip of his Scotch. "Was she really torn up after she stopped seeing the artist?"

Connor laughed and started for the kitchen. "Let me put it this way. One week after she'd stopped dating him she was dating a banker. One week after you and she broke up, she went into hibernation."

Rafe nodded, satisfied. "Yeah, I know. If it makes you feel any better, Connor, my social life followed roughly the same pattern during the past year."

"That's one of the reasons I agreed to help you get her back," Connor said. "Couldn't stand to see the two of you sufferin' like a couple of stranded calves. It was pitiful, just pitiful."

"Thanks, Lark. You're one of nature's noblemen."

OUTSIDE ON THE PATIO MARGARET helped herself to another round of salad while she chatted easily with several of the guests. She was answering a barrage of questions concerning publishing when Rafe's sister materialized with her friend the artist in tow.

Margaret had met Julie and Sean earlier in the evening and had liked them both although she had sensed a certain reserve in Julie. Rafe's sister was a pretty creature with light brown hair, her mother's delicate bone structure and dark, intelligent eyes.

Sean Winters was a tall, thin man who had an easygoing smile and quick, expressive features. He greeted Margaret with a smile.

"How's it going, Margaret? Cassidy find you? He was looking for you a few minutes ago," Sean said.

"He found me. He's inside helping my father with the ice. It's a lovely party, isn't it?"

"Well, hardly the sort of bash we weird, bohemian types usually enjoy. No kinky sex, funny cigarettes or heavy metal music, but I'm adjusting," Sean said.

Margaret laughed but Julie looked stricken.

"Don't say that," Julie whispered tightly.

Sean shrugged. "Honey, it's no secret your brother isn't all that enthusiastic about having an artist in the family."

Julie bit her lip. "Well, he's going to have one in the family, so he better get used to the idea. I won't have him insulting you."

"He didn't insult me. He just doesn't think I'm good enough for you."

"He's tried to play the role of father for me ever since Dad died," Julie explained apologetically. "I know he means well, but the trouble with Rafe is that he doesn't know when to step back and let someone make their own decisions. He's been giving orders around here so long, he assumes that's the way the world works. Rafe Cassidy says jump and everyone asks how high. He's totally astounded when someone doesn't." Julie glanced at Margaret. "The way Margaret didn't last year."

"I don't know what you mean," Margaret said calmly. "I followed orders last year. Rafe said to get out and I went."

Julie sighed. "Yes, but you were supposed to come back."

"So I've been told. On my hands and knees."

"Would that have been so hard?"

"Impossible," Margaret assured her, aware of the sudden tightness in her voice. Her pride was all she'd had left last year. She'd clung to it as if it had been a lifeline.

"My brother was in bad shape for a long time after you left. I've never seen him the way he was this past year and I admit I blamed you for it. I think I hated you myself for a while, even though I'd never met you. I couldn't stand what you'd done to him." Julie's dark eyes were very intent and serious.

Margaret understood the reserve she'd sensed in Rafe's sister. "It's natural that you'd feel protective of your brother."

"It was a battle of wills as far as Rafe was concerned. And he lost. He doesn't like to lose, Margaret."

Margaret blinked. "He lost? How on earth do you figure that?"

"He finally realized that the only way you were going to come back was for him to lower his pride and go and get you. It was probably one of the hardest things he's ever done. Mom says now that it was good for him, but I'm not so sure."

"Lower his pride?" Margaret was flabbergasted by that interpretation of events. "You think that's what Rafe did when he went to Seattle to fetch me down here?"

"Of course."

"Julie, it wasn't anything like that at all. Not that it's anyone else's business, but the truth is, I was virtually blackmailed and kidnapped. I didn't notice Rafe having to surrender one square inch of his pride."

"Then you don't know my brother very well," Julie said. She put her hand on Sean's arm. "But I shouldn't say anything. It's between you and Rafe. Mom may have been right, maybe Rafe did need the jolt you gave him. He's accustomed to having things his way and it's no secret that people cater to him. But that doesn't change the fact that he's human and he can be hurt. And he's got a thing about loyalty."

"I don't think you need to worry about protecting your big brother," Sean murmured. "Something tells me he can take care of himself."

Julie groaned. "You're right. Besides, right now I've got my own problems with him. To tell you the truth, Margaret, I'm inclined to sympathize with you at the moment. Rafe can be extremely bullheaded when it comes to his own opinions. I haven't dared tell him yet just how serious Sean and I are. He thinks we're just dating casually, but the truth is Sean and I are going to get married whether Rafe approves or not."

"Give Rafe a chance to know Sean." Margaret smiled at the artist. "He's really fairly reasonable about most things, once you get his full attention."

"If you say so."

"I'm sure you know as well as I do that folks in the business world have a hard time understanding people in the art world."

"True." Sean's eyes gleamed with amusement. "And the situation isn't improved any by the fact that Cassidy is basically a cowboy who happens to be a genius when it comes to business. Maybe I should invite him to a showing of some of my work. Then he could at least judge me on the basis of my art. If he's going to criticize me, he might as well know what he's talking about."

"But Rafe hates modern art," Julie exclaimed.

"He's fully capable of appreciating it if he puts his mind to it," Margaret said. She remembered the discussion she'd had with Rafe on good wine and good hotels. "He may be a cowboy at heart, but he's very good at moving in different worlds when he feels like it."

Julie eyed her thoughtfully. "You've got a point. My brother likes to play the redneck when it suits him, but I've heard him talk European politics with businessmen from England and West Germany and I've even seen him eat sushi with some Japanese distributors."

Margaret looked up at Sean. "Letting him see your work is not a bad idea at all, Sean. When's the next scheduled exhibition of your work?"

Julie interrupted before Sean could reply. "There's one on Monday evening at the gallery here in town that handles Sean's work. Do you think you could convince Rafe to come?"

"I'll talk to him," Margaret promised.

"Don't get your hopes up, Julie." Sean's voice was gentle. "Even if Margaret gets him there we can't expect him to instantly change his mind about me."

"No," Julie agreed, "but it would at least be a sign that he's willing to give you a chance. Margaret, if you can pull this off, I will definitely owe you one."

Margaret laughed, feeling completely relaxed around Julie for the first time since she had met her. "I'll keep that in mind."

Julie turned to Sean. "Look, the band is starting up again. Let's dance."

"All right. I could use a few more lessons in Western swing. If I'm going to marry a ranch girl, I'd better learn a few of the ropes." Sean put down his glass. He nodded at Margaret. "Thanks," he said as he took Julie's arm.

"No problem. Us non-business types sometimes have to stick together."

"You've got a point."

Margaret watched the handsome couple disappear into the throng of people dancing on the patio. She was idly tapping her foot and wondering where Rafe was when she suddenly became aware of Doug Hatcher standing behind her. She turned to smile brightly at him, thinking that he was about to ask her to dance. But his first remark dispelled that illusion.

"You're settling in very quickly around here, aren't you?" Doug's words were carefully enunciated, as if he was afraid of slurring them.

Margaret felt a frisson of uneasiness. "Hello, Doug. I didn't see you there. Enjoying the party?" She eyed the half-empty glass in his hand and the careful way he was holding himself and wondered if he was a little drunk. She realized she had never before seen him drink anything at all.

"You've definitely moved in on the Cassidy clan." Doug took a long pull on his drink. "You're changing things around here."

"I am?"

"Don't be so modest, Miss Lark." Doug stared at her and nodded, as if at some private understanding. "Yeah. You've changed him all right."

"Are we talking about Rafe?"

"He's different now."

"In what way, Doug?"

"Getting soft."

"*Soft?* Rafe?" She was genuinely startled by that comment.

"It's true." Doug nodded again, frowning. "When I first went to work for him he was like a knife. He'd just cut through everything in his path. But a year ago things changed. Oh, we put together a couple of good deals this past year, but it's not like the old days. I thought it was going to be all right for the first few months but then he decided he wanted you back."

"He talked about me to you?"

Doug shook his head, the gesture slightly exaggerated. "He didn't have to. I know him. I knew what he was thinking about and it wasn't about business. Like I said, he's gone soft, lost his edge. When he does think about business, he only thinks about one thing these days." He turned abruptly, caught himself as he nearly lost his balance and then vanished into the crowd.

Margaret took a deep breath as she dared to hope that the one thing Rafe thought about most these days was her. She didn't expect him to spend the rest of his life focusing entirely on her, she told herself. She fully understood that he had a major corporation to run and a ranch to manage. She had no intention of being unreasonable.

But it was comforting to know that there was growing evidence that she was finally important enough to him to make him alter his normal way of doing business. A year ago she had not been at all certain she held that much significance in his life.

"You look like you're enjoying yourself, Maggie, love." Rafe materialized out of the crowd and took her hand to lead her onto the dance floor. "Can I conclude that the thought of engagement parties in general no longer is enough to send you running for cover?"

She smiled up at him, aware of the sheer pleasure of being in his arms. His beautifully controlled physical strength was one of the most compelling qualities he possessed. She loved being wrapped up in it. "I'm having a great time at this one," she admitted.

"One of these days we'll start planning another one."

His certainty always left her feeling breathless. "Will we?"

"Yeah, Maggie, love. We will."

"I thought I was going to get plenty of time to make up my mind."

"I promised you a little time to get used to the idea of marrying me, but don't expect me to give you an unlimited amount of rope. Knowing you, you'd just get yourself all tangled up in it."

She shook her head in wry wonder. "You are always so sure of yourself, aren't you?"

"I am when I know what I want." Rafe came to a halt in the middle of the dance floor. "And now, if you'll excuse me, it's time to make the big announcement. I've been assigned to do the honors."

"Doesn't it seem a little odd that you're announcing your own mother's engagement?"

"We live in interesting times." He kissed her forehead. "Be back in a few minutes."

The crowd broke into loud applause and cheers as Rafe grabbed a bottle of champagne, vaulted up onto the diving board and strode out to the far end. He held up the bottle in his hand to get the crowd's attention.

"You all know why you're here tonight, but I've been told to make it official," he began with a grin. "I would therefore like to say that it gives me great pleasure to do as my Mama tells me and announce her engagement to one smooth-talking cowboy named Connor Lark."

A roar of approval went up. Rafe gave the crowd a couple of minutes to grow quiet once more before he continued.

"I'm here to tell you folks that I've got no choice but to approve of this match. It's not just because I've had Lark checked out and decided he can take care of my Mama in the style to which she has become accustomed—"

The crowd interrupted with a burst of applause.

"And it's not just because she seems to actually like the guy or the fact that he's crazy about her. No, folks, I am giving my heartfelt approval to this match because Lark has informed me that if I do not, he will personally drag me out into the desert and stake me out over an anthill. Folks, I am a reasonable man. I want you to know I can hardly wait for Connor Lark to marry my mother."

Laughter filled the air as Rafe let the cork out of the champagne bottle with a suitable explosion. Again the crowd yelled approval. Connor, standing at the side of the pool next to Bev, grinned broadly at Rafe as he held a glass up to be filled with bubbling champagne.

Rafe filled the glass with a flourish and then a second one for his mother and everyone toasted the guests of honor. Connor finished his drink in one swallow and kissed his fiancée. Then he gave a whoop and grabbed her hand.

"Honey, let's dance," Connor crowed, sweeping Bev into a waltz. She laughed up at him with undisguised delight.

"They make a great couple, don't they?" Rafe leaped lightly down from the diving board and went to stand beside Margaret. He put an arm around her shoulders and drew her close to his side.

"Yes," Margaret said, her eyes on her father's face. "They do. I think they're going to be very happy."

"No happier than you and me, Maggie, love, you'll see." Rafe kissed her soundly and then dragged her over to the section of the patio that was being used for dancing. He smiled down into her eyes as he whirled her into the Western waltz.

A moment later the patio was filled with dancing couples and Margaret gave herself up to the joy of the music that flowed around her like champagne. *Yes,* she allowed herself to think for the first time in a year, *yes, she could be very happy with Rafe*. She could be the happiest woman in the world.

Rafe saw Hatcher hanging back as the last of the guests took their leave. He scowled at his assistant, wondering if Doug had followed orders two hours ago and laid off the booze.

"You sober enough to get behind the wheel, Hatcher?" he asked bluntly as the two men stood isolated on one side of the front drive.

"I'm fine," Hatcher muttered. "Haven't had anything but soda for the past couple of hours. Just wanted to tell you I left the Ellington file in your study. You'd better take a look at it as soon as possible."

Rafe eyed him. "Something new come up?"

Hatcher nodded, his eyes sliding away to follow the last car out of the drive. "Today. I've updated the file so you can take a look for yourself. I didn't want to say anything before the party. Seemed a shame to ruin it for you."

"Since when have I ever asked you to shield me from bad news? That's not what I pay you to do and you know it."

Hatcher's jaw tightened. "I know, but this is different, Rafe."

"What am I going to be looking at when I open the file?"

Hatcher hesitated. "The possibility that we've got a leak."

"Damn it to hell. You sure?"

"No, not entirely. Could be a coincidence that Moorcroft came up with the numbers he did today, but we've got to look at the other possibility."

"Someone gave him the information."

"Maybe."

"Yeah, maybe." Rafe watched the last set of taillights disappear down his long drive. "I thought we had this airtight, Hatcher."

"I thought we did, too."

"When I find out who's selling me out, I'll do a little bloodletting. Hope whoever it is realizes what he's risking."

"We don't know for sure yet, Rafe," Hatcher said quickly. "It really could be a genuine coincidence. But regardless of how it happened, there's no getting around the fact that we've got to counter Moorcroft's last move and fast. Thought you'd want to run the numbers yourself."

"I'll do it tonight and have an answer in the morning. Nothing gets in the way of this Ellington thing, understand? It has to go through on schedule."

"Right, well, guess I'd better be off." Hatcher nodded once more and dug his keys out of his pocket. "I'll talk to you tomorrow."

Rafe stood for a while in the balmy darkness watching Hatcher's car vanish in the distance.

Vengeance was a curious thing, he acknowledged. It had the same ability to obsess a man's soul as love did.

"Rafe?"

He turned toward the sound of Maggie's soft, questioning voice. She looked so beautiful standing there in the doorway with the lights of the house behind her. His beautiful, proud Maggie. He needed her more than the desert needed the fierce storms of late summer. Without her, he was an empty man.

And if she ever realized what he was going to do to Moorcroft, she'd be furious. There was even a possibility she'd try to run from him again. He had to be careful, Rafe told himself. This was between him and Moorcroft, anyway. A little matter of vengeance and honor that had to be settled properly.

"I'm coming, Maggie, love." He started toward the doorway. "Mom and Dad still out waltzing by the pool?"

Margaret laughed. "Without a band? No, I think they gave up the waltzing in favor of getting some sleep before leaving for Sedona in the morning."

"Not a bad idea," Rafe said.

"What?"

"Sleep. I could use some myself and so could you. Good night, Maggie, love." He pulled her into his arms and kissed her.

Forty minutes later he watched from the other side of the patio as Margaret's light went out. For a short time he toyed with the idea of going to her room.

But the file waiting in his office was too important to ignore. He'd told Hatcher he'd have an answer by tomorrow morning.

Chapter Seven

MARGARET FOUND SLEEP IMPOSSIBLE. She tossed and turned, listening to the small night sounds that drifted through her window. Her mind was not cluttered with the bright images of the successful party or thoughts of her father and his new love. She wasn't thinking about any of the many things that could have been keeping her awake.

All she could think about was Julie Cassidy's remark concerning Rafe having overcome his hawklike pride in order to find a way to get Margaret back.

The notion of Rafe Cassidy lowering his pride for a woman was literally stunning.

Margaret stared up at the ceiling and realized she had never considered the events of the past few days in those terms. She had felt manipulated at first and there was no denying that to a great extent she had been.

But what had it cost Rafe to admit to himself and everyone else that he wanted her back?

She thought of all the times during those first few months after the disaster when she had almost picked up the phone and called him. Her own pride had stood in her way every time. She had nothing for which to apologize, she kept telling herself. She had done nothing wrong. She had tried to explain her side of the situation to Rafe and he had flatly refused to listen.

And then he had said terrible things to her, things that still had the power to make her weep if she summoned them to the surface of her consciousness.

No, she could never have made the call begging him to take her back and give her another chance. It would have meant sacrificing all of her pride and her sense of self-worth. Any man who required such an act of contrition was not worth having.

But it was a novelty to think that in some fashion Rafe's apparently high-handed actions lately bespoke a lowering of his own pride. Margaret realized she had never thought of it in that light.

It was true he had not actually admitted that he had been wrong last year. Other than to apologize grudgingly for his rough treatment of her, he had basically stuck to his belief that she was the one who was guilty of betrayal; the one who required forgiveness.

But there was also no denying that he was the one who had finally found a way to get them back together.

Of course, Margaret told herself, somewhat amused, being Rafe, he had found a way to do it that had not required an abject plea from him. Nevertheless, he had done it. They were back together, at least for now, and Rafe was talking about marriage as seriously as ever.

What's more, he really did seem to have changed. He was definitely making an effort to limit his attention to business. The Rafe she had seen so far this week was a different man than the one she had known last year in that respect. The old Rafe would never have taken the time to get so completely involved in organizing his mother's engagement party. Nor would he have spent as much time entertaining a recalcitrant lover.

Lover.

The word hovered in Margaret's mind. Whatever else he was, Rafe was indisputably the lover of her dreams.

She had missed being with him last night. She and Bev had sat up talking until very late and then retired. Margaret had toyed with the notion of waiting until the lights were out and then gliding across the patio to Rafe's room. But when she had finally glanced out into the darkness she had seen the two familiar figures splashing softly in the pool and quickly changed her mind. Her father and Bev had already commandeered the patio for a late-night tryst.

But tonight the patio was empty. Margaret pushed back the sheet and got out of bed. A glance across the patio showed that Rafe's room was dark. She smiled to herself as she imagined Rafe's reaction if she were to go to his bedroom and awaken him.

In her mind she visualized him sleeping nude in the snowy sheets. He would be on his stomach, his strong, broad shoulders beautifully contoured with moonlight. When he became aware of her presence he would roll onto his back, reach up and pull her down on top of him. He would become hard with arousal almost instantly, the way he always did when he sensed she wanted him. And she would ache with the familiar longing.

Margaret hesitated no longer. She put on the new gauzy cotton dress she had purchased while shopping with Bev and slid her feet into a pair of sandals. Then she went out into the night.

When she reached the other side of the patio it took her a few seconds to realize that Rafe was not in his room. She let herself inside and saw that the bed had never been turned down. Curious, she walked through into the hall.

The eerie glow under the study door caught her eye at once. An odd sense of guilt shafted through her. The poor man, she thought suddenly. Was this how he was accomplishing the job of proving he could love her and run a business at the same time? Had he been working nights ever since she got here?

She crossed the hall on silent feet and opened the door. The otherworldly light of the computer screen was the only illumination in the room. Rafe was bathed in it as he lounged in his chair, his booted feet propped on his desk. He had not changed since the party but his shirt was unbuttoned and his sleeves rolled up to his elbows. His dark hair was tousled.

There was a file lying on the desk in front of him and a spreadsheet on the computer screen. He turned his head as he heard the door open softly. In the electronic glow the hard lines of his face seemed grimmer than usual.

Margaret lounged in the doorway and smiled. "I know you think I'm a demanding woman, but I'm not this demanding. Honest."

"What's that supposed to mean?" Rafe casually closed the file in front of him and dropped it into a drawer.

"Just that when I said I wanted our relationship to get a little more attention than your work, I didn't mean you had to resort to sneaking around in the middle of the night in order to spend some time on the job. I do understand the realities of normal business, Rafe. I worked in that world for several years, remember?"

Rafe's mouth curved faintly. "Believe me, Maggie, love, our relationship has had my full attention lately. This—" he gestured at the computer screen "—was just something Hatcher wanted me to look at. I didn't feel like sleeping yet so I thought I'd take care of it tonight." He swung his feet to the floor and punched a couple of keys on the computer. He stood up as the screen went blank. "How did you find me?"

Margaret smiled into the shadows as he walked toward her. "I refuse to answer that on the grounds that you'll think I'm fast."

His laugh was soft and sexy in the darkness. "As far as I'm concerned, you could never be too fast for me, lady, not as long as I'm the one you're chasing." He stopped in front of her and drew a finger down the side of her throat to the curve of her shoulder. He smiled knowingly as he felt her answering shiver of awareness. "You went to my bedroom, didn't you?"

"Uh-huh. You weren't there."

"So you went looking. Good. That's the way it should be." He kissed her lightly on the tip of her nose and then brushed his mouth across hers. His voice deepened abruptly. "Promise me you'll always come looking for me. No matter what happens. Don't run away from me again, Maggie, love."

She touched the side of his cheek. "Not even if you send me away?"

"I was a fool. I won't make that mistake again. I learned my lesson the hard way. Promise me, Maggie. Swear it. Say you won't leave even if things get rough between us again.

Fight with me, yell at me, slam a few doors, kick me in the rear, but don't leave."

She caught her breath and then, in a soft, reckless little rush she gave him the words he wanted to hear. "I won't leave."

He groaned thickly and gathered her so tightly against him that Maggie could hardly breathe. She didn't mind. She felt his lips in her hair and then his fingers were moving up her back to the nape of her neck and into her loosened hair.

She wrapped her arms around his waist and inhaled the sensual, masculine scent of him. She kissed his chest where the black shirt was open and felt him shudder.

"Maggie, love, you feel so good."

Rafe moved backward a couple of steps and sank down into his chair. He eased Maggie up against the desk in front of him until she could feel the wooden edge along the backs of her thighs. His hands went to her legs.

"Rafe, wait, we can't. Not here, like this." She stifled a tiny laugh that was part anxiety at the thought of getting caught making love in his study and part joyous arousal.

"Why not here?"

"What if someone hears us?"

"What if they do?" He pushed the gauzy cotton hem of the dress up above her knees. Then he deliberately parted her legs with his hands and kissed the sensitive skin of her upper thigh. "Anyone with half a brain who might happen to overhear us should have enough sense to ignore us."

"Yes, but." Maggie shivered delicately as she felt his mouth on the inside of her leg. His hands had lifted the skirt of the dress up to her waist. She heard him laugh softly as he realized she was naked under the cotton shift.

"Ah, Maggie, love, I see you dressed for the occasion."

"You're a lecherous rake, Rafe Cassidy."

"No ma'am, just a simple cowboy with simple tastes. There's nothing I like better than taking a moonlight ride with you."

"A moonlight ride? Is that what you call it?"

"Yeah. You know something? I like you best when you're stark naked." He leaned forward again in the chair and dipped his tongue into the small depression in her stomach. Then his lips worked their way downward into the tight curls below her waist.

"Rafe. *Rafe*." Maggie's hands clenched his shoulders. She felt unbelievably wanton and gloriously sexy as she stood there in front of him legs braced apart by his strong hands. Her head was tipped back, her hair cascading behind her. She closed her eyes as his kisses became overwhelmingly intimate.

"So good. Sweet and sexy and so hot already." Rafe eased a finger into her.

Margaret tightened instantly and cried out softly. She could hardly stand now. She leaned back against the desk, letting it support her weight. Rafe's fingers stretched her gently and she dug her nails into his shoulders.

"That's it, Maggie, love. Let me know how it feels. Tell me, sweetheart."

"You already know what you can do to me," she whispered in between gasps of pleasure.

"Yeah, but I like to hear about it." His eyes gleamed in the darkness as he looked up into her face.

"Why?"

"You know why. It makes me crazy."

She half laughed and half groaned and tangled her fingers in his hair. "You make *me* go crazy, Rafe. Absolutely wild. I don't even feel like myself when you touch me like this."

"Good." He stood up slowly, his hands gliding along her hips and then her waist and above her breasts. He carried the cotton dress along with the movement, lifting it up over her head. When it was free, he tossed it heedlessly onto the floor.

Margaret had one last burst of sanity. "Your room. Just across the hall. We can…"

"No. I like you just fine where you are." He stood between her legs and lifted her up so that she was sitting on the desk. She reached back to brace herself with her hands as his mouth moved on her shoulders and traveled down to her swollen breasts.

Rafe's fingers went to the waistband of his pants. A moment later Margaret heard the rasp of his zipper.

"Aren't you going to at least take off your boots?" Margaret demanded in a husky whisper.

"No need. This'll work just fine."

She look down and saw that it would work just fine. "But what about…about the protection you always use?"

"Got it right here." He reached into his back pocket.

Margaret heard the soft sound of the little packet being opened. "You carry that on you?" she gasped.

"Every minute since the day you arrived. I want to be able to make love to you anywhere, anytime."

"Good heavens, Rafe." She giggled, feeling more daring and wanton than ever. "Isn't there something a bit scandalous about doing it like this—on top of a desk? With your boots on?"

"This is my office, let me run the show, okay?" He caught one nipple lightly between his teeth.

Margaret inhaled sharply. "Yes. By all means, go ahead. Run the show. Please." She sighed in surrender and ceased worrying about decorum.

Rafe eased her down until she lay across the desk in a blatantly sensual pose. Her legs hung over the edge, open and inviting. She shuddered as he moved closer.

Margaret looked up through slitted eyes as Rafe probed her tenderly with his thumbs and then slowly fitted himself to her. She felt the excitement pounding in her veins and wondered at the magic between them. It was always like this. When Rafe made love to her he took her into a different world, one where she was wild and free and deliciously uninhibited—one where she knew she was temporarily, at least, the center of his universe.

Margaret clutched at Rafe as he surged slowly, deeply into her. She tightened her legs around him as he braced himself above her, his hands planted flat on either side of her.

"Maggie, love. *Maggie.* You're so sweet and tight and, oh, sweetheart, I do love the feel of you. Incredible."

She watched the hard, impassioned lines of his face as he drove into her until she could no longer concentrate on anything except the tide of excitement pooling deep within her. She closed her eyes again, lifting herself against the driving thrusts and then she felt Rafe ease one hand between their bodies.

He touched her with exquisite care and Margaret lost her breath. Her body tightened in a deep spasm and then relaxed in slow shivers that brought an intense pleasure to every nerve ending.

"*Rafe.*"

"Yes, love. Yes." And then he imbedded himself to the hilt within her. His lips drew back across his teeth as he fought to control a shout of sensual triumph and release. A moment later he dropped back into the chair behind him and dragged Margaret down onto his lap.

Margaret huddled against him, aware of his open zipper scratching her bare thigh. Rafe's hand slid slowly, absently along her leg and up to her waist. His head was pillowed against the back of his chair, his eyes closed.

"You are one wild and wicked lady," Rafe said without opening his eyes. "Imagine just walking in here bold as you please in the middle of the night when I'm trying to work and seducing me on my office desk."

Margaret smiled to herself as a thought struck her. "You know something, Rafe?"

"What?" He still seemed disinclined to move.

"I couldn't have done that last year when we were together."

He opened one eye. "Couldn't have done what? Walked into my office and seduced me? You're wrong. I'm a sucker for you. I always was."

She shook her head. "No you weren't. We always made love on your schedule and when you were in the middle of some business matter I always had to wait until you were finished. I could never have interrupted you the way I did tonight and expected you to shut down the computer so that we could make love in the middle of your office. Last year if I'd tried anything like that you'd have patted me on the head and told me to go wait in the bedroom until you finished working."

"Are you sure?"

Margaret lifted her head and glared at him. She saw the laughter in his eyes. "Of course, I'm sure. I have an excellent memory."

"I must have been a complete idiot last year. I can't imagine ignoring you if you'd traipsed into my office wearing that light little cotton thing with nothing on underneath. You know what I think?"

"What?"

"I don't think you'd have even tried it last year. You'd have waited very politely until I was finished. Maybe a little too politely. You were a very self-controlled, very restrained little executive lady last year. Cool, sleek and quite proper. I think the career in romance writing has been good for you. It's made you more inclined to make demands on me."

"You think that's good?" Margaret was startled.

Rafe sighed, his eyes turning serious in the shadows. "I think it's probably necessary. You're right when you called me arrogant and bossy and tyrannical."

"You admit it?"

"I admit it. I'm used to running things, honey. I've been giving orders so long it comes naturally. I'm also used to putting work first. My father always did and there's no denying I was following in his footsteps. Mom let him get away with doing that. But somehow, I don't think you'll let me get away with it."

"And you don't mind?"

Rafe smiled slowly. "Let's just say I'm capable of adapting."

"It's not that I'm completely insensitive to the demands you face, Rafe, you must know that," Margaret assured him earnestly. "I spent enough time in the business world to know that certain things have to be done and certain deadlines have to be met. But I don't want your work to rule our lives totally the way it did last year."

He drew his fingers through her tangled hair. In the shadows his eyes were very dark and deep. "It won't, Maggie. And if it ever threatens to, you know what you can do about it."

She grinned in delight. "Walk into your office and seduce you?"

"My door is always open to you, Maggie, love." Rafe kissed her lightly on the mouth and gave her a small nudge.

"I'm being kicked out already?" Margaret reluctantly got to her feet and reached for her cotton shift.

"Nope. We're both going to retire for the night. It's late and you and I are going to get up early to see Mom and Connor off to Sedona, remember?"

Margaret yawned. "Vaguely. Going to walk me back to my room?"

"You're the one whose sense of propriety insists that you wake up alone as long as the parents are around. If I had my way, I'd just walk you back across the hall to my room."

"Going to sneak back here and work on the computer after you've tucked me in?"

Rafe shook his head as he led her back across the hall, through his bedroom and out into the moonlit patio. "No, I saw all I needed to see. I've got an answer for Hatcher."

"It's very sweet of you to not make a fuss about letting me spend the night in my own bed, Rafe."

"Anything for you, Maggie, love. Besides, things will be different when we have the house to ourselves, won't they? I'm a patient man."

Much later Margaret awakened briefly. She automatically glanced through the glass door and followed the shaft of moonlight that struck full into Rafe's bedroom. She couldn't be positive, but it looked as if his bed was still empty.

CONNOR AND BEV TOOK THEIR LEAVE immediately after breakfast the next morning. Margaret stood with Bev in the driveway as the last of the luggage was loaded into the car.

"We'll be gone about a week, dear," Bev said cheerfully. "We're going to stop in Scottsdale first. That's where I live most of the time now. This ranch is a little too isolated for my tastes. At any rate, I have some friends I want Connor to meet. And then we'll drive on to Sedona. It makes a nice break this time of year. Much cooler up there in the mountains. There are several galleries I always like to visit when I'm there."

"Have a wonderful time, Bev."

Bev searched her face. "You'll be staying on here with Rafe?"

"Do you mind?"

Bev smiled. "Not at all. I'm delighted. I was afraid you might head straight back to Seattle. In fact I told Connor that perhaps we should cancel our plans in order to encourage you to stay here with us a little longer."

"I told her, forget it," Connor said as he walked past with a suitcase under each arm. He was followed by Tom who was carrying two more bags. "I was willing to help Cassidy get you down here but he's on his own now. I refuse to help him with any more of his courting work. I'm too busy tending to my own woman."

Bev's eyes lifted briefly toward the heavens. "Listen to the man."

Connor chuckled hugely as he put the suitcases into the trunk. He looked over at Rafe who was coming through the door with one last bag. "Hey, Cassidy. Tell your mother you can handle my daughter on your own from here on in. She's afraid Maggie's going to take off the minute our backs are turned."

Rafe's eyes met Margaret's. "Maggie's not going anywhere, are you, Maggie?"

Under the combined scrutiny of Bev, Tom, her father and her lover, Margaret felt herself turning pink. "Well, I had thought I might stay a few more days but that decision is subject to change if the pressure gets to be too much," she informed them all in dry tones.

"Pressure?" Rafe assumed an innocent, injured air. "What pressure? There's no pressure being applied, Maggie, love. Just bear in mind that if you take off this time, I'll be no more than fifteen minutes behind you and I won't be real happy."

"In that case, I suppose I might as well stay. As it happens, I have a social engagement here on Monday evening."

That succeeded in getting everyone's attention.

"What social engagement?" Rafe demanded. "You don't know anyone here in Tucson except me."

"That's not quite true, Rafe. I also know your sister and her friend Sean Winters. I've been invited to a showing of Sean's work."

"You're going to some damned art show?"

Margaret smiled serenely. "I thought you might like to escort me."

Rafe's brows came together in one solid, unyielding line. He slammed the trunk shut. "Like hell. We'll discuss this later."

Connor Lark turned to his fiancée. "Something tells me the children won't be bored while we're gone, dear. I think they're going to be able to entertain themselves just fine without us."

Bev glanced curiously from Margaret's cool, deliberate smile to Rafe's thunderous scowl. "Something tells me you're right, Connor."

Rafe stood beside Margaret as Connor drove away from the house. When the car was out of sight he took Margaret's arm and turned her firmly back into the foyer.

"Now tell me what the hell this business is about attending an exhibition of Winters's work."

"It's very simple. Julie and Sean invited me last night before they left. I accepted." She took a deep breath. "On behalf of both of us."

Rafe propped one shoulder against the wall in the negligent, dangerous pose he did so well. He folded his arms across his chest. "Is that right?"

Margaret cleared her throat delicately. "Yes. Right."

"What the devil do you think you're doing, Maggie?"

"Manipulating you into giving your sister's choice of a husband a fair chance?" She tried a smile to lighten the atmosphere.

"Trying to manipulate me is right. At least you're honest about it. But you should know me well enough by now to know I don't like being manipulated, not even by you. And what the hell do you mean my sister's choice of a *husband?* She told you she's actually thinking of marrying that damned artist?"

"They told me their plans last night. I think they have every intention of following through, Rafe, with or without your approval. You'd better learn to accept the situation graciously or risk alienating your sister."

"Damnation." Rafe came away from the wall and plowed his fingers through his hair. "Marry him? I didn't know they were that serious. I thought Winters was just another boyfriend. Julie's always got one or two trailing around behind her."

Margaret eyed him with a feeling of sympathy. "You've been looking after her for so long you may not have noticed she's grown up, Rafe. Julie's an adult woman. She makes her own choices."

"Some choices. She hasn't even been able to choose a job she can stay with for six months at a time. The guy's an artist, Maggie. Why couldn't she have found herself a nice, respectable…" His voice trailed off abruptly and he slid a quick glance at Margaret.

"A nice, respectable businessman? Someone who wears three-piece suits and ties and travels two weeks out of every month? Someone who needs an attractive, self-sacrificing hostess of a wife to entertain his guests while he closes big deals?"

Rafe winced. "Is that what you thought I'd turn you into? The boss's wife?"

"It's one of the things I was afraid of, yes."

"You should have said something."

"I tried. You never listened."

"I'm listening now," Rafe said evenly. His gaze locked with hers. "Believe me?"

Margaret nodded slowly. "Yes," she said, "I think I do."

Rafe nodded once. "Okay, that's settled. But that doesn't mean I'm going to approve of Winters."

"Rafe, they don't need your approval. They're quite capable of getting married without it."

"You think so?" Rafe's mouth twisted. "What if Winters finds out Julie doesn't come equipped with an unlimited checking account and a handful of charge cards?"

"I don't think he's marrying her for her money."

"How do you know? You only met him once last night."

"I liked him. And even if he is marrying her for her money, there's still not much you can do about it. Your best bet is to stay on good terms with your sister regardless of whether her decision is right or wrong."

"I could always try buying Winters off," Rafe said thoughtfully.

"I don't think that would be a very smart thing to do, Rafe. Julie would hate you for it. Give Sean a chance first before you try anything drastic. Come to the gallery show with me."

"Why? What will that prove?"

"It will give you an opportunity to meet him on his turf, instead of yours. If you're going to have him in the family you should make an effort to learn something about his world."

"Stop talking as if the marriage is an accomplished fact."

"Rafe, you're being deliberately stubborn and bullheaded about this. Give the man a chance. You know you should."

"Yeah? Why should I?" he challenged.

"I thought giving the other guy a fair chance was one of those fundamental tenets of the Code of the West."

He scowled ferociously at her. "What the devil are you talking abut now? What's this nonsense about a code?"

She smiled again. "You know that basic creed you probably learned at your father's knee. The one he undoubtedly got from his father and so on. The one that's supposed to cover little things like vengeance, honor, justice and fair play among the male of the species."

Rafe swore again in disgust and paced the length of the foyer. He stopped at the far end, swung around and eyed her for a short, tense moment. "You want to play by the Code of the West? All right, I'll go along with that. We'll start with a little simple frontier justice. If you want to manipulate me into going to that damn gallery, you've got to pay the price."

Margaret watched him with sudden wariness. "What price?"

Rafe smiled dangerously. "In exchange for my agreement to go to the showing, you agree to let me announce our engagement. I want it official, Maggie. No more fooling around."

Margaret took a deep breath. "All right."

Rafe stared at her in open astonishment. "You agree?"

"You've got yourself a deal, cowboy."

Rafe gave a shout of triumph. "Well, it's about time, lady."

He took one long stride forward, scooped Margaret up in his arms and carried her down the hall to the nearest bedroom.

This time he took off his boots.

Chapter Eight

RAFE SADDLED HIS BEST CHESTNUT STALLION the next morning at dawn. Out of the corner of his eye he watched with satisfaction as Maggie adjusted her own saddle on the gray mare. He took a quiet pleasure in the competent manner in which she handled the tack and the horse. Connor had been right. His daughter knew her way around a barn.

Rafe wondered how he could have spent two whole months with Maggie last year and never learned that single, salient fact about her.

Then again, those two months had passed in a tangled web of sudden, consuming passion mixed with an explosive game of corporate brinksmanship that had involved millions. There had been very little time for getting to know the small, intimate details of his new lover's past. He had been far too anxious to spend what little free time he had with her in bed.

Money and love were a dangerous combination, Rafe had discovered. A pity he hadn't learned to separate the two before. But, then, in all fairness to himself, he'd never come across the two combined in such a lethal fashion until last year.

He knew what he was doing this time around. He could handle both.

"All set?" he asked as he finished checking the cinch on his saddle.

"I'm ready." Margaret picked up the reins and led her mare toward the barn door.

"We'll ride out over the east foothills. I want to show you some land I'm thinking of selling." Rafe walked the chestnut out into the early morning light and vaulted lightly into the saddle. He turned his head to enjoy the sight of Maggie's sexy jeans-clad bottom as she mounted her mare. The woman looked good on horseback. Almost as good as she looked in bed. Rafe nudged the stallion with his knee and the chestnut moved forward with brisk eagerness.

The day was going to be hot, Rafe thought. They all were this time of year. But at this hour the desert was an unbelievably beautiful place—still cool enough to allow a man to enjoy the wide open, primitive landscape. It was a landscape that had always appealed strongly to something deep within him. They had never talked about it, but he'd always sensed the land had affected his father and his grandfather in the same way.

They rode in companionable silence until they came to the point where a wide sweep of the ranch could be seen. Only a handful of cattle were visible. Here in the desert livestock needed vast stretches on which to graze. The cattle tended to scatter widely.

Rafe halted the chestnut and waited for Margaret to bring her mare alongside. She did so, surveying the rolling foothills spread out in front of her.

"How much of this is Cassidy land?" she asked.

"Just about all of what you can see," Rafe admitted. "It goes up into the mountains. My great-grandfather acquired most of it. My grandfather and father added to it. They all ran cattle on it and did some mining in the hills. The land's been good to the Cassidys."

"But now you're thinking of selling it?"

Rafe nodded. "Some of it. It would be the smart thing to do. The truth is, the cattle business isn't what it used to be and probably won't ever be again. The mines are all played out. If I had any sense I would have gotten rid of the stock five years ago and sold the acreage to a developer who wants to put in a golf course and a subdivision."

"Why didn't you?"

"I don't know," he admitted. "Lord knows I don't need several thousand acres of desert. I've made my money buying and selling businesses, not in running cattle. Compared to my other investments, running livestock is more of a hobby than anything else. But for some reason I haven't been able to bring myself to put the land on the market."

"Maybe that's because part of you doesn't really think it's yours to sell. You inherited it so maybe you think deep down that you're supposed to hold it in trust for the next generation of Cassidys."

Rafe was startled by that observation. She was right, he thought. Absolutely right. "Sounds kind of feudal, doesn't it?"

"A bit old-fashioned in some ways," Margaret agreed. "But I can see the pull of that kind of philosophy. When you look at land like this you tend to start thinking in more fundamental terms, don't you?"

"Yeah. When I was younger I used to ride out here and do a lot of that kind of thinking. Then I got away from it for a while. I got back in the habit this past year."

"Because of me?"

"Yeah."

Margaret looked down at the reins running through her fingers. "I did a lot of thinking, too. It nearly drove me crazy for a while."

"I know what you mean." Rafe was silent for a moment, satisfied that they had both suffered during the past year. "You know, I really should sell this chunk of desert. There are plenty of developers who would pay me a fortune for it."

"Do you need another fortune?"

Rafe shrugged. "No. Not really."

"Then don't sell. At least not now." Maggie smiled her glowing smile, the one that always made him want to grab her and kiss her breathless. "Who knows, maybe the next generation of Cassidys won't be as good at wheeling and dealing in the business world as this generation is. Your descendents might need the land far more than you need more money. No one can predict the future and land is the one certain long-term investment. Hold on to it and let the next batch of Cassidys sell it if they need to do so."

"You mean, tell myself I really am holding it in trust for the family?"

"Yes."

Rafe looked out over the vastness in front of him. Maggie's simple logic suddenly made great sense. It was a relief somehow to be able to tell himself that there was no overwhelming need to sell for business reasons. "I think that's exactly what I'll do. I wonder why I didn't think of it that way before now."

"You've been thinking in terms of good business, as usual. But there are other things just as important. A family's heritage is one of them. My father sold his land because he had no choice. He turned out to be a much better engineer and businessman than he was a rancher. But a part of him has always regretted giving up the land. You're not forced to make the choice, so why do it?"

Rafe reached across the short distance between them and wrapped his hand around the nape of her neck. He leaned forward and kissed her soundly. He had to release her abruptly as the chestnut tossed his head and pranced to one side. Quickly Rafe brought the stallion back under control and then he grinned at Maggie.

"Remind me to bounce the occasional business problem off you in the future, Maggie, love. I like the way you think."

"Praise from Caesar." Her laugh was soft and somehow indulgent. "You do realize this is the first and only time you've ever asked my opinion on a business matter?"

"I'll obviously have to do it more often." Rafe hesitated a few seconds, not sure how to say what he intended to say next. Hell, he wasn't even certain he wanted to say it at all. But for some irrational reason he needed to do it. "Maggie, about our bargain."

She glanced at him in surprise. "What bargain?"

He was annoyed that she had forgotten already. "Don't give me that blank look, woman. I'm talking about the bargain we made the other day. The one in which I agreed to go to Winters's gallery show in exchange for your agreement to let me announce our engagement. Or has that little matter slipped your mind?"

She blinked, taken aback by his vehemence. "Hardly. I guess I just hadn't thought of it as a bargain."

"Yeah, well, that's what it was, wasn't it?"

"I suppose so. In a way. What's bothering you about it, Rafe?"

He exhaled heavily, willing himself to shut his mouth while there was still time. But the words came of their own accord. "I don't want you agreeing to get engaged because we've made a deal, Maggie. I don't like having you feel you've got to do it to defend Julie from my bullheaded stubbornness."

"Oh, Rafe, I really didn't think of it quite like that."

"All the same, I thought I'd tell you that I'll go to that damned art show with no strings attached. I'll give Winters a fair chance. As for us, you don't have to make any promises to me until you're ready. I'm willing to give you all the time you need to make certain you want to marry me."

"You surprise me, Rafe."

"I can see that." He was still irritated. "You don't have to look so stunned. You think I can't be open-minded when I want to be?"

"Well—"

"You think I can't give a guy a fair chance?"

"Well—"

"You think the only way I work is by applying pressure whenever I see an opportunity to do so?"

"Well, to be perfectly honest, Rafe…"

He held up a hand. "Forget it. I don't think I need a truthful answer to that one. But I am doing my best to back off a little here, so let me do it, okay?"

"Okay." She smiled gently.

Saddle leather creaked as he studied her face in the morning light. "I want you to marry me. But I want you to come to me willingly, Maggie, love. Not because I've pushed you into it." Rafe drew a deep breath and got the rash words out before he could rethink them. "Take all the time you need to make your decision."

"So long as I come up with the right one?" Her eyes danced mischievously.

He grinned slowly, relaxing inside. "You've got it. So long as it's the right one." The sun was getting higher in the morning sky and the heat was setting in already. Rafe crammed the brim of his hat down low over his eyes and turned the chestnut back toward the ranch.

IT WAS OBVIOUS FROM THE MOMENT Margaret and Rafe entered the thronged gallery that the showing of Sean Winters's work was a resounding success. The large, prestigious showroom was filled with well-dressed people sipping champagne and commenting learnedly on contemporary art. Margaret saw Rafe's cool-eyed appraisal of the gathering and smiled.

"Not quite what you expected, hmm, cowboy?"

"All right, I'll admit the man apparently has a market. The place is packed. That must be his stuff on the walls. Let's take a look at it before Julie discovers we're here."

Sean Winters's work was clearly of the Southwestern school, full of the rich, sun-drenched tones of the desert. His paintings for the most part tended toward the abstract with an odd hint of surrealism. There was a curiously hard edge to them that made them stand out from the work of other artists dealing with similar subject matter. Margaret was instantly enthralled.

"These are wonderful," she exclaimed, a bit in awe in spite of herself. "Look at that canyon, Rafe. And that evening sky above it."

Rafe peered more closely at the painting she indicated. "Are you sure it's a canyon? Looks like lots of little wavy lines of paint to me."

"It's titled *Canyon*, you twit. And don't you dare play the uncultured, uncouth redneck cowboy with me, Rafe. This work is good and you know it. Admit it."

"It's interesting. I'll give it that much." Rafe frowned at the price on the tag stuck next to the painting. "Also expensive. If Winters can really sell this stuff for this kind of money, he's got quite a racket going."

"Almost as good a racket as buying and selling companies."

Rafe gave her a threatening scowl just as Julie came hurrying up to greet them.

"You made it. I'm so glad. I was hoping you'd get him here, Margaret." Julie turned hopeful eyes on her brother. "Thanks for coming, Rafe. I really appreciate it."

"Thank Margaret. She practically hog-tied me and dragged me here. You know I'm not into the artsy-craftsy stuff."

Julie's sudden glowering expression bore a startling resemblance to the one Rafe could produce so quickly. "I'm not going to let you dismiss Sean's work as artsy-craftsy stuff, Rafe. Do you hear me? He is a very talented artist and the least you can do is show some respect."

"Okay, okay, calm down. I'm here, aren't I? I'm willing to give the guy a chance."

Julie glanced uncertainly from her brother to Margaret and back again. "You are?"

"Sure. Code of the West and all that."

"What are you talking about, Rafe?"

Rafe flashed a quick grin at Margaret, who beetled her brows at him. "Never mind."

Julie relaxed and gestured at the art that surrounded them. "Tell me the truth, Rafe. Now that you've had a chance to see it, what do you really think of Sean's work? Isn't it wonderful?"

Margaret didn't trust the response she saw forming in Rafe's eyes. She stepped in quickly to answer Julie's query. "Rafe was just saying how impressed he was, weren't you, Rafe?"

Rafe started to comment on that, caught Margaret's eye again and apparently changed his mind. "Uh, yeah. That's just what I was saying." He looked around as if seeking further inspiration. "Big crowd here tonight."

"Oh, there always is for a new showing of Sean's work. He's had a steady market for some time but lately he's been getting a lot of attention in reviews and articles. His career is definitely taking off."

Rafe nodded. "Things blow hot and cold in the art world, don't they? Not a reliable line of work. An artist can be in big demand one year and dead in the water the next."

Margaret saw Julie's mouth tighten and she turned to pounce on Rafe. But the attack proved unnecessary. Sean Winters had come up in time to hear the remark. He smiled coolly at Rafe.

"Nothing's for sure in the art world or any other. That's why I've paid a fair amount of attention to my investments since I made my first sale."

"Is that right?" Rafe swiped a glass of champagne from a passing tray and gave Sean a challenging look. "What do you put your money into, Winters, paint?"

"I guess you could say that. I own that artists' supply house Julie manages. We grossed a quarter of a million last year and this quarter's sales are already overtaking last quarter's. Or so I'm told. I just read the financial statements. I don't actively manage things. Julie handles everything."

Rafe nearly choked on his champagne. Margaret obligingly pounded him on the back. He gave her a sharp look.

"Sorry. Did I hit you too hard?" She smiled at him with brilliant innocence.

Rafe turned back to Winters. "Julie works for you? You own that place she's been managing for the past few months?"

"Best manager I've got."

"How many have you got?"

"Two. New store just opened in Phoenix last month. Julie's going to be overseeing the management of both branches. I don't like having to worry about the business side of things so I've turned it all over to your sister. She seems to have inherited her fair share of the family talent."

"I see," said Rafe. He took another swallow of champagne and glared around the room. "We've been looking at the paintings. Maggie likes your stuff."

Sean grinned. "Thanks, Margaret."

"It's stunning. I love it. If I could afford it, I'd buy *Canyon* in a red-hot second. Unfortunately it's a little out of my range."

Sean winced in chagrin. "I know. Ridiculous, isn't it? For a long time I couldn't even afford to buy my own stuff. I leave the pricing of my work up to Cecil."

"Who's Cecil?"

"He owns this gallery and one in Scottsdale and let me tell you, Cecil is one ruthless son of a gun." Sean grinned at Rafe. "Come to think of it, you'd probably like him, Cassidy. The two of you undoubtedly have a lot in common. Want to meet him?"

"Why not? I'd like to hear a little more about the inside workings of this art business." Rafe handed his empty glass to Margaret and strode off with Sean.

Margaret and Julie watched the two men make their way across the room for a moment and then Julie looked anxiously at Margaret. "Rafe's going to grill Sean. I just know it."

"I wouldn't worry. I have a feeling Sean can take care of himself."

Julie looked briefly surprised and then she relaxed slightly. "You're right. It's just that I've been defending and protecting my dates from Rafe for so long, it's become a habit. I get nervous whenever he gets near one. He tends to stampede them toward the nearest exit. And now that I've actually decided to marry Sean a part of me is terrified Rafe will scare him off."

"No chance of that," Margaret said cheerfully. "Sean won't scare easily." She turned back to study *Canyon*. "Why didn't you tell Rafe you were actually working for Sean?"

"I wanted to make sure I could make a success of the job before I told either Rafe or my mother. This is the first position I've gotten on my own, you know. Rafe has always taken it upon himself to line up something for me. He had a job waiting the day I graduated college. Said it was my graduation present. Every time I quit one he used his business contacts to line up another one."

"That's Rafe, all right. Tends to take over and run things if you let him."

Julie sighed. "The problem is he's good at running business things. You can't deny he's got a natural talent for it. But when he gets involved in people things he's dangerous."

Margaret laughed. "I know what you mean."

"How are you two doing up there at the ranch without Mom or Connor to referee?"

"We're slowly but surely reaching a negotiated peace."

Julie smiled. "I'm glad. Difficult as my brother is, I want him to be happy. And he definitely has not been happy this past year. Margaret, I want to thank you again for what you've done tonight. You didn't have to go out of your way to help. It was very kind of you."

"No problem. Rafe is basically a good man. He just needs a little applied management theory now and then. When it comes right down to it, he did it for you, Julie. You are his sister, after all."

"No," Julie said with a smile. "He didn't do it for me. He did it for you."

RAFE SHUDDERED HEAVILY AND MUFFLED his shout of sensual satisfaction against the pillow under Maggie's head. The echo of her own soft cries still hovered in the air along with the scent of their lovemaking. A moment earlier he had felt the tiny, delicate ripples of her release and he had been pulled beyond the limits of his self-control.

She always had this effect on him, Rafe thought as he relaxed slowly. She had the power to unleash this raging torrent of physical and emotional response within him. When their lovemaking was over he was always left with an incredible sense of well-being. There was nothing else on earth quite like it.

Rafe rolled off Maggie's slick, nude body and settled on his back, one hand under his head. He left his other hand lying possessively on one of Maggie's sweetly rounded thighs.

For a long while they were silent together, just as they always were when they rode into the hills at dawn. In some ways making love with Maggie was a lot like taking her riding, Rafe told himself. He grinned suddenly into the moonlit shadows.

"What's so funny?" Maggie stretched luxuriously and turned onto her side. She put her hand on his chest.

"Nothing. I was just thinking that being with you like this is a little like riding with you."

"I don't want to hear any crude cracks about midnight rodeos."

"All right, ma'am. No crude cracks." He smiled again. "Midnight rodeo? Where'd you get a phrase like that? You've been sneaking around listening to country-western music stations, haven't you?"

"I refuse to answer that." She snuggled closer. "But for the record, I will tell you that you're terrific in the saddle."

"I was born to ride," Rafe said with patently false modesty. "And you're the only little filly I ever want to get on top of."

"Uh-huh. Keep it that way. Tell me what you talked about with Sean Winters tonight at the gallery."

"It was men's talk," Rafe said loftily and was promptly punished by having his chest hair yanked quite severely. "Sheesh, okay, okay, lay off the torture. I'll talk."

"Yes?"

"We discussed business."

"Business?"

"Yeah. The business of the art world. It's real dog-eat-dog, did you know that? Bad as the corporate world. We also talked about the fact that he fully intends to marry Julie. With or without my approval."

"And?"

Rafe shifted slightly on the pillow. "And what?"

"And did you try to buy him off?"

"That's none of your business."

"You did, didn't you?" Maggie sat up abruptly, glaring down at him. "Rafe, I warned you not to try that."

He studied her breasts in the moonlight. She had beautiful breasts he told himself, trying to be objective about it. They fit perfectly into his palms. "Don't worry, we got the issue settled."

"What issue?"

"Winters's paintings are for sale, but he isn't," Rafe explained succinctly.

Maggie flopped back down onto the pillow. "I told you so."

"Yeah, you did, didn't you? Has anyone ever told you that's a nasty habit?" Rafe asked conversationally.

"Saying 'I told you so'?" She turned her head and gave him a sassy grin. "But I'm good at it."

He gave her an affectionate slap on her sleek hip and yawned. "You're good at it, all right. I'll have to admit it looks like the Cassidys are going to have an artist in their ranks."

"You're beginning to like Sean, aren't you?"

"He's okay."

"And you're going to tell Julie you like him and approve of him, aren't you?"

"Probably," Rafe admitted. He was feeling too complacent and sensually replete to argue about anything right now.

Maggie giggled delightfully in the darkness. "I love you when you're like this."

"Like what?"

"So reasonable."

Rafe felt a cold chill go through him. The satisfaction he had been feeling a few seconds ago vanished. He thought of the file in his study and the moves he had instructed Hatcher to make that morning. He levered himself up onto one elbow and looked down at the woman beside him.

She sensed the change in him instantly. "Rafe? What's wrong?"

"What about when I'm not reasonable by your standards, Maggie?" he asked. "Will you still love me?"

She searched his face, her eyes soft and shadowed. "Yes."

Rafe inhaled deeply and told himself she meant it. "Say it straight out for me. I need to hear the words."

"I love you, Rafe." She touched his shoulder, her fingers gliding down his arm in a gentle caress. "I never stopped loving you although I will admit I tried very hard."

Rafe fell back onto the pillow and pulled her down across his chest. He drove his fingers through her tangled hair and held her head clasped in his hands. "I love you, Maggie. I want you to always remember that."

"I will, Rafe."

He lay there looking up at her for a while and then the tension went out of him. His good mood restored itself. "Does this mean we're finally engaged?"

She smiled slowly. "Why, yes, I guess it does."

"You're sure?" he pressed. "You're willing to set a date?"

Maggie nodded. "Yes. If you're very sure you want to marry me."

"I've never been more certain of anything in my life." He used the grip in her hair to pull her mouth closer to his own. When he kissed her, she parted her lips for him, letting him deep inside where he could stake his intimate claim. Rafe growled softly as he felt himself start to grow hard again.

Maggie giggled.

"What are you laughing at, lady?"

"You sound like a big cat when you do that."

He rolled to the edge of the bed, taking her with him. Then he stood up with her in his arms. Maggie laughed up at him as she clung to his neck. "What are you doing? Where are we going?"

"Swimming."

"But it's two in the morning."

"We can sleep late."

"We're both stark naked."

He grinned and eyed her body appreciatively. "That's true."

"You're impossible, you know that?"

"But you love me anyway, right?"

"Right." Maggie looked down as he reached the pool. She glanced up again in alarm as she realized his intentions. "I don't mind a late night swim, but don't you dare drop me into that water, Rafe."

"It's not cold."

She gave him a quelling look. "All the same, I do not like entering swimming pools by being dropped into them."

"Think of this as just another little example of simple frontier justice."

"Rafe, don't you dare. What justice are you talking about, anyway?"

"This is for trying to set me up at that gallery this evening."

Her eyes widened innocently. "But you agreed to go to the show with no strings attached. You said you liked Sean after you got to know him."

Rafe shook his head deliberately. "That's not the point. The point is you tried to set me up. Tried to manipulate me into doing exactly what you wanted. If you're going to play games like that, Maggie, love, you have to be prepared to pay the price." He opened his arms and let her fall.

She yelled very nicely as she went into the water. When she surfaced she promptly splashed him, laughing exuberantly as he tried to dodge.

Rafe grinned back at her and then dove into the pool thinking that this was probably one of the best nights of his entire life.

Chapter Nine

RAFE WAITED UNTIL MARGARET'S BACK WAS turned in the large mall bookstore before he strolled casually over to the romance section. He stood there for a moment, lost in a sea of lushly illustrated paperbacks. Then he spotted a familiar-looking name. Fuchsia foil spelled out Margaret Lark. The title of the book was *Ruthless*.

After another quick glance to make certain that Margaret was still busy browsing through mysteries, Rafe examined the cover of her latest book. It showed a man and a woman locked in a passionate embrace. The man had removed the charcoal gray jacket of his suit and his tie hung rakishly around his neck. His formal white shirt was open to the waist and his hand was behind the lady's back, deftly lowering the zipper of her elegant designer gown.

The couple was obviously standing in the living room of a sophisticated penthouse. In the backdrop high-rise buildings rose into a dark sky and the sparkling lights of a big city glittered.

Rafe opened *Ruthless* to the first page and started to read.

"It's no secret, Anne. The man's a shark. Just ask anyone who worked for any of the companies Roarke Cody is supposed to have salvaged in the past five years. He may have saved the firms but he did it by firing most of the management and supervisory level people. We're all going to be on the street in a week, you mark my words."

Anne Jamison picked up the stack of files on her desk and glanced at her worried assistant. "Calm down, Brad. Cody's been hired to straighten out this company, not decimate the staff. He must be good to have acquired the reputation he's got. Now, if you'll excuse me, I've got to get going. I've got a meeting in his office in five minutes."

"Anne, you're not listening. The guy's ruthless. Don't you understand?" Brad trailed after her to the door. "He's probably called you into his office to fire you. And after he lets you go, I'm next. You'll see."

Anne pretended to ignore her frantic assistant as she made her way down the hall, but the truth was, she was not nearly as confident as she looked. She was as aware of Cody's reputation as Brad was—more so, in fact, because she'd done some checking.

"Ruthless" was, indeed, the right word to describe the turnaround specialist who had been installed here at the corporate headquarters of Seaco Industries. Roarke Cody had left a trail of fired personnel in his wake wherever he had gone to work. He was nothing less than a professional hit man whose gun was for hire by any company that could afford him.

Three minutes later Anne was shown into the new gunslinger's office. She held her breath as the tall, lean, dark-haired man standing at the window turned slowly to face her. One look and her heart sank. She had been putting up a brave, professional front but the fact was, she had known the full truth about this man the first day she'd met him. There was no mercy in those tawny gold eyes—no compassion in that hard, grim face.

"Good morning, Mr. Cody," she said with the sort of gallant good cheer one adopted in front of a firing squad. "I understand you're on the hunt and you'll be having most of management for dinner."

"Not most of management." Roarke's deep voice was tinged with a hint of a Western drawl. "Just you, Miss Jamison. Seven o'clock tonight." He smiled without any humor. "I thought we might discuss your immediate future."

Anne's mouth fell open in shock. "Mr. Cody, I couldn't possibly..."

"Perhaps I should clarify that. It's not just your future we will discuss," he said smoothly. "But that of your staff, as well."

And suddenly Anne knew exactly how it felt to be singled out as prey.

"For heaven's sake, what are you doing?" Margaret hissed in Rafe's ear.

"Reading one of your books." Rafe closed *Ruthless* and smiled blandly. "Something sort of familiar about this Roarke guy."

To his surprise, Margaret blushed a vivid pink. "You're imagining things. Put that back and let's go get that coffee you promised me."

"Hang on a second, I want to buy this." Rafe reached for his wallet as he started toward the counter.

Margaret hurried after him. "You're going to buy *Ruthless?* But, Rafe, it's not exactly your kind of book."

"I'm not so sure about that."

She stifled a groan and retreated to wait near the door as Rafe paid for the book. A moment later, his package in one hand, Rafe ambled out into the air-conditioned mall. "Okay, let's get the coffee."

Margaret marched determinedly toward a small café near a fountain and sat down. "Are you really going to read that?"

"Uh-huh. Why don't you have your coffee and go shop for a while? I'll just sit here and read."

"Why this sudden interest in my writing?"

"Maggie, love, I want to know everything there is to know about you. Besides, I'm curious to see whether or not I save Seaco Industries."

"Whether or not *you* save it," she gasped in outrage. "Rafe, don't get any ideas about my having used you as a model for the hero in my book."

Rafe paid no attention to that as he dug *Ruthless* out of the sack and put it down on the table in front of him. "Come on, Maggie, love. Light brown eyes, dark brown hair and a Western drawl? Who do you think you're kidding?"

"I have news for you, Rafe. There are millions of men around who fit that description."

"Yeah, but I'm the one you know," he said complacently as he ordered two cups of coffee from a hovering waitress.

Margaret gave him an exasperated glare. "You want to know something? Most of my heroes look like Roarke Cody. And I wrote at least three of them long before I ever met you."

"Is that right? No wonder you fell straight into my hands the day I met you. I was your favorite hero come to life. The man of your dreams."

"Why you arrogant cowboy. Of all the…"

"Give me a hint," Rafe said, interrupting her casually. "Does the heroine sleep with this Roarke guy in the hope that she can persuade him not to fire her and her staff?"

"Of course not." Margaret was obviously scandalized at the suggestion. "That would be highly unethical. None of my heroines would do such a thing."

"Hmm. But he tries to get her to do that, right?"

Margaret lifted her chin. "Roarke Cody is quite ruthless in the beginning. He tries all sorts of underhanded, sneaky maneuvers to get the heroine."

"And?"

"And what?"

"Do any of those underhanded, sneaky maneuvers work as well as the underhanded, sneaky maneuver I used to get you down here to Tucson?"

Margaret folded her arms on the table and leaned forward with a belligerent glare. "I am not going to tell you the plot."

"Go shopping, Maggie, love. I'll wait right here for you." Rafe propped one booted heel on a convenient empty chair, leaned back and picked up *Ruthless.*

MARGARET SPENT OVER AN HOUR IN THE colorful, Southwestern-style shops. The air-conditioned shopping mall was crowded with people seeking to escape the midday heat.

The clothes featured in the windows tended to be brighter and more casual in style than what she was accustomed to seeing in Seattle. It made for an interesting shopping experience that she deliberately lengthened in the hope of causing Rafe to grow bored and restless.

But when she returned to the indoor sidewalk café, several packages in hand, she saw to her dismay that he was still deep into *Ruthless*.

She told herself she ought to find his interest in her book gratifying or at the very least somewhat amusing. But the fact was, it made her uncomfortable. He had guessed the truth immediately. He was the hero of *Ruthless* and of every book she had ever written.

Margaret had been in the middle of writing Roarke and Anne's story when she had met Rafe. She had finished it shortly after Rafe had turned on her and accused her of betraying him. It had not been easy to write a happy ending when her own lovelife was in shambles.

But a part of her had sought to work out in *Ruthless* the ending that had been denied to her in real life. Her own relationship might have gone on the rocks but she'd still had her dreams of what a good relationship could be. A woman had to have faith in the future.

"Not finished yet?" Margaret came to a halt in front of Rafe.

He looked up slowly. "Gettin' there. Ready to go?"

She nodded. "I could use a swim."

"Good idea." Rafe got to his feet and dropped *Ruthless* back into the paper bag. "You know this Roarke guy started out okay in the beginning. He had the right idea about how to save Seaco. You've got to cut a lot of dead wood when you go into a situation like that. But I get the feeling he's being set up for a fall."

"He's being set up for a happy ending," Margaret muttered.

Rafe shook his head, looking surprisingly serious. "The problem is, he's starting to let his hormones make his decisions. He's getting soft." Rafe chuckled. "Not in bed, I'll grant you, he's holding up just fine there. But when it comes to business, he's falling apart. Going to shoot himself in the foot if he doesn't get back on track."

"He's falling in love with the heroine and that love is causing him to change," Margaret snapped.

"It's causing him to act stupid."

"Rafe, for pity's sake, it's just a story. Don't take it so seriously."

"Real life business doesn't work like that."

"It's a story, Rafe. A romance."

"You know," Rafe said, looking thoughtful as they walked out of the mall into the furnace of the parking lot, "your dad was right. It's a good thing you got out of the business world, Maggie. You're not tough enough for it."

"My father said that? I'll strangle him."

"He said it during one of our early conversations and I agree."

"You're both a couple of turkeys."

"Maybe women in general just aren't hard enough to make it in the business world," Rafe continued philosophically. "You've got to be willing to be ruthless, really ruthless or you'll get eaten by the bigger sharks. Women, especially women like you, just don't have that extra sharp edge, know what I mean?"

Margaret came to a full halt right in the middle of the blazing parking lot and planted herself squarely in front of a startled Rafe. She was hotter than the blacktop on which she stood, her anger suddenly lashed into a fire storm.

"Why you chauvinistic, pig-headed, redneck cowboy. I always had a feeling that deep down inside you didn't approve of women in the business world and now at last the truth comes out. So you don't think women can handle it, do you? You don't think we'll ever make it in big business? That we aren't ruthless enough?"

"Now, honey, it was just an observation."

"It's a biased, prejudiced, masculine observation. I've got news for you, Rafe Cassidy, one of these days women are going to not only make it big in the business world, but we're going to change the way it operates."

Rafe blinked and reached up to pull the brim of his Stetson lower over his eyes. "Is that right?"

"Darn right. You men have been running it long enough and women are getting tired of playing by your rules. We're getting tired of cutthroat business practices and vicious competition—tired of playing the game for the sake of some man's ego."

Rafe shrugged. "That's the way it works, Maggie, love. It's a jungle out there."

"Only because men have made it into one. I suppose that after you got civilized and no longer had the thrill of the hunt for real, you had to create a new way to get your kicks. So you turned all your aggressive instincts into the way you do business. But that's going to change as women take over."

"Uh, Maggie, love, it's kind of hot out here. What do you say we go back to the ranch and continue this fascinating discussion in the swimming pool?"

"Your sister is a good example of the new breed of female businessperson. And Sean Winters has shown the good sense to turn his stores over to her to manage. You could take a lesson from him."

A small smile edged Rafe's mouth. His eyes gleamed in the shadow of his hat. "You want me to turn Cassidy and Company over to you?"

"Of course not. I don't want anything to do with that company. I've got my own career in writing and I like it. But I swear to God, Rafe, if we have a daughter and if she shows an interest in the family business, you'd darn well better let her have a hand in it."

Rafe grinned slowly. "It's a deal. Let's go home and work on it."

Margaret stared at him in frowning confusion as he took her arm and steered her toward the Mercedes. "What are you talking about?"

"Our daughter. Let's go home and get busy making one. I want to see this brave new world of business once the women take over. The sooner we get started producing the new female executive, the sooner we'll see if it's going to work."

Margaret felt as if the wind had been knocked out of her. She struggled for air. "A daughter? Rafe, are you talking about a baby?"

"Yeah. Any objections?"

She cleared her throat, still dazed by the abrupt change of topic. A baby—Rafe's baby. A little girl to inherit his empire. Margaret recovered from her initial shock and began to smile gloriously.

"Why, no, Rafe. I don't have any objections at all."

RAFE WAS FEELING EXCEPTIONALLY GOOD two days later when he walked down the hall to his study. He had no premonition of disaster at all.

But, then, he'd been feeling very good every day since Margaret had arrived. Now that they had the house to themselves he was indulging himself in the luxury of waking up beside her in the mornings. He loved that time at dawn when they lay together in tangled white sheets and watched the morning light pour over the mountains.

One of these days he really was going to have to start going back into the office on a regular basis, he told himself. But all in all, if the truth be known, he was slightly amazed at how well things were going with him on vacation.

He chuckled to himself at the thought that he might not be as indispensable at Cassidy and Company headquarters as he'd always assumed. Maggie wouldn't hesitate to point that out to him if he gave her the chance.

He rounded the corner, glancing at his watch. Hatcher had gone back out to his car to get another file. They had been working for the past two hours before taking a break and now they were going to finish the business. Rafe was looking forward to joining Margaret out by the pool.

Rafe walked through the door of his study, frowning slightly as he realized he must have left it open. Perhaps Hatcher had already returned from the car.

But it wasn't Doug Hatcher standing beside the desk staring at the open file and the computer printout lying alongside. It was Margaret. One look at her face and Rafe knew she had seen too much.

He sighed inwardly. He would much rather she hadn't found out what was going on, but it wasn't the end of the world, either. She loved him and this time around she was firmly in his camp.

"What are you doing in here, Maggie? I thought you were going swimming."

She was staring at him with wide eyes. A storm was brewing rapidly in their aqua depths. "Doug said you were in here. I wanted to talk to you. But I found this instead."

She gestured angrily at the open file. "What in the world is going on, Rafe? What are you up to with this Ellington takeover? Why all these references to Moorcroft?"

"It's just business, Maggie, love. I'll be finished in another half hour or so. You told me you were willing to be reasonable about the amount of time I spent on work. Why don't you go on out to the pool?"

"This is what you were working on that night I found you in here after the engagement party, isn't it? This is why Hatcher comes here to see you every day. I demand to know what is going on."

"Why?"

"Why? Because it's clear Moorcroft is involved in some way and I know you have no liking for him." Her eyes narrowed. "I also know that you're quite capable of plotting revenge. Tell me the truth, Rafe. Are you in competition with Jack to take over Ellington?"

He shrugged and sat down behind the desk. "You could say that."

"What do you mean by that? Are you or aren't you?"

Rafe closed the damning file and regarded her consideringly. She was getting mad but she wasn't going up in flames. "As I said, Maggie, this is just business. It doesn't concern you."

"Are you sure? If this really is just business as usual, you're right. It doesn't concern me. But if this is some sort of vengeance against Jack, I won't have it."

Rafe rested his elbows on the arms of his chair and steepled his fingers. His initial uneasiness was over and he was starting to get annoyed by her attitude. "You think you have to protect Moorcroft? The way you did last year?"

She flinched at that. "No, of course not. I don't work for him any longer and I don't owe him anything, but—"

"You're right. You don't owe him anything, especially not your loyalty. That should be crystal clear this time around. So let him take his chances out there in the jungle, Maggie. He's been doing it a long time, same as me."

"Rafe, I don't like this. If you're up to something, I think I should be told."

"You're a romance writer these days, not a business executive. You don't need to know anything about this."

"Damn you, Rafe, don't you dare patronize me. I don't trust you to treat Moorcroft the way you would any other business competitor. Not after what happened last year. I want to know—" She broke off abruptly, glancing at the open door.

Rafe followed her gaze and saw Hatcher standing on the threshold. He looked uncertain of what he should do next. "I'll, uh, come back later, Rafe."

"No," Rafe said. "Maggie was just leaving. Come on in, Hatcher. I want to get this Ellington thing finished today. Sit down."

Margaret hesitated a moment and then apparently thought better of making a scene in front of Hatcher. "We'll discuss this later, Rafe." She turned and stalked out the door, the elegant line of her spine rigidly straight with anger.

Hatcher stared after her, looking more uneasy than ever. "She knows about the Ellington deal?"

"She walked in here and saw the damned file lying on the desk."

Hatcher paled. "Sorry. I know you didn't want her to find out about it."

Rafe bit off a curse. "It wasn't your fault. Never mind, I'll deal with Maggie later. I can sugarcoat the facts and calm her down. Let's get back to work."

Hatcher drew a deep breath. "Rafe, I think there's something you should know."

"What?" Rafe jabbed at a key on the computer console and narrowed his eyes as a familiar spreadsheet popped onto the screen.

"There's been another leak of information."

That caught Rafe's attention. He swung his gaze back to his assistant. "Bad?"

"The latest set of offer figures. The ones we drew up this week. My inside information tells me Moorcroft has them."

"This time around we were very, very careful, Hatcher," Rafe said softly. "Only you and I knew those numbers and they existed only in this file. We wiped them out of the computer after we ran the calculations."

Hatcher studied the desktop for a long moment before he looked up. There was a desperate expression in his eyes. "You're going to have my head if I say what I have to say next, Rafe."

Rafe looked at the man he had trusted for the past three years. "Just say it and get it over with."

"There's been someone else here in your house with access to these figures for over a week. I hate to be the one to point this out to you, but the fact is the really bad leaks began after she got here."

Rafe was so stunned he couldn't even think for a moment. The accusation against Margaret was the last thing he'd been expecting to hear. He had prepared himself for something else entirely.

For an instant he simply stared at Hatcher and then he came up out of the chair, grabbed his startled assistant by the collar of his immaculate shirt and yanked him halfway across the desk. "What the hell are you trying to tell me?"

Fear flashed in Hatcher's eyes. "Rafe, I'm sorry. I shouldn't have said anything. But someone has to point it out to you. And as long as it's gone this far, there's more you should know."

"More?" Rafe's hand tightened.

Hatcher looked down at the corded muscles of Rafe's forearms and then up again. "My sources tell me she saw him shortly before leaving Seattle to come down here."

"Hatcher, I swear, I'll break your neck if you're lying to me."

"It's true," Hatcher gasped. "I've known about the meeting for a couple of days but I've been afraid to tell you. But now you're practically accusing me of being the leak and I've got my own reputation to consider. Ask her. Go on, ask her if she didn't talk to Moorcroft before she flew to Tucson."

"There's no way she would have talked to that bastard."

"Is that right? Ask her if Jack Moorcroft didn't offer her a nice chunk of change to find out what she could about what we're up to. You want to pinpoint the leak? Don't look at me. I've been your man since the day I came to work for you. I've proven my loyalty a hundred times over. Try looking close to home, Rafe."

"Damn it, Hatcher, you don't know what you're saying."

"Yes, I do. I've just been afraid to say it out loud for several days because I knew you didn't want to hear it. But you've never paid me to be a yes man, Rafe. You've always said you wanted me to speak my mind and tell you the facts as I saw them. All right, I'm doing just that. She betrayed you once and she's betraying you again."

Rafe felt himself hovering on the brink of his self-control. He hadn't been this close to going over the edge since the day he'd found Margaret with Moorcroft.

He made himself release his grip on Hatcher. Doug inhaled deeply and stepped quickly back out of reach, smoothing his clothing.

"Get out of here, Hatcher."

Hatcher glanced nervously at the file. "What about the Ellington deal? We need another set of numbers and we need them fast. We've got to make the final move within the next forty-eight hours."

"*I said, get out of here.*"

Hatcher nodded quickly, picked up his briefcase and went to the door. There he paused briefly, his expression anguished. "Rafe, I'm sorry it turned out this way."

"Just go, will you?"

Hatcher nodded and went out the door without a backward glance.

Rafe stared for a long while at the far wall before he yanked open the bottom desk drawer and pulled out a glass and a bottle of Scotch.

Very carefully he poured the liquor into the glass and then he propped his feet on the desktop and leaned back in the chair. He took a long swallow of the potent Scotch and forced his mind to go blank for a full minute.

When he felt the icy calm close in on him he knew he had himself back under control.

"Rafe?"

He didn't turn his head. "Come in, Maggie."

"I heard Doug leave." She walked into the room and sat down on the other side of the desk. Her beautiful, clear eyes met his. "I want to have that discussion now, Rafe. I want to know what's going on and what you're planning to do to Moorcroft. Because if you're bent on getting vengeance on him for what happened last year—"

"Maggie."

Her brows drew together sharply as he interrupted her. "What?"

"Maggie, I have a couple of simple questions to ask you and I don't want any long, involved lectures or explanations. Just a simple yes or no."

"Rafe, are you all right? Is something wrong?"

"Something is wrong, but we'll get to that later. Just answer the questions."

"Very well, what are the questions?"

"Did you have a meeting with Jack Moorcroft in Seattle before you caught the plane to Tucson? Did he ask you to spy on me?"

The shock in her lovely eyes was all the answer he needed. Rafe swore softly and took another long pull on the Scotch.

"How did you know about that?" Margaret whispered in disbelief.

"Does it matter?"

"Yes, it bloody well matters," she shouted, slamming her fist on the desk. "I'd like to know what's going on around here and who's spying on me. I'd also like to know exactly what I stand accused of."

"Someone's been leaking information on the Ellington deal to Moorcroft. You, me and Doug Hatcher are the only ones who've had access to the file in the past few days. Just how badly did you hate my guts after what happened last year, Maggie, love? Bad enough to come back so that you could get a little revenge?"

"How dare you?" Margaret was on her feet. *"How dare you?"*

"Sit down, Maggie."

"I will not sit down, you deceitful, distrusting, son of a…" She gulped air. "I will not go through this a second time. Do you hear me? I won't let you tear me apart into little pieces again the way you did last time. You don't have to throw me out, Rafe. Not this time. I'm already gone."

She whirled and ran from the room.

Rafe finished the last swallow of Scotch and threw the glass against the wall. It shattered into a hundred glittering pieces and cascaded to the floor.

Chapter Ten

RAGE, A FIERCE, BURNING RAGE THAT WAS an agony to endure drove Margaret from the study. Behind her she thought she heard the crash of breaking glass but she paid no attention. She fled down the hall to her bedroom, dashed inside and slammed the door.

She was gasping for breath, the hot tears burning behind her eyes as she sank down onto the bed. An instant later she leaped up again, hugging herself in despair as she paced the room.

How could he do this to her a second time? she asked herself wildly. How could he doubt her now?

She had to get out of here. She could not bear to stay here under Rafe's roof another minute. Margaret ran to the mirrored chest and threw open the doors. She found her suitcase, dragged it out and tossed it onto the bed. Spinning around, she grabbed her clothes and began throwing them into the open suitcase.

He didn't trust her. That was what it came down to. After all they'd each been through separated this past year and after finally rediscovering their love for each other, Rafe still didn't trust her. He was prepared to believe she'd come here as a spy.

Damn Moorcroft, anyway. If only he hadn't looked her up that day in Seattle. If only she hadn't agreed to have coffee with him.

But if it hadn't been that unfortunate incident, it probably would have been something else sooner or later. Rafe was obviously ready to believe the worst.

And apparently he had a reason to worry about a Moorcroft spy, Margaret thought vengefully. He was plotting some form of revenge against his old rival. She just knew it. She was caught in the middle again between the two men and she was furious. They had no right to do this to her.

She would take the Mercedes, Margaret told herself. The keys were on the hall table. Rafe could damn well make arrangements to get his car out of the airport lot.

It was intolerable that he had dared to question her reason for being here in Tucson. He was the one who had forced her to come down here in the first place.

Margaret tossed one sandal into the suitcase and looked around for the other. She dropped to her knees to peer under the bed and to her horror, the tears started to fall.

It was too much.

She cried there on the floor until the rage finally burned itself out. Then, wearily, she climbed to her feet and went into the bathroom to wash her face.

She grimaced at the sight of herself in the mirror and reached for a brush. She wondered if Rafe was still in the study.

It flashed through her mind that he probably wouldn't come after her a second time. No, not a chance. In his own way he had sacrificed his pride once before to get her back and that was all anyone could reasonably expect. He was, when all was said and done, a tough, arrogant cowboy who was as hard and unforgiving as the desert itself.

And she loved him.

Heaven help her, she loved him. Margaret stared at herself in the mirror knowing that if she walked out this time, he would not come after her.

There was only one chance to salvage the situation. She was woman enough to know that this time she would have to be the one who rose above her own pride.

She forced herself to think back on the past few days. She clung to the knowledge that Rafe had changed since last year. He had tried hard to modify his work habits and to realign some of his priorities. He had worked hard to please her, to make her fall in love with him.

In his own way, he had tried to prove that he loved her.

Slowly Margaret put the brush back down on the counter. Turning on her heel, she went back through the bedroom and into the hall. The first few steps took all the willpower she had. Her instinct was to turn and run again but she kept going.

She rounded the corner and saw Rafe leaning in the open doorway of the study, thumb hooked onto his belt. In his other hand he coolly tossed the keys to the Mercedes. He watched her with an unreadable expression. Margaret halted. For a moment they just stared at each other and then Rafe broke the charged silence.

"Looking for these?" he asked, giving the keys another toss.

"No," Margaret said, starting forward deliberately. "No, I do not want the keys to the Mercedes."

"How are you going to get to the airport? You expect me to drive you?"

"That won't be necessary. I am not going to the airport."

"Sure you are. You're going to run, just like you did last time."

"Damn you, Rafe, I did not run away from you last year, I was *kicked out.*"

"Depends on your point of view, I guess."

"It is not a point of view, it's a fact." Margaret came to a halt right in front of him and lifted both hands to grab him by the open collar of his shirt. She stood on tiptoe and brought her face very close to his. "Listen up, cowboy. I have a few more facts to tell you. And you, by heaven, are going to pay attention this time."

"Yeah?"

"Yeah." She pushed him backward into the study, too incensed and too determined to pursue her mission to notice just how easily he went. She forced him all the way back to his chair and then she put her hands on his shoulders and pushed downward. Rafe sat.

Margaret released him and stalked around to the other side of the desk. She planted her hands on the polished wood surface and leaned forward.

"If this were a romance novel instead of the real world, this little scene would not be necessary. Because of our great love for each other, you would trust me implicitly, you see. You would know without being told that I would never go to bed with you and then turn around and spy on you so that I could report to Moorcroft."

"Is that right? Your heroes can read minds?"

"The bonds of love make them intuitive, sensitive and insightful and don't you dare mock me, Cassidy."

"I thought I made it clear I'm not one of those modern, sensitive types."

"All right, all right, I accept the fact that this is not a romance novel and you are not exactly the most perceptive, intuitive man I've ever met."

"I'm no romance hero, that's for sure."

She ignored that. "I also accept the fact that I cannot expect you to come after me if I leave here today. You gave us both a second chance, Rafe. It's my turn to give us a third. I only hope this does not indicate a pattern for the future. Now then, let's get one thing straight. I did not make any deal with Jack Moorcroft."

Rafe waited in stony silence.

This was going to be hard, Margaret thought. Resolutely she gathered her courage. "I had not seen or heard from Jack Moorcroft since that debacle last year until he showed up out of the clear blue sky on the Saturday before I was due to come down here."

"Just a friendly visit, right?"

"No, you know very well it was not a friendly visit. He said he thought you might be plotting against him. He told me that since last year he's had the impression you were gunning for him. He thinks you're out to get him."

"I never said Moorcroft was a stupid man. He's right."

"He also said that he would give a great deal to know exactly what you were planning."

"Why didn't you mention the little fact that you'd seen him before you came down here?"

"Are you kidding? The last thing I wanted to do was mention Moorcroft to you. Keeping quiet was an act of pure self-defense. The last time I got between the two of you I got crushed, if you will recall."

"Damn it, Maggie…"

"Besides, I told him to take a flying leap. I made it clear I considered myself out of it. I did not work for him any longer. I owed him nothing this time around. I told him I was going to Tucson for my own personal reasons and that was that."

"And he accepted your answer?"

"Rafe, I swear I haven't communicated with him since that Saturday and I certainly have not handed over any of your precious secrets to him. I don't even know any of your secrets."

"You saw the Ellington file."

"I saw it for the first time this afternoon." Margaret closed her eyes and then opened them to pin him with a desperate gaze. "Rafe, I can't prove any of this. I am begging you to believe me. If Moorcroft has numbers he shouldn't have, then you must believe he got them from someone else. Please, Rafe. I love you too much to betray you."

"Revenge is a powerful motivator, Maggie," Rafe finally said quietly.

"More powerful for you than for me, Rafe."

"Are you sure of that?"

"I love you. When you came back into my life you opened up a wound I had hoped was healed. I was angry at first and frightened. And I didn't know if I could trust you. But I knew for certain the first night I was here that I still loved you."

"Maggie…"

"Wait, let me finish. Julie said something about what it had cost you in pride to find a way to get me back. She was right. I realize that now that I'm standing here trampling all over my own pride in an effort to get you to trust me enough to believe in me. Please, Rafe, don't ruin what we've got. It's too precious and too rare. Please trust me. I didn't betray you."

"You love me?"

"I love you."

"Okay, then it must have been Hatcher, after all."

Margaret blinked. "I beg your pardon?"

"I said it must have been Hatcher who gave Moorcroft the numbers. He's been acting weird for the past six months or so, but I wasn't sure he would have the guts to actually sell me out. Hatcher's not what you'd call a real gutsy guy. Still, you never can tell, so I put some garbled preliminary information into the Ellington file to see what would happen."

"Rafe, will you please be quiet for a moment. I am having trouble following this conversation."

His brows rose. "Why? You started it."

She eyed him cautiously, uncertain of his mood. For one horrible second she thought he was actually laughing at her. But that made no sense. "Are you saying you believe me?"

"Maggie, love, I'd probably believe you if you told me you could get me a great deal on snowballs in hell."

She was dumbfounded. Slowly she sank into the nearest chair. "I don't understand. If you believe me now, why didn't you believe me a while ago when you asked if I'd seen Moorcroft?"

"Maggie, I did believe you," he reminded her patiently. "I asked you if you'd seen him before you left Seattle and you, with your usual straightforward style, told me you *had* seen Moorcroft, remember? You didn't deny it."

"But you didn't let me explain. You told me I had to answer yes or no."

"All right, I'm guilty of wanting a simple answer. I should have known that with you the explanation would be anything but simple. There are always complications around you, aren't there, Maggie? And you ran out the door without bothering to try to explain. What was I supposed to think?"

"That I would never have come down here for revenge," Maggie declared in ringing tones. "You should know me well enough to know that."

"Maggie, I know for a fact to what lengths a person will go for revenge. I also know how much I wanted you. It was entirely possible I'd deluded myself into thinking I'd really succeeded in convincing you to come back to me. God knows I want you back bad enough to tell myself all sorts of lies. But when you didn't deny the meeting with Moorcroft…"

"Never mind," Margaret said urgently. "Don't say it. I'm sorry. I should have stood my ground and yelled at you until you believed I was innocent."

Rafe's mouth curved gently. "You don't even have to yell. I'm always ready to listen."

"Hah. What a bunch of bull. You didn't listen last year."

"Yes, I did." Rafe sighed. "Maggie, last year you told me the truth, too. I listened to every damn word. When I caught you in Moorcroft's office you admitted immediately you'd just told him I was after Spencer, remember? You said you'd had to tell him—that it was your duty as a loyal employee of Moorcroft."

"Oh. Yes, I did say that, didn't I?"

"Our problem last year had nothing to do with your lying to me. You were too damned honest, if you want to know the truth. I'll tell you something. I would have sold my soul for a few sweet lies from you last year. More than anything else in this world I wanted to believe you hadn't felt your first loyalty was to Jack Moorcroft instead of me."

Margaret closed her eyes, feeling utterly wretched. "Are you ever going to be able to forgive me for that, Rafe? I don't know if we can go on together if you aren't able to understand why I did what I did."

"Hell, yes, I forgive you." Rafe pulled two more glasses out of his desk drawer and splashed Scotch into each. He handed one glass to Margaret who clutched it in both hands. "I hate to admit it, Maggie, love, but I was the idiot last year. You want to know something?"

"What?" she asked warily.

"I didn't think I'd ever say this, but I admire you for what you did. You were right. In that situation your business loyalties belonged to Moorcroft. You were his employee, drawing a salary from him and you believed you'd betrayed his interests by talking too freely to me. You did the right thing by going to him and telling him everything. I only wish I could count on all of my employees having a similar set of ethics."

Margaret couldn't believe what she was hearing. A surge of euphoric relief went through her. "Thank you, Rafe. That's very generous of you."

Rafe took a swallow of Scotch. "Mind you, I could have throttled you at the time and it took me months to calm down, but that doesn't change the facts. You did what you thought was right, even when the chips were down. You've got guts, Maggie."

She grinned slowly. "And out here in the Wild West you admire guts in a woman, right?"

"Hell, yes. No place for wimpy females around here."

"I thought you said I was soft. Too soft for the business world."

"That's different. You're a woman. Being soft doesn't mean you don't have guts."

Margaret got up, put her glass of Scotch down on the desk and walked around to sit on Rafe's knee. She put her arms around his neck and leaned her forehead down to rest against his. "You are a hopelessly chauvinistic, anachronistic, retrograde cowboy, but I love you, anyway."

"I know," he said, his voice dropping into the deep husky register that always sent shivers down Maggie's spine.

"I've been fairly certain of it all along but I knew it for sure when you grabbed me by the shirt a minute ago, shoved me into this chair and begged me to listen to you."

"I did not exactly beg."

He smiled. "Pleaded?"

"Never. Well, maybe a little."

His smile widened into a grin. "It's okay, Maggie. I love you, too. More than anything else on God's earth. And just to prove how insightful, sensitive and intuitive I can be, I'll tell you that I understand what you went through a while ago when you came in here and pinned me down."

"You do?"

"Honey, I know first hand what it's like to stomp all over your own pride."

"Actually, it's not quite as bad an exercise as I thought it would be."

"I don't know about that. Personally I wouldn't want to have to repeat it too many times. Once was enough for me."

She relaxed against him. "What about Hatcher?"

Rafe tipped her head back against his shoulder and kissed her exposed throat. "Don't worry about him. There's no real harm done. I told you I've been letting him see bad information. The Ellington deal is safe."

"Yes, but, Rafe, don't you think you should try to understand why he did it?"

"I do understand. He's a yellow-bellied snake."

"But, Rafe…"

"I said, don't worry about it." He kissed her full on the mouth, a long, slow kiss that made her tremble in his arms. "That's better," Rafe said. "Now you're paying full attention."

He got up with her in his arms and carried her out of the study and down the hall to her bedroom.

A LONG WHILE LATER MARGARET STIRRED amid the sheets, opened her eyes and blinked at the hot, lazy sunlight that dappled the patio outside the glass door. She knew without lifting her head to see his face that Rafe was wide awake. His arm was around her, holding her close against his side but his gaze was on the bright light bouncing off the pool water.

"You're thinking about Hatcher, aren't you?" Margaret asked.

"Yeah."

"What are you going to do, Rafe?"

"Fire him."

She didn't move. "And the Ellington deal?"

"It'll go through."

"This isn't just a case of beating Moorcroft to the punch, is it?"

"No."

"Rafe, tell me what you're planning. I have to know why this Ellington thing is so special to you."

"It doesn't concern you, Maggie, love. Let it be."

She sat up, holding the sheet to her breasts and searched his face. "It does concern me. I can feel it. Please tell me the truth, Rafe. I have to know what you're going to do."

He regarded her in silence for a long moment. "You won't like it, Maggie. You're too gentle to understand why I'm doing it."

"I've got guts, remember? *Tell me.*"

He shrugged in resignation. "All right, I'll spell it out. But don't say I didn't warn you. The Ellington deal is the first falling domino in a long line that's going to end with Moorcroft Industries."

Margaret froze. "What are you talking about?"

"I've lured Moorcroft way out on a limb. He's mortgaged to the hilt. Going after Ellington will weaken him still further. There's no way he'll be able to fend off a takeover when I get ready to do it."

"You're going to put him out of business? Destroy Moorcroft Industries?" Margaret was appalled. "Rafe, you can't do that."

"Watch me."

Horrified, Margaret grabbed his bare shoulder. "It's because of me, isn't it? You're going to ruin Jack Moorcroft because of what happened last year. He was right. The business rivalry between the two of you has escalated into something else, something ugly."

"This is between Moorcroft and me. Don't concern yourself."

"Are you nuts? How can I help but concern myself? I'm the cause of this mess."

"No."

Margaret shook her head. "That's not true. Answer one question for me, Rafe. Would you be plotting now to take over Moorcroft Industries if that fiasco last year hadn't occurred?"

He eyed her consideringly. "No."

"So you're doing this on account of me."

"Maggie, love, don't get upset. I told you you wouldn't understand."

"I do understand. I understand only too well. You're bent on revenge. You have been all along."

"He's got to pay, Maggie. One way or another."

She could have cut herself on the sharp edges of his voice. "You can't blame him because I felt loyal to him. Rafe, that's not fair. I'm the one you should punish."

"It wasn't your fault you felt loyal to him," Rafe said impatiently. "I told you that. If it makes you feel any better, I don't blame Moorcroft, either. At least not for your sense of loyalty."

"Then why are you plotting to destroy him?" Margaret asked wildly.

"Because of the things he said and implied about you after you left his office that morning."

Margaret was truly shaken now. "Oh, my God. You mean that stuff about me having been his mistress? But, Rafe, he was lying."

"I know. I'm going to see he pays for the insults and the lies he told about you."

"You're doing all this to avenge my honor or something?" she gasped as it finally sank in.

"If you want to put it that way, yes. He shouldn't have said what he did about you, Maggie."

Dazed, Margaret got out of bed and picked up the nearest garment to cover herself. It was Rafe's shirt. She thrust her arms into the long sleeves, sat down on the edge of the bed and clasped her hands. The enormity of what he was planning in the name of vengeance nearly swamped her.

"Rafe, you can't do it," she finally whispered.

"Sure I can. Code of the West and all that, remember?"

"This is not funny. Don't try to make a joke out of it. Rafe, I can't have this on my conscience." She shook her head. "An entire company in ruins because of a few nasty remarks made by some male flaunting his latest victory. I can't bear to be the cause of so much destruction. I fully agree Moorcroft shouldn't have said those things to you."

"Damn right."

"Look, he was deliberately taunting you because he knew he'd won on the Spencer deal. You know how men are, always pushing, jostling, shouldering each other around. They see everything in terms of victory and defeat and when they see themselves as winners, they like to rub it in."

"Thank you for giving me the benefit of your deep, psychological insights into the male sex, ma'am. I think I like the Code of the West approach better, though. It's simpler."

"That's because you like to think in terms of black and white. Rafe, my father himself said that whole mess last year was one big area of gray and he's a great one for preferring things in black and white. If he can let it go, you can, too. We have each other now. That's all that really counts."

"Moorcroft has to pay, Maggie, and that's all there is to it. Stay out of it."

"I can't stay out of it. I caused it. You've said so yourself, often enough. Think about what you're doing. Granted Moorcroft was out of line in the things he said, but he doesn't deserve to be destroyed because of it. He's put his whole life into Moorcroft Industries, just as you've put yours into Cassidy and Company. Furthermore, there will be dozens of jobs on the line. You know that.

These things always cost a lot of jobs. Innocent people will get hurt."

"For God's sake, don't try to make me feel sorry for the man or his company."

"Then try feeling sorry for me," she snapped. "I'm going to have to bear this burden on my conscience for the rest of my life."

"Hell. I was afraid you'd feel that way. I told you, you're too soft when it comes to things like this, Maggie. This is the way the business world functions and that's all there is to it."

"You mean this is the way men function."

"Amounts to the same thing. We still run the business world."

Margaret leaped to her feet in frustration. "I can't stand it. I have never met such a stubborn, thick-headed, unreasonable creature in my whole life. Rafe, you are being impossible. Utterly impossible."

"What the hell do you expect me to do? Act like that dim-witted Roarke Cody in *Ruthless* and let a multimillion-dollar deal go down the toilet just to please a woman?"

Margaret faced him from the foot of the bed, her hands on her hips. "Yes, damn it, that's exactly what I expect."

Rafe watched her with hooded eyes. "And if I don't agree to do what you want?"

"I will be furious."

"I don't care if you get mad. The question is, are you going to walk out on me?"

"No, I am not going to walk out on you, but I am going to be very, very angry and I will not hesitate to let you know it," she shouted.

"Prove it."

"Prove what? That I'm mad? What do you want me to do? Take a swing at you? Break a lamp over your head? Believe me, I'm tempted."

"No. Prove you won't walk out on me."

"The only way to prove it is to let you go through with this crazy revenge plan. And I won't agree to do that. I'm going to fight you every inch of the way, Rafe, I promise you."

Rafe laced his fingers behind his head and leaned back against the pillows. "You still don't understand. I want you to marry me. Now. Tonight. We can take a plane to Vegas."

Margaret took a step backward, shocked. "Marry you? Tonight? Why? What will that prove? You already know I love you. What's the rush?"

Rafe's smile was dangerous. "Maybe I still feel a little uncertain of you. Maybe I want to know you won't threaten to postpone the marriage as a means of manipulating me into doing what you want. Maybe I want to know that this time you love me enough to marry me even though you're madder than hell at me."

Margaret exploded. "You sneaky son of a... You weren't satisfied with the way I bloodied my knees in that little scene down the hall a while ago, were you? You want me to trample my pride right into the dust, don't you?"

Rafe shook his head. "No. I just want to know that you'll marry me even knowing you can't change me and that you aren't always going to like the way I operate."

Margaret threw up her hands in a gesture of exasperated surrender. "All right, I'll marry you."

"Now? Tonight?"

"If that's what you want. But I promise you I am going to argue this thing about crushing Moorcroft with you all the way to Vegas and back."

Rafe grinned. "It's a deal. Get dressed while I phone the airlines and see how soon we can get out of here."

Chapter Eleven

TWO DAYS AFTER HIS MARRIAGE, RAFE strode past two startled secretaries and straight into Moorcroft's office. Moorcroft looked up at the intrusion, his expression at first annoyed and then immediately cautious.

"Well, hello, Cassidy. What brings you to San Diego?"

Rafe tossed the Ellington file onto the desk in front of the other man. Then he removed his pearl gray Stetson and hung it on the end of the sleek Italian-style desk lamp.

"Unfinished business," Rafe explained, dropping into a black leather chair.

Moorcroft hesitated and then opened the file. He scanned the contents, absorbing the implications quickly. When he looked up again, his mouth was tight. "So you knew about my pipeline into your office all along? Knew Hatcher was keeping me informed?"

"I figured something was going on. He used to be a good man. One of the best. But he's changed recently."

"Probably because you've changed." Moorcroft leaned back in his chair. "And he didn't like the change."

"Is that right?" Rafe casually put his silver-and-turquoise-trimmed boots on Moorcroft's richly polished desk. "What didn't he like?"

Moorcroft sighed mockingly. "Don't you understand? You were his idol, Cassidy. The fastest gun in the West. Hatcher thought he was working for the best and he liked being on the winning side. But during the past year he decided you'd lost your edge."

"No kidding."

"Afraid so. In his opinion you'd become obsessed with a certain woman and that obsession had weakened you. A young man on the way up does not like discovering his idol has an Achilles' heel. You were no longer the hotshot gunslinger he'd gone to work for three years ago. No longer the toughest, meanest, fastest desperado on the coast."

Rafe nodded. "I think I get the picture."

"Apparently for the past six months all you've done is plot revenge against me and worked on ways of getting Miss Lark back into your bed. Revenge he could understand, but not your single-minded desire to bed one specific lady."

"Looks like I failed as a role model."

"Something like that. It bothered him, Cassidy. When I contacted him on the off chance I could buy him, I discovered he was ripe for the picking."

"And you offered him a way to prove his newfound loyalty to you."

"What did you expect me to do?"

"Exactly what you did do, I suppose."

Moorcroft shrugged. "You'd have done the same. We live and die on the basis of inside information in this business, Cassidy. You know that. We take it where we can get it."

"True. Going to give him a job when he comes looking for one?"

"Hell, no. The guy's proven he's the type who will sell out his own boss. What do I want with him?"

"Figured you say that."

Moorcroft glanced at the Ellington file. "But in this case it looks like Hatcher may have been a little premature in writing you off. He's been feeding me false information almost from the start, hasn't he?"

"Yeah."

"And especially for the past week or so. It's too late for me to counter now, isn't it? Congratulations, Cassidy. Looks like you win this one." Moorcroft reached behind his chair and opened a small, discreet liquor cabinet. "You drink Scotch, according to Hatcher. Can I offer you a glass?"

"Sure."

Moorcroft poured Scotch into two glasses and pushed one across the desk to Rafe. Then he raised his own glass in a small salute. "Here's to the thrill of victory. I guess this makes us even, doesn't it? I got Spencer last year. You get Ellington this year."

"It's not quite that simple, Moorcroft. Check the printout at the end of that file."

Moorcroft hesitated and then reopened the Ellington file. He flipped to the last page and scanned the detailed financial forecast and spreadsheet he found there. Then he looked up again. "So?"

"So Ellington was merely the first."

"I can see that. Brisken was next?"

"And then Carlisle."

Moorcroft's eyes narrowed. "Carlisle? What do you want with it?"

"Guess."

Moorcroft slowly closed the file again. "Carlisle has a major stake in Moorcroft Industries at the moment. You take control of them and you have a chunk of me."

"You've got it."

Moorcroft swallowed the remainder of his Scotch in one long gulp. His fingers were very tight around the glass as he carefully set it down in front of him. "I was right, wasn't I?" he asked softly. "You are gunning for me."

"That was the plan," Rafe agreed. He studied the San Diego skyline outside the window. "Ellington, Brisken, Carlisle, and then Moorcroft. Dominoes all lined up in a neat little row."

"Why are you telling me this in advance? You're giving me time to maneuver. Why do that?"

"Because I'm canceling my plans. I've changed my mind. I'm not going to topple my little row of dominoes after all. I just wanted you to know what almost happened." Rafe's mouth curved faintly. "It's about the only satisfaction I'm going to get."

"To what do I owe this unexpected generosity of spirit?" Moorcroft looked more wary than ever.

"My wife. She didn't like being the reason for the collapse of an empire the size of yours. She's a soft little creature in some ways." Rafe grinned and took a sip of Scotch. "Plenty of spirit, though. Feisty as hell. You haven't been through anything until you've been through a wedding night with a bride who wants to lecture you on business ethics."

"We're talking about Margaret Lark, I take it? You've married her?" Moorcroft looked a little bewildered.

"Day before yesterday."

"Congratulations," Moorcroft said dryly. "You're a lucky man. I guess I am, too, if the reason you're calling off the revenge bit is on account of her. Looks like she saved my tail. So she was worried enough about me to make you change your whole battle plan. Interesting."

"Don't get too excited," Rafe advised. "It wasn't you she was concerned about. It was all the other innocent people who would go down with you. There's always a lot of blood-letting in the case of an unfriendly takeover. You know that."

"She wouldn't want that on her conscience."

"No."

"She's a real lady, isn't she?"

"Yeah. She's a lady all right. You forgot that last year."

Moorcroft nodded. "I shouldn't have said some of the things I did last year."

"No," Rafe agreed, his eyes still on the view.

"You know why I said them?"

"Sure. You wanted her and you knew you'd never have her," Rafe said succinctly.

"Never in a million years. She never gave me any sign of being interested in all the time she worked for me. Totally ignored every approach I tried to make. Then you appeared on the scene and she fell right into your hands."

"Yeah, well, if it makes you feel any better, I had something going for me you didn't have."

"What's that?" Moorcroft glanced in disgust at Rafe's hand-tooled boots.

"I was the man of her dreams. Straight out of one of her books."

"Women."

"Yeah." Rafe put his glass down on the desk and smiled fleetingly. "Maggie says they're going to take over the business world one of these days and show us how to run things right."

"I can't wait." Moorcroft looked at the Ellington file and then at Rafe. He frowned. "Is this business between us really over, Cassidy?"

"Almost." Rafe slid his boots off the desk, got up and peeled off his jacket. Then he started to roll up his sleeves.

"What the hell do you think you're doing?" Moorcroft got slowly to his feet.

"Finishing it." Rafe smiled. "You get to keep your company but I can't let you get off scot-free after insulting my wife's honor. One way or another you've got to pay for that, Moorcroft. You know how it is. Code of the West and all that."

"I suppose it won't do me any good to remind you she wasn't your wife at the time?"

"Nope. Doesn't matter. She still belonged to me. She has since the day I met her, whether she knew it or not. You want to take off your jacket so it doesn't get messed up? Looks like nice material."

Moorcroft eyed him for a long moment. Then he sighed again, shrugged off his jacket and unfastened the gold links on his cuffs.

Rafe went over to the door and locked it.

When he walked out of the office ten minutes later he paused briefly to tug his Stetson low over his eyes. He smiled brilliantly at the two secretaries. "Your boss won't be taking any more appointments today, ladies."

"YOU'RE MARRIED? WHAT THE HELL DO you mean, you're married?" Connor Lark roared at his daughter as he climbed out of the car and went around to the passenger side to open the door for Bev. "We go away for a few days to give you and Cassidy a chance to work out your differences and you up and get hitched. Couldn't you at least have waited until we got back?"

"Sorry, Dad, Rafe was in a hurry. Hello, Bev. How was Sedona?"

"Just lovely." Bev gave her a quick hug and then stood back to look at her new daughter-in-law. "Did that son of mine really marry you while we were gone?"

"It was real cheap and tacky, Bev. A Vegas wedding, no less. But it was for real." Margaret smiled warmly at the older woman but a part of her was waiting to make certain Bev approved. *You'd make him a better mistress than a wife*.

"My dear, I couldn't be more delighted," Bev said gently. "You'll make him a wonderful wife. And Rafe knew it all along. We'll have to give him credit for that, won't we? Don't worry about the cheap and tacky wedding. We'll make up for it with a lovely reception. I can't wait to start planning it."

"Well, there's no rush," Margaret assured her dryly. "The groom isn't even in town."

Connor plucked a suitcase out of the trunk. "Where the devil is he?"

"Took off this morning with hardly a goodbye kiss. Just announced at breakfast he was catching a plane to California. I haven't seen him since. Can you imagine? And after all those promises he made about not letting his business dominate his life anymore, he no sooner gets my name on a marriage certificate than he takes off. I guess the honeymoon is over."

Bev frowned. "Is that true, dear? He's gone off on business? I can't believe he'd do such a thing."

"I can." Margaret grinned. "But in this case I'm going to let him get away with it. I think I know where he went."

"Yeah?" Connor turned his head at the sound of a familiar car coming up the long, sweeping drive. "Where was that?"

Margaret watched the Mercedes come toward them, a sense of deep satisfaction welling up within her. "He had to take care of some unfinished business in San Diego."

The Mercedes came to a halt and Rafe got out. Margaret raced toward him and threw herself into his arms. "It's about time you got here," she whispered against his chest as she hugged him fiercely.

Rafe sucked in his breath and winced slightly. "Easy, honey."

Margaret looked up in alarm. "Rafe, are you all right?"

"Never better." He was grinning again as he bent his head to kiss her soundly.

"I was afraid you wouldn't get home this evening."

"Hey, I'm a married man now. I've got responsibilities here at home." He looked at Connor and Bev and nodded a friendly greeting. "Looks like we're going to be one big happy family again tonight. Damn. I was hoping for a little privacy. This is supposed to be a honeymoon, you know."

"Don't worry, Cassidy, your Mom and I won't be staying long," Connor assured him. "We're on our way to California. Just wanted to check up on you two and make sure you hadn't throttled each other while we were out of town."

"As you can see, Maggie and I have worked out our little differences. Hang on a second."

Rafe released Margaret to open the rear door of the Mercedes. He reached inside to remove a large, flat parcel.

"What's that?" Margaret asked curiously.

"A wedding present."

Margaret quickly dragged the package into the house and ripped off the protective wrapping while everyone stood around and watched. She laughed up at Rafe with sheer delight as she stood back to admire Sean Winters's *Canyon.*

"It's beautiful, Rafe. Thank you."

"I still think it looks like a bunch of squiggly lines but I'll try to think of it as an investment in my future brother-in-law's career."

MUCH LATER THAT NIGHT MARGARET SNUGGLED up beside her husband, drew an interesting circle on his bare chest and smiled in the shadows. "You went to see Jack Moorcroft today, didn't you?"

Rafe caught her teasing fingers and kissed them. "Uh-huh."

"You told him he was off the hook? That you aren't going to ruin him?"

"That's what I told him, all right."

Margaret levered herself up on her elbow to look down at him. "Rafe, I'm so proud of you for being able to handle that situation in a mature, reasonable, civilized fashion."

"That's me," he agreed, his lips on the inside of her wrist, "a mature, reasonable, civilized man."

Margaret studied his bent head and experienced a sudden jolt of unworthy suspicion. "You did behave in a mature, reasonable, civilized way when you went to see him, didn't you, Rafe?"

"Sure." He was kissing her shoulder now, pushing her gently back down onto the pillows.

"No Code of the West stuff or anything?" she persisted as she felt herself slipping under his sensual spell. "Rafe, you didn't do anything rash while you were visiting Moorcroft, did you?"

He kissed her throat and then raised his head to look down at her with gleaming eyes. "Maggie, love, I'm a businessman, not a gunfighter or an outlaw. Your romantic imagination sometimes gets a little carried away."

"I'm not so sure about that. Where you're concerned, my romantic imagination tends to be right on target." She reached up to put her arms around his neck and draw him down to her. "Remind me in the morning to send a telegram to some friends."

"Sure. Anything you say, Maggie, love. In the meantime what do you say we go for another midnight ride?"

"That sounds wonderful," she whispered, looking up at him with all her love in her eyes.

KATHERINE INSKIP HAWTHORNE GOT HER telegram while she was eating papaya at breakfast with her husband on Amethyst Island. Sarah Fleetwood Trace found hers waiting for her when she got back from a treasure-hunting honeymoon.

Married a cowboy. Definitely an old-fashioned kind of guy. Code of the West, etc. A little rough around the edges but fantastic in the saddle. Can't wait for you to meet him. Suggest we all vacation on Amethyst Island this year.

Love,
Maggie

Sarah reached for the telephone at once and dialed Amethyst Island. "*Maggie?* She's let him talk her into letting herself be called Maggie?"

Katherine laughed on the other end of the line. "Obviously the woman is in love. How about that vacation here on the island?"

"Sounds like a truly brilliant idea to me," Sarah said, glancing at Gideon. "We'll all go treasure-hunting."

"It seems," said Katherine, "that we've already found our treasures."

"I think you're right."